F
G97   Gustafsson, Lars.
            Bernard Foy's third
        castling.

ALSO BY LARS GUSTAFSSON

THE DEATH OF A BEEKEEPER
Translated by Janet K. Swaffar and Guntram H. Weber

THE TENNIS PLAYERS
Translated by Yvonne L. Sandstroem

SIGISMUND
Translated by John Weinstock

STORIES OF HAPPY PEOPLE
Translated by Yvonne L. Sandstroem and John Weinstock

FUNERAL MUSIC FOR FREEMASONS
Translated by Yvonne L. Sandstroem

THE SILENCE OF THE WORLD BEFORE BACH:
NEW SELECTED POEMS
Edited by Christopher Middleton

Lars Gustafsson

BERNARD FOY'S THIRD CASTLING

TRANSLATED BY YVONNE L. SANDSTROEM

"Wer spricht von Siegen? Überstehn ist alles."
("Who speaks of victory? To survive is all.")
Rilke

A NEW DIRECTIONS BOOK

Originally published as *Bernard Foys tredje rockad* by P.A. Nordstedt & Söners Förlag, Stockholm, in 1986. This English translation is published by arrangement with Carl Hanser Verlag, Munich.

Manufactured in the United States of America
New Directions Books are printed on acid-free paper.
First published clothbound by New Directions in 1988
Published simultaneously in Canada by Penguin Books Canada Limited

Library of Congress Cataloging-in-Publication Data

Gustafsson, Lars, 1936–
    Bernard Foy's Third Castling.

    Translation of: Bernard Foy's tredje rockad.
    I. Title.
    PT9876.17.U8B4713   1988   839.7'374   88-17968
    ISBN 0-8112-1086-3 (alk. paper)

New Directions Books are published for James Laughlin
by New Directions Publishing Corporation,
80 Eighth Avenue, New York 10011

Dedication

Mr. Bernard Foy is a businessman living in Houston, Texas. During World War II, he was a paratrooper with the 82nd Airborne and took part in the battles in North Africa, Sicily, and Italy. He was captured in France on D-Day and incarcerated in a German prisoner of war camp until he was liberated by the Russians. On his return to the U.S., he entered the civil service, first as a customs inspector and then as a customs agent.

He has certain things in common with the hero of this novel: courage and determination, great generosity, a sense of humor and, of course, a name suggestive of the French word for belief: *foi*.

In return for his kindness in letting me borrow his name, I dedicate my novel to Mr. Bernard Foy of Houston, Texas.

Contents

Bernard Foy's Third Castling
Detective story and reconstruction of *Les Fleurs du mal* by Charles Baudelaire

I / OCTOBER'S ROOF HANGS LOW   1

1. The Severed Head   3
2. The Worpswede School   18
3. The Mystery of the Two Briefcases   31
4. The Jester of Rue des Petits-Champs   43
5. Bernard Meets a Lady   56
6. In the Passage des Panoramas   62
7. Night without Stars   69
8. The Players and the Clock, the Pit and the Pendulum   73
9. You Don't Have to Die If You Can Play   80
10. The Two against Terlingua   85
11. The Eagles over Mesa Aquilas   91
12. The Head of Medusa   97

II / WHEN PETALS STILL FELL IN THE SPRING   103

1. Lost Days   105
2. October Exercise   113
3. Putting Out Bread and Milk   118
4. Dress Rehearsal   122
5. The Tribulations of a Prince of Poetry   127
6. Visit from a Literary Admirer   133
7. A Sight of Undeniable Beauty   140
8. More about Forgetfulness: Art and Life   145
9. What the Briefcase Did Not Contain. And What it Did Contain.   151
10. The Sweet Draught of Forgetfulness   155
11. Winter Resort   161
12. Death and the Maiden   168
13. Master and Servant   171
14. Bernard Foy Meets a Stranger   176
15. There's Something Profoundly Demonic about Mirrors   179
16. A Zeppelin Rises, at Long Last, through Clouds of Restless Birds   184

III / THE AGE OF MATURITY   189

  1. The Last Swan Flies Up from the Rushes   191
  2. Sentimental Landscape Description   196
  3. It Was the Time When Our Pockets Bulged with Fruit . . .   202
  4. Medusa and the Mirror   207
  5. The Pit and the Pendulum   212
  6. Hans von Lagerhielm Goes in Search of Bernard Foy   217
  7. The Hierophant   221
  8. The Voices of the Whist Players in the Arbor   225
  9. The Hanged Man   230
10. Images at the Beginning of Night   232
11. Invitation to the Voyage   235
12. Guide to the Underworld   239
13. In This Kind of Landscape: A Walk Underground   242
14. A World of Interiors   246
15. Mysteries of a Bedroom Town   250
16. The Whist Players Move Up on the Porch   254
17. The Oracle Is Silent, Snow Falls   258

The first gate is opened:

OCTOBER'S
ROOF
HANGS
LOW

1. The Severed Head

A man lights a lamp for himself in the night, when the light of his own eyes is extinguished. The living man touches the dead in his sleep; the waking man touches the sleeper.

When the twenty-nine-year-old rabbi, Bernard Foy from Houston, Texas, lay down at last in the lower berth of a first-class sleeping compartment on the Stockholm–Paris train, he had a hard time falling asleep. The copious events of the short October day were still surging through his memory like so many autumn clouds, chased by a strong wind across a low sky.

For a brief moment he remembered his morning run, which had taken him from his apartment at Hornsplan along Söder Mälarstrand, by Slussen and Riddarholmen, then back by way of Marieberg, across the two Essinge bridges, across the big new bridge that carried Route E-4 and whose name he didn't know, and finally home through the Gröndal district with its quiet public library and small industry.

The two most powerful memories of his run were first of the wind, in the early dawn light, driving the fallen leaves across the surface of the Pål Sound with surprising speed; the second was something he'd seen for a moment when he was climbing down the spiral-shaped pedestrian stairs from one of the Essinge bridges in order to gain the bike path that would take him to Gröndal by way of the huge new bridge.

He'd seen an iron door open, a door gratuitously placed in a pillar, a pillar standing far out in the ice-cold Lake Mälar bay. It opened, and then it closed again just as quickly and surprisingly. Who needed a door to get into the pillar? What could there be inside? Electric wiring? A secret defense construction? Repair equipment, possibly? The bomb that would be used to blow up the bridge the day when, God forbid, the Russians came.

My forefathers were Russians, too, he thought absently.

There was very little in this strange city where—not without learning a thing or two, he's served as assistant to the chief rabbi in the Conservative synagogue on Wahrendorffsgatan for the past three years—that would have surprised Bernard Foy.

That door, however, had appeared so strange to him that he'd braved the October wind and, in his sweaty running suit, leaned over the railing of the lower bridge to see whether it wouldn't open once again.

The wind, the October wind with its peculiar, damp smell of smoke from distant garden fires and damp, plowed earth from still more distant autumn fields, had played with the complex and completely artificial labyrinth of parabolas and hyperbolas executed in concrete where he now found himself, played with them the way one might blow into a seashell. Although Bernard Foy was warm from his brisk run, and although he was wearing a blue knitted cap with the legend JÄRLÅSA CONCRETE on his head, he soon started to feel cold.

Just as he was about to continue his run, the iron door in the pillar opened for the second time on a scene so bizarre and at the same time so horrifying that—lying under the warm Compagnie Internationale des Wagon-Lits blanket on a peaceful overnight train which at this very moment was rolling across the big bridge at Södertälje Canal—he still felt a shiver going through his body. The hollow sound of the train going over the bridge, the experience of sudden, deep empty space under him, the slight flutter of the curtain in the faint breath of night air from the window, made him sit up in his berth and turn on the small reading light.

At the end of the bed he could see his big, wide-brimmed hat and the long wool scarf his mother had knitted for him when he left hot and humid Houston for the cold, matter-of-fact climate of Brandeis University.

The autumn rain was louder out there; the train seemed to be slowing down. His hat, which had been wet through when he boarded the train, had left a damp ring on the evening paper *Expressen*.

In spite of the fact that he'd read it on the subway on his way to the train station, he picked up the newspaper and started to skim its damp pages again. Like many other foreigners who have learned Swedish only with effort and at a mature age, he appreciated its almost childishly simple language and simplified vocabulary.

Two decapitated meter maids had been found floating in the Pål Sound—apparently there was a gang in Stockholm which, for the past month, had been spreading terror among the meter maids in the city, decapitating them on dark autumn nights. According to the paper, it might be a kind of cult of the goddess Kali, introduced by fanatical Hindus. Bernard Foy clutched his forehead. He hadn't noticed the item the first time he read the paper.

It wasn't just the horridness of the information that made him shiver. He recalled that he must have looked out on the approximate place where the bodies had been found that very morning and seen nothing but the arrow-swift flight of leaves across the water, alternately smooth and rippled.

With a renewed shiver—he wasn't coming down with another cold on his way to Paris?—he turned the still damp page. The seventy-eight-year-old member of the Swedish Academy, the poet Jacob Brumberg, had delighted and astonished the critics with a new collection of poems with themes from his childhood and his school years; the name of the book was *When Petals Still Fell in the Spring*.

What I pity I never had time to buy it, Bernard Foy thought.

A schoolboy from Sankt Larsgatan in Uppsala (his name, of course, wasn't mentioned in the article) had used his home computer to enter the main computer at the office of the Uppsala County Council; he'd removed all of his father's tax liabilities and arranged early retirement as county councilor, at 30,000 kronor a month, for his alchoholic older brother.

4

Newspaper items such as that one were not uncommon nowadays. The boy had apparently escaped the Child Welfare authorities at the last moment and left the country, equipped with sufficient knowledge of information retrieval to make his way anywhere in the world, one would assume.

Right then, the man who already occupied the upper berth when Bernard Foy entered, and who must be the owner of the large pigskin briefcase that now blocked the sink, woke up and said in a firm but not unfriendly voice, "Would you mind turning out the light so we can go to sleep?"

"Just a moment," Bernard Foy said absent-mindedly in English, for he'd just noticed another item more fascinating than any of the previous ones.

"Are you American?" asked the man in the upper berth.

"Of course," Bernard Foy said.

A hairy leg in silk pajamas came climbing down.

"Please forgive me if I sounded a bit brusque," the man said. He had an intelligent but rather ordinary face and looked about fifty. Bald, clean-shaven, with blue, somewhat watery eyes.

"Oh, I don't mind turning out the light," the rabbi said, hoping at the last minute to avoid being drawn into a conversation that would bore him. Since he didn't even follow American politics when he was in the U.S., except as fragments on the TV program *Washington Week in Review*, he always got annoyed when all sorts of Swedes would ask him about American activities in Latin America, and even more so when they tried to make him defend particular incidents. It isn't easy to defend even Israeli politics at all times, and those he did read about in the thirty-five journals which any normal rabbi receives every month from various Jewish committees and associations.

"So you're an American on your way to Paris?"

"I'm on my way to a job interview at the synagogue on Rue Copernic," Bernard Foy said. "It's almost, but not quite, the same thing."

The bald man fell silent. Without more ado, he sat down on the berth beside Bernard Foy, who found his behavior rather presumptuous but made room for him.

"I've got a problem," the man said. "My name is Hans von Lagerhielm, I'm a lawyer, and I'm also chairman of the Swedish Chess Association. That's why I'm going to Paris."

"Oh," Bernard Foy said with newly awakened interest. "Is there going to be an international conference?"

(At auspicious moments, his Swedish became surprisingly idiomatic.)

"No," the lawyer said dully. "I'm meeting with a very small group—it's a conference of the chairpeople of the West European chess associations who are meeting in Versailles."

"How interesting," said Bernard Foy.

"We're in the process of changing some rules."

"You aren't going to do away with the bishop or prohibit castling or anything stupid like that?"

(Bernard Foy would sometimes exhibit a youthful impertinence that made his father, the bar owner and army veteran Jacob Foy in Houston, Texas, completely beside himself. Jacob Foy himself was a quiet, but not totally quiet, man, proprietor of Burnie's Saturday Beer Garden, a terrible place on Canal Street, where the monotonous ring marks from glasses or burns from dropped cigarettes that had been allowed to smolder on the brown counter were only interrupted by two large aquariumlike glass containers, one of pickles and one of hard-boiled eggs. It was rather a fun little bar frequented by sailors, pilots from the small, rustic airlines at nearby Hobby Airport, and a large number of platinum blonde prostitutes.

The latter were demanding but profitable customers. Some of them would routinely bring along baby carriages with small children which were parked in the quiet corner between the men's room and the slot machines. Not infrequently, Jacob Foy would have to heat bottles of formula on the hot plate above the wondrous Italian espresso machine some Italian business friends had given him, once upon a time.

Sometimes this quiet but strong-willed man, a former member of the 82nd Airborne, who had participated in the Sicilian invasion in July 1943 and in the attack it had inaugurated, two days before the main offensive, against primary targets in Normandy in June 1944, might be seen feeding some baby or other its formula with his own hands, when it became obvious that its mother had somehow been detained.)

"Of course not. Big rule changes in chess are hardly possible, and it's probably been a thousand years since the last one," Hans von Lagerhielm answered with unaltered patience.

In the opinion of several chess historians, the last rule change to occur was precisely castling, this remarkable maneuver which allows the castle to assume the position of one of the main pieces at a suitable moment in the game, creating new points of departure for the subsequent winding up of the end game.

"No, no," the evidently talkative and pedagogically inclined chess association chairman continued, "we're not concerned with such big rule changes nowadays. It's mostly rules to do with rest days during world tournaments that we have the opportunity to address."

"How interesting," said the rabbi absently. He hoped that this voluble lawyer wouldn't prevent him from reading some more of his evening paper and a book he had brought along, before he went to bed.

He was only moderately interested.

The peculiar events of the morning were still passing through his mind.

That strange iron door, peculiarly placed just by the water line, had actually opened a second time.

Perhaps the person who opened it the first time wanted to assure himself that there was nobody around? There wasn't, either, except for Bernard Foy. It was much too late in the fall for any pleasure craft to pass. High above him on the bridge, fast cars thundered past. Down here on the spiral stairs leading to a lower walkway which eventually joins another highway bridge in the direction of the pleasant district called Gröndal, there wasn't a single human being. No one except Bernard Foy standing in the shadow of the upper bridge, elbows against the railing, waiting curiously to see if that heavy iron door had actually been opened, or if he'd simply been the victim of an optical illusion.

From the door down there it must be very hard to see someone standing up here in the shadows.

Bernard had just decided that it must all have been his imagination—he'd started feeling so chilly that he realized he'd get a bad cold if he continued to stand there.

What happened now happened so quickly and was so scary that, just a minute later, Bernard had to clutch his forehead to assure himself that what he'd seen was actually what he'd seen.

Right then, there was a gust of wind from the Mälar inlet to the north, one of those lurching, dark gusts which, in October, seem to create shadows that have a life of their own. When a shadow merged with the shadow under the bridge and the water around the pillar rippled, the iron door opened again.

Out comes an arm which, for a brief, tantalizing moment, holds something in the opening, then lets it fall into the dark, autumnal waters, where it disappears as fast and as heavily as a rock.

At the same time, heavy traffic rumbled across the bridge.

Bernard couldn't have been mistaken; the moment he saw the object falling, disappearing into the depths, he knew what it was. The shock was so great that it sent a shudder through his agile, well-conditioned body. At the railing, perhaps thirty or forty meters above, he'd let a cry escape him. Perhaps it had been unwise to utter this cry, since it seemed he'd attracted the attention of the person down there inside the iron door. It didn't close right away but only after an interval which lasted for two seconds or for an eternity, depending how you looked at it.

There was no doubt. What Bernard has seen was the head of a woman, pale, beautiful, with a full mouth and classically straight nose, a head whose shape was more apparent because the hand holding this head held it by its long, black hair. This way, the forehead was exposed.

The next moment there was nothing to see. Just water and wind, an iron door in a pillar, as closed as it had always been. How strange, Bernard Foy thought. I must have been hallucinating. What I saw, of course, was some careless repairman working on the electrical equipment inside the bridge. The long black hair must have been tough strands of insulating tape, and the pale face must have been a bag where the tape was kept. But how can I have interpreted it as the severed head of a woman, of a very beautiful woman, even?

When the rabbi continued his interrupted run, as the first drops of a dark, melancholy October rain started to fall, he continued to see the dead woman's face in his mind's eye. He could still see her eyes, and those eyes had a gaze that seemed to respond to his, but not in the ordinary manner. It wasn't him they saw.

They knew something about him that he didn't know about himself, some threatening and doleful truth. He shivered in the rain, trying to shake off the unpleasant feeling of reality that seemed to be tied up with his stubborn hallucination.

He tried thinking about all kinds of things to do with the day which had just begun, his impending trip to Paris and everything connected with that, but nothing could quite free him of this strange vision.

Remarkable, he thought. She still sees me. Although in all probability, she's never existed but is only a hallucination, this woman looks at me with her dead, broken eyes. The unpleasant, sort of milk-white excitement of this encounter stayed with him all day. And the whole time, some famous lines of Charles Baudelaire's echoed in his ears:

> *Un regard vague et blanc comme le crépuscule*
> *S'échappe des yeux révulsés.*

> (A gaze, vague and white like the dusk
> Flees from these rolled-back eyes.)

"So you're going to get a job?" the chess association chairman asked for the third time, with the polite patience often encountered in good lawyers.

"Job interview. I'm from Houston, Texas."

"An interesting place."

"Not at all."

"You're a rabbi?"

"Unfortunately, not all Texans are in the oil business, as people seem to believe here. There are poor small farmers with black goats in Texas. And little Jewish watchmakers. And bar owners in the waterfront area, like my father. And rabbis, for that matter. As you can see, I'm a rabbi. I'm not going to Texas, however, but to Paris. There I'll have a job interview with the chief rabbi in the synagogue on Rue Copernic, a Mr. Charles Williams."

For some reason incomprehensible to Bernard Foy, Swedes were always startled when he told them he was a rabbi. After years of experience, he knew that their reaction wasn't due to any kind of anti-Semitism; it was just that any indication that people had a religious life put them into a state of frozen affability. The conversation would literally make their faces turn to stone on such occasions.

This lawyer (and during the later unfolding of events, Bernard Foy would send him a kindly thought solely because of his attitude in this instance) was evidently someone who'd seen a lot of life. He just said,

"Wonderful. Orthodox?"

"No. Conservative."

"Oh yes."

There was a moment's silence.

"Listen, Rabbi, would you do me a favor?"

"Of course. If I can, that is."

"The thing is, I have such a hard time getting to sleep when I'm in the upper berth. In sleeping compartments. I've always been like that."

"Yes," Bernard Foy said. "It can get very hot up there. Do you want to switch bedclothes as well?"

"Is that really necessary?"

"And our luggage?"

"I suggest," said von Lagerhielm, "that we leave everything the way it is."

"Like philosophy," Bernard Foy said, a joke that amused him a lot.

"I don't understand," the lawyer said.

"Wittgenstein, the philosopher, says that philosophy leaves everything the way it is."

"How interesting. Do you mind if I turn out the light now?"

"Of course not. But first, please tell me which bag you want the customs people to regard as mine, just so I know. I always feel confused when I'm woken up in the middle of the night."

"But please . . ."

"Just tell me. I won't say anything. I'm on the side of humanity. Once I hid someone. No. I won't tell you that story."

"It's the pigskin briefcase."

"Then let's hope the the customs people don't know too much about Jewish laws and customs. I don't use pigskin."

"I should hope not."

"It's on behalf of a client, I presume."

"Yes. A most deserving case."

"Have you thought of something," said Bernard Foy consideringly. "In a country such as this, where everyone has secrets, or where everyone suspects everyone else of having secrets, you always know, almost instinctively, what the secrets are. But perhaps life's always been like that."

In his dream the woman's severed head turned its white gaze on him again. His hairline tickled, as from a light touch, as she regarded him. Suddenly her eyes looked into his eyes. Her eyes were open, but not pale and dead. They lived. They were dark blue, very cold wells.

What excellent advertisements they'd be for a bar in Houston on an August night when the air throbs with heat, the rear lights of the cars run like a ribbon of glowing coals down Telegraph Drive, and the smell of burnt grass permeates the city, a night like that, when you might . . .

With practiced discipline he interrupted this thought, for the dream of opening a bar in Houston is not appropriate for everyone, and he said his evening prayers.

As often before, it struck him how easily, just before we fall asleep, we forget our occupations, our duties, our pasts, our hopes, returning like actors after the play is done to an older, more elemental face which lends itself to everything or nothing.

9

For the experienced traveler in Sweden—and Foy belonged to the experienced—there is a way to know when the train is approaching Helsingborg. That's when all the Serbian cleaning women board the train at Klippan. Not unlike old-fashioned Norns, they sit in the corridors of Swedish overnight trains, wherever they can find a spot for a period of glum brooding, swathed in shawls from which only the glowing tips of cigarettes peer like magic eyes.

When Bernard Foy stepped out into the corridor around 4:30, there were no Serbians, for the conductor in the international sleeping cars doesn't let them in, but since, to his astonishment, he found both lavatories occupied, he left the territory belonging to the Compagnie Internationale des Wagon-Lits and entered Swedish Railways' more ascetic sleeping car to Copenhagen in order to find a lavatory. Here was the smoking, nodding row of Serbian cleaning women just as usual. Not even a hint of dawn was discernible through the half steamed-up windows, but when Bernard Foy walked through a connecting passage between the cars on his return trip, he experienced such an overwhelming odor of damp, heavy earth, rotting leaves and distant pig farms that for a moment, the whole landscape swam in his nose like its own molecular signature. At such times, this quiet young Texan felt something almost akin to love and a sense of belonging in the Nordic landscape.

He looked at his watch. They were due to arrive in about ten minutes.

As soon as he'd closed the door behind him, carefully so as not to wake the sleeper, Bernard Foy felt there was something radically wrong in the compartment.

It was unlocked while I was in the lavatory. A thief must have availed himself of the opportunity. There are a lot of thieves on Swedish trains since it's a poor country with a lot of unemployment, the rabbi thought. I only hope they didn't take my briefcase.

For some years, he'd been working, under the direction of an advisor he hardly ever saw and didn't hear much from either, on a doctoral dissertation about the great medieval mystic Isaac Luria. The only valuable thing Bernard Foy carried with him on his journey, except for the traveler's checks safely secreted in the inside pocket of his jacket, was the first three chapters of his dissertation.

The briefcase was still there, standing in the corner by the sink, beside the hat, which had fallen down. In the light of the faint blue ceiling lamp, Bernard Foy looked about him with eyes which only slowly adjusted to conditions.

With a sigh of relief his increasingly well-adjusted eyes also discerned the flat, square, businesslike briefcase of polished pigskin apparently so important to his fellow passenger. It now reposed on the small luggage rack at the foot of Bernard Foy's upper berth.

The swift feeling of uneasiness, the impression of a creeping presence, of something foreign, which Bernard Foy had felt the moment he stepped into the compartment, was contradicted by the order, quietness, and silence that still prevailed.

That's it, the rabbi thought. It's more *silent* in here than it was before.

With great care, he put three fingertips against the shoulder of the sleeping lawyer. Not even with his most sensitive touch could he feel any movement.

He turned the light on full.

There wasn't a lot of bleeding from the broad, heavy hunting knife, a German bayonet model, protruding from the left shoulder of the chess association chairman.

"I knew as soon as I met him that he was deadly," Bernard Foy said silently to himself, while he rushed to the small cubby hole of the sleeping car conductor, his pajama jacket flapping behind him. A frail, narrow-shouldered blonde girl, of a type often encountered in Finland, smiled nervously and stepped aside. She smelled of Givenchy Nr. 3. For an instant, he brushed against her hip, and enjoyed it.

Just then he became aware that the train was about to leave the station, where it had made a brief stop. The compact crowd of cleaning women, each in her garish shawl, flowed toward the exit along with some workmen dressed in the quilted jackets typical of the country.

It's somehow remarkable, Bernard Foy thought, that somewhere underneath a shawl like that, smoking a damp little cigarette, walks a man who believes himself to be my murderer. His heart beats fast under the coarse woman's coat he's wearing, and he's quite sure he's killed me and that he'll get his reward.

It's true that it is written, "Make a plan. It will come to naught."

"How can I help you, sir?" asked the sleeping car conductor, with a trace of impatience in his voice. He spoke a German which betrayed the Dane.

"I've taken the liberty of pulling the emergency brake. I will now notify the station master while you lock the door of this car at both ends."

The sleeping car conductor—normally, one might guess, a substantial and calm individual—lost his composure.

"What the hell do you think you're up to?" he asked.

"I realize that my action right now can be interpreted as high-handed," Bernard Foy said. "But a man has just been murdered in my compartment."

He threw himself off the train without waiting for an answer. To himself he thought: Although it might appear pedantic, I'd very much like to find the murderer.

For there's reason to believe it was my death he carried with him.

And who could defend himself against the temptation of momentarily touching his own death?

Nobody seemed particularly shocked, least of all the sleepy police patrol which soon appeared. Rather, Bernard got the impression that events of this kind were an everyday occurrence on this railroad. After an almost grotesquely short interrogation, during which he had to give his immigration number and his Stockholm address, Foy was allowed to separate his luggage from that of the dead man.

At the other end of the car, the dead man had already been carried out on a stretcher. Strangely enough, it seemed he had bled very little. To Bernard's sur-

11

prise, the murder car was evidently supposed to continue on with the train. The station inspector, a half-awake, red-faced man, only seemed irritated at having to delay one of the southbound trains for a period that would spell chaos for the whole morning schedule.

"But aren't you going to save any clues? No investigation of the scene of the crime?" Bernard was speaking to one of the policemen, a gigantic young man wearing overalls of almost military cut, with the Three Crowns insignia on his sleeve, rubber boots on his feet, and a heavy flashlight in his hand.

"The criminal police aren't on duty tonight. We're from the district police. The criminal police have had too much overtime lately." He looked impatiently at his watch, a Rolex on a gold band. It now showed 5:10.

"It's a *union issue*," he added, with an expression not unlike that of a learned man citing a well-known passage of the Mishnah to support his actions.

"*I understand*," said Bernard Foy, struck by how often this expression means its own opposite.

"Anything else?" asked the policeman, handing over the black briefcase and the garment bag.

"I'd appreciate it if I could put some clothes on in the conductor's compartment."

"You have to show us which clothes are yours," said the constable, and Foy realized, with a shudder, that his coat and hat and the dead man's were still hanging together in brotherly fashion on the wall and that no one would be able to tell them apart.

In a way, his death is my death, and in him I touch my own death and will for a long time to come.

From now on I have, so to speak, two bodies, one living and one dead, and the secret is that not just anybody can tell the living one from the dead one, Bernard Foy thought silently to himself.

Aloud he said,

"Give me that camel's hair coat with the blue scarf. That one, that's right. And the dark suit on the left. That's it. Thank you, I've already got my socks and shoes on. I've just got to retie them. The shoes, I mean. But please hand me my briefcase. No, not that one. The pigskin one over there. That's right. Yes, I often travel with two briefcases."

They'd promised to put him on the train ferry to Helsingör right away so that he could get a new direct train to Hamburg. He saw Helsingborg disappear in the first faint morning light, with the long pier called the Parapet where the Helsingborg exhibit had once been held. He'd read about it in a novel that had recently been recommended to him, *Funeral Music for Freemasons*, by Jacob Abrahamson.

Kronborg Castle where, according to legend, Prince Hamlet had once performed the deeds described in *Gesta Danorum*, would soon appear on the other shore.

He doubted that Hamlet's castle would have been so baroque and elegant.

This was an important place for the Swedes. One of the classic routes out of their sad, elongated country. A back way of course, because only someone lacking in historic sense could help seeing that Stockholm, nowadays so strangely placed on the backside of Europe, in the shadow of the frightening and implacable Russian empire, would once have been the center: the center of quite a different realm which had stretched from Lake Ladoga in the east—from Pomerania and Reval—to Värmland, on the Norwegian border, in the west.

In this vanished watery realm, the placement of the city had been natural. Nowadays it was mostly a nuisance.

Since all economic life north of Dalälven was state supported these days, the capital might just as well have been Helsingborg, resulting in sharply reduced transportation costs.

Oh well, Bernard Foy thought, it's not my problem.

Anyway, I've got a cousin, Benjamin Foy, who flies jumbo jets three or four times a month from Los Angeles to Tokyo for Pan Am.

He always starts his workday by flying to Los Angeles the night before, just as if it were a suburb of Austin. One shouldn't be too impressed by geography. It's a good old Jewish rule: One diaspora is like another.

While he, so to speak, calmed his heated imagination with these inoffensive thoughts, leaning across the ferry railing, he suddenly realized that he must look ridiculous, standing there with a briefcase in either hand, one old, black, and worn, the other stiff and shiny, of polished pigskin. Only now did he notice that it was the type with a combination lock. How would he be able to get the combination?

And wasn't there a kind that exploded if you tried to force it open?

He recalled having seen something of the sort in an exciting display case of listening devices and spy cameras at the Frankfurt airport.

Perhaps it had been an unfortunate idea to take the dead man's briefcase, but wasn't it his duty to try to understand what had happened, understand it thoroughly?

Still preoccupied with these thoughts, he went into the coffee shop where, in spite of the early hour, there were a goodly number of Swedes who wanted either coffee and Danish or open sandwiches and export beer for breakfast. Bernard Foy, who was very particular about everything he ate, not only because of his occupation and his traditions but also by temperament, had a cup of tea and a cookie.

Only when he started drinking his tea did he shiver a little. He realized that the broad knife that had been so deeply embedded under the left shoulder blade, placed with anatomical precision right in the heart muscle, had almost certainly been intended for himself.

Or did it have to be that way?

Perhaps the lawyer, Hans von Lagerhielm, had also had an enemy on board the train? It was obvious that the answer must be inside the elegant briefcase, and he wasn't able to open it.

In Paris, Bernard Foy thought, there is, on Rue Claude-Bernard, somewhere between 40 and 46, a shop that boasts it can open *anything*; the window is always full of the strangest objects: old cameras, umbrellas, steam engines, and locks. I'm sure I've seen locks there. They'll be able to open the briefcase.

He was again struck by the capacity of terror to diffuse thoughts, to drive them aside, the way a good back will drive an attacking forward to the sides in a soccer game.

We're willing to accept that we're mortal, but we're less prepared for someone seriously trying to annihilate us, Bernard Foy thought. Perhaps because there's such tremendous conceit in wanting someone else's death, Bernard Foy thought.

Once more he glanced across the coffee shop. The ferry ride was very short; the loudspeakers were already exhorting the passengers to resume their seats. On his way down the steep stairs, he was struck by something very unpleasant. Tired and also wrought up by the night's events as he was, he'd thrown the dead man's camel's hair coat across his shoulders as he passed the coat rack at the entrance to the coffee shop, donned his Burberry hat (it felt ridiculously small and strange compared to his own large, black one, from which only the intimation of mortal danger had been able to part him), and by force of habit, he'd picked up his own worn old briefcase, foolishly leaving the other, elegant one behind.

Feeling that it would already be too late, he dashed up the stairs again; it wasn't easy going against the thickening crowd of passengers anxious not to miss the train. He didn't need many seconds to see that the briefcase was gone. The hat rack and the space under it were empty now. He decided to go back to his compartment.

In spite of everything, he thought, I have my mission in Paris. It's my future, and I can't miss that.

After all those adventures, where the loss of the strange briefcase felt more like relief—an equation that had been tidied up, so to speak, to contain a smaller number of unknown quantities, even though some cheating might have been involved—he was almost surprised to be able to change trains in Copenhagen without difficulty.

The Paris train was waiting, and there was an almost unlimited supply of empty seats in the elegant French first-class compartments. Bernard Foy sat down opposite a friendly Belgian couple, Belgian Jews apparently, who greeted him with absent-minded smiles. They seemed completely immersed in discussing the psyche of a somewhat problematic teenager, probably a grandchild.

Annoyed that he hadn't availed himself of the opportunity to buy the Danish morning papers—*Politiken* was often more intelligent and better edited than the increasingly state-influenced *Dagens Nyheter* in Stockholm, and he probably could have got a copy of the *Herald Tribune* in the main hall—he watched the train glide into Danish farming country through suburban tunnels. The sky was as heavy as the day before, the temperature the same characterless but fragrant mean between warm and cold that he'd experienced the previous morning during his strange run across the five bridges in Stockholm.

It's odd, he thought. Either nothing happens to me for months on end, or else

14

everything starts happening in a mad whirl, everything at once. There are times when I'm absolutely convinced that I call it up myself.

I should read the new article on Luria's Manichean sources I've got a xerox of in my briefcase, he thought, taking it out immediately to execute his intention. But his youthful physique and the hardships of the night won out, and soon Bernard was in a deep sleep.

He dreamed that he was in a ramshackle wooden house in a really old, residential area of a Swedish town, a solid lower-middle-class neighborhood. In the garden there were apple trees so old that they'd easily fall victim to any November storm; in their midst stood a gigantic pear tree which, in his dream, was so tall that you couldn't see all the way up to the top.

Or perhaps the sky was hanging very low.

When, in his dream, he walked through the creaking door of the house, he noticed the smell of dampness and of old, rotting wood, not unpleasant, not even obtrusive, but still a reminder that everything that's been built will also deteriorate.

There seemed to be no one in the house, except possibly in the cellar, because now and then the cellar steps would be lit up by the kind of white lightning flashes that occur when the electrode in an electric welding gun comes into contact with the object you're working on and the arc lights up.

The face of the plumber wasn't visible, since he had on an immense, old-fashioned face shield. He had heavy gloves on, and with his left hand, the one that didn't hold the soldering iron, he seemed to be intimating to Bernard Foy that he should come on down and help.

Bernard nodded politely and shouted, "I'm coming, Mr. Plumber, just one moment and I'll be down there to help you with the frozen pipes."

All of a sudden, however, the steps seemed terribly long and steep; rather than ordinary, everyday cellar steps they suddenly seemed like a ladder into a deep well. Bernard Foy felt dizziness starting in the pit of his stomach.

There weren't many things in the hallway. Just a large metal cupboard of the kind used to store oil cans in gas stations.

Without hesitation, Bernard Foy opened the cupboard. There stood, apparently frozen in a pose of horror, a man in an SS uniform. Judging from the stripes on his sleeve, he was some kind of noncommissioned officer.

As often happens in a dream, Bernard Foy surprised himself by not getting the least bit scared at this apparition.

It's Master Sergeant Ernst Lutweiler from Stalag 216 in Zwillerheyde, he said calmly to himself. The master sergeant is supposed to stand there, because that's where my dad has put him. And he's going to keep on standing there for a long time.

He carefully closed the door on the ghostly shape, whose oddly staring, cold blue eyes seemed to bear witness to a condition that was neither death nor life, but at the same time more frightening than either.

Now running steps came from farther inside the house and descended through what must be an old-fashioned butler's pantry. Bernard Foy suddenly sensed that he was no longer alone on this floor. He rushed into the kitchen.

The person he glimpsed when he rounded the corner was the same blonde girl he'd seen that morning in the corridor of the overnight train.

"But she can't be the same girl," Bernard Foy mumbled to himself in his dream. Why not? Good and evil at the same time. I'm simply mixing up two girls. From two different contexts.

Of course that means that I'm dreaming. But on the other hand, I doubt that. I'm thinking, that's the only thing I can rely on under the circumstances.

With this thought, Bernard Foy woke up.

The train was evidently passing through the suburbs of Hamburg.

We don't have that far to go now, Bernard Foy thought. It should be about ten o'clock, or perhaps eleven, and seven o'clock tonight I should be in Paris. Then I'll take the Metro, as usual, to Hotel Jeanne d'Arc on Rue de Jarente. That might seem like a strange place for a rabbi to stay, but that's the way the Irishman's secretary wanted it.

If I remember correctly, Saint Joan fell into the hands of the English in 1430, after John of Luxemburg and the duke of Bedford lowered the portcullis behind her in Compiègne. I wonder, by the way, whether the dukes of Bedford were already living in Woburn Abbey at that time?

He realized straight off that this violent sequence of ideas, attacking him time after time subsequent to the night's events, was only a symptom of profound terror, something he'd seen and didn't want to face up to, and that it was time for him to call up some mental self-discipline to curb what was already developing into a bad habit.

"What a lot of unnecessary knowledge I've got," he said sternly to himself.

The train was already gliding onto the large cast-iron structure that was Hamburg's Hauptbahnhof. The corridor was full of passengers on their way out, tremendously corpulent German ladies, old gentlemen with suitcases, well-trained Westphalian youths with blond bangs on leave from the Bundeswehr, somewhat high on beer. Just such a familiar cross-section of the West German population as is usually found on intercity trains, right now anxious to get all their bags off in Hamburg, where it's so difficult to change trains because you have to drag everything up and down steep stairs.

"But good Lord," Bernard Foy exclaimed, getting up from his seat so precipitously that the Belgian couple couldn't help jumping with fear.

A single gaze at what he'd glimpsed was enough. He threw on the yellow coat that he's already developed a serious aversion to, pushed the Burberry hat determinedly over his forehead, slung the garment bag over his right shoulder, the old oxhide briefcase in his left hand, and elbowed his way through businessmen and elderly ladies.

"*Sehr wohlerzogen,*" said a very angry lady in a green hat with five inches of pheasant feather proudly waving from its crown.

The rabbi was just vaulting her three heavy suitcases.

16

Of course he didn't have a chance. The blonde lady, with the unfortunate Hans von Lagerhielm's elegant pigskin briefcase in one hand and a small weekend bag in the other, had gotten off the train before Bernard Foy had a chance to catch up with her.

On the platform, it wasn't as easy as he'd thought to find her again. Probably she, with her light luggage, moved considerably faster than he did.

Porters with heavy trolleys shouted impatiently at him to move aside, newsstands and the little platform offices of the train employees obstructed his view; the Italian express train came in, filling the already narrow space on the platform to overflowing. Close to despair, he suddenly caught sight of the lady descending the stairs again.

Apparently she'd gone the wrong way. There was no doubt that she was the frail blonde girl of Finnish type with narrow, rather high forehead, cold blue eyes, and the late Hans von Lagerhielm's pigskin briefcase in her hand.

Bernard Foy hid discreetly behind the small stand where miniature bottles of cognac are sold, seizing the opportunity to buy two with the ten-mark bill he knew, from that morning, to be reposing in an inner pocket of the lawyer's coat.

Watching the blonde lady, who was apparently waiting for a local to Bremerhaven, he pulled out the ten-mark bill and something fell on the platform. He picked it up.

It was a library card for the reading room in the Bibliothèque Nationale in Paris. The fee for 1983 had been paid, as evidenced by a small red sticker. The photo showed a lady. She wasn't blonde but had long, dark hair falling across her shoulders, almost like a hippie. Elisabeth Frejer, her name was. Elisabeth Frejer was still very young, born in 1961.

What business would Hans von Lagerhielm have had with a student in Paris? Thoughtfully the rabbi replaced the card, this time in his wallet, and pushed a miniature bottle of bad German brandy into each outside coat pocket. The train for Bremerhaven was just getting in; the blonde girl boarded it, seemingly unaware that she was being observed.

Rabbi Foy decided to get into the compartment next to hers, even if this should entail a risk, or into the same compartment if there were open cars, so that he would discover in time if she were to get out before Bremerhaven.

He was now absolutely determined, not quite aware of where the determination had come from, to recover the pigskin briefcase, to open it, to—if necessary by force—wrest from it all its secrets.

Purposefully, as if she'd made the trip many times before, the blonde girl stepped into a first-class coach. Unlike the second-class coach, which was filled with smoking, noisy high-schoolers, it had compartments.

Against his will, he admired the slender, elegant line of the girl's hips under her light poplin coat. Good and evil, all of it.

Was it the murderer of the lawyer and chess association chairman Hans von Lagerhielm he saw in front of him? And faithfully followed?

Or, a thought which he could only pursue with a shudder: his own murderer?

2. The Worpswede School

People often fool themselves when it comes to recognizing what's obvious. Take Homer, for example, the wisest of all Greeks who, according to Heraclitus, was still tricked by some boys killing lice.

They said, "What we see and catch, we leave behind. But what we neither see nor catch, we carry with us."

Where Bernard Foy is standing now, anxiously rocking back and forth in the corridor at one end of a train from Hamburg to Bremerhaven, between herds of horses and heavy old trees becoming more and more sparse the farther the train gets, he's about to overlook something vital. What we neither see nor catch, we carry with us.

The next stop on the route was Osterholz-Scharmbeck; the girl, who seemed sleepy and had nodded off for a while over a book that was invisible to the rabbi, now started to get her things together, from hangers and shelf. At this time of the morning, she looked like quite an ordinary girl. Did she still have the mysterious briefcase of light pigskin with a combination lock which she'd probably taken from Bernard on the Helsingborg ferry?

Yes, it was coming off the shelf.

The fog thickened around the train, which was slowing down. Bernard realized that for two reasons it was important to get off quickly. One was that he didn't want to get into a discussion with the conductor. His experience of German conductors, in particular after a year as librarian at the Jewish Center on Fasanenstrasse in Berlin, was that those discussions might go on for at least three stops longer than the traveler wanted. The other reason was that he thought he'd be able to keep an eye on the blonde lady if he got off before she did.

When he got off the train at the old-fashioned Osterholz-Scharmbeck station, with its wild Viking gables and strange wood carvings, Bernard Foy had no inkling that he was on the outskirts of the fascinating marshy landscape in the northwest corner of Germany called Teufelsmoor, one of the most desolate parts of Central Europe, colonized as late as the 1850s, when the Elector princes of the Niedersachsen province started sending some of their least prosperous subjects here to dig the heavy, damp turf from the moor, to sail it to Bremen in black-tarred, flat-bottomed boats beneath pitch-coated and much-patched sails made of homespun, and to cultivate white buckwheat in the few places where there was enough soil.

Here, between sky and marshland, where rivers and canals sketched their silvery lines under an endless summer sky in which thunderstorms died like distant ships, where crowds of birds moved in gigantic whirls as in Dante's *Divine Comedy* (*The Inferno*, Canto V, 31-86, we hasten to add, so as to win the tireless group of pedants and precisionists to our side), here where the fog encloses eve-rything during October, November, and December, where lanes linked with birches march rhythmically from one insignificant place to the next, the great Rainer Maria Rilke stayed in the artist's colony of Worpswede a number of times around 1900. During the first years of the twentieth century, Mackensen, Modersohn, and Vogeler painted clouds, light, air, and space here. In the strange *art nouveau* studios of Worpswede the pictures of heavy turf boats and glum turf farmers grew on the gigantic canvases of the time. Rilke's young wife, the accomplished sculptress Clara Westhoff, stands, in her blue dress, so pure and clear and still against the summer sky that every spectator is moved to catch his breath.

In 1900, Fritz Overbeck paints his large canvas *Summer Day in the Hamme-Niederung*. The large, pregnant summer clouds of the marshland traverse the sky like cattle; the quiet, desolate Hamme River with its soft, grassy shores solemnly progressing toward the west, where low-lying Weyerberg rises humbly to the horizon. The water in the river mirrors the sky in a cool, crystalline fashion.

Far off, at the foot of the unassuming mountain, lies Worpswede. A glance at map number L2718, *Osterholz-Scharmbeck*, from the survey carried out in 1961 by the Landesverwaltungsamt Niedersachsen, tells us that the artist, in order to depict the river just as it branches off at the Waakhaus Canal, with the mountain directly to the west, must have set up his easel just west of the bridge spanning the highway, where the ancient inn called Tietjen's Hut still rests under large, peaceful elms.

At the end of October, this landscape is enveloped in billowing fog. Sometimes a stork will fly across the slow water of the Hamme River on heavy, sad wings; a group of horses will move in a deep-green field; a distant car will disappear into the namelessness with fading headlights.

Otherwise all is quietude, anonymity, forgetfulness, as the October fogs seep in over the marshland. The Hades of the ancient Greeks might have looked like this.

The souls might have looked like the jogger who is now moving along the verge of the highway between the glider airfield on the southern outskirts of Osterholz-Scharmbeck and Tietjen's Hut, where a yellow country bus had stopped to let off a single tourist and his luggage.

Or perhaps the souls might look like the two cyclists, both wearing yellow sweaters, and not that visible from here, who've stopped right behind the bus to make sure their packs are securely fastened on their bikes.

Tourists on bikes are rather uncommon in this damp, quiet Hades country.

What do the souls in Hades know of what they once were?

The small, crooked man out in the field who's pouring fresh water for twelve thoroughbreds into an old, beat-up enameled bathtub; he thinks he was once a dictator, the ruler of a mighty people, his prisons full of tortured prisoners; his secret police forced apartments open and carried people off in the early, gray dawn.

And he doesn't know anything about it.

Or perhaps he dreams that he was such a dictator, when all his life he was a browbeaten, rather alcoholic accountant at United Laundry Inc. in Stockholm, and never hurt a fly.

It isn't easy to know those things.

This tourist, carrying a worn black briefcase and a garment bag, walking up the path to the weekend hotel Tietjen's Hut, nowadays rather elegant, often visited by fashionable couples from Bremen and Hamburg in need of a few days' quiet and a change from big city life in a pleasant rural inn with fat Hamme carp on its menu, this unassuming visitor has a vague memory of recently having been the assistant rabbi in the Stockholm synagogue on Wahrendorffsgatan.

But why does he have to be precisely that?

Couldn't he just as well be something else?

Why not an American businessman, living at 8806 Brummel Drive, Houston, Texas 77099, U.S.A.? Or an escaped sex murderer?

Only One knows our true name.

The hostess, a reddish-blonde Frau Carola Matthiessen, graciously conducts him to his room, which he finds almost too romantic for a solitary business traveler to Teufelsmoor, with its large elms outside the window, the Hamme disappearing into the fog, a handsome blue couch in the corner.

Frau Matthiessen is a woman of the world who seldom evidences surprise at her guests, but she can't help raising her eyebrows a bit when in the next half-hour, here at the end of October, two cyclists arrive and demand a room. One is a dark-haired young man of about thirty; the other is probably ten years older, but apparently in good physical condition, with noticeably large ears. A wrestler, she thinks.

It isn't only the season that surprises her. It's something else as well. Something that doesn't add up. These people don't seem—how should she put it—open enough, keen on nature, to be interested in bike trips.

In order not to be accused of needless mystification, we have to retrace the plot somewhat.

Bernard Foy had hardly left the railroad station before he realized how difficult it would be to hide from someone in the empty square outside, where three different buses leave from three different stops.

He realized his only chance was the telephone booth, placed off to one side close to the station. Consequently, he started leafing through the Yellow Pages of the local telephone directory while studying the passers-by.

The interesting thing was that when the blonde lady at last emerged into the square in front of the station, she was no longer carrying the pigskin briefcase—or any other luggage. Dressed against the fog in her warm poplin coat, a wool scarf covering her hair and held against her mouth to prevent the raw October air from entering her lungs, the blonde lady seemed to be waiting for the bus.

Bernard Foy, fervently hoping that no other traveler would come along wanting to use the telephone, jumped up and down on cold feet in his thin shoes, frantically leafing through the directory.

Now a bus came, but it proved to be a military one. It belonged to the American Air Force. Was there an American air base out here in the marshes? Some American soldiers with duffel bags over their shoulders hurried into the warmth of the railroad station. The blonde lady remained, looking as if she, too, felt the cold.

It's incredible, Bernard Foy thought to himself. Quite incredible. What had she done with the briefcase?

Just then, a Mercedes turns into the bus stop. A man in plus fours, a short English sports coat, and tweed cap gets out. He embraces her with what seems like more than fatherly affection for several minutes, then politely holds the car door for her. Bernard Foy watches the man ceremoniously securing the blonde lady's safety belt, and the car disappears before he can get out of the booth.

To his astonishment, a friendly young man with glasses was suddenly standing next to him.

"Are you through?" the young man asked.

"What do you mean, 'through,' " Bernard Foy said, right then feeling that nobody is ever through with anything.

"With the telephone," the young man said, still polite.

"Oh, the telephone. Of course. By the way, can you tell me who the man with the tweed cap was, the one who picked up a young lady in a Mercedes right now? I felt so definitely that I know him."

"Of course. That's Count Hansdorff of Westerwede."

"Really. Where have I seen him before?"

"On television, of course."

"Perhaps the blonde lady was his daughter?"

"No. I don't think so."

"Please excuse a tourist, but may I ask another question?"

"Of course."

"Where is Westerwede?"

"It's an estate near Worpswede. The great Rainer Maria Rilke lived there around 1900. Didn't you know that?"

"One last question, and then I won't bother you; I'm sure you're anxious to use the telephone."

"Please."

"You said I'd probably seen Count Hansdorff on TV? But landowners from Teufelsmoor don't usually appear on TV, do they?"

"No, that's quite true. Ministers of Defense, however, often do. Perhaps this has escaped your notice, but Count Hansdorff is the Minister of Defense for the Federal Republic of Germany."

"Gosh, I'd no idea. How interesting. Tell me, does that bus go to Worpswede?"

"Yes, it does."

"Are there any decent hotels there?"

"Several. Worpswede is still an artists' community. The best hotel, however, is actually Tietjen's Hut, a little closer to where we are."

Since the bus wasn't due to leave for fifteen minutes, Bernard Foy went into the station again. There were no luggage lockers to be seen. He had to knock several times on the glass pane of the small ticket office before a clerk appeared. He turned out to be a red-faced older man with thin, gold-framed glasses on his nose.

"Tell me, is there some place to check your luggage here?"

"Yes, what do you want to check?"

"I don't want to check anything. The thing is, my wife just checked her luggage, and by mistake, she left my light-colored briefcase as well."

Bernard Foy inhaled deeply—the whole thing was somewhat hazardous—and continued:

"My wife is the blonde lady, she's waiting in the car."

The man in the ticket office looked him up and down. Then he disappeared inside the station. Had he gone to call the police? Bernard Foy was the only one in the waiting room, not counting a rough-haired dachshund curled up asleep next to the stove.

The discreet snores of this animal were interrupted by sudden knocking and rumbling behind Bernard Foy's back, which made him turn around with the hair-trigger resolve of a stuntman on American TV.

Evidently, the clerk belonged to the peculiar kind of state employee you sometimes run into, who prefers to communicate by gestures rather than by words, as if to demonstrate his superiority to the general public who are paying his salary.

It seemed the checkroom was on the opposite side; there stood the clerk, waving the desired briefcase of light pigskin, because of which the chairman of the Swedish Chess Association might have been murdered just twelve hours ago.

"Thank you, that's very kind of you," Bernard Foy said, walking with controlled haste to the yellow country bus that had just stopped under the *Worpswede* sign.

Blessing the One who, already in his mother's womb, provided him with such a clear and clever head, the rabbi sat down in one of the rear seats. He put his own luggage beside him. He couldn't resist the temptation to finger the combination lock cautiously. He wasn't able to suppress a small cry of surprise when, this time, the briefcase opened by itself.

"But of course that's how it had to be," Bernard Foy said to himself.

A faint smell of Givenchy Nr. 3, familiar to Foy, rose from the briefcase. To his surprise, it was almost empty. There were just three objects: an unopened package of elegant Christian Dior pantyhose in a—to Bernard Foy—very appealing dark brown, almost black, shade; a minicassette-player, a Panasonic; a small pocket diary.

Was he holding the possessions of Elisabeth Frejer rather than of Hans von Lagerhielm in his hands?

"Tietjen's Hut!" shouted the driver, stamping the floor impatiently as Bernard Foy collected his belongings.

After a delightful shower, the Rabbi ordered tea and cookies, settling down comfortably on the blue couch, in his light-colored dressing gown, to review the von Lagerhielm briefcase.

The pocket diary was completely uninformative. Strangely enough, it was manufactured in Belgium, and it was in French. It took a while before Bernard Foy realized that it contained two entries.

One was for Thursday, October 27, 1983.

"*M. Bibliothèque Nationale*," it said. The day was not far off.

"Strange," Foy mumbled between clenched teeth. "This is either Elisabeth Frejer's entry or her lover's. Be that as it may, I'm the one who's got her card to the Bibliothèque Nationale."

Right then the rabbi jumped, shutting the briefcase as it he were a schoolboy found playing forbidden games.

But it was just the girl, a shy, nervous, skinny blonde girl who seemed taken straight from the fog of the marshland, bringing his tea. Bernard Foy regarded her small breasts under the black dress with benign interest as she poured milk into his tea.

She wore a neat, old-fashioned white apron, of a type nowadays mostly seen in English manor houses, over her dress.

Hardly had she curtsied from the room before Bernard Foy hurried back to the contents of the briefcase. The scent of perfume was deep and sensual, and Bernard Foy turned over the package of elegant pantyhose. When would their owner discover that they were missing?

The second diary entry concerned the Friday of the same week, that is October 28, and it was even more puzzling.

"*International Utilities. Ranch Road 22 22—Rt. 10 Exit après La Grange*," it said. Bernard Foy didn't deny himself the pleasure of smacking his lips in the manner of a botanist who has at long last discovered a really interesting poisonous fungus on some old, damp tree trunk on a warm promontory in Lago di Como, or like a collector coming upon a folder of the early drawings of Carl August Ehrensvärd, the eighteenth-century author and illustrator of *Travels in Italy*. Only his religion prevented him from saying, "That's a hell of a thing."

The cassette-player was less informative. There seemed to be something the matter with it. Instead of the chirping sound that usually results when you run the tape back and forth, there was only a shrill, high sound, the same on both sides of the tape, not unlike a fourth octave C-sharp played on a flute.

For safety's sake, Bernard Foy removed the cassette and put it in the pocket of his suit jacket. He could hardly explain why he did this. As often happens, he had a thought too swift and too subtle to be pinned down in words.

To about a million people, sitting in a friendly hotel room by the Hamme River, the scent of tea slowly rising from the pot, the fog moving in bands

23

alternating between thick and thin under the heavy trees outside, the entry "*International Utilities. Ranch Road 22 22—Rt. 10 Exit après la Grange*" would mean nothing at all, or possibly "something French." Especially since the previous entry apparently fixed the day for an appointment at the French national library.

But this was not the case with Bernard Foy.

"Gosh. I must have seen that place a hundred times. It's a strange kind of factory just after Bastrop Forest. It's a place in central Texas between Austin and Houston. How in the world will the owner of the diary be able to keep two appointments the same week, one in the middle of Paris, one in the central Texas countryside?

He decided to use the already darkening late fall day for a walk, pulled on the dead man's coat, tied the scarf around his neck, and put the Burberry hat on his head.

"I'm going for a walk," he said to the hostess at the desk. "I'd like a table for dinner," he added. "At eight o'clock."

"We have two restaurants," the hostess informed him with a friendly smile. "One is French, and the other has German country cooking."

"I'd like a table in the French restaurant," Bernard Foy said, realizing with some regret that this was the night he should have been welcomed in Rabbi Charles Williams' hospitable home on Rue Copernic.

Walking out on the steps outside the hotel and shutting the glass door behind him was like walking into a different world. Immediately, the fog lay on his cheeks and forehead like a greeting from German baroque poetry. The smell of decaying turf, dark autumnal water, river meadows, and horses, perhaps also of cows hidden out in the fields, was overwhelming.

Bernard Foy made his way to the road and started walking to his right. It was a bit unpleasant crossing the narrow bridge across the Hamme, since several cars were just passing each other when he got there. Bernard Foy jumped onto the stone wall and noticed a row of nice old motorboats with cabins moored below the hotel.

Strange that they don't take their boats out for the winter, he thought.

It was quickly getting dark. A swirl of birds moved toward the mouth of the river and the sea. A pair of storks glided heavily over the bend in the river.

Europe is mysterious, Bernard thought. More mysterious than people generally believe, if they've only seen the mule tracks on the mesas above the Santa Margarita Canyon in Big Bend or have only heard the canyon swallows whirring in the green twilight. The thought that there were two such different worlds made him happy. Like all young people, he was convinced that he needed more than one world to be happy and free.

Behind him he heard the low conversation of two cyclists, whose swift, narrow tires whizzed on the fog-slick asphalt. This brought him back to Europe.

So, Europe is mysterious. But there's something else that's mysterious, too. If I could only think what it is.

24

If a lady steals a murdered lawyer's briefcase, maybe even kills the chairman of the Swedish Chess Association, in order to get hold of his briefcase, then attempts to carry this briefcase, which contains some kind of secret message, to Osterholz-Scharmbeck, where she apparently is trying to seduce the Minister of Defense of the Federal Republic of Germany, for God knows what obscure reason, it is then likely that she will put her pantyhose in this briefcase?

If, on the other hand, the chairman of the Swedish Chess Association, a seemingly most correct and generally well-behaved gentleman, is so anxious to smuggle a pigskin briefcase out of the country that he's willing to change berths with an American rabbi to escape the notice of the authorities, why, in heaven's name, does he put an unopened package of Christian Dior pantyhose in his briefcase?

And, if there are also a pocket diary and a minicassette-player in the briefcase, how do you know whether they belong to the murderer or to his or her victim?

Perhaps the original contents of the briefcase had been exchanged in order to mislead him? But when would that have happened? There's something here that doesn't hang together, doesn't make a pattern. There's something wrong somewhere.

Most people don't think of things in the order they encounter them, and they don't recognize what they actually experience. They only believe in their opinions, Bernard Foy thought.

Then something occurred to Bernard Foy with an ice-cold—perhaps one might say crystal-clear—certainty, something he'd always known. And at the same time, not known. Such things happen. Only by concentrating with Talmudic discipline was it possible for him to live through the events again in the order they had actually occurred.

He had missed the briefcase at the coat rack on the ferry. Yes.

For some reason, he'd thought that's where he'd put it. But it now occurred to him with icy certainty that you don't have to have put something in a certain place because that's where you miss it.

"I have to get back to the hotel right away. Because if my hypothesis is correct, then, strangely enough, it . . ."

The lightning-swift and, to an outside observer, quite unmotivated turn he made probably saved his life.

The cyclists, who were coming up on either side of him, seemed rather oddly, considering the lateness of the hour, to be wearing some kind of dark swimming goggles. They were swinging something in their hands which Bernard Foy interpreted as rolled-up newspapers.

Perhaps they're paperboys, he had time to think, before one "newspaper," heavy as a lead pipe, landed on his padded shoulder, which still hurt him considerably. If he hadn't turned at that moment, the pipe would have hit his unprotected head. It was hard to believe he'd have survived.

For the second time in twenty-four hours, Bernard Foy experienced the profound, righteous indignation felt by every healthy person when threatened with extinction. Bernard Foy was a peaceful, well brought-up man, educated at good universities, with all the affability of the yeshiva in his body, ever willing to discuss opinions that seemed to him repugnant or, at first glance, incomprehensible.

This brutal murder attempt, however, made him beside himself with fury.

When Bernard Foy was small, his parents lived in the Telegraph Drive neighborhood, where young Mexicans, Jews and, to some extent, Blacks engaged in street fighting. Bernard Foy had learned many things between eleven and sixteen, for example the value of trying to hit your opponent's nose so hard at the beginning of the fight that he's blinded by pain. This was exactly what the boy, still present in the body of the man, did. Bernard Foy hit like a true street fighter, not with his knuckles (they are much too fragile for such things and can only be used if covered by protective boxing gloves) but with the flat of his hand, the way the old Etruscans fight in their grave paintings and the way all sensible American boys, brought up in the border country between the different ethnic groups in the big cities, fight when they're attacked on their way home from school.

He now had the satisfaction of feeling his adversary's nose crunch the proper way under his right hand and seeing him bend forward. The man was actually wearing swimming goggles, which made it hard to determine his looks or age, especially since his rather large face was contracted by pain and his nose started bleeding.

"*Make a plan. It will come to naught*," Bernard Foy quoted piously to himself from a medieval *Havdala* ritual he'd learned to love over the years.

His enemy was folded over by the railing, the bike fallen in the road. The bleeding, howling man's only striking characteristic was his huge, oddly doglike ears, which stuck out almost in points from his bald head, visible now that the man had lost his knitted cap.

Now the other cyclist approached from the opposite direction with frightening speed. The rapid turn of events had obviously taken him by surprise. He was no longer surprised but already swinging his "newspaper" like the cuirassier did his saber during the last, desperate French cavalry attack at Waterloo. Bernard Foy, possessed by the icy calm of great fury, quickly seized the fallen man's bike—a nice light Peugeot—still lying in the road with its wheels spinning and threw it stiff-armed at his attacker. The result was spectacular. Instead of losing his balance completely, as Bernard had hoped, the man slipped on the damp, slick surface of the bridge, ran into the low right-hand stone wall at full speed, and disappeared with a splash into the ice-cold autumnal water of the Hamme River.

Meanwhile, the first attacker was trying hard to get up again. His face bleeding, he attempted to gain his feet.

Bernard Foy was in no way reconciled with his attacker, quite the opposite: the events of the past twenty-four hours had developed in him a mixture of cold fury and curiosity that, as his father could have told anyone who inquired, would not dissipate for a good while. Quickly he made his way to the opposite side of the road, collected what remained of the first attacker's bike, its front wheel now twisted into a figure eight, and worked the fallen man over, using the whole bike as his weapon, to such good effect that he soon collapsed onto the railing again.

"It's my fervent hope that the Angel of Death will come for him."

In answer to this barely articulated wish, the low rumble of a truck was heard in the distance. Other than that, everything was quiet. A cow lowed in the darkness, receiving an answer from the other side of the road. In the water under the bridge the splashing had stopped. The whole world was again brooding on its own riddle.

"Now I'll have to be quick," Bernard Foy said to himself.

It's funny, he thought. I'm really up to situations of this kind. And strangely enough, I'm well trained for them too.

What else did you watch on TV all through your childhood?

He was in a better mood than he'd been for a long time.

The hotel employees seemed quite frantic when he walked into the foyer, where Frau Matthiessen was using the phone behind the oak counter. An open fire burned.

"Of course, Mr. Lutweiler," she said. "Of course not, Mr. Lutweiler. But of course, Mr. Lutweiler. It's just that a dinner for thirty at a half-hour's notice is a bit much, even for Tietjen's Hut. Of course, Mr. Lutweiler."

Didn't the beautiful red-haired hostess with the heavy breasts and the broad hips look a little pale as she hung up?

"Some problem?" Bernard Foy asked, smiling his winning, youthfully shy smile.

"You might say so. Mr. Lutweiler's daughter has announced her engagement, suddenly, tonight."

"But how nice."

"No. It isn't nice at all. He wants to have a family dinner here, at half an hour's notice."

Bernard Foy thought intensely.

It seemed he'd heard the name Lutweiler somewhere before. But where? And how?

"When are the guests arriving?"

"At nine o'clock. But of course you'll have your dinner, Mr. Foy. Perhaps you could dine a bit earlier?"

"Pardon my asking, but who is Mr. Lutweiler?"

"Mr. Ernst Lutweiler is one of the biggest landowners around here. Well, actually he's in industry. But he also has an estate here. He's very demanding and he's a very good customer, so I like to accommodate him."

"Of course. You have to, naturally. What's the name of Mr. Lutweiler's company?"

"Oh, if I could only remember. It's a multinational concern. They have offices in Hamburg, Paris, and New York. Utilities . . . something."

"International Utilities?"

"That's it. *International Utilities*, that's the name."

"I'm sorry, but I must tell you that I've had to change my plans," Bernard Foy said. "I'll have dinner in ten minutes, if that's possible. Then I'll ask you to make out my bill. Of course I'll pay for an extra night's lodging if necessary. But I've got to have cab for, let's say, twenty minutes to eight."

27

"What a pity, Mr. Foy."

Her large, strangely *warm* green eyes looked as if they meant it.

Fortunately, they hadn't had time to get to his room. Everything was where it should be, even the *Siddur* on the night table. His own briefcase leaned against a corner of the blue couch, and the pigskin briefcase was in the other corner.

He opened the old-fashioned wardrobe of brown walnut on its creaking hinges. His garment bag was hanging there, unopened. When would he have had time to change his clothes, anyway?

It was of highly intelligent American construction, navy vinyl, not very expensive but durable and roomy. A big, vertical zipper gave access to his three suits and five shirts. Down below were two compartments for shoes that opened with horizontal zippers.

The dinner, which was quite excellent, started—with a bit of bad conscience on Foy's part—with fried eel and scrambled eggs. He skipped the wine. Strangely enough, to him it was more important that the wine was kosher than that the fish was.

The penetrating sound of an ambulance was heard in the fog.

"There seems to have been an accident on the bridge," an elderly gentleman at the next table said to his wife. "The ambulance stopped up there."

"How awful," his wife said. Even in the dining room, she wore her green hat with the bird feather.

"I wouldn't mind some more of the eel," Bernard Foy said to the shy girl.

He looked discreetly at his watch.

Frau Matthiessen herself came bustling into the dining room. Waiters were pushing tables together for the engagement dinner, dazzling white tablecloths were spread, silver and crystal were polished one last time, folding chairs were dusted off.

"Oh yes," she said. "I don't know what to do. I haven't been able to order a cab for you, Mr. Foy."

"Oh," said Bernard. "Is there such a lot of traffic in Osterholz-Scharmbeck at this time of night?"

"No," Frau Matthiessen said. "That is to say, I don't know. The problem is that there must be something the matter with the telephone."

Bernard Foy couldn't suppress a whistle. The second hand rushed across the face of his Olympic.

Probably there were some risks connected with a departure along the ordinary route. He pushed the curtain aside and looked out. The fog was still thick. The ambulance had disappeared from the bridge. This time his adversary, whoever he was, would realize that you don't attack Bernard Foy with impunity.

"I thank you, Lord, for taking on my enemies so magnificently," he said, with a formulation he'd started using on his way home from high school along Telegraph Drive at the time when the Mexicans had just started to move in on the borders of the Jewish district.

He turned to the patiently waiting Frau Matthiessen.

28

"In that case I'll stay the night. It's no problem, Mrs. Matthiessen. But I'd like to leave my credit card and have you imprint it on my bill in case there should be an improvement in the telephone service."

The dessert was an excellent mocha ice cream. He ate it without enthusiasm. The racket from Mr. Lutweiler's engagement dinner increased.

"Strange," Frau Matthiessen said when she came to pour more coffee.

"Strange, how?" Bernard Foy asked affably.

"All the guests are here, but the host is missing."

"Mr. Lutweiler?"

"Yes, isn't it strange?"

"I hope he hasn't met with an accident. It did look as if there was an ambulance here."

"Oh, what a terrible thing. It seems a car ran into a couple of cyclists in the fog. Those cyclists are often very careless. They travel late at night even in October, and without reflecting lights."

That's funny, Bernard Foy thought, some twelve minutes later. This time last week I was teaching schoolchildren to read Hebrew characters and making calls to find a speaker for Library Night, and now I'm sitting on a sloping tin roof in Niedersachsen.

It wasn't hard to get onto the roof. Just a short step down from his window.

Carefully, he dragged his luggage behind him as he inched forward on the fog-slick surface. The roof sloped toward the garden, and behind was the Hamme River and the small-boat dock which was Bernard Foy's next goal. The park was poorly lit; the fog surged thickly through it, and only a streetlamp, half choked with mist, gave any hint of directions.

Down by the entrance from the main road it sounded as if a large truck, or perhaps some farm vehicle, was backing into the hotel driveway. Angry voices and shouts could be heard. Apparently, it wasn't easy to back the vehicle in. Now it suddenly showed between two lime trees, a big furniture van with the logo *Harry W. Hamacher, Berlin*.

How strange, Bernard thought. Who'd want to move this time of night?

Now he was at the edge of the roof. He let his luggage fall into the raspberry bushes, first his own worn briefcase, then the elegant one, and finally the garment bag, which fell with a surprisingly heavy thud.

He landed fortunately, last year's raspberry canes under him.

That doesn't matter, he thought. They'll only have to be removed and burned, anyway.

At the same time he became aware of how frightened he was. His heart thumped, his neck felt cold. His inner tide was rising.

It took two trips to the dock and a lot of nervous searching in the dark before he found what he wanted. A good-sized motorboat with a sturdy cabin at the stern. Without hesitation, he took the screwdriver someone had obligingly left between two of the planks on the dock and broke the padlock on the cabin door.

The smell of gasoline led him to the reserve tank; with sensitive fingers, surprisingly sensitive, he found the tank lid, pulled the choke upright, and pressed the electric starter button.

The sound of the moving van on the gravel turnaround in the front of the hotel was so hellishly loud that Bernard Foy would easily have been able to start the engine of the old boat, if only it had wanted to start. Frantically, he again pressed the starter button.

A memory awoke in him of his father always disconnecting the ignition cable to the lawn mower out of consideration for the children before he put it into the untidy toolshed on Brummel Drive on Sunday afternoons.

He was right: not just one but two ignition cables were hanging loose. After what seemed like a ten-minute search, he had them in place. Meanwhile, the hellish din of the moving van had abated.

Astonished, Bernard Foy looked out through one of the many holes in the tarpaulin through which rain water was streaming into the boat.

In the light of the lamps in the drive Bernard Foy, his eye teared equally by the wind blowing through the canvas and the effort of looking, saw that practically a whole platoon of German riot police, with helmets, bullet-proof vests, and machine guns with short, air-cooled barrels of a type Foy had thought existed only on TV news programs, ran quickly down the loading dock, evidently intending to surround Tietjen's Hut.

"Frightening, there must be some dangerous terrorist about," Foy said to himself, with the inner joy only occasioned by a profoundly ambiguous situation, letting the boat glide quietly onto the dark water.

Carefully, he used an oar to maneuver the boat down the Hamme and into the shadow of the bridge. New police cars seemed to be arriving with hooting sirens, and he took the opportunity to start the engine.

It wasn't easy to find the main channel in the fog and darkness, and more than once, it was only at the last minute that Foy saw a clump of alders emerging from the darkness.

My goal, he thought, has to be to get through the labyrinth of tributaries and canals to the main channel of the Weser, which has to be to the west. I should be able to get to Bremerhaven somehow.

As Bernard Foy's eyes got used to the darkness, steering became easier. He made friends with the quietly putt-putting motorboat; it was no longer as hard to find the main channel; you could sense it in the rudder if you paid close attention.

If only the fog doesn't lift so that they can send up helicopters or some other kind of nuisance, they'll never catch me, Bernard Foy thought.

Unhesitatingly identifying with the criminal, the hunted man, the outsider, the rabbi steered with increasing and blind certitude into the strange, marshy world of willows, channels, high-water dikes, and long-abandoned turf railroads.

In the darkness before him coots, grebes, and mallards flew up, and Bernard Foy thought that it would be wonderful to be able to fly up like that and, almost soundlessly, move through the silent, damp landscape in order to alight, shadowless and swift, on some quite different, remote canal.

30

3. The Mystery of the Two Briefcases

In truth, eyes and ears are poor witnesses for those who don't understand their language. Now, at four o'clock, the drawing room at Westerwede Castle seemed so quiet, so pleasant: a butler, assisted by one of those shy, slim, serious blonde housemaids who always seem as if they've been taken from early illustrations by Lucas Cranach the Elder, served tea in blue cups and the afternoon papers were brought in. Still, there was no escaping the fact that the atmosphere in the room was thunderous.

Count and Defense Minister Hans Hansdorff walked back and forth in the room with silent steps, as if he wanted to measure the expanse of Oriental rug between the rococo armchairs. His private secretary, knowing his employer's silence did not bode well, waited reverently in the background. Apparently the precarious party coalition was on the verge of splitting again under the pressure of KGB-financed peace demonstrations in strategic spots. In the Bundestag, large-scale rebellion against the missile placement policy seemed to be percolating.

As if that weren't enough, unsettling reports of terrorists striking only ten kilometers away, subjecting two of his own security men to an almost fatal assault (he must remember to send flowers; they were both in the military hospital in Bremerhaven). All of this was bad enough, but on top of everything else, there'd been that awful fight with Amelie at breakfast and her departure at ten.

Then more annoying letters from his lawyer about the paltry sum he'd carelessly accepted during the last election campaign. What he needed was a business secretary.

The weight of all these events sent a slight, throbbing pain, only too familiar, under the left edge of his waistcoat where his ribs started. Damn it all, was *that* nuisance going to start up again? And these women, with their insinuating, soft, shimmering negligees, their tailored suits, their scents! Always so ecstatic to begin with, and then lots of trouble when they had their periods, headaches, mysterious mental blocks, and neurotic foolishness, all stemming from their damn father fixations.

On the whole, woman is a lie, he thought. A sack full of worms, that's what a woman is. *Of all women, I've loved sleep the most.*

The last phrase seemed familiar to him, a quotation from one of the classics, but for the moment, he wasn't able to place it. Could it be from a Rilke sonnet?

His train of thought was interrupted by the security guard—an insignificant young man, who received, scrutinized, and announced the guests—proclaiming the arrival of Rabbi Bernard Foy.

Of course, it was that American tourist, who was a *rabbi*, on top of everything

31

else, and who'd gotten Amelie's briefcase by mistake. The minister expected a man with long sidelocks, broad-brimmed hat, and kaftan, or something along those lines, and was consequently somewhat surprised.

Before him stood, in a correct suit of Scottish wool, what looked like an American college student in excellent physical shape, his red hair cut rather short. His eyes were alight with intelligence and perhaps also with ironic interest.

Good Lord, the minister thought, life would certainly be a lot easier if I had assistants like this boy! The thought made him blush, because for one hundredth of a second it had touched on something forbidden. The minister soon switched his attention to the object Foy held in his hand, a pigskin briefcase, with some damp spots here and there, but unquestionably still very elegant.

"Please sit down, we're just having tea," the count said with a sudden upsurge of good will. In the same breath, he gave his secretary gracious permission to sit down.

"Milk or lemon?" the butler asked attentively.

"Milk, please," Bernard said.

He turned to the minister.

"Please forgive my intrusion, but I've been able to establish that a briefcase given to me by mistake in the checkroom at the Osterholz-Scharmbeck station yesterday belongs to one of your guests, a lady. I'd like to return it to her so she'll have the opportunity of determining that there's nothing missing. Here's my card. However, I'll be getting a new address soon. I'm going to start work in Paris, with Rabbi Williams at the synagogue on Rue Copernic."

He handed the briefcase over. The minister, who didn't seem particularly inhibited by the sanctity of private property (but then ministers seldom are), opened the briefcase with the expression of an experienced old customs officer. He examined the red leather diary that Bernard Foy had already subjected to close scrutiny, replaced the plastic pack of Dior pantyhose with a grimace of distaste, and played absent-mindedly with the buttons on the minicassette-player.

"My cousin Amelie left this morning. But of course I'll let her know as soon as possible that her luggage has been retrieved. Now, please tell me how you find Teufelsmoor. Isn't it an interesting landscape?"

"Magnificent, Count Hansdorff," Bernard Foy replied politely. "The only thing I regret is that I can't ride here. It must be wonderful to ride across the moors. But I'll have to postpone that pleasure. I've got a cab waiting, actually."

"Hans," the minister said to his security guard. "Go down and give a coupon to the driver. Of course Rabbi Foy mustn't suffer economically because he's being helpful. I really can't understand why my cousin left her briefcase at the station instead of bringing it with her here. Mr. Foy, are you quite"—he looked up with tired, very cold blue eyes while Bernard Foy stirred his tea pensively— "quite sure that it's Amelie's briefcase?"

"According to the station inspector, I and the blonde lady you picked up yesterday are the only people who could have left it."

"Odd. By the way, who saw that it was I, personally, who picked her up?"

"The station inspector."

"Oh, I see. That's fine, then."

"Thank you for inviting me in. By the way, there's another small detail . . ."

The minister no longer seemed interested. Instead he scrutinized the briefcase minutely.

"I can't find Amelie's name in it anywhere, and no other name either."

With sudden suspicion, perhaps with the intuitive feeling for *what doesn't add up* which he had practiced during his life in the political subcommittees, lobbies, and corridors of the Bundestag, the count added,

"Are you sure it isn't yours, Mr. Foy?"

"Rabbis aren't in the habit of using pigskin briefcases."

A thoughtful silence fell in the room. Through the tall French windows in the drawing room a cow was heard lowing in the distance.

"Please forgive me. I've forgotten something," Foy said. "Something important."

"The cab's waiting and we're paying for it," the security guard announced as he reentered the room.

"Excellent," Foy said, "I have to continue my journey to Paris with the night train this evening. But there was something else which I put in my breast pocket for safe-keeping. It's a minicassette for the tape-player."

"Is there anything on it?" the count asked with interest, quickly extending his hand to receive it.

"No voices," Foy said, "but please play it—just a moment, I'll help you, I think this is the way to insert it. If you listen carefully, you'll notice something."

A high whining and falling note was heard in the room. Sometimes it would change to short squeaks, then go back to its more continuous whine. The squeaky periods evidently occurred at indeterminate intervals.

"Modern music?" the count suggested. "Something like Stockhausen's *Gesang der Jünglinge*?"

"I'm no expert," Bernard Foy said. "But when I was a student I sometimes worked on the main frame at the University of Texas. My work mostly consisted of cleaning the heads of disk drives and getting beer for the operators. However, I did pick up a few bits of information. This tape contains a data bank or a computer program, or both."

"And the three signals that recur?" the butler asked, somewhat surprisingly.

"It might be a signal to a satellite where the particular string has something to do with a maneuver, a turn, perhaps . . . *no, I'm being really stupid.*"

He fell silent and started to think. What is it that maneuvers this way, at irregular intervals, across a large mass of other information, that swings back and forth, above a forest of isolated data, in sudden, jerky movements?

"Please excuse me, Count Hansdorff, but there's *something* the matter with your cousin Amelie. If this briefcase actually belongs to her, you have to do a painful reevaluation of your relationship to your young relative."

"What do you mean, young man?"

"What she hid as an ordinary tape cassette is *the program for a cruise missile.*"

33

"Good Lord!"

The minister blanched. He collapsed with his face in his hands. Bernard Foy moved his chair closer.

"If I can help you, I'd like to."

Just then a housemaid entered, the same housemaid in black and white who had helped serve the tea and whose stern, Gothic face made a strange impression on Bernard Foy. It was as if the sternness of the moorland itself, its melancholy and bleakness, its suddenly rising birds and its dogs baying in the night, had found a mirror in her gray eyes. They were like autumnal wells, reflecting a gray sky from which leaves fall, singly, silently.

"Mr. Lutweiler is on the phone," the housemaid announced.

Only in the Metro, en route from the Gare du Nord to Place Victor Hugo, surrounded by North Africans, American tourists, and the kind of ineffable book-reading women students found nowhere but in the Paris Metro, did he feel safe again. The fog's grip eased. In the long, echoing, tile corridors at the Barbès-Rochechouart you could hear a solitary flute player, immersed in the slow movement of Bach's suite in A-minor.

This flute melody seemed to be trying with endless patience, like some lonely, groping hand, to test the wall of the world to see if one of its stones might be loose.

To his astonishment, Bernard Foy discovered that the trees around Place Victor Hugo, mostly plane trees, were still almost green. He had the feeling of going from a colder room to a warmer one. Restaurant guests were still sitting outside. A mild sunlight blessed the scene.

Rabbi Williams, red-haired, freckled, terribly busy on two phones at once (he spoke a forceful English into one of them, to someone who apparently concerned himself much too closely in the affairs of his almost grown-up daughter, and a very elegant French into the other one, to the managers of an indoor tennis court he was hoping to rent for an evening event for his congregation) welcomed him with a gesture appropriate for a public school friend, rather than a yeshiva friend.

Bernard Foy looked around the room, brimming with books, while his new boss now and then acknowledged his presence with a friendly nod, at the same time continuing to speak more and more sternly into one telephone and more and more politely into the other.

The excellent 1933 Berlin edition of the Babylonian Talmud lay open on the table, and Bernard recognized chapter and verse with a sudden feeling of having come home. Evidently it was the extensive Talmudic essay "Shabbat" that had caught the rabbi's interest. A folder of letters that needed his signature, a pile of unread newspapers and periodicals, and a picture of the rabbi with his very beautiful wife on a visit to Venice completed the picture.

All this, and a thousand other small details characteristic of a rabbi's study wherever you are, from Tunisia to Texas, was familiar and gave Bernard Foy the same feeling of comfort and homecoming that coffee and cinnamon buns give a forester in Västmanland. Discreetly placed among all those familiar and comfortable things—the calendar from the World Jewish Congress, the black volumes of Torah texts and commentaries, the cozy Windsor cups on the table, the rabbi's well-seasoned Dunhill pipe, placed in a green ashtray decorated with a meander border and Chinese dragons—there was, however, one object which in its mysteriousness, its total strangeness, sent a new shiver down Bernard Foy's spine. It was as if the ice-cold fog of the marshland had for a moment penetrated the warm, carpeted, booklined room.

Leaning against one of the legs of the rabbi's desk, as if it were an object that had to be kept under particular observation, there, *once again*, was the gold-brown pigskin briefcase which faithfully, like a dog, seemed to have followed Bernard Foy from the moment he'd taken it from the murdered lawyer and chairman of the Swedish Chess Association, Hans von Lagerhielm.

"Of course it isn't my briefcase," Bernard Foy said, very silently and determinedly, to himself. "It's just my imagination, shaken by the bizarre and dangerous events of the last few days, that makes me believe it is. Now let me get a *firm* hold on my common sense and try to summarize the briefcase situation *before I go mad.*"

Rabbi Williams concluded the angry English telephone call and now completely immersed himself in the French one. Consequently he had, so to speak, *more capacity* left over to devote to Bernard Foy. He smiled at him welcomingly, examined him in brotherly fashion, his eyes alight with benevolence and intelligence; the promise of a long, rewarding conversation was behind these gestures which Bernard Foy tried to return with smiles just as winning, wise, and dutiful, so as to convince his new boss that he'd made a good choice of assistant.

Concurrently, in a small, ice-cold spot somewhere in Bernard Foy's brain, someone possessed a computerlike precision and lack of imagination was making a spread-sheet that looked something like this.

PIGSKIN BRIEFCASES

1. DELIVERED BY HANS VON LAGERHIELM, ATTORNEY, SHORTLY BEFORE HIS DEMISE ON THE EXPRESS OVERNIGHT TRAIN STOCKHOLM-HAMBURG, LOST ON THE FERRY HELSINGBORG-HELSINGÖR; NEVER RECOVERED AND NEVER OPENED.

2. THE PROPERTY OF A STRIKING BLONDE LADY, FORMER MISTRESS OF THE COUNT AND DEFENSE MINISTER OF THE FEDERAL REPUBLIC OF GERMANY, HANS HANSDORFF, CONTAINING, AMONG OTHER THINGS, A COMPLETE GUIDANCE PROGRAM FOR A CRUISE MISSILE. DELIVERED, ACCORDING TO CORRECT PROCEDURE, TO THE GOVERNMENT OF THE FEDERAL REPUBLIC OF GERMANY, I.E. ITS DEFENSE MINISTER, FOR FURTHER ACTION.

3. LEANING AGAINST THE FRONT RIGHT LEG OF RABBI CHARLES WILLIAMS' DESK IN RUE COPERNIC; INEXPLICABLE.

QUESTION: IS 3. IDENTICAL WITH 1. OR WITH 2.? OR IS IT POSSIBLE THAT 3. HAS ITS OWN IDENTITY?

That stupid computer might have continued to spit out its silly observations forever in the back of Bernard Foy's head if Rabbi Williams hadn't concluded his second conversation, too.

"Welcome, my dear Foy. Have you had lunch?"

"No, not yet. I feel a bit as if I've been floating in the rushes. I had a few problems on the trip."

"I heard about that, my dear Foy."

"From *whom*?"

"From the Danish consul general. He called this morning. But now let's go to a nice kosher restaurant called Wolkonskies at the corner of Avenue Kléber."

For a moment, the affable Irishman's features became stern. He added,

"Of course you keep to a kosher diet, my dear Bernard Foy?"

"Of course, Rabbi Williams, of course I do."

"I ask because I was thinking of your *baggage*. The Danish consul general called this morning to ask if he could send your briefcase along. Apparently you left it on the train to Copenhagen?"

"How did he find it?"

"The Danish police contacted the police in Helsingborg. It seems that, unfortunately, you shared your compartment with a man who was the victim of a crime?"

"Yes," Bernard said, "a most unpleasant affair."

"I can understand that," Williams said. "At any rate, the crime was what made the Swedish police remember that the briefcase was yours. And now they've been good enough to send it along from Copenhagen."

"Has anyone opened it?" Bernard Foy asked, perhaps somewhat thoughtlessly.

"I don't know. I . . . ."

"Because if no one has opened it, I don't know if it's mine."

"My dear Foy, before we go to have lunch and start our job interview, which we of course *hope* will be quite brief, just a formality, perhaps I should mention something. I'm known as a liberal, I'm sure there's no one in either Ireland or in Paris who'd characterize me as a 'fanatic' . . ."

"Of course not," Bernard Foy interpolated obligingly as the two men donned hats and overcoats.

"But you see, my dear Foy, we have some older members in our congregation here, not to mention the Board . . . And to them it might not seem so obvious that a rabbi should carry his books, perhaps even his prayer books and his sermon, in a pigskin briefcase. Even," he hastened to add, "if I have to admit that your briefcase is very elegant."

"Of course I'll change my briefcase right off," Bernard Foy said. "I can't understand why I didn't think of it myself. But lately I've been so preoccupied with my dissertation on the Gnostic-Manichean roots of Isaac Luria. However, I know of a little shop on Avenue Claude-Bernard, close to Rue Vauquelin, which boasts that it can repair *just about anything*. It's between a butcher's and a shop for advanced microelectronics. I'm sure they'll have some nice old brief-cases."

Secretly he thought: *They'll help me find the combination for that lock.*

Just as they stepped into the street, the rabbi said:

"You seem to be man of broad interests, my dear Foy?"

Rabbi Foy found it most expeditious not to answer this question for the time being.

After a lunch at which the two learned men did not deny themselves the pleasures of this world, from gefilte fish to kugel, and where some glasses of Calvados contributed to the creation of a peaceful and pleasant atmosphere, Bernard Foy emphasized that it was important for him to have enough free time to finish his dissertation on Isaac Luria's theory of the creation.

This remarkable medieval teacher who had once had the audacity to assume that the original work of creation had been interrupted by a subtle kind of breakdown, comparable to a just-awakened computer refusing to display the inserted software program, instead sadly communicating, FAILURE TO LOAD APPLICATION or some such thing, interested the two rabbis equally. As so many readers through the centuries they, too, had felt the cool, almost ironically calming breeze of nega-tion theology in Luria's works. The idea that the original harmony between Creator and Creation could only be restored by an effort on the part of the Created, that man has in his power to recreate, not God, but the contact with the obverse of the dark world, where God dwelt, hidden in the black depths of negation, wasn't that in fact an idea with profoundly liberating implications?

Oughtn't Bernard Foy to have access to the excellent collection of medieval Hebraica in the Bibliothèque Nationale so that, for a few afternoons a week at least, he might further his knowledge? Should he also read around, quite exten-sively, in the works of other cabbalistic writers to show what was original with Luria and what wasn't, what was an expression of specific, political disappoint-ment at the tragic expulsion of Jews from Spain and a much older element, per-haps older than what's called Gnostic and Manichean impulses, in the rich web of medieval Judaic concepts?

Perhaps the American cultural attaché might even be persuaded to write a letter of recommendation to the stern ladies presiding over the reading room at the Bibliothèque Nationale?

When the conversation reached this point, it struck Bernard Foy that he had good reason to believe he'd been accepted as the assistant rabbi of one of the wealthiest and in all respects most excellent of the Jewish congregations in Paris.

He parted from Rabbi Williams on the best of terms in order to, as he put it, "Go to his hotel and get some sleep."

A neutral, benign autumnal sunshine was falling on the city, and Bernard had not the slightest inclination to go to his hot little room (he knew what they looked like) at the Hotel Jeanne d'Arc on Rue de Jarente. The yellow briefcase weighed heavily in his hand after the meal. What was he going to do with it?

Throw it into the river? Forget it on a park bench? Try to sell it?

But suppose it contained something valuable? The currency regulations of the present Swedish government, which were hardly successful in economic terms, enforced by means of prison sentences and house searches, were almost on par with the currency regulations of the Nazi regime in 1939. Of course this led to some rather naive attempts to carry property out of the country. Perhaps the dead lawyer had tried to get money out of Sweden in this clumsy manner, for himself or for one of his clients? Wouldn't it, in that case, be unethical not to try to save the money, perhaps by contacting the dead man's estate?

In the Metro Bernard Foy was already—with the youthful ability to stimulate himself with strange fantasies characteristic of him—becoming convinced that the weight of the pigskin briefcase must be due to it being packed with paper money. Perhaps it contained millions? Why else would the lawyer have been so anxious?

He was not unaffected by the temptation inherent in the thought that he might be the only person in the world who knew the whereabouts of this briefcase. He became aware of how heretical this thought was when he looked up and realized that a gang of Moroccan youths in the Metro also knew that he had the briefcase in his possession. Bernard Foy loved a fight—he regarded it as a moral imperative—but he didn't have the slightest wish to get into a fight with four unemployed Moroccans in the Paris Metro over a pigskin briefcase about whose contents he knew nothing and which might contain a million dollars, but which, however, did not belong to Bernard and which consequently had to be restored to its proper owner.

He got off at the next stop, finding to his relief that the young Moroccans had not followed him, and made his decision quickly.

The small shop in Rue Claude-Bernard which he'd passed many times in the late '70s and taken amused notice of, since the advertisement in the window, printed on a piece of cardboard in careful, old man's penmanship, actually promised to *repair anything*, proved still more amusing when you got inside. Behind an old-fashioned counter you got a glimpse of a workroom with lathe, anvil, and pipe-cutting machine. On the shelves and depending from hooks in the ceiling here and there was a collection of objects that would have made the Aragon who wrote *Le Paysan de Paris*, the Marcel Duchamp who once selected the bottle washer of le Bistro Rue du Bac as the object for a museum collection, wild with enthusiasm.

Baby carriages from the '20s co-existed with cameras from 1910. Two dolls with cold, beautiful, and probably refurbished china faces sat on a shelf with a huge mahogany music box whose lid featured a Moor with crossed legs, wearing a red cap.

Why am I suddenly pursued by *Moors*? Bernard thought.

Beside the music box and the dolls was a German Peoples' radio set from

World War II, probably a collector's treasure, some tin soldiers of the rounded Spanish type: a Roman centurion, stern, holding his commander's staff; a slender, athletic Greek hoplite with sword and dagger, almost in a dance position; and furthest off a Viking, big, heavy, and blond, who seemed to have lost his shield and was going to have it glued on again.

A tiny bell had sounded on the rabbi's entrance to the shop. The small man, in slippers and with strongly magnifying gold-framed half-glasses on his nose, was so like the last portrait of Dr. Walter Benjamin, from Svendborg in 1939, that for an instant, Bernard Foy imagined that he was seeing a ghost.

"Monsieur," Bernard Foy said in a French that had some American roughness, but which was fluent and accurate, "I have a stupid problem . . ."

"People usually do when they come here."

"The thing is, the combination lock on my briefcase doesn't want to open. I've tried to remember the combination, but I've forgotten it."

"Monsieur, please allow me to ask you a question which may be impertinent, but which I'm afraid I have to ask. Is this briefcase actually *yours*? Have you yourself opened it at some time? I only ask because sometimes the owners of these modern briefcases have explosives built into them, so that the contents will be destroyed by an explosion if someone who doesn't know the briefcase starts fiddling with it."

Bernard Foy squirmed with embarrassment.

"Of course it's my briefcase. But you might also say that it isn't. The thing is, it belonged to my uncle, the Swedish lawyer Hans von Lagerhielm, chairman of the Swedish Chess Association. It came to me on his death. Consequently I am not quite able to preclude your conjecture, Monsieur . . .?"

"Klock."

"Excuse me?"

"Jean Christophe Klock."

"Thank you. My name is Bernard Foy, and I come from Stockholm."

"I can hear that . . ."

"Hrrmm, be that as it may, I'm not able to preclude your *conjecture*, Monsieur Klock. But at the same time I have to say that I'd be very much surprised if Uncle Hans had actually done anything so foolish."

"Thank you, Monsieur Foy, that's all I wanted to know; now I am reassured. I'll be back in a minute."

Monsieur Klock disappeared into the interior of the shop. At first, Bernard Foy expected a deafening explosion to rend the silence of this strange place, where only the ticking of a wall clock somewhere divided the Bergson time into mechanical units. There was no explosion. But neither did Monsieur Klock return. Bernard started to feel somewhat uneasy.

Hopefully, there was no back door through which Klock might have disappeared with millions of dollars? Ridiculous. Here he was, back again, but with a worried look behind his gold-framed half-glasses, the briefcase in one hand and a tiny, very narrow screwdriver in the other.

"Your uncle, Monsieur Foy, must have been both a very wealthy and a very careful man."

"What do you mean?"

"The lock of his briefcase isn't mechanical. It looks like a mechanical lock, but it's electronic."

Bernard Foy didn't find his own reply particularly intelligent.

"What can we do now?"

"Please take your briefcase to my young nephew, three shops up the street. He does electronics."

As distinguished from his uncle, the young man had a harder, more business-like attitude which hardly seemed softened by Bernard's reference to his uncle.

"What have we here?"

"A briefcase with a combination lock."

"I can see that. What am I supposed to do with it?"

"It's got an electronic lock."

He whistled and gave the other young man in the shop a meaningful look. Then he disappeared without further comment.

Bernard Foy would never have believed there could be so many bizarre electronic bugs and paraphernalia. Here, packaged as simply as if they'd been stereos, were contraptions to put in your own or someone else's telephone. Then you could call from Paris or Singapore and, by dialing an extra digit, turn the telephone into a sensitive microphone that would disclose everything that was being said in the room.

Bernard Foy felt slightly bored. Who'd be that interested in knowing other people's secrets?

The nephew returned.

"Do you think the briefcase is rigged?" he asked.

"No, I don't," the rabbi answered. "However," he added with a chilly smile, "I can't vouch for the fact that it isn't."

The nephew disappeared and returned triumphantly.

"It isn't that hard when you've got a good computer that can give you all the permutations in ten minutes. Frankly, your uncle's briefcase is already somewhat *obsolete*," he said.

"That's why I went to *your* uncle first," Bernard Foy said, "so that the uncles might have a chance to solve the problem between them, so to speak."

Back in his narrow, cozy hotel room, he opened the briefcase. He had expected anything, *practically anything*, except *exactly* what he found when he loosened the two side locks and slowly opened the lid on the silk-lined interior.

The reason it had felt so heavy was that it contained books. In colorful jackets, charmingly in period if a bit worn, lay a row of adventure stories and sensational thrillers from the late nineteenth century, carefully packed, spines up.

Had the dead man been a collector? Were those old softcover books actually so valuable that someone had been willing to kill the lawyer to get them? Or—an icy thought traveled down Bernard's spine—was it at him the knife had been aimed after all?

He took the books out of the briefcase, one by one. There weren't as many as it had seemed at first. Here was Vidocq's *Les Vrais Mystères de Paris* from 1844.

And here, more elegant, in several volumes, apparently intended for a more sophisticated audience, was X. de Montepin's *Les Viveurs de Paris*. P. Bocage's *Les Puritains de Paris* seemed duller. And this one, Gaboriau's *Les Esclaves de Paris*, seemed positively scholarly.

Bernard seriously doubted that the reading of those volumes would render his evenings in Hotel Jeanne d'Arc happy. One by one, he put them on the bedside table. Had Hans von Lagerhielm in fact intended to open another bookstall among the many already in existence on the Left Bank of the Seine?

Bernard's attention to and interest in this briefcase, which for days had embittered and complicated his existence, was again awakened when his tired eyes fell on the only hardcover book in the briefcase. It seemed to be a volume of the periodical *Nouvelle Revue Française*, the glorious periodical started by André Gide and Roger Martin du Gard with the elder Monsieur Gallimard, the source of not just a literary tradition but also of an important Parisian publishing house. This was evidently the handsomely bound Volume I for January-May of 1937.

Thoughtfully, Bernard turned the volume over. But what was this? The book belonged to the Bibliothèque Nationale! No doubt about it; no one could mistake the gold lettering on the spine and the emblem imprinted on the title page.

The rabbi's head felt quite *empty*, the great emptiness you feel when you open a volume with cuneiform text, or are confronted with the task of reprograming a menu written in Lisp when you don't know Lisp. Why would a respected Swedish lawyer steal books from the Bibliothèque Nationale? And if he did, why would he want to return them? Had he had an attack of bad conscience?

But, *supposing* that he wanted to steal books from the Bibliothèque Nationale, why then wouldn't he steal something valuable instead of this periodical volume you could probably buy for thirty francs in any secondhand bookstore?

He leafed quickly through the book. He couldn't see anything remarkable about it. The Bibliothèque Nationale. When had this concept first surfaced during his journey?

He put his hand into the inside pocket of his jacket and fished out the small library card that had been and, strictly speaking, still was, the property of a beautiful young lady with long dark hair, Elisabeth Frejer. Had the lawyer known her? Probably.

Perhaps he'd meant to return the book on her behalf? But in that case, she must have stolen it, for you don't take books out of the Bibliothèque Nationale; you sit solemnly and decorously at one of the long library tables to the right or to the left under the handsome iron ornaments in the big reading room Labrouste completed in 1868. You sit there looking at the beautiful beech forest, painted against a background of blue sky, which adorns the wall panels of mild-colored murals, or you look down at your books, or you look at the beautiful graduate student sitting opposite. But you wait for the attendant to come with the book you have ordered.

Perhaps Elisabeth Frejer had stolen the book, and her more responsible lover had persuaded her to return it? But why should a beautiful young student, evidently the lover of a wealthy Swedish lawyer, risk scandal and expulsion from university and library in order to steal an insignificant, relatively modern periodical worth at best fifty francs?

For the first time in the last few days, Bernard Foy had the feeling that he'd reached a dead end. This riddle was like a ball of yarn in which it's impossible to find the loose thread.

But hadn't the Bibliothèque Nationale turned up somewhere in Worpswede? In quite a different context?

Of course! Tomorrow, Thursday, October 27, the blonde lady who, in all probability, had carried the guidance program for a cruise missile in her tape recorder, the attractive but apparently dangerous lady whom Count Hans Hansdorff, probably with less than perfect truth, had characterized as his cousin Amelie, was to meet someone at the Bibliothèque Nationale.

But what did this blonde Soviet spy, whom he had flushed out because of a stupid mix-up, have to do with the person or persons who'd killed the chairman of the chess association, or with Elisabeth Frejer's library card to the Bibliothèque Nationale? Coincidences, patterns, configurations that looked as if they had a meaning but didn't.

Stretched out on his hotel bed, his head a veritable ants' nest of hypotheses and counterhypotheses, Bernard Foy left this tangle of riddles for a long, invigorating nap.

When he woke up, blue dusk had already started falling over Les Marais. The chirping voices of the schoolchildren on their way home from Lycée Charlemagne had woken him up. He pulled the curtain aside and looked out on the street. The housewives were going in and out of the *boulangerie*.

The whole thing is quite simple, it occurred to him. It's like a *boulangerie*, actually. You carry in something very small, very insignificant, that's never been there. And you take something else away. You exchange something with someone else. *1937 Vol. I of NRF* is nothing but a mailbox. And if one proceeds carefully and doesn't make any mistakes, he'll find out what it contains.

Tomorrow Bernard Foy will be at the Bibliothèque Nationale.

Fortified by this idea, he went out into the soft blue of the Parisian autumn night. He wanted to have dinner in a small restaurant at the Exchange, on Rue Saint-Marc, which he remembered as inexpensive, pleasant, and cultured. It was called Le Petit Coin de la Bourse. *Luxe, calme, volupté*, he thought involuntarily.

4. The Jester of Rue des Petits-Champs

The name of the bow is life; its work is death.

In Rue des Petits-Champs, between the Palais Royal and the Bibliothèque Nationale, on beautiful afternoons in late fall, a strange figure can be seen sitting on the stone ramparts or strolling nonchalantly up and down the little steps outside the Palais-Royal Passage, swinging a champagne glass in one hand and a bottle of Veuve Clicquot, renewed each day, in the other. He's dressed in evening clothes which have seen better days, with correct white bow tie and a waistcoat that used to be whiter; his pants are tight on his calves, as if they've been subjected to too many violent rainstorms, and he wears them pulled high at the waist.

This gentleman, making the kind of gestures only seen in roguish Viennese barons in light opera of the '90s, enmeshed in merry duets with coquettish ladies—although in this instance, his gestures are silent—sits on his stage, which sometimes is the steps to the shortest passage in Paris, sometimes the rampart of one of the palaces from the age of Colbert which line the narrow street.

Who is he? A gentleman who's fallen on evil days? A hero from a novel Balzac intended to write but forgot about in his haste and who now, abandoned for more than a hundred years, wanders about in search of his author? One of those men peculiar to Paris, one of those holy jesters whom the abolutist era tried to lock up on the grounds of the old saltpeter mines on the Left Bank, in the cradle of modern psychiatry called La Salpêtrière? It's impossible to keep the madmen of Paris under control, or its magicians, sword dancers, and fire-eaters either: this city has a subconscious.

There seems to be a continuous, silent operetta going on inside the madman of Rue des Petits-Champs. Who knows whether the city is not in fact dependent on its being performed precisely and silently, as dependent as on the proper performance of Racine plays on the other side of the Palais Royal? On this particular Thursday in October, the gallant gentleman, an operatic hero in tatters, would meet with the kind of misfortune that's always unpleasant for an artist, perhaps particularly so for an artist in search of perfection: namely, not to be the most interesting spectacle around, overshadowed by an even more bizarre spectacle.

But at 8:43 that morning—that is seventeen minutes before the Bibliothèque Nationale will open and admit the hopeful crowds of gentlemen with coats and umbrellas, slim-hipped women students in leather skirts and long, rain-soaked hair, substantial older ladies with something that looks like market baskets, all of them standing there waiting for admittance as Bernard Foy passed through the Passage du Palais Royal after a pleasant stroll under the arches, up from the Metro station down by the Comédie-Française—at this time the operetta duke

43

still knew nothing of his fate. He only saw a youngish rabbi, apparently red-haired under his black, new-looking, broad-brimmed hat, with a briefcase of—rather surprisingly—yellow pigskin in his hand. The rabbi hurried down the street with determined step, making an energetic effort not to notice the jester.

In actual fact, Bernard Foy was worried that he might be late. More than worried: he had the strong feeling we all experience at times, that the day would somehow be decisive, that this was the kind of day when a long-nurtured, irritating mystery will at last have its solution. He'd slept fitfully in his narrow bed in the Hotel Jeanne d'Arc, wound in thin, gray blankets that had barely kept out the dampness of the autumn rain which fell through the night. Would the simple letter of recommendation from Rabbi Williams, the only thing he'd been able to scrounge up in such a short time, guarantee him free passage into the big reading room's silent forest of wrought-iron pillars? Would the *Nouvelle Revue Française*, Vol. I, 1937 (he carefully safeguarded the probably spurious library copy he'd found in the dead lawyer's briefcase) in fact turn out to be a mailbox for secret agents?

Would the blonde lady in Worpswede, who had had in her possession a vital piece of software for a cruise missile, turn up for the meeting in the library?

And, to add the most difficult of all the day's difficult questions to the compilation of mysteries: Was it one or two mutually independent, secret organizations he was looking for? The answer was not unimportant, for if there were two, it was quite possible that one of them sought his own death.

"All living things suffer," he thought, in the consoling words of the Talmudist.

The stern lady in the glass cage examined him carefully, demanding a hundred-franc note in exchange for the small red sticker which, after a rather funny photo ceremony, was affixed to his elegant new library card. He noted in passing that it was his last large bill.

I'll have to ask Rabbi Williams for an advance, he thought, but the thought changed direction right away: "Everything is in our service. But we have to be able to grasp it."

That was what Rabbi Eliezer had once said, consolingly.

He was the last one admitted before the usual morning line formed. With a sigh of relief, he received a white card with the number 242. So he was going to sit on the left side of the reading room. He sat down, putting his briefcase reverently under the green lamp. A heavy, almost shapeless gentleman with huge, doglike ears had settled himself on Bernard's left. On his right was a woman student, of course in a skirt of soft kid leather, angora sweater, and long, billowing, dark hair, the kind of girl who always seemed to end up beside Bernard Foy in libraries and who, with her reminder of the beauty and richness of creation, often drew his attention from the theology of Isaac Luria.

He mustn't start dreaming. In the catalog room, which he knew well from his early youth, this strange, subterranean catalog room, it took some time before he, alone in his corner, could find the periodical. He'd forgotten that the

Bibliothèque Nationale catalog is divided into a horrendous number of subdivisions, almost like annual rings, or centennial rings, according to different eras.

It was still early down here. A small man moving about in squeaking shoes, on crutches, frightened him strangely.

What a peculiar place, he thought, as he passed the table reserved for the editors of *La Revue Bibliographique*, where two ancients with long, pointed beards seemed to nod at each other as they wrote in pointed script on lined paper. *As if they were part of some funny old-fashioned mechanical toy,* Foy thought. They nod at each other the way the pendulum wags in old clocks.

After he had left his order for the strange volume of *NRF* that already reposed in the briefcase on his table, he cautiously looked around the room. The young woman on his right seemed absorbed by a volume on art history which she could probably have found in any library. Those damn young girls, Foy thought, spoiled daughters of rich daddies, who use the Bibliothèque Nationale for their little seminar papers.

It's as if I'd use an electric saw to slice my breakfast butter, the rabbi thought. Her hips were mysteriously present in his anger. She seemed mostly preoccupied with sharpening her pencils. There were many of them.

The man on his left exuded an unpleasant, sour smell, like an old, unaired barracks where sweaty wool uniforms had been allowed to dry without being washed, a smell of camphor, essence of vinegar, foot deodorant, iodine for infected wounds, and something else that Bernard Foy found deeply disturbing but which he couldn't place.

With his notebook in front of him, Bernard Foy tried to escape from the smell into a world of objective observation. Somewhere in the reading room, the blonde German lady would turn up, any minute now, for her meeting. But where? Perhaps by the counter, where all the readers had to leave and pick up their numbers? Perhaps in the Ladies'? Why not in the big periodicals room, quite a distance from where he was sitting? Why not in the catalog room? What was the signal? Provided the meeting was actually going to take place, how would he be able to find the right spot?

In his notebook, sacred to a higher purpose and filled with endless Hebraic quotations from various medieval authorities, one page contained a single phrase: *Ernst Lutweiler.*

Ernst Lutweiler was the businessman who'd disturbed his peaceful dinner at Tietjen's Hut—and who might have tried to kill him.

"Herr Lutweiler is on the phone," the German Minister of Defense's maid had said, as Bernard rushed out of the house. Not only that—here, under the tempting green branches of the mural frescoes, he suddenly remembered with absolute certainty where he'd first heard the name of Ernst Lutweiler.

It wasn't just once, but hundreds of times, in a bar on Canal Street Houston.

Bernard's father, Jacob Foy, hadn't presided over the cash register at Burnie's all his life. When he, now in his late sixties, presided over his clientele of sailors, pilots, and dubious housewives with platinum hair, he might reasonably have been characterized as a well-traveled man who'd seen a lot of life. The large glass jar of pickles looked like some strange aquarium for otherworldly delicacies; a small, strange toy orchestra on the wall, a Big Band in the Glenn Miller style, played on dainty toy instruments at regular intervals.

In this bar there was also a picture from the Normandy invasion, a framed newspaper cutting showing soldiers of the 82nd Airborne in their descent over France.

After a wild time in the youth gangs only too typical of Houston in the '30s, Jacob had ended up as a noncommissioned officer in the San Antonio paratrooper regiment of later fame. He remembered his youth as the smell of wet khaki, gun oil, clouds of Texas dust, shrill whistle commands, and leather straps cutting into his shoulders.

From this environment, Jacob had, so to speak, been thrown into empty space above Sicily; after a few days of unmitigated hell with bursting shells, machine-gun fire, and mounds of melancholy dead piled in the shimmering Italian summer heat, he'd suddenly found himself in possession of the Congressional Medal of Honor. The step from black sheep of the family to hero was so swift that it was almost impossible for him to grasp it. His own paratrooper platoon, a collection of uncommonly stubborn young men, often known to each other from meetings in barrooms in early youth and slowdowns among tough gangs in late '30s Houston, suddenly found themselves on the front pages of *The New York Times* and *Collier's*.

They'd had the good, or perhaps bad, luck to run into an unusually well-defended and numerically superior German unit in Sicily. It had killed some of his comrades and given the survivors Purple Hearts and Distinguished Service Medals from a distant U.S. which, until now, they'd hardly been aware of except in the shape of motorcycle policemen and harassment in the juvenile courts.

The first Germans he saw were dead ones. It surprised him that those weather-beaten, emaciated, proletarian faces had held malice toward him. But that was how it was. The first reports of the extermination camps were already being published in Jewish community papers.

He returned from Sicily a hero, eventually being transferred to England. His platoon was put ashore forth-eight hours before the Normandy invasion. It was a clear night in early summer when he jumped, and all would have been well if the platoon hadn't chanced to land right in a training camp for SS officers, some of the parachuters smack on the tent roofs. Jacob didn't have a chance to get off many shots that night. A black eye and a broken rib as his prize, he managed to survive the day. Blood group B on his dog tag stood for "Baptist," he convinced the interrogating officer (this wasn't the first time angry men in boots and uniforms had submitted young Foy to a bellowing interrogation). He ended up on the Red Cross list and, a few days after the invasion, he was conducted through Paris, a defeated prisoner.

It was an instructive experience. Even forty years later, when the TV in the corner of the bar (it was always turned on, talking and making a racket) showed documentary footage from the Allies' triumphant entry into Paris, as sometimes happened, Jacob Foy always had the feeling that the world history being shown must have taken place on some other time-line in some other possible universe.

Jacob Foy, too, remembered triumphant faces, jubilant Frenchmen, uniformed men with beautiful young women by their sides. But they did not rejoice because he and his comrades had come to liberate them but because they were captives: the women spat in their faces and the men laughed with scorn; the whole time, they were surrounded by trucks where the cameras whirred.

The white-haired, nowadays rather quiet Jacob Foy would then muse in his bar: Where had all those who rejoiced that he and his comrades were captives disappeared to at the Liberation? And where had all those *liberated* people come from, the ones you saw on CBS documentaries? No matter how old he got, he feared he'd never get it right. His son, who was a clever, educated man, might do so, but for one thing, his son wasn't home much nowadays, and for another, Jacob was too shy to ask questions. Perhaps the boy would think he was stupid?

In 1944, Bernard Foy wasn't born yet. The man who would become his father was a prisoner of war in a large camp, conventionally divided into three parts, with Russians and Americans on the two sides and Englishmen at the center. It was in Zwillerheyde.

It was a flat landscape, sometimes beautiful in the morning light. When the weather was clear, one could see, far beyond the barbed wire, woods and hills where fog was rising. The winters were incredibly cold: the prisoners survived by sleeping in each other's arms at night, and that was no joke. Frequently, two prisoners would make common cause, dividing the small bread rations with each other, sharing their blankets and Red Cross packages. It was a kind of symbiosis which, due to simple laws of economics, made survival more probable.

Jacob Foy's particular tormentor was Sergeant Lutweiler. This gentleman, whose SS cap seemed to be kept in place only by his awful protruding ears, must have been in the same age group as his victim. Jacob Foy could remember the close-cropped back of his head.

Asked what he did with Lutweiler in 1945, when the Allied troops were in the vicinity of the camp, most of the guards had fled, and the prisoners were already in revolt, old Jacob Foy would answer, tranquilly, an expression of childish glee in his face:

"Lutweiler? I killed him. I remember chasing him down a passage with a large piece of firewood, and at the end of the passage there was nothing but a big delousing cupboard. I opened the door—it was a heavy metal door—and I made him step into the cupboard. I've always wondered why he obeyed me. Then I set the dial to delousing. Arsenic powder and hot steam rushed in. Yes, that was the end of Lutweiler."

As a small boy, Bernard Foy had listened with undisguised admiration to his father's narrative, which—it must be admitted—got more dramatic with the passing years. He'd imagined the door closing forever before the eyes of that pale SS man; he'd seen him standing there, like a mummy in its case. What would happen if someone, some fine day, found that delousing cupboard at some abandoned dump?

(For some reason, abandoned dumps played a large part in the fantasy life of Bernard Foy, along with culverts, long underground tunnel systems under hospital buildings and similar large buildings, culverts and the realistic electronic games that one might play in such structures. What was slightly odd was the fact that in real life, Bernard Foy never visited either dumps or underground culverts.

However, something in him was stimulated by the thought that in actual fact, he was nothing but a participant in one of those stupid computer games young people seemed so obsessed with nowadays.)

Would the terrible man still be standing there, now with a white, grinning cranium under his SS cap? Responding to the look of the living with the distracted, milky eyes of the dead?

Or suppose there was nobody there? Suppose he'd gotten out the other side, in some strange way? What other side? Where would it be, in that case?

"Unthinkable, son," Jacob Foy would say with his confident laugh, when the eleven-year-old Bernard cautiously introduced this possibility during his father's magnificent storytelling sessions in the bar. "Completely unthinkable."

There were huge bolts that were shot home when the delousing cupboard was used. "And in back of them, you see," he continued, lovingly touching the back of his son's head, while the guests at the bar listened with bated breath, "in back, you see, my young friend, there was nothing but the wall. *The wall*, you know, sonny!"

And his laughter resounded across the bar counter.

But perhaps this execution of the prisoners' tormentor was nothing but a daydream, a never-realized revenge fantasy which the quiet man had thought up long after he left the prison camp? Something very determined, very hard in his father's personality, which hardly ever surfaced in ordinary life, but which at certain times became visible with the same sharpness and solidity as a shell fragment in the bark of a friendly old tree, that something told Bernard that perhaps it wasn't a fantasy after all.

Bernard Foy sank into musings and dreams. The beautiful foliage in the ceiling frescoes, which conveyed such a pleasant feeling of being in a forest, was kind to the eye. The impression of forest in this handsome reading room, which had seen so many brilliant essays and books written at the long tables with the friendly green lamps, was reenforced by the subdued rustling of thousands of pages turning simultaneously under the cupola.

It sounds like a summer wind passing through aspens, Bernard thought.

If it hadn't been for the unpleasant—what shall we call it: barracks smell—of the man on his left, Bernard would have found everything very agreeable.

I won't be able to stand it much longer, Bernard thought. At the risk of having to stand in line again, I'll have to ask for another seat. Very disagreeable! But unwashed people is something I've never been able to put up with, he said to himself. The young lady on his right, who'd recently exerted such a clear sexual attraction in her leather skirt and her narrow, well cared-for hands, nervous as two fluttering young swallows, was now seated elsewhere turning the leaves of Walter Benjamin's *Passagenwerk* in the new Suhrkamp edition. She seemed to have reached the only possible conclusion: One simply could not remain sitting next to that stinkbag with his smell of infantry soldier and police barracks wool.

I certainly hope, Bernard thought, that she didn't think the smell was coming *from me. That* would be too painful.

Look, she seems to have forgotten an envelope on the table. But perhaps it would be impolite to move it? Perhaps she'll be coming back? Perhaps I'd better leave it at the circulation desk. He put the envelope, evidently containing a photograph or some other very stiff paper, on top of his notebook.

He was sitting in the foliage shade of the ceiling paintings. Here Walter Benjamin had once, in the last few years before the war, frantically collected his excerpts and quotations for the big book on Baudelaire he never had time to put into final form. But when this reading room was inaugurated, on June 16, 1868, Charles Baudelaire had been dead for a year.

Here learned works, querulous magazine reviews, brilliant debate contributions had been written. Here doctoral dissertations, dictionaries of Old Sumerian and Chaldee had been written. And in the endless storage rooms slept all those books no one reads anymore; strange old novels like the ones in the pigskin briefcase.

Bernard was recalled from his vague musing by a light touch on his elbow.

It was the guard, the polite young man whose duty it was to distribute the requested books. Sometimes this gentleman will arrive bearing a small green card that tells you the book you've asked for has already been given to someone else. Sometimes you're lucky enough to get your book. It's like a lottery. One morning's absence could mean the irretrievable loss of a book for which you've waited several weeks.

But that wasn't the case this time. He was handed Volume I, 1937, of the *Nouvelle Revue Française*, frightening in its twin-likeness to the volume, bound in exactly the same way, which Bernard had found in the locked briefcase. Simultaneously, the young man collected the copy Bernard had already put on his table.

It happened so fast that Bernard didn't have a chance to demur. And what would he have said if he'd had the chance? That copy, too, belonged to the Bibliothèque Nationale. It's not a brilliant beginning of a young rabbi's Parisian career to be accused of book theft in the national library. Clenching his teeth, Bernard suppressed his shock and disappointment and started to leaf through the new copy.

Here was Roger Martin du Gard, and here was André Gide. Here the big prewar debates were acted out, here was the eternal, always tedious struggle between the kind of intellectual who admires Power—in one of its incarnations— and the kind of intellectual who opposes it. Here vitalism and communism met, psychoanalysis and the remainder of the thin ideology of *les hommes de la bonne volunté* in what might, somewhat irreverently, be referred to as blessed confusion.

And here there should be an essay on Paris by an interesting young critic, Roger Caillois. *But what was this!*

Seldom has a rabbi been as close to emitting a raucous whistle beneath the venerable cupola of the Bibliothèque Nationale as was Bernard Foy from Houston on this particular afternoon. He had valid reasons, however. What he'd discovered was nothing less than a perfect spy mailbox.

For in the place where Roger Caillois' interesting essay "Paris, Mythe Moderne" was to have begun, that is, on page 668, the most monotonous cryptogram of figures started, arranged into groups of five:

85739 97878 24659 25375 36645 35332 97748 . . .

and so on, page up and page down, in such terrible monotony that it would have induced spleen in even the most wide-awake reader, and this compact mass of figures stretched to exactly the point where the next article quietly began.

This interleaving was so elegantly carried out that, from the outside, the faint difference in color at the edges of the leaves could only be noticed if you held the book very close to the light.

There was no doubt. Evidently there was someone who was able to smuggle out volumes from the Bibliothèque Nationale, there was someone who produced skillful facsimiles with long, coded messages which, at the right moment, were exchanged at a table in the reading room.

But how could they be smuggled out again? Wasn't the risk that they'd be discovered by the stern controller at the exit too great? Had there been a similar message in the book he'd carried into the library, the one that had been in the briefcase of the murdered chess association chairman? He couldn't recall that he'd seen anything in that volume which departed from the usual. It was true, however, that he hadn't actually looked for interleaved pages.

But who, in this age of xeroxes, could have an interest in making these careful reports? You only do that, it occurred to Bernard, if you want to smuggle something across a national border. Nobody steals books, or reads them either, least of all customs officers, if they look like that. A book like that doesn't raise expectations of pornography.

Bernard realized clearly that he was in danger. Perhaps someone was watching him, right now, from one of the passages in the upper galleries? It was hardly advisable to keep sitting here, on this chair, and try to copy this enormous mass of figures, and hardly advisable, either, to try to carry the book out under his coat.

Evidently this text was important: here was a text to be saved.

Bernard's thoughts now returned to the magic word which had just passed through his tired brain: Xerox!

With determined step, he walked to the library's reproduction department, situated behind the left-hand circulation desk.

It was the time of day when there are no long lines. He might have stood there for three, or at most five, minutes (a period of time that would later prove surprisingly significant) before it was his turn to talk to the friendly little Vietnamese girl who received his book.

She carefully counted the number of pages to be copied, estimated the cost, showing not the least surprise that those pages contained nothing but a seemingly endless row of figures.

Bernard paid the required eighteen francs with equanimity, noting in passing that he didn't have much money left; it was true that he hadn't undertaken any financial activity for a while, and his extended excursion to the wet marshlands and autumnal canals of Worpswede certainly had not enriched him.

On his return to the reading room, a single glance was enough to convince him that something very unusual must have taken place there. Not a single reader remained in his seat; instead they formed mumbling, whispering, chattering groups, still very low-voiced. The middle of the room was dark blue with the uniforms of gendarmes, and still more were flowing in.

He already *knew it*: it was around his former seat that the police, standing in a ring, were making a discreet screen. From the steps to the reproduction department—providing him with a better view than he would otherwise have had—he saw, only too clearly, the heavy body being carried out on a stretcher.

Frightened but at the same time incorrigibly curious, the readers and learned men of the library, shuddering but surprisingly dilatory, made way for the two policemen who carried the body out. Only too clearly, Bernard saw the handle of the very large, broad dagger which had been the death of the innocent reader.

It must have been the hapless reader who'd been next in line to get a seat who'd ended up there. It was because I took my notebook when I went to the copy room that the knife hit him instead of me, Bernard said to himself, a thought which only slowly overwhelmed him with its frightful conclusion. Because of that, someone had erroneously deduced that the seat was unoccupied.

For the second time in a week, someone's tried to murder me. And someone else has been killed instead. Both murders committed the same way. I'm starting to feel really scared.

Quickly, he surrendered the *NRF* volume and his numbered ticket. Holding the xerox copy of the strange essay, his notebook, and the envelope the girl had left behind, he hurried to the exit. I'll look at the envelope as soon as I get a chance, but now I've got to get out before the exit is barred, he thought.

The courtyard of the national library, bathed this day in the same kindly, autumn sunlight which had blessed Paris for a few days, is, as we know, a handsome rectangular courtyard in the block to which the great Colbert brought the collections from Rue de Laharpe in 1666, and in this courtyard smoking is prohibited nowadays. Currently, it was inundated with policemen and scholars who did not seem to know whether they wanted to get into or out of the library. In the street outside, several large, black police cars were parked. The kindly man to the left in the archway, who sells the early edition of *Le Monde* to the scholars

51

as they exit from the library in the afternoon, seemed to be the only person on the block who hadn't allowed himself to be frightened.

He shouted something which made Bernard quickly, in full flight, unearth one of his last francs from his pocket and buy a copy. Reading, he stumbled into the street.

He hadn't heard wrong. The man who had been found dead, lying head down in one of the inner ponds in Bois de Vincennes, was the West German Defense Minister, Hans Hansdorff.

Evidently he'd been paying a private visit to Paris. His death, probably suicide—there was talk of stress, depression, mental confusion—was viewed with great concern in NATO circles.

I knew it, Bernard thought as he crossed the street, half in a trance, sitting down at the small marble table in the first café in the narrow Rue Rameau, right across from the entrance to the library.

I knew it. I could see it in his eyes. He committed suicide.

Once again, he counted the few coins in his pocket, finding that he probably had enough for a *citron pressé*. For a moment, the pattern in the marble table top caught his tired eyes with singular force. There was something in the marble that looked like *the elegant tendril of a woman's hair*.

"I don't have the strength to read more about this dead man," Bernard told himself. "Not right now. Let me see, instead—and here's my *citron pressé*, sugar bowl and all—what's in the girl's envelope. Perhaps I'll be able to return it to her. Perhaps there's an address inside. She was a very pretty girl. She would move the tip of her index finger back and forth across her upper lip, with a caressing movement, that I found intensely attractive and exciting.

"Not to speak of the faint rustling sound as her nylons moved against the inside of her leather skirt. She had a habit, which I've often noticed in very young girls, of sitting with now one, now the other, leg folded in back of her, under the seat of her chair. How fortunate that she left before that awful thing happened.

"And I don't want to think about that anymore. Not right now. Later, perhaps."

The envelope was not sealed. There was just one thing in it, a photograph. It represented himself in sweatsuit and woolen cap, seen obliquely from below, his elbows against the railing of a bridge, with a stiff but at the same time fascinated expression, staring straight into the camera. The photo must have been blown up considerably.

The strange thing, Bernard thought, *is that people often look so dead around the eyes in photographs. We depict them in such a way that they don't have a chance to look back at us.*

So Hans Hansdorff had been found dead in a pond in the Bois de Vincennes. That was it, not much to be done about it. A man who for some unknown reason had taken his, Bernard's, seat in the Bibliothèque Nationale had been killed in that seat while he himself was in the reproduction department. It was serious, quite serious.

Because either this man had been killed by mistake for him or else . . . or . . .

His thought was lost in the slight, rising panic in him. There was great hurry now. His thought became as small as a dot. But . . .

The girl who'd just been sitting on his right had left his photograph of *the moment when he'd seen too much*. That was probably the most serious fact. What could it mean?

A thought, so fantastic that he couldn't, even now, take it seriously, glimmered in his inner vision.

Suppose, let's suppose (without any *ontological obligation*) that the heavyset man with the doglike ears—a decidedly unintellectual type—sitting on my left was dispatched by the same gang that tried to murder me in the vicinity of Minister Hansdorff's castle in Westerwede, a gang I thought I'd escaped by going to Paris.

Now let's *suppose* that the girl, the strikingly attractive girl sitting on my right, was from the other gang, the ones who tried to kill me on the train.

And *suppose* (something which is the only reasonable supposition in this tangle of vague supposition, unsupported hypotheses about identities and differences, the whole loose, lax ontology which characterizes any philosophy developed in a state of panic and hurry, but is there any philosophy to which that doesn't apply?) that neither of the two groups did, in fact, have any idea of the existence of the other one.

In that case, isn't it *possible* that the two killers, the clumsy KGB man on the left and the beautiful, slim girl on the right (representing God knows what), had gotten in each other's way in some strange fashion?

I've got to find a way out of this! No matter what, I've got to figure out what's going on. He took out his notebook, where he usually entered ideas for his dissertation on the Manichean roots of Isaac Luria, found his pencil, whose bluntness had already irritated him in the reading room, and noted in his pedantic, concise handwriting:

It appears I have *four* clues at my disposal and *one* of them has to be the key to the whole thing:
1) A ticket to the Bibliothèque Nationale, belonging to a lady by the name of Elisabeth Frejer, about whom I only know that she's beautiful and that, for some reason, her library card was in the possession of the chairman of the Swedish Chess Association, the lawyer Hans von Lagerhielm. Also, mark well, a tape which may have contained the guidance program for a cruise missile. Stolen, somehow, from the now defunct minister of defense of West Germany, Count Hansdorff. Or perhaps not stolen *from* him but on its way *to* him? How to establish that difference?
Somehow, this lawyer is in the midst of a *very sick, very dangerous* international conspiracy. However, it may well be that he was the victim of a murderer's dagger, and that the one holding the dagger knew nothing of the conspiracy. Perhaps he died because he chanced to change berths in a sleeping compartment with a man who looked innocent but

who was actually condemned to death because he'd seen something he wasn't allowed to see.

2) The strange pigskin briefcase with the peculiar old novels. The only thing I know about it is that it was equipped with the latest in locks, as if harboring state secrets. And perhaps it did?

At any rate, it's clear that one of the books in this briefcase was instantly exchanged for another in the Bibliothèque Nationale, and that the other book contained a long cryptogram, arranged in groups of five numbers.

I've still got the books, with the exception of the one exchanged in the Bibliothèque Nationale, and—

3) *The cryptogram* remains as a xerox copy, meaningless to me, meaningless the way all texts are before you've found the key to interpreting them. Worthless to me as well, but so valuable to someone else that he may kill me in the next few minutes to get his hands on it. (This is instructive, and some day I'll use it in a sermon on the Torah.)

4) The photograph that was left behind, showing me in a sweatsuit, leaning on the railing of a bridge. It scares me more than any picture I've ever seen, yes, more than anything else in this murky case.

For that picture shows that someone saw me while I saw.

Around him the city was moving; Paris, this masterwork of human thought, existed, breathed, teemed. Sea, labyrinth, great listening sea shell, all at once. Blue buses stopped, spewing diesel fumes almost up to his table. Scholars en route from the library to their afternoon coffee crossed the street eagerly. Labyrinthine, mysterious, the life of the great city spread in every direction, as the first evening breezes started to blow, a little heavily, a little slowly, like businessmen rising from their armchairs.

Was it the demons of the night starting on their flight? What was it that made the street signs rattle, caused a momentary rustling in the Venetian blinds?

Now warmth was rising from the open doors of the restaurants, now the first prostitutes appeared, oddly unreal in their make-up, since they weren't ordinary women, but disguised as "women" the way a coarsened, shabby, lower-class imagination wanted to see them. And perhaps in the gathering dusk there was also the pickpocket, on his way to work, the safecracker with his tools. Yes, perhaps . . . Perhaps also the hired killer, with the razor-sharp blade hidden in the pocket of his dark coat . . .

All of this great city, this labyrinth, this great sea shell, was simply living its own life. And in this sea of human endeavor, gestures, passions, communications, he was quite alone with his murderer.

With a celerity uncommon in a rabbi, Bernard paid for his *citron pressé.* He looked carefully all around him. He knew, only too well, where his photograph had been taken. It had originated at the moment when he did his last run across the five big bridges in Stockholm, when he stopped and *saw too much.*

That enemy, too, has followed me here.
We're a complement now, so to speak.
The play may begin!

Was it due to an overheated, sick imagination, this feeling he had of being watched as he turned into Rue des Petits-Champs? He looked around him cautiously.

It looked the same, but not *quite* the same. Something, a lightning-swift perception at the back of his head, told him that something wasn't quite right.

The farthest part of the street, the end closest to the very short Passage du Palais Royal, was blocked by a huge moving van. A line of cars, seemingly unable to move in either direction, sounded their horns aggressively and unremittingly, but to no avail. There seemed to be something the matter with one of the tires on the moving van. At any rate, there were two men in overalls engaged in loosening the right rear-wheel nuts, as if in the process of taking the wheel off. They didn't seem to be in any particular hurry. But the worst thing was that a Mercedes, the large, limousine size, with smoked-glass windows, the kind used by ministers and other shy people when they have to brave the traffic, was standing parallel to the moving van.

The Mercedes had evidently tried to get past the van, and now it was squeezed so tightly between the van and the canopy of the nearest restaurant that not even the slimmest of pedestrians could have squeezed past.

Bernard was turning to the right instead, toward the small, arch-shaped Passage du Palais Royal which, with its two shops, leads to the beautiful arcade. Right then, four men flung themselves from the Mercedes, surrounding him.

For one dizzy moment, he thought he recognized one of them. Wasn't that the coarse man who, in the foggy autumn night, had been forced to take a well-deserved swim in the Hamme River, after Bernard had thrown him from the bridge outside Tietjen's Hut in Worpswede?

What did he have to put up against those four heavy, presumably well-armed and, this time, probably better prepared men, in all likelihood murderers and henchmen of the Soviet slave state?

Only my imagination, Bernard thought. I have to come up with something, and quickly, too.

The only thing that looked the same was the strange jester in his worn tails, his top hat and split kid gloves, in other words, the jester of Rue des Petits-Champs. As usual, he was engaged in his autistic little operetta number with the champagne bottle on top of a stone rampart beside the short flight of steps leading to the passage.

"There," said Bernard Foy involuntarily, so loudly that the four doglike faces approaching him heard him distinctly and stepped back momentarily, "*there is the man I need.*" And he pointed dramatically at the jester.

And this gesture was so compelling that for an instant, they all looked in his direction.

5. Bernard Meets a Lady

A man's character is his fate. In Bernard Foy's character, there was a quickness. More than once during this journey it would be of help to him.

Such was the case now. In a single leap, he joined the jester in tails up on the stone ramparts, and for safety's sake, he made another leap, up onto the perilously high balustrade, so that now this strange man, the atrociously skinny, torn and worn '80s parody of an 1850s dandy, was below him.

With a loud laugh, Bernard divested him of the champagne bottle, still not completely empty, swinging it in the air in strange, seemingly magical circles above his head. The poor man did not seem to appreciate the joke. His face was bluish red with fury; with high, annoyed leaps, not unlike an angry little lap dog, he tried to jump up to the level where the big rabbi in his dark coat and wide-brimmed hat was standing.

People were already starting to assemble below. The sight of a rabbi snatching his champagne bottle from a curiously prancing, dandyish alcoholic, letting it dance provocatively in front of his eyes, immediately split the audience into two parties: the ones who were against what seemed to be happening and the ones who felt it was high time for exactly this sort of thing to happen. Their shouts and loud comments, some of which, to Bernard's great distress, did not seem completely free from a slight anti-Semitic tinge, rose as from the depths of an amphitheater. With the difference, however, that here the audience was in the depression and the actors were in an elevated position.

The jester had now started shouting loudly. There was undoubtedly something of the prima donna about him, a prima donna who discovers that right in the middle of the big tenor aria, someone has taken over just prior to the first reprise, singing in a voice twice as rich and twice as strong.

It wasn't easy to tell just what he was shouting about so loudly. His elegance had undeniably cooled several degrees in just a few seconds; now there only remained a weepy little madman jumping about his adversary's knees. Bernard had the uncomfortable feeling that the man might start biting them at any moment, since there was nothing else around for him to bite.

At the same time, he kept a discreet watch—if such a thing is possible in the kind of situation in which Bernard now found himself—for the four men who, just a minute ago, had been so sure that the rabbi could be flung into their dark-windowed Mercedes like any old package.

Make a plan. It will come to naught.

No, this jester in his worn tails was no team player. Bernard was already getting tired of him. He alternately shouted incoherently and bit the soiled thumb of his kid glove. With his once-shiny, black patent-leather shoes, he kicked the stone of the balustrade angrily and made huge leaps, sometimes at Bernard's coat tails, sometimes at the champagne bottle. More and more people gathered around them.

Street theater? A piece about the decline of capitalist society? Perhaps the man in tails symbolized industrial capital trying to regain control of society, wresting it from the noble M. Mitterrand? Or perhaps it was the dastardly Mitterrand who kept their rightful property away from French industry by means of various social controls? Several other interpretations reached Bernard in his elevated position.

It seemed the audience had now decided that what was going on was street theater. But who can tell the difference between theater and madness, drama and scandal? Bernard Foy, ordinarily an unassuming and retiring individual, for an instructive moment felt the double fascination of playacting and of madness.

Suddenly he noticed a movement in the crowd which made him freeze. The four murderous types from Worpswede, Mr. Lutweiler's henchmen, now seemed to have recovered from the shock, made a new plan, and regrouped. They evidently thought Bernard would not be able to keep all four of them under surveillance at the same time. What would happen now? Perhaps they intended for someone to pull him, or the madman, down from the stone ramparts. In the ensuing confusion, it would be easy to carry him off to the car. The spectators? Bah, they'd probably take it as the natural conclusion of the spectacle they were presently enjoying. The favor of the public, Bernard told himself, should never be confused with friendship. It was something different. Almost the opposite, in fact.

In the favor of the public there was always a hope for your death.

The four men were now quite close. They stood frozen into strange poses. Among the exulting spectators, engaged in lively debate, they stood out because of their frozen stance. They might have been robots programed for exactly this kind of situation. Or something to do with the play. Weren't they frighteningly alike in their Burberrys and pulled-down felt hats?

Tired of the goings-on and unable to understand why someone should want to deprive him of the small joy of his life, the man in tails whom Bernard had so quickly made into his colleague now started howling, like an old-fashioned Russian greyhound. The noise was so authentic, so terribly mournful, that nobody doubted he was in earnest. A shudder passed through the crowd, recently so merry—one of those mood reversals characteristic of crowds in their cheap favor and equally cheap ire.

With a chivalrous gesture, Bernard finally relinquished the champagne bottle to the howling man, who immediately put it to his mouth, like a baby who at last has gotten his bottle back, and in the flabbergasted silence which followed he shouted loudly (it was important to make himself heard above the angry hooting of the traffic in the street which was now completely blocked):

"Come closer, friends!

"Come closer, come closer!

"Our magical street theater has only made its modest beginning. Our emsemble, led by Mr. Gypsy Baron and Former Count, Rudolfino von Zapfenstreich, straight from Vienna, and myself, Bernie Foy, straight from Houston, Texas, ask your permission to introduce a world sensation: the knife-throwing troupe The Four KGB, well-known from Moscow and Worpswede, where they recently gave a highly acclaimed performance at Westerwede Castle. And that's not all! In a moment you will see, discreetly in the background, but indispensable and irreplacable—yes, there he is—the former SS Obersturmführer, now Grand Commissar of the Order of the Red Star with the right to carry a red bulb in his fly, Ernst 'The Knife' Lutweiler.

"Let's give him a big hand!"

Ernst Lutweiler—for it was really he—dressed in an elegant black leather coat and Tyrolian hat, pulled far down over his forehead like the other gentlemen's somewhat cheaper headgear, approached with morose steps, his hands demurely folded across his fly; this gentleman didn't seem amused by the lively clapping that greeted him from all directions as the crowd parted obligingly to allow him to participate in what they assumed was to be a brilliant comic escapade. The four knife-throwing acrobats, now actually holding razors, were as still as statues, nervously watching their boss. It seemed they were waiting for him to take some kind of initiative.

At this moment he lost courage, perhaps because some small boys started asking for his autograph—did they feel they'd seen him before, perhaps on TV?—and, in fact, Mr. Lutweiler started beating a retreat to the Mercedes, quickly followed by the four knife-throwers. General confusion ensued, and Bernard did not hesitate to avail himself of it to get down from the ramparts.

The five gentlemen, who'd managed to get into their elegant car with commendable speed, now tried putting it into reverse, darting back and forth desperately, something which did not please the already bad-tempered and disappointed crowd. You could already see the marks of violent kicks in its recently gleaming doors and fenders.

Because of the crush and the shoving Bernard, through no fault of his own, had ended up practically in front of their windshield, through which he glimpsed Ernst Lutweiler himself, frantically working the gear box. It now struck Bernard that a hard object thrown at the windshield at this point might work miracles. It would turn the windshield into a milky surface, a myriad of small cracks. But where to find a weapon? Now he, in his turn, could have howled for the champagne bottle. For a moment, Bernard contemplated running back to the glamorous and self-centered madman in the alley, once again snatching his beloved champagne bottle away. Fortunately, he realized how immoral such behavior would have been: for it is impossible to deprive your fellowman of a pleasure just to hurt an enemy.

Bernard never had to ponder this central problem of the Halakah and of moral philosophy, for right then, practically under the big rabbi's armpit, appeared a white-haired, very short, primly dressed old lady of the type who owns an apart-

58

ment on the Place des Vosges which her nephews, with ingratiating smiles, try to "help" her sell to Arab and other potentates for fantastic amounts; in the course of this transaction, the old lady is apt to end up in some nursing home run by pious sisters.

It's possible that some Darwinian mechanism is triggered, turning such old ladies into spirited fighters. It's also possible that there is some other explanation; be that as it may, the black leather handbag the old lady handed Bernard must have contained a piece of lead pipe or something of that sort. Through the impenetrable racket, Bernard signed to his unexpected helper, whose eyes were alight with enthusiasm and mild admiration, to watch out for his backswing. (As a golfer, Bernard was known for his excellent backswing.)

And he gave it everything he had. The result exceeded his expectations. The whole windshield of the Mercedes instantly turned into a continuous membrane of impenetrable white glass; the same white light that filtered through the glass roofs of Paris' passages, dirtied by birds and flies, Bernard thought. "Lumière blanchâtre," as Louis Aragon expresses it in his exemplary 1926 book, *Le Paysan de Paris*.

Now everything happened very fast. From inside the Mercedes issued loud oaths in German and Russian. Whom God wishes to destroy, he first makes blind. But it can be wise to make use of the blindness, Bernard thought.

Swiftly, with a perhaps absent-minded word of thanks, he handed the heavy handbag to the shrewd old lady. This little lady is undoubtedly a character, he thought. Her nephews won't find it so easy to get the better of her. Can she really be walking around with lead pipe in her handbag? Or why not a bar of gold? The lady accepted her bag with a contemplative little smile, opened one of its many side compartments, and abstracted a visiting card, which she placed in Bernard's hand with another gentle smile. Bernard put it in an inside pocket and rushed off as fast as he possibly could in the direction of the river. Only when he got to the Le Petit Coin de la Bourse restaurant, where he stopped to consider his situation, did it occur to him that the yellow pigskin briefcase was no longer in his possession.

For a moment he almost felt as if he'd lost a friend, a companion. He calmed down, though. No matter how large the loss is, I've still saved my life, he thought. But where could he have left it? At the cafe with the marble table where he'd had his *citron pressé?* Or on the stone ramparts, with that madman in Rue des Petits-Champs? In that case, Mr. Lutweiler might now know exactly how much Bernard knew.

No. Not quite. He still had the two most important items in his inside pocket, the xerox copy of the cryptogram from the book in the spy mailbox in the Bibliothèque Nationale and that girl's, Elisabeth Frejer's, library card. Oh, if he could only find her!

Half running, he assured himself that he still did have those papers in his pocket. They were there, all right. But what was this? oh yes—of course. The white-haired lady's card. Because it was hers, of course?

STERN

Graveur depuis 1857
Le Prestige
d'une gravure traditionelle

Ateliers et bureaux:
47, Passage des Panoramas
75002 PARIS

It couldn't possibly be anything else. Was the old lady an engraver? How improbable and how strange! Or perhaps it was one of her nephews she wanted to recommend? Or—the thought hit him with staggering suddenness—perhaps it was no coincidence that she had been there just then? In that case, who could have sent her? While those thoughts went through his head, Bernard kept running. For who knew what perils surrounded him? Who could tell friend from foe any longer?

He found himself very close to the entrance of the Passage des Panoramas. In some strange way, he felt more secure when he'd entered the milk-white light of the passage. There were still a lot of people in the passage. In these blocks behind the Exchange, people probably work late, he thought. Most of the people seemed to be elegant, busy secretaries. For a moment, he stopped in front of a shop window. He did look rather disheveled, with his large black hat askew and his tie pulled loose.

Discreetly, he rearranged his clothing. More and more people seemed to be moving down the passage on their way to the nearest Metro station. A man's character, as we've already pointed out, is his fate.

Such would also prove to be the case in this instance. For when Bernard, at once conceited and sensitive, turned back toward the passage, this strange exterior which is also an interior, he saw, walking past him swift as lightning, the most beautiful woman he'd ever encountered. The experience had something of the immediacy of a flash of lightning. That is, her gaze, dark, defiant, at once hot and cold, hit him long before the thunder which would logically have followed.

She was dressed in stately mourning. A gloved hand raised her old-fashioned, long, wide skirt, as if she wanted to keep its ruffled hem from being soiled by the dust of the passage. For a single moment, he glimpsed her leg, its sculptured whiteness, its frightening marble whiteness.

A few moments later, when he entered Stern's engraving shop at number 47 and heard the small doorbell give its subdued jingle among all the engraved sheets with ducal crests, invitations to private concerts, opening exhibits, and stock certifications for new, interesting banks on the Cayman Islands, in this peaceful shop where a very short, completely bald gentleman, dressed in an old-fashioned swallow-tailed coat, inquired politely how he might serve him, Bernard was still numb with shock.

It seemed like a distinguished concern. Samples of their production were everywhere: handsomely engraved stationery with ducal and marquisal crests, magnificent letterheads for old-fogyish legal firms with many partners. And behind the counter, surprisingly, a framed photograph. It appeared to be a picture of an antique zeppelin, floating above pure white, arctic snow. It was a very old photograph, somewhat yellowed. He wondered where it might have come from.

Actually, he didn't want to see any of the things he was seeing in here. Still, the only thing he saw was the lady he'd met outside, in the milk-white light of the passage. What he knew of this woman was that he might have loved her. And, it struck him, as he stood leaning his arms against the counter top, trying to regain his power of speech, she knew it.

The kindly gnomish gentleman behind the counter regarded him with attentive sympathy. It struck Bernard that he didn't really know why he was in this shop. The old lady who had so conveniently produced the right weapon to save him from the persecution of Mr. Lutweiler had given him a card with this address. Since she had saved his life, she must—for some reason or other—be well disposed toward him. Consequently, he'd come here. That was all there was to it.

6. In the Passage des Panoramas

It is hard to fight against passion. Whatever it wants, it buys. Even at the expense of the soul.

The quiet, slightly gnomish man, evidently the owner of the pretty little shop for engraved and crested stationery in the middle of the Passage des Panoramas, now also leaned across the counter, until he was sitting on his small chair with his elbows resting on the counter. There were the two gentlemen, leaning from different directions, scrutinizing each other closely. Did the engraver have the audacity to imitate Bernard? Or was he unaware of the almost ridiculous similarity of their posture?

When he spoke at last it was in an agreeable, surprisingly cultured voice, the voice of an old teacher at the École Normale Supérieure rather than of the proprietor of an engraving concern.

"Welcome. It's a pleasure to see you here. Very few have succeeded in getting as far as you've done. I have to congratulate you on your brilliant disguise, Mr. von Lagerhielm. What an amusing idea, dressing up as a rabbi."

Bernard felt a great emptiness. Almost absent-mindedly, he fingered the cryptogram in his pocket, lying there with the girl's—Elisabeth Frejer's—library card to the Bibliothèque Nationale. What would he try first?

"It wasn't all that easy," Bernard said. "In Rue des Petits-Champs in particular I was grateful for the help I got."

"But of course," the voluble little engraver said quietly. "I had a lot of people there. With radios and all kinds of equipment. There was never any danger. But they were *most* amused by the performance. It would be safe to say that Monsieur von Lagerhielm has already received great reviews as director of street theater. By way of ultrashortwave radio," he added affably. "As soon as I realized that you had reached the rendez-vous, Baron von Lagerhielm, I put everything in motion."

Bernard almost gave in to the temptation to ask where the rendez-vous was. Evidently he'd once again been mistaken for the dead chairman of the chess association, Hans von Lagerhielm, lawyer and baron. God, how bizarre! But *where* had the rendez-vous been? And did he know what side those people were on?

"I found something strange in the Bibliothèque Nationale," Bernard said.

To his surprise, the engraver seemed totally uninterested in this remark. Either he was a very clever actor or else there was some colossal misunderstanding.

"Oh yes, the Bibliothèque Nationale contains a lot of remarkable things. You could spend half your life there, hunting for new discoveries. I remember in my youth, how I dreamed of some day finding one of Hegel's lost manuscripts. Or perhaps an unknown sonnet by Baudelaire," the little man said.

"By the way, have you thought of something, Baron von Lagerhielm? This is a time *without values*. People are capable of anything, so to speak. The only thing they respect is the victor, raw power. When they stopped believing in progress, in moral tendencies, in a World Spirit dialectically and laboriously struggling to free itself from its chrysalis, then they started believing in rough, raw chronology instead.

"If only a power is stronger for the moment, people will kiss the tips of its boots, don't you agree? The same thing now as in the days of Collaboration. And those pacifists with their stupid mass demonstrations are the worst. They love violence, if it's the strongest violence. They say 'peace at any price'—have you heard that? So they give themselves to violence, they join it, identify with it, if they can only become quite convinced that the violence they're fondling is the newest, the strongest: in short, the *unavoidable* violence. Just make sure that you appear successful, and there's no atrocity you can commit without acquiring warm-hearted, humane supporters. That's what's happened to Hegel, the idol of my youth, the great master from Jena, whose ideas were once so brilliantly expounded to me and other *normaliens* by the great Professor Alexandre Kojève.

"But here I stand talking away without even offering you a seat; how awful!"

"Not at all," Bernard said politely.

Was he being sarcastic? Or was he really, if he knew so many other things, completely ignorant of what had happened at the library? Was this a case of some absurd mix-up?

"What orders would you like to give, Baron von Lagerhielm? In addition to the ones I've received already, I mean?"

The thing here seemed to be to keep going, as quickly as a Swede who has gotten onto thin spring ice and realizes that he'll have to almost run so the ice simply won't have time to break under his feet.

"If you would be so kind," Bernard said,"as to repeat all my instructions, so that I can be sure there's been no misunderstanding."

"Of course. A briefcase with the money is ready in locker A 345 66 at the Charles de Gaulle Ouest airport. That's Air France. You're booked on the New York Concorde tonight at 11:15."

"The money?"

"Yes. Your remuneration, Baron von Lagerhielm."

"Excellent! And how do I know that the amount is correct?"

"Excuse me, what do you mean, 'correct'?"

"That you haven't dispatched too small a sum."

"But it's the usual sum. Exactly the same as last time."

"Excellent," Bernard said. He realized that he really needed to step carefully.

"And after that I'm routed to—?"

"Houston, as usual."

Something haunted his memory *Ranch Road 22 22—Rt. 10 Exit après La Grange*. That's what had been in the pocket diary he'd taken over from the dead lawyer. Surely there would be some connection with the fact that he was booked to Houston? But what could it mean?

"La Grange?"

"Pardon?"

"*La Grange*," Bernard said, with cautious emphasis.

"I'm sorry, but I don't know any such person," the engraver said, shaking his head regretfully.

Was there a trace of suspicion in his affable accents? It was probably important to act before it was too late. Bernard literally staked everything on one card. The one in his inside pocket, where he let the cryptogram rest in peace.

"Is that all?" Bernard asked.

"That's all, Baron von Lagerhielm."

"Excellent," Bernard said. "Then I'd like some help with two things. One is that the bookings have to be changed to a new name: *Bernard Foy*."

"Of course. Would you spell it, please?"

Bernard did, not without dread. He had the feeling that the world around him was a bit *too* quiet, that any time, something he said or did might cause a terrible blow-up.

"There's one more thing." He picked up the card to the Bibliothèque Nationale with the photo of the girl, Elisabeth Frejer.

"I'd appreciate it if you could tell me where I might find this lady: Elisabeth Frejer. Do you know where she is?"

The gnome did not seem at all surprised. Did a small, momentary shadow flit across his sensitive earlobes? Was he getting the scent of something strange going on? Who was he? And whose side was he on?

"She expects you as usual. In room 32, Hotel Moussorgski."

"Very good. Then I'll go straight there. Thank you once again for your invaluable help."

"Oh, my dear Baron, we are the ones who should be thankful. What you're doing for us is completely invaluable and quite indispensable."

"Really?" Bernard smiled wryly. "It isn't all that remarkable, is it?"

"If you have a moment, I'd like to tell you something."

The thoughtful engraver leaned across the counter.

"You've made *tremendous* problems for them."

"Really?"

"Yes, this last thing you sent really did it. Soon there'll hardly be a single *program* that's *not* affected. It's spreading by leaps and bounds. Like an old-fashioned plague. They can't get it out of the memories. And it multiplies so rapidly, from one spot to another. The silly fools are always looking in the wrong place. They've just thrown some two-bit smugglers in Stockholm in the drink, with their feet in cement."

"That's nice to hear," Bernard said uncertainly. "People often tend to look in the wrong place, don't they?"

"The next time they'll probably take one of their higher-up contacts in

Stockholm. Rather amusing, don't you think? They can't make head or tail of it. I don't suppose they'd credit how simple the whole procedure is if we told them."

"So there'll be a great demand for cement in Stockholm in the near future?"

"I'm afraid so."

Was there a mildly critical note in Bernard's voice? Wasn't he in fact getting rather tired of this strange squabble between forces of unfathomable power, incomprehensible in their limitless complications and ramifications? Did he, poor simple rabbi from Houston, even know what side he was on? Ordinary American citizens are only too uninterested in foreign policy, he told himself. This means that the whole thing is turned over to the experts. And those experts have a strange ability to *complicate* everything.

His most pressing problem, however, was something else. The awful absence, the negation—*Nothingness*, as Jean-Paul Sartre would have called it—of the beautiful lady he'd let get away in the passage was spreading through his soul. The world was full of strange plagues and riddles, and this moment was one at which he didn't give a damn for any riddle except the one which right then *was* his life. Why had she been dressed in mourning?

"I'm going to my hotel," Bernard said. "I expect you won't lose touch with me."

"Of course not; your safety is provided for from now on until you reach Houston. So far, we've done our best. But please be careful. We cannot guarantee *everything*. If I'm not mistaken, you're only at the beginning of an expedition which might prove quite hazardous."

"Really?"

No doubt about it, Bernard sounded rather hesitant.

"As I've said already: few have gotten this far. And the sequel might be really dangerous. It is, so to speak, more poorly mapped."

"Excellent," said Bernard, still more doubtfully.

It was with a certain relief he opened the squeaking glass door of the little engraving shop. There seemed to be fewer people going through the passage now.

He stopped for a moment in front of a second-hand bookstore to check discreetly in the reflection in the window for anyone following him. Unwittingly, his attention was caught by the yellowed old books in the window. In fact, they were not unlike the books he'd found in the yellow pigskin briefcase and which now were lost forever. Where do they go, all those old masterpieces that the critics of every generation exhort us to read with such flushed enthusiasm? And thirty years later, no one has ever heard the name of the author? In what laundry basket in what attic in Rue du Bac does the last known copy of the "thrilling, fabulous, and ambiguous"(*La Presse*) Vidocq's *Les Vrais Mystères de Paris* from 1844 lie hidden? Where is Xermand de Montepin's elegant *Les Viveurs de Paris*? On which dusty shelf on the porch of a closed beach hotel in Normandy dwells "a

65

passionate and brilliant unique story-telling tour de force" (*Journal des Débats*) like Pierre Bocage's *Les Puritains de Paris*, not to mention Marcel Gaboriau's "bitter but crystal clear wisdom of life" (*Le Figaro*) in his once highly praised five-hour comedy *Les Esclaves de Paris*? In what dusty, unused theater attic do its once elegant costumes hang?

While all those things are continuing, and perishing, in strange ways defying the critics' promises to us poets about immortality, pieces of the past—quite unexpected and at one time not particularly appreciated—manage to survive one world war after the other.

A good example is the insignificant Hotel Moussorgski. German occupation, Algerian explosives, all this and much else had come and gone in Paris without anything really having changed inside the milk-white light of the hotel lobby. Perhaps because there's evidently something appealing about the idea of a hotel that is *inside*, deep in the fork of two passages. Fundamentally, doesn't a place like that remind us of the maternal womb?

Such perfection: to retire, on a dark autumn night, to your room in such a hotel, fill the ancient bathtub on its four lion's paws with hot water, place a steaming cup of coffee on top of the marble sink, and then to crawl voluptuously into the hot water and forget the busy world outside the huge body of the passage.

Or to step out into the early morning, after a croissant and a café au lait, and to encounter, instead of an evil sky full of rain, the milk-white light of the passage above, a silent cleaning-man sweeping the marble floor.

Bernard stepped into this strange hotel lobby after ascending the short flight of stairs that leads up from the marble floor of the passage. The gentleman at the reception desk was, as a person, still more remarkable than the gnomelike engraver Bernard had just left. Only as he got closer did he realize that the completely bald man with thick, sensual lips, heavy, sleepy eyelids, behind which a pair of red, exhausted eyes moved drowsily, was actually a dwarf. The dwarfish part must have to do with his legs, disproportionately short in relation to his remarkably powerful torso.

The dwarf, who, for no perceptible reason, made a vaguely frightening impression on Bernard, seemed engrossed in the hotel's bookkeeping, and it took more than a clearing of the throat to make him notice that he had a visitor in front of him.

His hands had the short, strong fingers and powerful wrists ordinarily found only among skilled tennis players. Were there dwarfs who played tennis? On the whole, the man had something undefinably Asiatic about him. It's hard to see what continent people come from when they don't have hair, Bernard told himself.

"I'm looking for Mademoiselle Elisabeth Frejer," Bernard said. "Is she in, by any chance?"

Since the dwarf seemed to take such a long time answering, Bernard repeated his question.

"You might say she's in," said the dwarf. "One might also say she isn't. Have you been announced?"

Bernard hesitated. The dwarf examined him with eyes as sharp as the needle in a syringe. There was something profoundly unpleasant about this cripple.

"Room 32. It's on the third floor, the attic floor under the roof."

The stairs were steeper and more difficult than Bernard Foy had imagined. They seemed never to end. When at last he reached the third floor, he saw that the ceiling was the same ceiling of milk-white glass as the ceiling of the passage itself. Of course, that's the way it has to be, he thought.

It was strangely quiet up here. Could it be that Elisabeth Frejer was the only guest on this floor?

He knocked once, very decisively, on the door. Then he opened it. The sight confronting him was one of those incomprehensible sights which at first make us feel that we're seeing a *picture*, perhaps the sketch of some unknown master, a drawing from some forgotten illustrated book, rather than a piece of reality.

Some things we've seen we don't allow to enter our memories; we prefer to locate them in someone else's.

The room was large, more a long, narrow studio, with a ceiling that had to be twice as high as usual. Under the ceiling was a gallery, which at present seemed to serve no purpose, but which must once have housed paintings. Everything was bathed in the indefinite milk-white light filtering through the dirty glass roof of the studio, which was also the roof of the passage. If you listened closely, you could hear the distant cooing of pigeons up on the roof. Their blurred shadows moved back and forth. Like some species of elemental phenomena seen through a microscope of great magnifying power.

The room was luxuriously furnished. Among a number of perfume bottles on the large side table, reflecting the pale light of the ceiling with an opalescent sheen, there were also carafes of wine, some burnished brass bowls, a handsome marble sculpture. Some surprisingly heavy oil paintings in characteristic Second Empire style decorated the walls. One of them could have been a small Delacroix; it represented an Oriental rider on his horse, with his scimitar lifted above his head.

A lily languished solitary in a vase. The room was too warm.

Still, nothing of all this held Bernard's attention. As if caught by a magnetic current, his gaze kept returning to the magnificent bed at the far end of the room.

The faint cooing from the roof wasn't, after all, the only sound. There was another one, more distinct, which slowly impinged on his consciousness and then seemed to increase in power: a low, regular drip. As from a faucet that hasn't been properly shut off. It emanated from the still copiously bleeding opening where the head should have been on the naked and still, in its terrible pallor, beautiful, decapitated female body which, knees far apart, occupied the middle of the bed, turning it into a swamp of red blood that slowly dripped onto the floor.

Fascinated, Bernard noticed her small breasts, the red sock still on one foot.

It was attached to a garter which must have been some kind of souvenir: the garter was studded with diamonds.

The strangest thing, however, was the head of this woman; on the night table, like a ranunculus, radiating an immense, milky-white emptiness, an emptiness like that of the world before Creation.

There was no longer any doubt. Those milk-white eyes belonged to the girl on the library card for the Bibliothèque Nationale: Elisabeth Frejer.

And, for one lightning-quick second, her dead gaze coincided with the living gaze of the woman dressed in mourning he'd met in the passage, the one who'd seen him for a brief moment.

Right now, it felt as if the world, for just one single moment, expected some kind of decision from him. He turned away. Slowly, falteringly, he started saying *Kaddish* over the dead woman.

7. Night without Stars

What awaits the dead, Bernard thought, is something they neither expected nor can imagine. For me, on the other hand, the thing is to get away from here quickly. It's obvious that if death has caught up with this beautiful young woman, there's no reason to believe it won't catch up with me as well.

He made his way cautiously around the growing puddle of blood by the bed. This deep red, frightening blood was in fact already finding its way to the door. What would happen if the unpleasant desk clerk called the police right now and he was found here with the dead woman?

How would Bernard Foy be able to prove his innocence? How would his testimony stand up against that of the horrible little man? But on the other hand, did the desk clerk know that Elisabeth Frejer had become the victim of a terrible crime?

What had he said to Bernard, word for word? It was impossible to remember it at this time. Carefully, he put his hand on the door handle, and only then did the unpleasant thought strike him that perhaps he should avoid leaving finger-prints in a room where a murder had evidently just been committed. But who would get the bizarre idea of suspecting him, Bernard Foy, a young Texas rabbi, on his way from Stockholm, of such a terrible crime? Or was he exactly the kind of person who'd be suspected?

The incredible is just the thing that often escapes recognition. Perhaps one ought to proceed according to exactly that principle? Frightened and upset, he depressed the handle again.

To his astonishment, the door refused to open. It was simply locked. Someone had locked it noiselessly while he'd been preoccupied with the horrible inventory of the room. He was caught in a trap! Or was he?

Up on the dirty glass roof of the studio, which also was the roof of the passage, the pigeons were still conversing in their quiet fashion. A few steps brought him to the gallery. Here there was an old-fashioned skylight of the kind that opens if you pull on a string from below. If he stood on the oak railing, it should be possible to get out through the skylight. Bernard examined the contraption with the string more closely. The string ran over a pulley. It was dirty but evidently still usable.

Just then a shadow fell for one short, almost unnoticeable moment across the glass roof whitened by generations of pigeons. Was it a cloud? Impossible. A large bird passing swiftly between the sun and the roof? Hardly that, either. There are no Texas turkey buzzards or eagles in Paris.

So someone was moving about up there. Obviously, every single step here might be booby-trapped. Bernard stood very still, pressed into the shadow on the inside of the gallery. A large, handsome porcelain vase down there gave him an idea. Full of horror at the thought of once more having to approach the dead woman but still unable to free himself from the impression made by this paradoxically virginal body, the cut-off head which would never be reunited with its body, Bernard stole down the steps, carefully lifted the heavy porcelain vase from its place on the table next to the dead woman, and carried the vase back up the steps.

He put his large black hat on the vase, opened the skylight slightly, and moved the vase cautiously outside the opening. The damp, autumn evening air penetrated into the room, pleasantly cool. Only now did Bernard realize how terribly hot it must have been inside the whole time. The noise from the traffic on the boulevards sounded distant; it was the hour when twilight starts to fall.

With extreme caution, standing as close to the railing as he could, balancing nervously with his tongue between his teeth, Bernard turned the vase with the hat a little to the left, and now the thing happened which, two minutes earlier, he'd astutely foreseen. The squeaking sound of sword against porcelain was almost more than Bernard could stand.

Automatically, the rabbi relinquished his grip on the lower part of the vase, and the horrible dwarf from the reception desk, not unlike a hideous, flapping elf owl, but of almost human size, fell through the window. He ended up next to the bed with the poor decapitated dead woman, on well-trained feet, so it appeared. There was something about this dwarf which immediately made you think of a circus performer.

Dr. Mabuse with his artistes under the big top, so to speak, Bernard thought. A sign of the times! The dwarf was already standing. And that wasn't all. He was coming up the steps, still unvanquished, uttering one of his awful cries. In an almost magical way, his weapon was back in his hand: a Turkish scimitar, gleaming blue.

Meanwhile Bernard had hardly had time to do more than get up on the railing. He swung himself onto the glass roof, shut the window behind him at what must have been the last possible moment, only to realize that the immense expanse of glass on which he now found himself, the roof of the Passage des Panoramas—its long track of pigeon-spattered glass not unlike a Dutch canal, hard-frozen and stilled by a severe winter—had to be still more fragile than newly frozen ice, and that keeping his balance on the rusty old wrought-iron framework between the glass panes would require the utmost delicacy. The swiftly falling dusk did not make his task easier. Bernard spotted a couple of magnificent chimneys about thirty meters to his left and started inching forward in their direction.

Far from vanquished, the dwarf emitted another of his awful cries. The sound traveled through the pane, glassy, mournful, and wild, and perhaps it was the kind of cry that can shatter glass. Whether he cried because he was shut up or because he'd discovered the dead woman was hard to tell.

All living things suffer, Bernard told himself, stretching a cautious hand toward the next cast-iron stanchion. It struck him that it had to be contemporaneous with the World Exposition in 1855.

At that exact moment, the whole structure gave way under him.

This is the end of everything, Bernard told himself. He'd probably stepped through the roof in a spot right above the passage and would fall perhaps twelve or thirteen meters straight onto the hard marble floor. He shut his eyes in anticipation of the inevitable. If I end up at the intersection of two corridors, perhaps I'll land smack in the middle of one of those big ornamental roses of black marble, Bernard thought.

He didn't in fact fall that far, perhaps only two meters, and he landed in an immense cloud of dust in a very dark room on top of something that felt like a pile of rolled-up old rugs. The only light here came from the opening he himself had made by falling through the milk-white roof of the passage. The pigeons calmed down again up there, his eyes slowly grew accustomed to the light, and from the other side of the room, where a stronger shaft of light crept in under a door, he heard an annoyed voice asking somebody else, whose name seemed to be Caratti, to shut off a machine: *"Ecco—Caratti, ferma la macchina!"*

The sound of what was probably a noisy vacuum cleaner of the large model used in barrooms and other public places ceased accordingly.

In his half reclining position, Bernard tried a cautious semiturn. One knee hurt; it had absorbed the first impact against this pile of rolled-up rugs. Miraculously, nothing seemed to be broken. He decided to be very quiet. Those Italians on the other side of the door had probably heard the thud but without realizing where it had come from. Now they'd shut off the vacuum cleaner to listen for other sounds.

Breathlessly silent, Bernard was fascinated by what the light revealed of the rolled-up rug against which his left cheek was resting. It wasn't a rug but a rolled-up painting. It had been taken down so carelessly and so stupidly that the painted surface was on the outside. In the shaft of light from above, now growing dimmer as dusk fell, Bernard discerned next to his left elbow a precisely painted, tiny windmill. Beside this windmill, cavalry with the characteristic helmets of French Guard cuirassiers, with Greek horse tails on top, charged across the canvas squadron by squadron, small as tin soldiers.

Was it a scene from some battle? Perhaps Marshall Ney's big, desperate cavalry charge at the battle of Waterloo?

Fantastic, Bernard told himself. No doubt about it. I've ended up inside of one of the old panoramas. Once they could be seen in almost every door of this long passage, those innermost, glowing, cells of *La Ville Lumière*; panoramas, dioramas, cosmoramas, diaphanoramas, navaloramas, pleoramas, Fantasma-Parastasies, *Expériences fantasmagoriques et fantasmaparastatiques*—picturesque voyages in space, views of historic battle grounds, submarine scenes, cycloramic paintings which, through wax figures and animals, approach the viewers, coming right up to their feet.

Sometimes swiftly advancing troops from the windmills on the horizon right up to the dying, stuffed cavalry horses, rearing up and emitting inaudible death cries, and the wounded cuirassiers in their uniforms, spattered with blood and gunpowder, right up to the railing of the wooden platform, still in darkness, where the spellbound spectators are standing. On the horizon, smoke, burned villages, blown-up bridges.

Sometimes submarine landscapes, the burning color-play of deep-sea fauna, not unlike ladies' jewelry in a salon. What looked like a band of water lit from within along the walls of the large hall, dark in the middle. Sometimes Indian landscapes where seraglios are reflected in moonlit waters. Sometimes white nights in empty parks, where, at the end of a solemn, old-fashioned poplar avenue and a pond in which the white façade is mirrored, you recognize the old castle of Saint-Leu, where the last Condé was discovered hanging in a window in 1830. The Vatican in summer light. Baden-Baden with elegant strolling couples in the dusk, a diorama of Dr. Enzensberger from Munich. The dead yellow light and the wind-tossed, restless clouds above Géricault's raft with the shipwrecked unfortunates from the *Medusa*, copied and equipped with cleverly inserted light effects by Maître Weiss from Rue du Bac.

But most beautiful of all: *wax candles*. In the dusky dark of old cathedrals—only the discreet sound of jackdaws flocking outside the tall windows with their indistinctly glimpsed glass paintings—rests, surrounded by quietly fluttering wax candles, the just murdered Le Duc de Berry, the wax candles so exquisitely and naturally copied by Maître Delblanc on Rue du Vieux Cirque that you can hardly believe your eyes. Oh the sweet, illusory life of art!

How strangely those cycloramic paintings create their own world. How profoundly they resemble the secret revolving stage of our own dreams, these landscapes opening on Parisian passages around 1857, these windowless windows, these illusory horizons, rooms within rooms. The same way a dream is always a room enclosing a much larger room inside its walls. How strangely you mislead us, you artificial paradise, you interior universe, you creation labyrinth, with your Optic Picturesques, your Cinéoramas, your Phanoramas, your chic Stereoramas, and these ultrafashionable Cycloramas.

How am I going to get out of here? Bernard asked himself, rising a little higher from the seemingly endless pile of old cycloramic paintings. What kind of panorama will my next scene be?

Perhaps a *Panorama Dramatique*? Or perhaps a *Pleorama Aeronautique*? Or perhaps—morbid thought—a *Diaphanorama Necrophilique*?

His eyes, which had slowly gotten used to the light, now discovered another door at the far end of the room, where light entered through a crack. This crack, through which he had just heard the Italians conversing merrily, and through which a vacuum cleaner had made itself heard, was now obliterated.

My problem, he told himself, is that I've fallen into childishness. Everything that captures my eye has also, in the most ridiculous, undisciplined fashion, captured me as well. I've been in an infantile stage. That's the sad truth.

With determined steps, he went toward the other door. It allowed itself to be opened without the least difficulty.

8. The Players and the Clock, the Pit and the Pendulum

The incredible always escapes discovery. And so he entered, unembarrassed and with a rather strained smile on his lips . . . The room was deep, lit by a row of crystal chandeliers; momentarily, it seemed huge. The first sound he heard was the subdued metallic clanking of jewelry on the thin, desiccated bosoms of some very ancient, blue-haired, probably American ladies as they leaned across the green tables to pick up new cards from the shoe the croupier was passing around. In their narrow, pleated polyester dresses—the kind that are easy to get washed overnight in hotels that cater to group tours—they might, in the (despite the crystal chandeliers) rather subdued light, be mistaken for aging courtesans. But that kind of courtesan hardly existed in present-day Paris.

In an Empire clock on the side wall the pendulum was going back and forth.

Aha—a game room, Bernard thought. Or perhaps one should say a game salon. For at the far end there's another beautiful clock whose slow pendulum catches the eye in a special way. Here they play blackjack, like they do in Las Vegas. Of course, it used to be that people always played games of chance in the Paris passages. It was one of the things they were famous for. It must be because of the foreign tourists that they still have those game rooms. Americans in particular like that sort of thing.

Leaning against the doorpost, he looked around cautiously, taking in more and more details of the strange picture, not unlike a dream, which opened before him.

Around the green tables faces without lips, lips without color, toothless gums. But the suppressed restlessness of their hands, which seemed to open and close as if searching empty pockets, or perhaps their own restlessly heaving bosoms, contrasted with the pallor. It was as if a demonic power had taken their thin bodies to itself, filling them with alien life.

It's terrible how skeletonlike elderly American tourists can look in places like this, Bernard thought.

Leaning his elbows against a table at the far end of the room, evidently not being used for play but rather for supervision by the management, was a pale man who seemed cold, mute, and envious. His face was handsome but had a masklike stiffness about it. His eyes were large and soulful but strangely sunk in on themselves. When he slowly looked up from the table and at Bernard, whose arrival he appeared to have noticed immediately from across the room, straight through the crowd of playing ladies and gentlemen, he smiled a small smile not totally free of malice.

With a very discreet gesture, the gesture of a dandy one might say, he indicated that Bernard should come over to his table. Bernard elbowed his way through the crowd of ladies and gentlemen, who didn't seem willing to lift their heads from the green tables for even a moment.

Close up, the pale little man seemed familiar, but Bernard couldn't remember where he'd seen him. He exuded a faint but noticeable scent of some chemical preparation. Could it be laudanum?

"You're the manager of this establishment?"

"Not at all. It simply amuses me to sit here with a glass of lemonade when I get tired of the cafés in the passage. It amuses me to look at the faces of the players. It is, so to speak, part of my profession. And you, my dear Baron? Back, for I don't know which time, to *La Vie Parisienne*, is that right? You certainly are indestructible."

The voice in which this was said was a strangely tired voice, the voice of someone who seemed to have experienced everything the world over, not once, but many times before. Perhaps it was the peculiarly dead fall at the end of each syllable which gave this impression.

"By the way, I hear that you spent the morning at the Bibliothèque Nationale?"

"Oh," Bernard answered cautiously. This gentleman did not inspire him with a great deal of confidence.

"It was rather dangerous, wasn't it? But that seems to be the rule when you turn up. The last time, when we said goodbye to each other at the Gare du Nord, I really didn't expect that we'd have another chance to meet. That horrible dwarf was rather close to the mark in that studio on Reimersholme, wasn't he? He wiped out your secretary. How awful! Please accept my condolences."

The handsome, pale gentleman who averred that he was just sitting there looking, paused rhetorically. Then his face assumed, more and more strongly, the character of an immobile mask Bernard had noticed. It occurred to Bernard that it was exactly the face of a person who has decided, once and for all, never to grow up, someone who'd sooner hide his real face forever than, even momentarily, expose himself to the horror of *being seen*.

"And two meter maids, by mistake, isn't that so? It's ridiculous actually." He gave a chilly laugh.

Now the rabbi gained the upper hand of all possible and impossible characters within Bernard.

"I don't think," he said with youthful indignation, "that the deaths of two innocent young women under macabre circumstances and, as you say, by mistake, is actually *comic*."

The pale gentleman kept laughing unperturbedly, actually so merrily that Bernard almost had the impression that the death of these women afforded him a *particular* pleasure.

"There are no innocent meter maids," he giggled into his elegant lace handkerchief. "If you only knew what they allow themselves here in Paris, what excesses they can be involved in, sometimes even voluntarily, you'd see things from a less moralizing point of view," this strange dandy continued. "You really have an exquisite sense of humor, my dear Baron von Lagerhielm," the other man giggled without restraint. "Saying that after what *you* allowed yourself the last time we saw each other. Fie on you! Have you really forgotten the enchanting young Moroccans in Pontoise? You're a terrible hypocrite! Or that little Negress, don't you *really* remember her? The one you promised to take on a trip to the West Indies? If only she did what you wanted her to? The finely polished furniture? The quiet rooms? The slow ships in the canals? My dear Baron. Don't you remember what exquisite advertising language you used to describe it all: *Luxury, holiday calm, voluptuousness!*"

He put his head back, laughing so hard that tears flowed from his cold blue eyes.

"It didn't turn out quite that way, if you remember. *Hypocrite!* And *you*, my fine friend, talking about meter maids, *you* . . . oh no, it's too ridiculous."

Bernard couldn't help an involuntary blush. So, he thought, it's easy to blush on account of someone else's crimes. It's only criminals who never blush.

"Oh well, those were different times," the pale gentleman resumed, getting his breath back after his paroxysm of laughter.

"Here in Paris things are getting straightened out, and several problems have been resolved. Of course, this didn't come about without some sacrifice. But now we're rid of most of the people who burdened our organization for such a long time. A good thing, right?"

"Of course," Bernard said, perhaps too doubtfully. "Of course that's true."

"You've got the code from the Bibliothèque Nationale? The miracle, the all-important code, the one the Secretary of State himself had such a hard time— that's it, he's the one. Who *else* did you think? The code that'll decapitate all the fat intercontinental missiles, the warheads of Medusa herself, petrifying all warriors, even in death. Medusa herself, with snakelocks of peace, so to speak. Oh, I really wish I could go with you to Terlingua and bash it into place in that stupid computer brain. It would compensate me for a lifetime of defeats and disasters."

This is frightening and fantastic, Bernard thought. Here's the start of another story. There's hardly anything here that jibes with my conversation with that engraver in the Passage des Panoramas. The engraver didn't know that I'd been to the Bibliothèque Nationale, that I was within a hair's-breadth of getting killed in that library.

With every turn of this story, it takes on a new interpretation, with new friends, new enemies, new tasks. It's grotesque! But the whole time, there seems to be some reason to kill me. When it comes to arguments *against* me, there's no shortage. But isn't it about time someone found an argument *for* me?

"So everything's set for the next step?"

"Oh yes," Bernard said.

"*Terlingua.*"

The truth is that, lately, I've been too much occupied with childishness, Bernard said to himself. It's time for me to stop. But without a doubt, there are matters here that need unraveling. Any blockhead can see it. I'm not a blockhead, am I? Or am I going mad? Is the whole world going mad and becoming unsurveyable?

For example, how come they wanted to get me in the Bibliothèque Nationale? Perhaps because I revealed too obviously that I knew about the strange mail drop for the exchange of secret documents someone had appropriated? Perhaps for some other reason? Perhaps it even was the way I thought it was when I got out, that two independent organizations who both had an interest in killing me got in each other's way in their eagerness?

I'm not sure I can take much more of this kind of thing.

This strange dandy treats me like a friend. The engraver treated me more like a boss. To this man, the awful dwarf seems to be an enemy to reckon with; no Lutweiler has turned up. The engraver has a large sum of money waiting at the Charles de Gaulle airport. He seems to believe I'm on my way to Houston. The dandy speaks of a still more deadly, desolate, and strange place, Terlingua, down by the Mexican border, where once upon a time a Yankee called Perry operated the old mercury mines, a place that's nothing but a ghost town out in the Big Bend massif, with an abandoned cemetery where the wooden crosses of the Mexican laborers who perished from malaria are blowing in the sand. That's what my father, Jacob, told me when I was a boy.

Sometimes things seem to tally, and sometimes not at all. One thing they all have in common is that they mistake me for Hans von Lagerhielm, although it's quite clear that I don't resemble him in the slightest.

Wherever I turn there's a parallel interpretation. And each interpretation only reveals some new threat against my life. As if that were the purpose of the interpretations. Recently, it was on Rue des Petits-Champs where I was almost killed. And then, all of a sudden, it's the Bibliothèque Nationale that counts. Now it's severed heads. Just before, it was the guidance program for cruise missiles. How to explain it all? Was Hans von Lagerhielm a double agent? Or was the world full of this kind of double theory? Tallying *in part but not completely*?

And why did everyone insist on confusing *him* with the dead double agent when there wasn't the slightest resemblance between them?

"Of course. Where else?"

"You can't mean the old mercury mine west of Big Bend?"

"But *what else*?"

Was it his imagination? Or did the other man's eyes suddenly grow narrow and suspicious? In that case, his quickness and composure were remarkable. This odd, pale dandy rose took a backward step and opened his arms in ironic admiration.

"*What else*, dear friend. *Young* friend perhaps I should say? You haven't gotten a day older. Quite the contrary; you actually look younger than before. How do you *do* it? You know, when you were standing there by the door, for a *fantastic* moment I really believed that you were that charming rabbi we ran into . . . in Stockholm, wasn't it? Now, what was his *name*?"

If this was a trap, it was too simple for an intelligent man like Bernard to walk into. Perhaps he knows who I am, went through him with ice-clear insight. Why does he keep playing with me in this strange way?

"No, I really can't remember," Bernard said, with the desperate ease of someone who has already said goodbye to hope.

"Bernard Foy, isn't that right? Now *Foy*, don't be stubborn. You understand that a lawyer from Stockholm wouldn't know such details about the landscape around Big Bend. That takes a specialist. And I don't know what brought you here, but now that you're here, and when the double agent Hans von Lagerhielm is dead, once and for all, perhaps it's just as well to ask you if you want to take charge of this case. Are you a good American patriot, Foy?"

It was almost impossible to tell whether the man, sitting pale and ironic at the edge of the green table, swinging his foot up and down, unperturbed by the low conversation and nervous excitement of the players, was being ironic or not. A more obvious noise, a rising but still relatively subdued racket, was heard in the background.

Bernard had heard it before. On top of everything else, that horrible dwarf has picked up my tracks and landed among the panoramas, Bernard thought. Will I be spared *nothing* this grotesque day?

The awkwardness of revealing that you're being pursued by such a ridiculous, disgusting enemy as this dwarf was, in fact, more repugnant to Bernard than the thought of the dwarf's terrible scimitar and what it might be used for.

"Of course I'm a good patriot," Foy said. "Whoever you are, don't imagine anything else. Do you hear what I hear, by the way?"

"Of course."

"Isn't it coming this way?"

"Now listen carefully," the dandy said. "The cryptogram you took charge of in the Bibliothèque Nationale is no cryptogram, as you believe."

"He's coming closer! He's hammering at the door!"

"It's actually a microcode that can be written into ASCII if you use CALL. But don't employ USER on any account. Will you be able to remember that, Rabbi Foy?"

Foy sweated with horror at the thought of meeting that terrible dwarf again. There was something about this awful, baldheaded apparition with the scimitar he simply couldn't bear to think of.

"I think so. I'm no programmer. Actually not."

"In the old mercury mine in Terlingua, which everybody thinks has been abandoned, a group of morally depraved, totally irresponsible American programmers, most of them probably addicted to some drug or other, or else victims of blackmail, poor souls, are working on the microcode of a new Soviet cruise missile with a multiform head. It's a cruise missile which will be used against all the cities and villages in Europe. This group is under the direction of quite a bad type, Dr. Ernst Lutweiler, former Nazi and Obersturmführer. Sometimes their programs will be smuggled out via Mexico City, and sometimes via blond, pacifist Stockholm. Like many other little things that the Slave State itself is too stupid or too sterile to engender . . .''

The hubbub at the other end of the game room had become so violent that even the roulette-playing American ladies were looking up.

"Now what's disturbing you? What I've got to say is important, you see . . . Oh, that terrible dwarf—little Dr. Mabuse, we call him. I'll take care of him. No problem. He comes from a brothel around here. It's only theater. God, how stupid to let yourself be disturbed by him now. But each man has his particular horror, as one of my friends says."

"It's not that I'm scared of him," Bernard burst out. "It's just that I find him disgusting."

"Your task is to get into their computers and, via CALL—for CALL is much more certain than USER—write in, between the lines in their ASCII, the lines that are simply an Escape Sequence. You've got them, from the Bibliothèque Nationale. If you're successful, every one of their rockets will eventually activate a sequence where it literally loses its head and that in such a way that it will fly in a wide loop back to its own base, bombing it. Clever, isn't it? You've already got the sequence in your pocket, don't you?"

"But why should I . . .?"

"My dear Bernard Foy. People have asked that question since Troy. But you said you're a good patriot."

"Tell me," Bernard said. "Hans von Lagerhielm was a double agent, but whose side was he on? Theirs or ours?"

"Honestly, Bernard, I don't know . . .''

In the silence that followed, it struck Bernard that the repulsive, at once hysterical and aggressive cries at the other end of this truly infernal room had ceased. The far door, through which Bernard had made his unwitting entrance, was open, but instead of the disgusting, armed loudmouth of a dwarf Bernard had expected there was a distinguished-looking gentleman, dressed in livery and white gloves, who gave a vaguely *Italian* impression.

It was probably one of those Italians who'd been cleaning while Bernard made his perilous landing. Apparently a member of the sparse but elegant personnel of this gambling establishment. Right now, he looked lost for some reason.

"*Caratti! Caro, come sta?*" Bernard's new friend, who was evidently well acquainted with the man, exclaimed at the same time as he quickly approached the end of the room where this gentleman was, a more hesitant Bernard following in his steps. Was this pale gentleman just roaming around, a temporary guest? Right now, he was acting like the boss of the place. The games-playing tourists seemed as engrossed in their activities as ever. At one table, a white-haired lady in black moiré was exchanging more bills for markers. Even this lady seemed to be a functionary. Not even she looked up for as much as an instant.

The servant opened the door and let them look in. With reluctant fascination, Bernard looked over his new friend's shoulder.

High under the ceiling the dwarf was hanging, slowly dangling back and forth like the pendulum of a clock. One of his own suspender straps had got caught up in the framework of the broken passage roof the moment he tried to get down the same way Bernard had. And the suspenders had tangled so unfortunately around his thick neck, now quite blue and swollen, that he'd been hanged in this strange position.

"*Just as in the tarot deck*," the dandy, evidently always equally ice-cold, remarked to his speechless companion. "A good omen for your journey, Rabbi Foy."

When Bernard finally stepped out into Rue Saint Marc, it was already night. And no stars.

9. You Won't Have to Die If You Can Play

One hot October night in western Texas, in the gaunt, dramatic border mountains close to the Mexican high plateau, two men riding mules were traveling between the Chisos Mountains and the St. Elena Canyon. In the evening light, their two shadows, hugely magnified by the almost horizontal sunset light, moved like two grotesque, mythological mounted figures against the deep red cliff wall of the high mesa which is the first mountain on the Mexican side: Mesa Aquilas.

A cactus wren sang its sudden shadow song in a big, dusty tamarisk; a crash in the mesquite shrubs announced that a family Porcopino, the lovable javelinas of the Mexican desert, with the boar in the lead and the sow bringing up the rear, each of the piglets holding onto the tail of the one in front of it, were about to cross the red laterite dust of the road, with all the solemnity and slowness of an academic procession.

A deep-rose sunset, incredibly beautiful, outlined mighty Mesa Aquilas, whose high, piled-up walls really look like the walls of an inconquerable fortress. The peace of the evening descended in blue-black shadows over the blocks of marble, basalt, and lava that looked as if they'd been carelessly flung across the ground. Anyway, the air temperature was ninety degrees, as is most often the case on October evenings in such regions, and the younger of the two riders wearily wiped the sweat from his forehead, red and peeling from a sun tan too quickly acquired.

"I wonder if it isn't time to make camp, light a fire, and put the kettle on; there won't be anything but tea left," Bernard Foy said.

For it was none other than he.

"A good idea," the older man said. "I think I'm getting saddle sores. Also, that old wooden sign says there's supposed to be a well here. I've stopped here and gotten water before. But that was a long time ago."

"You know it isn't possible to step twice into the same river," Bernard answered with a tired smile.

The older rider didn't answer; this white-haired man with tanned skin and strong, chiseled features dominated by heavy eyebrows and a large but still sensitive mouth seemed completely preoccupied with tying his somewhat recalcitrant mule to the nearest mesquite shrub so he'd have a chance to take off the saddle-bags where water bottle and teakettle had probably been packed at the dinner stop.

It's late, Bernard thought, looking at his watch, which showed half past seven. The road that brought us here was long. We had a long way to go. And there's a long way still to go. Tomorrow will be decisive, since it's Friday. What we haven't accomplished by sundown tomorrow, when the Sabbath starts, we will never accomplish. At any rate, it looks extremely difficult to get this thing straightened out. And what will we run into over there? Dogs, perhaps? Barbed wire, trip wires, minefields, high-voltage lines? If I didn't know that this job has to be done, I'd certainly prefer to devote myself to something different.

If only we had the stamina and could find our way in the pitch black, we should try riding all night so as to arrive undetected at the old mercury mine in Terlingua by sunup, but I can't figure out how to do it. The road's full of potholes and steep hills and bends, even in daylight. He shook his head slightly as he gave his mule the last of the stale, mud-smelling water from the gallon jug. That was the way water always smelled in his childhood. Even the tap water in the poor Houston suburb. In the summer especially, when usage was heavier. But sometimes when he'd been playing baseball all afternoon in the dust on the suburban dirt road, his mother had given him rootbeer instead.

I wish I had a rootbeer now, he thought spontaneously. In a way probably typical of someone who has just realized that he has an insolvable problem before him, Bernard Foy let his thoughts return dreamily to the immediate past, as if that would help him find an answer to the questions the immediate future was posing for him.

How had he managed to escape with his life from Paris, suddenly hostile and threatening, where just about every street corner, every arcade, every Metro station seemed to be hiding an enemy?

Now these childish things have to stop, he'd thought, when he was back on the boulevard.

And I might just as well forget about the wonderful lady dressed in mourning once and for all, because I'll never see her again.

Neither dead nor alive.

"I'll have to call the congregation on Rue Copernic from the airport and tell them I'm ill, that I'll be a little late, but that I'm sure I'll be back soon. In a week, no, in ten, fifteen days, perhaps three weeks . . . in any case, that I'm leaving and that I'll be back."

With rapid steps, he entered the small Metro station just behind the Exchange, appropriately named La Bourse.

Only at the turnstile did he discover that, no matter how many times he turned his pockets inside out, only twenty-five centimes remained in the by now rather battered dark suit he'd proudly purchased in Stockholm for his job interview.

If it had been in the States, he'd probably have been able to ask the man at the turnstile simply to let him through. But this guard, from some Third World country or other, looked at him with the merciless gaze with which functionaries, especially in poor and unhappy countries, usually regard their fellowman.

(*"A briefcase with the money is ready in locker A 345 66 at the Charles de Gaulle Ouest airport. That's Air France. You're booked on the New York Concorde tonight at 11:15."*

"The money?"

"Yes. Your remuneration, Baron von Lagerhielm."
"Excellent! And how do I know that the amount is correct?"
"Excuse me, what do you mean, 'correct'?"
"That you haven't dispatched too small a sum."
"But it's the usual sum. Exactly the same as last time.")

Just one Swedish mile from here, he thought, as he frantically turned his pockets inside out, searching among the receipts and visiting cards in his wallet. In locker number A 345 66 at Charles de Gaulle Ouest there's a huge sum of money. And a ticket for Houston, a ticket to the chance of getting hold of my father and asking him to help me with that terribly difficult task, with my awful duty, What Has to Be Done in Terlingua, Operation Medusa. And here I stand, helpless, a complete fool.

The sole result of this inspection was a steel comb in his right jacket pocket and a thin piece of paper, the receipt for some money Bernard had exchanged on his arrival at the Gare du Nord.

The paper wasn't absolutely ideal. It was a bit too stiff, but when he wrapped it around the comb and tested it, he managed a fairly decent note. With a determination perhaps typical of the whole Foy family, he sat down by the unpleasantly bare, tiled wall opposite the turnstile, spread his reasonably clean handkerchief on the ground beside him instead of the hat he'd lost, so that his audience would know where to put the coins, and started playing with the determination of a music director who has to play the Swedish national anthem on June 6, Swedish Flag Day.

Even as a yeshiva boy, Bernard had been considered very musical. He had always received some of his highest grades in music, noticeably higher than in more philosophical areas. Right now, more people were walking by, some of them chic secretaries from banks in the vicinity, probably those who had worked overtime, and some of them elegant gentlemen from the Exchange, the kind that make up the late clientele in the innumerable small bars thereabouts. He started with "Yankee Doodle," but since it didn't seem to inspire any sentimental feelings among the passing stockbrokers and their secretaries in correct business suits, he switched to Beethoven's violin concerto, the first movement, with the three rapid, strangely assonant octave leaps that introduce the first solo, while his right foot, tapping the concrete floor, indicated the orchestra part.

A very blonde young woman who looked as if her name were Clara and as if she were a Swedish *au pair* or something of the sort, stopped to watch the rabbi with wide, social-psychologically compassionate eyes, generously putting a whole franc on the handkerchief. Now all he needed was four girls like that to finance his ticket to Charles de Gaulle.

Since he, like most healthy people, disliked generating such a problematic, dangerous feeling as compassion, either in a beautiful woman or in anybody at all for that matter, he decided to interrupt the violin concert long before the cadenza of the first movement and instead started to play some Country and Western. That turned out to be the right decision. In no time at all, a small, devoutly listening group had gathered about him. It might even be that he caused some stockbroker or other to be late for his capitalist dinner.

The coins fell onto the handkerchief, tinkling merrily; one or two rolled a little way across the floor, but there was always someone to pick them up for him. A couple of bills joined the coins, and Bernard started feeling two kinds of apprehension. First, that one of the two—as it seemed equally dangerous—organizations which, independently of one another, had decided to kill him would find him here, in front of the turnstile in this space which for him had only a single exit. The second apprehension, oddly enough, was much sharper: that Rabbi Williams or somebody else knew him professionally would come across him here.

He therefore interrupted the concert long before he'd had time to play all the merry melodies he remembered from countless radio programs in the Texas of his youth. When he'd paid for his Metro ticket to Charles de Gaulle, a distance for which the astonishing sum of six francs was being charged, he still had thirty-eight francs left.

Perhaps I should have listened to my mother and become a musician instead of a rabbi, he thought as the train, much to his relief, at last arrived at the platform and carried him away.

It was as if this music had changed the magnetic field of his whole existence in some strange way. It was as if all his enemies had vanished, or as if he'd managed to *play* them away. From now and to Houston this was the most trivial, most clear-cut trip in the world.

Locker A 345 66 opened immediately with the key Bernard took out of his waistcoat pocket and inserted into the lock. He wasn't particularly surprised to find that it contained a briefcase of the exact same kind as the two that pursued him earlier in this narrative. This third briefcase opened without any trouble, and he hurried to close it right away. It did not contain a bomb. This time, there were no interesting old books, either. There was only one object. With the terrible monotony of a madman who can only hold a single thing in his mind, but who repeats this poor, single thought over and over with fearful anxiety, this pigskin briefcase, the third of its kind during Bernard Foy's travels, held fresh, never folded, precisely stacked hundred dollar bills.

There must be a million in the briefcase. I'll have to donate it to some suitable organization, Keren Kayemeth for example. Unless my father has gone bankrupt again, that is. He usually does, every time I come home.

Somewhat shaken by his discovery but with the confident manner that nothing except money and true love engenders, he strolled over to the Air France counter and picked up his first-class ticket to Houston; it was there, as expected, properly booked in the name of Bernard Foy.

In a slightly turbulent night wind, the big plane lifted and steered across Belgium, Ostende, and the dark, autumnal waters of the North Sea. The stewardess clinked the ice for the evening drinks encouragingly, and Bernard was soon engrossed in the prayer a devout man always says before embarking on a journey.

Before sinking into a well-deserved sleep, he had time to think: For my old father in Houston, this will mean a turning point. For a long time, he's expressed a desire to leave his horrid bar. Now he'll get the chance.

But for me it means something quite different, something I can't foresee right now. You're only allowed to castle once in every game, he thought, falling asleep. But the airplane, rolling slightly in the evening turbulence over Ireland, lost itself with increasing speed in the extended night that awaited it.

10. The Two against Terlingua

The dawn was lead-gray and hot. Yawning, unwashed, he stepped from the big Boeing 747 that had brought him to his featureless hometown which, gray and sleeping, stretched for miles in every direction: highways, factories, office buildings, clusters of skyscrapers, cosy little hamburger joints. Atlantic bog country caressed by the gray, autumn warmth coming up from the Gulf of Mexico, just as a gray house cat rubs against the legs of an ugly giantess.

The white-haired man in passport control welcomed him and his battered passport with a brief nod. Bernard asked what the weather was like, and the functionary slowly shook his venerable head. Those strange metereological questions that only Japanese and Yankees asked! If Bernard called the number of the weather station at the airport, he'd get the current forecast.

It was a great relief to see that the customs officers, at this early hour, seemed as uninterested in the obtrusive differences and surprises in life as everyone else.

At Hertz he managed to find a car to rent. In the heavy morning traffic, he soon found his way to six-lane Interstate 45, observing without emotion, but also without regret, a number of new skyscraper profiles on the horizon, profiles that had nothing to do with the Houston he'd left a few years ago. It was always like that. Nothing stayed the same. That's why cities like Stockholm and Paris, where everything stayed the same for centuries, were preferable.

After an hour's drive, however, the landscape started exhibiting familiar features. Even the street names started to sound familiar: Humble Road, MacCarthy Drive, Jensen Drive. Instead of parking next to the bar on Canal Street, he preferred to park on Irvington Street and walk the last bit in a flanking movement.

Time in life is a child playing, moving his chess pieces. What Operation Medusa is about is cutting off a fearsome head, using its killing gaze as a weapon against a still greater monster. In other words, changing the systems code in the program that guides the new Soviet intermediate distance missile, Burglar III in CIA slang, changing it so that the interference not only makes the rocket inoperable but also has a peripheral effect that spreads throughout the concurrent computer systems which constitute the Russian supreme command system.

By means of slightly altered copies, which may be copied in their turn, and which also wipe out millions of megabytes of other data in the files, this virus—such is the intention—will spread, by wireless and by modem, by computer commands and by debugging programs, like some awful paralysis throughout the Soviet war monster's horrendous, ice-cold soul; not just deadly but dead, from the moment of its inception.

But this missile program is written by a group of morally and humanly degenerate programmers in some carefully isolated rooms in the old abandoned mercury mine in Terlingua. Bernard is the one who'll cut off the head and turn its petrifying gaze on its creator.

In his inside pocket, in a form not intelligible even to him, Bernard carries the code he will write into the evil soul of Medusa. But how will he get a chance to write his fateful little figures among all the hundreds of thousands of lines already in the program? How will the living speak to the dead?

Carefully, a habit he'd had since boyhood and which was perhaps particularly well justified on this hot, humid morning when he was carrying such a large amount of money, he opened the door to the bar very carefully. It took some time for his eyes to get used to the perpetual dusk. The only person inside was a resolute black woman with a noisy vacuum cleaner. Bernard didn't recognize her. Her hair was grizzled. She didn't seem to have noticed him. The faint light from the ceiling fixture felt different, somehow, from the way it had in his childhood. Yes, that was it: instead of the nice old brass lamp, there was now an impersonal fluorescent tube concealed behind opaque glass, which for a moment made Bernard remember his adventures in the Passage des Panoramas with a shudder.

The cold light illuminated bottles and chairs quite differently from the way the kindly evening lamp used to do. In his youth, he'd worked here in the afternoons and studied for his philosophy courses in the bar. He remembered that he used to amuse himself by identifying different philosophers with different bottles. Spinoza was Bols egg liqueur. Leibniz was Jack Daniels, Descartes Jim Beam. Husserl was Smirnoff's blue-label vodka, while the somewhat weaker Jean-Paul Sartre was Smirnoff's red. It was even possible to describe cocktails this way: by their philosophical ingredients. The strange thing, however, was that they frequently agreed quite well with the history of ideas. Bertrand Russell, for instance, was a mixture of Frege, Leibniz, and McTaggart.

The woman seemed to be quite deaf, or perhaps simply not interested in Bernard. She still seemed unaware that he was standing there with his briefcase. Not without distaste, he viewed the glass jar with yesterday's boiled eggs and the pickle jar, equally huge, which in this light looked like an exhibit in a teratological museum.

If only he could have a cup of coffee. And if only it didn't look so pathetic. So this was his childhood kingdom. This was what he'd been told he could look forward to inheriting some day, and improving. He had to shout, practically in the ear of the old lady, before she took any notice of him.

"Where's my father?"

She shook her head as if she'd never heard anything so stupid.

"Where's my father?" Bernard asked again, more loudly. "What have you done with my father, you stupid old woman?"

She turned to him with ancient brown eyes, simultaneously starting to fill a bucket with water from the tap in the bar.

"Young man," she said, "how am I supposed to know who your father is?"

"My father," Bernard said, not without a certain offended dignity, "is the owner of this place."

"I don't believe you can be sure of that. If you mean that rascal Jacob Foy, who hasn't even paid my salary for five weeks, you're too late."

"What do you mean?" Bernard asked with pretended calm.

"They're coming to foreclose on the bar this afternoon. It's gone through the courts."

Bernard wasn't altogether surprised. Unpaid bills and a loan balance tottering on the verge of the unimaginable were familiar from his childhood where his father's affairs were concerned. But it hardly ever got this far.

"Where is he now?"

"If you go down the street and across you'll find a place called Northwestern Fitness Center. Go in there."

Bernard, who hadn't been in Houston for more than four years, looked around as he emerged into the daylight. It seemed dazzling to someone used to the mild autumnal light of Europe. He realized how terribly dusty the windows in the bar must have been.

Down the street there should have been a drugstore, one of those really big ones where you can buy just about anything you're ever likely to need, an Eckers. But it was no longer there. Above the glass doors at the entrance, where traces of the old legend could still be seen, there was a new, coldly blue neon sign with the message: *Northwestern Fitness Center.*

Bernard Foy, still pondering the significance of "Northwestern" as he entered the door—in his youth, he'd never have applied that concept to this part of Houston, where, as late as the '60s, a bar customer such as himself would simply have been characterized as having come to the wrong place. He held a piece of luggage in each hand, the almost frighteningly valuable briefcase and the worn garment bag.

The platinum blonde behind the desk couldn't have been less than fifty.

"Membership card?"

"I don't have a membership card. I'm Rabbi Foy. I've come to see if my father, Mr. Jacob Foy, is here by any chance."

"We don't like to disturb our clients when they're working out."

Her stern countenance softened as she looked at the son's features. Could it be that there was a resemblance between Jacob and Bernard?

"You don't have any sneakers, Rabbi?"

"Unfortunately not."

"Let me see if I can't lend you a pair. You have to have sneakers in here. And you have to have a T-shirt."

The lady was as implacable as she was flirtatious. Soon Bernard stood there in sneakers. Where was he to put his own shoes? He tried balancing shoes and luggage as weightlessly and discreetly as possible along to the next room, so as not to indicate that they were a bit too precious to leave with even this particular receptionist.

The room he entered bore a surprising resemblance to a medieval torture chamber. From one wall to another, there were the most bizarre machines, and the victims, mostly very fat men in gym shorts and T-shirts, were sitting, lying on their stomachs, straddling odd, vaguely obscene leather seats. They groaned, some even cried out, as they lifted and let down the most horrendous weights, mounted here and there in the machines, by means of handles, leather-covered levers, chains, and pulleys. Bernard Foy had never seen anything like it, for there hadn't been anything of the kind in Houston when he left the city, and the thought of his father occupying himself with something like this seemed completely crazy.

Some of the victims (or participants) cried as loudly as if someone had tried to draw and quarter them, limb from limb, and the whole thing made such a bizarre impression on Bernard that he had to ask himself whether he was awake or asleep. Not even during his most perilous adventures in Paris had he seen anything as odd as this. He looked from one of those newfangled sportsmen to another, then bent down to ascertain whether a certain gentleman, exhibiting the deep blue hue of someone about to choke to death, oppressed by some kind of lever that was going to send a wheelbarrelful of lead pieces into the air, might be his father.

This did not seem to be the case. He felt extraordinarily bizarre and misplaced in this environment. But right then his father came out, apparently from some inner room. He carefully closed the door, with a discreet PRIVATE, behind him. As distinct from all the others, he was wearing a fishnet undershirt that looked as if it hadn't been laundered for some time. He was just buttoning his fly in the deliberate way of an old man. He'd aged, but not a whole lot. His hair had turned white, though.

"Dad! Are you the owner of this horrible place *as well*, now?"

"Of course, son," the old paratrooper said calmly. "Until this afternoon, anyway. I've had a few problems. Those machines are more expensive than you think. But Bernard" (Jacob Foy speeded up, as if he couldn't leave this tiresome topic too soon) "*what* are you doing here? I thought you were in Stockholm."

"I was. I was even in Paris for a while, but it didn't work out for me to stay anywhere."

"I know," Jacob Foy nodded consideringly. "It's hard for young people to put down roots. I was the same when I was young."

"There's something I'd like you to help me with. We've got to go to Terlingua tomorrow."

"You're crazy. Terlingua, in my old heap? But listen, it might be fun. There's such a lot of people dunning me right now; it might be nice to get away from them for a bit. But you know, I think we'll have to rent a car."

"First of all," Bernard said, "I want to know how much money you owe other people."

His father didn't seem willing to discuss it. He squirmed in a way Bernard recognized from his early childhood. That was exactly how Jacob used to squirm when his mother was still alive and asked him at the door what he'd done with the five dollars she'd given him the day before.

"Then you'll have to tell me everything you know about Lutweiler."

"But Bernard! Lutweiler? Lutweiler's dead. You know that, don't you?"

A happy smile crossed his face.

"I *killed* him. I killed him with my own two hands in April 1945. I locked him up in the delousing cabinet in the camp at Zwillerheyde and turned it on. I've told you that story I don't know how many times."

"Are you *absolutely* sure?"

"*Absolutely,* son."

"Can we go in your office and talk privately?"

"Is that absolutely necessary?"

"What do you mean, *necessary*?"

"Well, it's a bit *untidy* at the moment."

Instead of arguing, Bernard discreetly opened his newest and, without a doubt, most precious briefcase. His father looked, caught his breath, and said shortly:

"Come right in, son."

He waved a platinum blonde girl out of the room. She disappeared, hair disheveled, a towel around her beautiful body. For some reason, she didn't seem to like getting slung out in such unceremonious fashion.

He quickly pulled Bernard into the office without taking any notice of her. That was his way. Unquestionably, the office was very small. He said sternly:

"Son. You were never supposed to get into that sort of stuff. Your mother didn't intend for you to, either. That's why you got the education you got. But if you have to get into that sort of stuff, it's a good thing you turned up today."

It wasn't long before they glided onto the big west-bound loop, this time in an elegant medium-blue rented Saab Turbo.

"As far as weapons are concerned," his father said, "I've got my old reliable bar gun along."

"The Peacemaker, you mean you've still got it?" Bernard felt his chest swelling with sentimental warmth. That was the gigantic revolver he'd admired as a small boy. Sometimes on Sundays they'd go to a shooting range by the new drainage dikes, where his father, when he was in his sunniest mood, would occasionally let the boy fire a shot or two from the heavy, dangerous old revolver. It could make a hole in a man like a drainpipe. Bernard had already learned that as a boy. He could still remember his surprise at the violent recoil that first time, which almost threw the weapon from his childish hands.

What are we going to do when we get there? Bernard asked himself, beginning to feel increasingly uncertain about the whole escapade.

Operation Medusa didn't resemble anything he had come up against in his whole life. Would he be able to make himself deliver the killing blow? How would they got there without being noticed? Wouldn't the wisest thing be to rent mules for a few days, for instance in Big Bend National Park, which was so close?

And how would the code he had in his possession be turned into a systems code for a complicated computer program?

"Dad," Bernard said, "the tea water's boiling."

His father seemed sunk in thought. He looked almost gigantic in his leather hat as he stood slowly patting the mule on its grayish mane.

"You say you believe that Lutweiler's still alive. That's crazy, son. I promise you he was dead as a doornail the day I shut the iron door on him at the Zwillerheyde camp. A very dead doornail. And the idea that things for the Russians' terrible missiles and other murder weapons of the New Pharaoh would be made in Terlingua is a bit odd. I don't suppose you can conceive of what it looks like out there. For example, do you know that when that Yankee, Perry, started his mercury mine, the one that cost so many poor, innocent Mexican mine workers their lives, they had to bring drinking water in convoy, on mules, and later on, they trucked it in—just imagine. I don't see how you can be right. Isn't it about time we turned around?"

At this moment, their conversation was interrupted by a strange engine sound. It was very loud; it moved almost right above them, as if it had been an airplane, probably rather large, but it moved far too slowly for it actually to be an airplane.

Doubtful, wondering, and irresolute, the two men looked at each other in the narrow circle of light from their fire.

11. The Eagles over Mesa Aquilas

They reached the environs of Terlingua around noon the following day. There was literally nothing to see here; their shadows were sharp and painful like the shadows at a Texan border gun duel. With biblical gravity, the red border mountains shaded those gray hills where hardly a mesquite shrub, not even a blade of grass, nothing but agave and hundred-year-old cacti had found a foothold.

About an hour and a half before Terlingua, they'd passed a kind of temporary town of hovels roofed with corrugated iron where Mexican illegals had evidently found an inadequate well with brown water and a couple of old telephone poles to hang their clotheslines on. The multicolored garments flapped restlessly in the hot, constant desert wind from the western mouth of the valley. The place was dusty, dry, impossible. Half-naked children played in the dust, a couple of black goats cried in God knows what kind of pain behind one of the sheds, an unrusted but beaten-up '50s Buick evidently served as a cage for the flapping, cackling black hens. Only campesinos would be made to endure such a place.

They had dismounted from their mules and chatted for a while, explaining that they were tourists on their way from Big Bend National Park going to see the old ghost town in Terlingua. An ancient Mexican woman with high Indian cheekbones and very dark eyes had warned them loudly: "Don't go there whatever you do!" The other Mexicans standing in a group around them, smoking their cheap cigarettes with almost expressionless faces, had nodded in agreement.

There was something uncanny about the old ghost town in Terlingua, something that wasn't the way it should be, not quite right, but just what was hard to get out of them. People? No. Spirits? No. Demons? Deep old mercury excavations to fall into? It wasn't easy to get sensible answers from them.

"In Hades souls can find things out by smell alone," Jacob Foy quoted in a low voice. He was speaking more to himself than to his son. When they got to the place, it had something frightening about it in its exposed loneliness. Bernard and Jacob Foy weren't the first people to have noticed it.

This was one of the most insignificant, most abandoned places anywhere in the Chisos Mountains. Straggling groups of Pueblo Indians on their way up from the river must have noticed the strange red color of some of the rocks. Perhaps they'd used the rare red cinnabar, in which there was mercury, for their ritual celebrations?

The conquistadors had come and passed by. (Their swords, once forged in the cool night wind by the river in Toledo, are still found by archeologists in the capricious sandbanks of the river, Spanish swords made from the unique steel which could only be forged by the old masters when the warm breeze from the south blew across the river, so that the metal didn't cool too fast when it was carried from the forge to the tempering bath, where an apprentice always stood prepared to read from the prayerbook those prayers required for the tempering to be done properly: not too long and not too short a time. That's how the swords of the conquistadors were forged, and in the dark and bloody history of Mexico, they wrote an indelible text. One, found a few years ago, bore the inscription POR MI REY on one side and POR MI LEY on the other. It means "For my king" and "For my law." That's what the swords of the conquistadors were like.)

But here they'd passed by, hungry, greedy for a single thing: silver.

But the Swedish geologist Johan August Uddén, who came here for the first time in 1903 with the Texas Mineral Survey, understood what the rich deposits of cinnabar meant. If those rocks were heated, they'd sweat mercury. And mercury was becoming a valuable substance. Three years later, he was back with Howard E. Perry, the strange little industrialist from Chicago, to build sintering furnaces and dig mine shafts in this desolate country. Everything had to be brought over trackless country from Marathon and Terlona. There were sad stories of men and mules dragging huge steam boilers for months on end on sleds through the terebinths of the boulder country.

The mine was dug in unstable rock; cave-ins were frequent and sudden. Steam boilers blowing up, plagues and, above all, the horrible diseases that mercury, this precious and deadly poison with its dead full-moon sheen, always caused, took their toll. The poor had been the losers, as always in this world. People had died cruel deaths here, for very little or for nothing at all. The simple wooden crosses in the cemetery with the many Spanish names were now mostly piles of dried wood. The winter winds didn't leave much standing in this valley.

The truth was that Terlingua had probably always been Hades.

And now it was a very long time since anyone had mined mercury here. After Perry, the strange, small master of the place, almost a dwarf, pursued by creditors and by the public prosecutor, who wanted to know why he'd dug underground passages under the mines of his competitors, gave it all up at the end of 1944—after his bankruptcy—Terlingua became a ghost town, though there'd been plans for development from time to time, of course. Howard E. Perry had died in December of that year, 1944. The dwarf was gone forever, and only the wind played with the crosses of the dead Mexicans.

Wasn't that his fancy mansion you got a glimpse of, with closed shutters, badly battered by winter storms, on top of the gray, grassless hill? They were so close that they could even read the big signboards at the entrance of the mine: DANGER OF CAVE-IN. ABSOLUTELY NO ADMITTANCE it said in both Spanish and English in large, distinct letters.

They dismounted at the foot of the hill with the mansion. The mules kicked listlessly at the gravel. A stubborn wind was still passing through the valley. The wind must once have pulled the smoke of the smelters in long, poisonous clouds over the little schoolhouse, the post office, and the police station, all of which stood pathetically alone, rapidly decaying, leaning against each other here, below the hill.

Bernard shuddered. "In Hades, souls can find things out by smell alone."

"There isn't a damn thing here," Jacob Foy said angrily. "I really appreciate that you came back from Europe with money to assist the family finances a bit. But I don't appreciate being dragged along on this kind of meaningless errand, for no good reason."

"Patience, Dad," Bernard said quietly. "I think if we only wait patiently, something will happen here."

His father grunted something inaudible.

The same stubborn wind passed through the valley. Now three eagles turned up, recognizable more from their manner of flying than from their profiles, for they were very far off, hovering just where they ought to, over Mesa Aquilas.

"It's a good thing," Bernard thought, "that those eagles are there. If what I expect comes from that direction, the eagles will warn me in time."

"Do we really have to stand out here in the sun? Can't we at least get into some shade?"

"Yes," Bernard said, "as soon as possible. I just want to look around a bit along the horizon."

"You could easily be seen yourself," the old paratrooper said scornfully. "How many men with binoculars do you suppose could hide in those crevices before anybody'd notice them?"

"A lot, Dad," Bernard said. "A whole lot. And we'd never notice them."

"Perhaps, taking that into consideration, it might be a good idea to be a bit more *careful*," his father said glumly. "For example, we might get into that haunted house up there. I'd actually *rather* be surrounded by ghosts than stand out there beside this hill, making myself a target for guns with telescopic sights."

"But sometimes it can be a good idea to be seen," Bernard objected.

They stood beside each other, father and son, and right then they were very much alike. Only the father's crewcut white hair and the numerous tiny wrinkles around his eyes, typical of a man who has spent most of his life in strong sunlight, set them apart. Where they stood they were suddenly strong, heavy as rocks, almost bearing a resemblance to the heavy desert mountains around them.

An enemy would have found them awesome. Had the wind picked up? Suddenly there was something happening with the eagles out on the mesa; after having circled so long on those same air currents rising continuously from the bottom of St. Elena Canyon, probably on the lookout for small game, they flung themselves out of their course and disappeared in the sunlight in a southerly direction toward the Mexican high plateau.

"Now," Bernard said, "now I actually think it's time to go into that house. It might be high time, actually."

They half ran up the slope. It wasn't altogether easy; the loose gravel kept sliding under their feet, the shrubs acted as if they'd had fingers. It was to be hoped they'd find no sleepy rattlesnake in their path.

The closer they came to the house, the more frightening it appeared with its strange terraces, its rotting railings, and its glass verandas covered with heavy shutters. The small, quick lizards disappeared, like forbidden thoughts taken by surprise. The smell of dry, decaying wood was suddenly everywhere.

"I think it would be best," Bernard said, "if you'd lend me your gun, Dad. I'll go first."

"Nonsense," his father said. "I'll go first. Besides, there's nothing here."

The door wasn't even locked. It was obvious from a long way off that it had been broken a long time ago. Perhaps by some roving, hungry little Mexican family, vainly hunting for something of value, perhaps by a gang of drug-smuggling hippies coming through from the other side of the Rio Grande?

Without hesitation Jacob Foy marched into the house, followed by Bernard. To begin with they couldn't see anything, but then their eyes slowly accommodated themselves.

"There's nothing here, just like I said," grumbled Jacob Foy, "nothing but an old wicker chair. But what's this! There's a man sitting in the chair! He's alive! Why doesn't he move? Why doesn't he speak? I wish we'd brought a flashlight. I can hardly see anything."

"You're starting to get very nearsighted, Dad," said Bernard, who'd already started cutting the ropes which held the almost unconscious man's cold and probably fiercely aching hands tied to the back of the chair. He loosened the scarf around the man's neck and helped him spit out the rag that had prevented him from speaking, saying calmly:

"Hans von Lagerhielm, the lawyer, I presume."

"*How did you know that, Rabbi Foy?*" the other man asked in an almost inaudible voice. His whole oral cavity must have been terribly dry.

"At the railroad station, when the police constables carried your body out," Bernard answered calmly. "Of course I was a bit surprised that there was so little bleeding. But I'm a clergyman, not a histologist. Then the constables gave me a real jolt. Just as they were stepping off the train I discovered that all of them were wearing Rolex watches with gold bands. No ordinary policeman in 1980s Sweden can afford that. Still less with a gold band . . . But it wasn't until Tietjen's Hut that I realized it *had all been staged just for me, to get me to take on the job*. You were too well known by the other side, weren't you? That was when I realized that *someone was helping me*. Someone was on my side. That boat engine, for example, in the canal on the Hamme. The engine in a boat whose owner has left it for the entire cold month of October in the fog won't start at the first try."

"Excuse me for interrupting your convincing exposition, Rabbi Foy," von Lagerhielm said, "but when you speak here of a German canal landscape in October I almost go mad with thirst. Can I have a swig from your pocket flask?"

Somewhat embarrassed by his self-absorption, at a time when he should have been concerned with offering help, Bernard held his flask to the lips of the dehydrated lawyer.

"Do you hear that engine noise?" asked Jacob Foy. "I've never heard such a strange noise. It sounds like a diesel train on the Santa Fe line, one of those with three or four locomotives. But it can hardly be that. Tanks? Unthinkable. Not here."

"It's an airship, a zeppelin," the lawyer said in a new tone, expressing horror and determination at the same time. "He's on his way, against all odds. Foy, you've lured him here."

"That's exactly what I wanted to do. But I wasn't sure, not until I found you here."

"Foy, now we'll have to fight for our lives. Do you still have the code in your inside pocket?"

"I do," Foy said. "But as far as I understand," he added quickly, "it isn't a microcode. I can't understand what it'd be good for."

"It's something better than that," the lawyer said. "It's a compiler which gets swallowed precisely because it *looks like* a microcode. Only in the belly of the dragon will this superior angleworm turn into microcode. You'll see how it works. *That is, if we survive the next ten minutes.*"

His father was already outside the door. To Bernard's surprise, it was no longer light outside. It seemed as if a solar eclipse had taken place while they were inside the house with its smell of old wood. The changed landscape around him was incomprehensible to begin with. Wherever he looked, an immense, metallic shadow hung over him.

It took perhaps ten seconds for him to realize that what darkened the sun was the enormous, boat-shaped passenger gondola of a still more enormous zeppelin. The propellers were spinning slowly on the three engine gondolas; apparently the zeppelin hovered right above the house, rocking slightly back and forth in the wind.

How interesting, Bernard thought. I've never seen anything like it up close. That strange, long cable that hangs down, dragging after the tail, must be an extreme longwave antenna. Then we aren't altogether wrong.

At the same time, the blinding white flash from the muzzle of Jacob Foy's heavy Peacemaker, discharged just half a meter away from him, reached Bernard's unprepared eyes.

The man he'd shot at had been thrown at least two meters by the impact. The horrible entry wound in his stomach, from which his guts were spilling out, was as large as a saucer. The man already seemed to be dead. "Blessed art Thou who divides light from darkness . . ." Bernard thought.

"Lutweiler," he heard his father shout as through a fog of unreality.

"Lutweiler," the old paratrooper cried with sudden merriment. "No doubt at all. Isn't it strange? Don't imagine I've forgotten anything. I remember it all: the latrines I had to scrub with a nailbrush, the rats in solitary, the whippings. I've killed you once, but since you were begging for it, I've killed you again. Strictly speaking, it's a lot of *fun* killing you."

"We've no time to lose," Hans von Lagerhielm shouted through the engine noise. "Go up the rope ladder and in, quick as a flash. We have to take her up to at least eight thousand feet before the radio antenna is fully extended. Then we can start sending."

"But tell me something—why does it have to be extreme long wave?"

"Because the idea is it won't be subject to interference from the electromagnetic storm that is a consequence of an atomic explosion. Lutweiler was not only a traitor and a top agent. He was a supremely well-equipped traitor. This zeppelin is probably a part of the back-up equipment that the Soviet nuclear military forces maintain for any eventuality. They want to keep their immense network of strategic computer programs going even after the cities have been destroyed and the underground staff doesn't have any radio antennas and telephone lines left. It's exactly this circumstance that's our ace in the hole. It makes it possible to send the microcode you've got in your pocket right into the heart of the Soviet system."

"It is written: *Make a plan. It will come to naught.*"

That was about all Bernard could say. For the rope ladder was really awfully high to climb up; it swung back and forth under the quick movements of the three men, and Bernard, who had a tendency to suffer from vertigo, hadn't detested any part of the past week's hair-raising adventures as much as this one. The faint movement as the zeppelin lay rocking in the wind made the ladder twist and turn.

"But which of us," he shouted to the lawyer who was above him and about to enter the opening in the gondola while Jacob climbed unconcernedly on underneath him, his gun ready in one hand, *"which of us can fly a zeppelin?"*

12. The Head of Medusa

Lightning pilots everything. In the same way, determination may pilot someone who has a real task to perform. Defying his vertigo, on the perilously twisting and swinging rope ladder, Bernard threw himself into the gondola of the free-floating zeppelin. He'd never been in such a place before. It looked like a boat, with aluminum walls, round windows as in an old-fashioned sailboat, an instrument panel in front with complicated controls for altitude and for lateral movement, steps going up to the mysterious cigar-shaped covering that kept everything suspended, now at more than twenty meters above the ground. The engines were idling just like before, seemingly prepared for an instant start.

Bernard noticed the three gauges for air-intake pressure, the hands of the tachometer trembling far down in the lowest part of the dial, the three regulators for rich and thin fuel mixture, red the way they are in small aircraft, so that it would be impossible to make any fatal mistakes. The VOR was set to Luckenbach's radio tower, at 151 degrees. The signal was STV, just as when Bernard was a teenager.

What primarily captured Bernard's attention, however, wasn't these instruments but the three computer consoles that occupied the whole space in the middle of the zeppelin. Was this where his task would be accomplished? Would he finally get the chance to write his text into the mysterious, invisible, but still very active, charged, and powerful darkness spreading like a black thundercloud behind those screens?

He felt in his jacket pocket. Yes, the paper was there. Would this zeppelin, with its dragging radio antenna, really function as a wireless modem and write his terrible text into the foreign system, the gigantic network of strategic enemy computer programs? Why not?

Hadn't a teenager in Ohio recently managed to destroy not just all his physics teacher's Apple programs, but also almost all such programs in the computer stores in town, because he'd grafted a small, unnoticeable, malicious self-copying loop, a demonic little worm, into the interior of the Apple?

How long would his text repose there in the foreign system like some dried, brown papyrus fragments, until the right rain came to loosen those letters from the papyrus, turning them once more into living text? Into letters of fire, into divine language, written—as the mystics once said about the still unwritten Torah—"with letters of fire on a ground of fire." For this little text would run through the foreign system like a conflagration; one moment it would be its subservient slave, and the next (precisely because of its subservience) it could become the supreme master, judge and, at last, its executioner . . . For this new text would turn the foreign strategic network of programs into something not unlike an old wool sweater unraveled by a pulled stitch.

Bernard shuddered, for he thought he comprehended something about The Text and What Is Written he'd never understood before. It could live in secret until its hour came. There might be a text that was written and still not written. Living in secret almost forever, until a new text, yes, as little as a new word, again gave it life.

If I survive this, Bernard thought, I'll be able to write a better dissertation than I'd ever have expected.

He heard the loud rumbling behind him as Hans von Lagerhielm dragged, more than helped, his father into the gondola. A bit red-faced from his exertion, the old paratrooper still held his gun ready.

"Careful with the gun, for God's sake, Mr. Foy," Hans von Lagerhielm said. "One shot in here and ten thousand hectoliters of hydrogen gas above us will explode in one white flash."

"But do modern zeppelins actually float on explosive hydrogen gas?" Jacob protested. "I thought—that is to say, I was just reading in *Popular Science* that after the explosion of the Hindenburg, modern zeppelins just use helium."

"Anyway be careful, Dad," Bernard said. "You can't be *absolutely* sure that this is a modern zeppelin, can you now? If you look around, you see that it doesn't *look* particularly modern. It's got a '20s look"

"Ridiculous," his father said, still merrily waving the heavy revolver in the air. "Are those VAX terminals from the '20s, too? I'm telling you, this is the fastest and most modern computer equipment you can buy anywhere in the world."

"I know that rabbis love to dispute," Hans von Lagerhielm said with a slightly irritated note in his voice, laboriously bolting the door behind him. It, too, was of a surprising construction. "Now is the moment. We have to take her up to eight or ten thousand feet above the mesa, check that the longwave antenna is straight out behind us at a speed of about eighty miles an hour, and then pray to God that the radio modem is functioning and that we have the right acceptance code and user password. But if we succeed in all that, well, then we'll make history this afternoon."

"History is created every moment. By us all," Bernard said.

"Who's going to take us up to ten thousand in this old ship?" Jacob asked.

"I'll take care of that little detail. I practiced for it in the Arizona desert all last winter."

It actually seemed as if the lawyer and chairman, perhaps one should say, *former* chairman, knew of what he spoke, for when he sat down at the rather surprisingly shaped altitude and lateral rudders and, with careful glances out the slanted side window, turned the gas on full, the airship obeyed him as if he'd never done anything else. The prow rose and the stern sank, but not unpleasantly so, rather less steeply and more softly than when a modern airplane starts. It didn't feel like an airplane at all. A submarine rising must come closer to this experience, Bernard thought, leaning over the shoulder of the marvelous air skipper.

Mr. Perry's house down below, the dead Lutweiler with a rapidly spreading pool of blood around him, the hill, the slag heaps, the decaying old schoolhouse built for the little Mexican children, the post office and the police station—everything disappeared very fast. Lutweiler, down there, looked very dead. Would he be able to return from the dead this time as well? Like the dragons in *Beowulf?*

He should be gone for good this time.

The view from the zeppelin was magnificent. Before them lay mighty Mesa Aquilas, and in a light that was already starting to acquire some of the mild, rosy color of evening, the huge rock walls rose swiftly toward them. Deep down there was St. Elena Canyon with its merry little brook, hidden far below in the deep verdure where the canyon swallows now rose in quick, fluctuating clouds, disturbed by the rumbling of the zeppelin engines. Far to the north, where the landscape appeared almost seductively green and level compared to the mountains and the desert dryness to the south, three of the mesa's brown eagles were flying majestically. Soon they would be far below the horizon. Right under them were the ancient mule tracks of the mesa, smugglers' paths, terebinth shrubs, radiating the warmth of the late day the way great libraries radiate history. It was a wonderful, dangerous evening.

Not without apprehension, Bernard saw the evening clouds assume this warmer red color. That meant that there was only half an hour left until the sabbath. It's now or never, he thought.

"Is it time to write?"

"No," von Lagerhielm said. "We've got to get up at least three thousand more feet."

His face was tense. The engines were now singing with a stronger sound, as if the propellers had been set at a higher rate of revolution. Which might have been the actual fact.

Majestically, still more grayish brown, still more distant mesas appeared in the evening light. Was it an illusion or not that the gondola was getting colder? Wasn't the air starting to feel thinner?

"I'm putting her into a circling pattern now. You can sit down at the terminal. No, not that one. The one in the middle."

The only thing visible on the big, dark screen was a rhythmic, blinking prompt. That's reassuring, Bernard thought, like the rhythmic brass pendulum in an old clock.

He noticed that von Lagerhielm was wearing stout flying gloves. He took them off and started writing at the left-hand console. Suddenly Bernard's console lit up, too. TERMINAL CONFIGURATION, it said, and an awful lot of numbers and sums and questions that had to be answered yes or no passed across the screen.

Bernard's fingers were so stiff from cold that he wondered whether he'd actually be able to write with them. New, difficult words appeared, like BAD

COMMAND, SIGNAL ERROR, HANDSHAKE, and other, still stranger things that couldn't be described in ordinary typographical terms. Suddenly Bernard noticed with a shudder, more intense than he would have expected, that all of a sudden every letter moving across the terminal screen was Cyrillic.

"Can I start to write soon?" Bernard asked impatiently.

"Not quite yet, but soon. Everything's going well."

So they were in actual contact with the other side?

Hans von Lagerhielm, who had to be an astonishingly expert computer operator for a Swedish lawyer, continued going through one configuration menu after the other, calmly and methodically. The fact that they were now in Russian didn't seem to bother him at all.

This time, anyhow, Jacob and I, two complete dilettantes, must have ended up among real professionals.

Bernard was just about to make this remark to Jacob when he noticed that his father had disappeared. Strange. He could hardly have gone out through the door? Bernard looked around. The only possibility, of course, was the steps to the hydrogen gas tank and the ballast above the gondola. Could he have gone up there out of curiosity? Bernard wasn't particularly anxious to go after him, especially since the circular movement the zeppelin was now describing was making him feel a bit seasick. At the same time, he couldn't suppress a lingering worry. Hadn't his father been here just a moment ago?

Hans von Lagerhielm seemed completely absorbed in a particularly intricate part of his computer configurations. I'll go look up there, Bernard thought.

The steps were a light metal ladder. It disappeared through a manhole and, to his horror, he noticed that it didn't stop there. Instead it went straight up to the gigantic gas tanks and ended on the dizzying platform that had only a wire railing and which, probably for the purposes of inspection, stretched along the whole horizontal axis of the zeppelin. A couple of fluorescent tubes created a faint, grayish white light up there. It's a good thing, Bernard thought, that the light isn't stronger, or my vertigo would be worse.

He saw no sign of his father. At the end of the passage, Bernard saw a sight that made his heart stop. There was a lady whose black hair and dark eyes he recognized quite well. How could this be possible? Without thinking, seized by an almost metaphysical passion for solving the riddle, he rushed down the passage. There could be no doubt: this head with its dark curls was the same head he'd seen severed last Sunday, held by someone in the dark little service opening in a bridge support in Stockholm.

Now the head was safely attached to a lady whose beautiful figure did justice to her custom-tailored suit. How could the same woman have her head severed from her body one Sunday morning in Stockholm and, the next Friday afternoon, stand there, whole and healthy, inside a zeppelin currently in a circling pattern over northern Mexico? Bernard was now so close to the mysterious lady that he could make himself heard above the noise of the engines. Strangely enough, the noise was more obtrusive up here than down in the gondola.

"Where's my father?"

"Where's your father?"

She turned toward him with inscrutable, at once coldly nearsighted and hot, dark eyes, simultaneously approaching him with calm, almost dancing steps. Somewhere from the depths of her suit she produced a small, egg-shaped object which she was now holding in her hand.

With chilled surprise, Bernard realized, long before he'd really seen the object, that it was a hand grenade. She'd already brought her right hand to the safety ring to pull out the pin. I guess she's left-handed, Bernard thought.

"Don't do that," Bernard said in a shaky voice. "In a zeppelin no one will survive. Not even you. Everything will just go up in one great, white flash. It'll be visible far into Mexico."

"Young man," she said, as if in passing. "How in the world could I know who your father is?"

"My father," Bernard said, not without a certain offended dignity, "is the man in charge of this zeppelin. Or was, just a moment ago. When the people in the villages down on the dry Mexican sierras and mesas see the great white flash that'll be the result of the hydrogen gas in this zeppelin exploding, they'll think that the nuclear war has started."

"How are we to know that it *hasn't* started?"

"By the way, I've seen you twice before. You're very beautiful. But I also believe that you're very evil."

"Twice?"

(How long would her slim, aristocratic, well-manicured hand still hesitate on the little safety ring and pin of the hand grenade?)

"In the Passage des Panoramas."

(Did she perhaps blush just a tiny bit?)

"And in Stockholm."

"You're lying."

(Why did she react so violently to his last remark? Suddenly, with lightning clarity, Bernard realized the facts of the matter.)

"Lutweiler fooled you. Your twin sister," Bernard said, slowly and with great emphasis, "your twin sister who worked for that industrialist you hope to meet in La Grange as soon as you get rid of me and my friends, your twin sister, Mademoiselle Frejer, will not be coming."

"Why?"

"Because she was decapitated in Stockholm last Sunday."

"It isn't true. You're lying. You horrible male chauvinist, you Zionist, you CIA agent. How do you know?"

"I've seen her severed head."

"You're lying."

"I've got her library card for the Bibliothèque Nationale. Look here."

Her reaction was quite unexpected, or perhaps not quite unexpected for Bernard who, in spite of his youth, knew a thing or two about people. The girl simply collapsed in tears on the platform. Bernard crouched next to her, put his arm protectively across her shoulders and pried the hand grenade from her convulsively closed, very cold left hand. Carefully he started to lead her down the steps.

"Bernard, what have you got there?" his father shouted when Bernard had half carried, half dragged the girl's body, paralyzed by grief and exhaustion, down the ladder. It was a tough job.

And it would be a still tougher job to lead this poor, betrayed, misled, seduced girl back to life. *All living things suffer*, Bernard said to himself, feeling a strong conviction that the Talmudic word expressed the case as crudely, as simply, and as hopelessly as the reality of it called for.

"You're too late to write," Hans von Lagerhielm said. "I couldn't wait. In your absence, I copied in the whole code from your paper. I thought that was the safest thing to do."

"So everything's written now?"

"Everything's written. And in the same script."

"And sent?"

"Yes."

"And where were you, Dad?"

"I managed to find the head, finally."

"So it's all over?"

Nobody answered Bernard, for the answer was only too obvious. The girl's convulsive sobs made her shoulders shake, but the sound of the engines drowned out the sobs themselves. Thank God, Bernard still had the secured hand grenade in his pocket. He wondered how he'd be able to get rid of it. Then he noticed that the tremendous, deep red Mexican sun was halfway below the horizon.

"Ferma la macchina!"

"But why are you speaking Italian?" Hans von Lagerhielm asked.

"I don't know. But do as I say. Hurry up now. Shut down the engines. But hurry."

Hans von Lagerhielm brought his gloved hand to the red throttle and shut off the big, heavy gas engines, one by one. Just then, the very last of the sun's disk disappeared below the horizon, above which the first two stars seemed to emerge from an infinite, warm, and velvet-blue darkness.

Not the faintest breath of wind moved the zeppelin from its position.

"I understand what you mean," he said kindly. "You mean that the sabbath has arrived. And I think you've earned it."

The second gate is opened:

WHEN
PETALS
STILL FELL
IN THE
SPRING

1. Lost Days

Such was the bizarre spy thriller the eighty-three-year-old poet, knight, and member of the Swedish Academy, Bernard Foy, spent the long afternoons writing in the winter months of 1983, behind drawn curtains in his large, silent, dull apartment on Malmskillnadsgatan in Stockholm.

Such afternoons, spent in his glum, brown-toned library, the telephone was turned off and his wife Amelie carefully instructed that no one was to disturb him, least of all herself. For, it was rumored, behind the closed doors with the ornamental Art Nouveau carvings the second volume of the aging poet's memoirs—promised for twenty years and anticipated with general excitement —*October's Roof Hangs Low*, was being composed.

The first volume, *When Petals Still Feel in the Spring*—printed by Albert Bonnier's publishing house as early as 1961—had been an unexpected, almost spectacular success he'd never really understood. It had surprised even him. Ever since his first volume of poetry came out, he'd been used to his work attracting unstinting praise from the reviewers, receiving lavish awards from foundations and academic institutions, and selling no more than a thousand copies. However, there was no obvious explanation why his book should sell thirty thousand copies. (Twenty years later, the comparatively handsome Foy with his white temples, his high thinker's forehead, and his broad, manly shoulders was still something of a favorite with the ladies' magazines solely because of this book.)

When Petals Still Fell in the Spring had aroused new interest in a poet already regarded as somewhat old-fashioned. His description of a childhood on the idyllic Svanå estate in Västmanland, with its water-lily ponds, deep pine woods, and enchanting forest ponds full of scuttling crayfish (which could be caught and brought home in lantern light during the warm nights of early fall), the artless, friendly story of boyhood years at Västerås *gymnasium*, had brought him his first real literary success. The heavy bells of the old cathedral tolling in the darkening, late-fall evenings as you dashed home to your cheap boardinghouse room while the shadows lengthened in the cemetery outside, the first literary attempts, the contact with Gunnar Mascoll Silfverstolpe and other poets in the early '20s, of romantic friendships and nocturnal conversations, the spring ball at the *gymnasium* with the scent of fresh young girls, their skirts billowing like flowers in the first waltz—all this had seemed so exotic, so foreign and attractive in 1962 that people couldn't help sighing and feeling a faint twinge in the pit of the stomach confronted with this hopelessly lost world of long ago.

The idea was that the next volume would be published quite soon. It was to have covered his military service at the Royal Uppland Regiment in 1919;

Bernard's friendship with the brilliant Hans and Veronica von Lagerhielm, the brother and sister at Flogsta, both of whom unfortunately died young; studies in Uppsala, the friends on the folk dancing team Philochoros, the start of his studies in art history which would eventually lead to a doctoral dissertation on the Worpswede School, which was much acclaimed at the time.

And it would all have culminated in the meeting with his wife-to-be, Amelie Jensen, during a research trip to Copenhagen in 1924.

This rich material should in a few years have become a book just as acclaimed and appreciated as the previous one, with sales to match. A bit sooner than in twenty years, at any rate. But of course there were explanations for the delay. Some of them were simple and natural, as for example Bernard's duties in the Swedish Academy and his wife's lovable but at the same time obstinate insistence on at least some small share of his attention.

The real obstacle, however, was unknown even to himself. Lately, especially this past winter, he'd experienced unusual and strange disturbances of his short-term memory (that episode of the forgotten yellow pigskin briefcase at the Royal Library, and all that it had brought with it of odd happenings and telephone calls, still hadn't stopped distressing him). He hoped there was no actual breakdown in the thin, eccentric membranes of nerve fibers, soaked in bizarre chemicals and probably severely damaged by a long life of whiskey drinking and late nights and fat cigars, which constituted his brain. So far he'd been able to keep this thought at a comfortable and proper distance. How much longer he'd be able to he didn't know.

Furthermore, and this bothered him almost as much, there was nothing in his faltering short-term memory to explain how twenty years could have rushed by at such a damn rate without the second volume having been written. There was not the least thing wrong with his long-term memory.

For example, didn't he remember, perfectly well, the peculiar blond veining in a marble table at a café outside the Comédie Française, not unlike the tendril of blond hair which had been so powerfully on his mind that beautiful September afternoon in 1924?

A tendril in the marble that might still be there? What happened to French marble café tables, anyway? Did they ever wear out?

And wasn't it true that he remembered, with almost hallucinatory clarity, the landscape painter Modersohn sitting one November day in Worpswede at a window whose pane was already mirror-deep with darkness, and how his huge, heavy, farmer's hand had shunted a little female spider in the right direction so that she could find her lost egg-sac?

"It's an extraordinary feeling when you can make one of the very *least* creatures happy," Modersohn said with his knowing turf-digger's smile.

Sometimes he'd tell himself that it was a surplus rather than a shortfall of memory that troubled him; that the floodgates of memory must be shut, one by one, if they were not to drown him in a single, terrible inundation from his past.

It was the present, not the past, that was affected and, in a most bizarre manner, torn apart by the widening, increasingly frightening and sudden rifts in the fragile curtain of his memory.

Days when it was so cold and frosty that the ice on the sidewalks was less slippery and the risk of breaking his hip consequently less, Bernard would trudge down to the Royal Library with slow, solemn steps, his faithful old briefcase in hand, officially to look at some source material, but actually mostly to chat a bit with the old gentlemen smoking cigarillos in the vestibule.

He wouldn't tell anyone that he also spent a lot of his time consulting medical encyclopedias to find out what might actually be happening to his memory.

There were a few different possibilities. One was called Alzheimer's disease, or something like that, and seemed to be one of the least appealing. It took you by stealth, starting with forgotten keys and telephone calls. Finally the sufferer would forget things that nobody would believe it possible to forget: how to use toothbrushes and toilets, spoons and forks. Of course this would lead eventually, if you weren't fortunate enough to die from something else in the meantime—for example, from having forgotten what pedestrian crossings were for—to a condition which meant you literally didn't know, from one moment to the next, who you were and why you were where you were.

Bernard wondered quite a bit what such a condition would feel like. In principle, it should be possible to draw strength from it, too.

For example, was it possible to *know* that you didn't know anything? Or would you be like a puppy, quite a new puppy that is, rushing back and forth sniffing everything in the world without having the least idea what kind of world it was in?

Perhaps it wouldn't be so bad to contract Alzheimer's?

But what would happen if it hit you in the middle of the street and you no longer knew where you lived? Or if you got it during dessert at a Palace dinner and knew neither that the phenomenon you witnessed was a Palace dinner, nor that what you held in your right hand was a knife, nor that the object in your left hand was a fork?

It seemed to Bernard that this situation might give rise to some strange complications. Suppose you turned to your neighbor at the table, some round little wife of a county councilor from Norrland, saying:

"Excuse me, perhaps the little lady might tell me what this is?"

(Waving his fork with abandon.)

"Excuse me, what's this under your skirt? It makes such a funny snapping noise when you pull it. Oh, you don't like it, my dear—what was your name again? Yes, there are so many modern inventions nowadays. Many modern refinements in underwear. Oh, you mean I'm not supposed to do that? *Really* not? But see here. You're quite wet already. Remarkable. Then you do like it, just the same. You aren't as uninterested as you pretend to be, then? Little thing. What are you squeaking about now?

"Oh, you like it, but not *here*. Where are we, then?

107

"No, really? Dammit, I'd forgotten. I hope no one's *watching* us. Your face has turned quite red. You aren't coming down with a cold, are you, girlie? Your eyes seem to be getting quite glazed."

Bernard was undoubtedly rather fascinated by his own fantasies.

Since he was in fact a poet, we don't of course have to point out how ambiguous his whole relationship to his own problems actually was.

If it was in fact the case that a swift, progressive brain disease was dissolving all of his short-term memory, ultimately affecting still deeper hierarchies of his personality, he was not completely alien to the new possibilities for happiness offered by such a situation. And, in a way that's probably typical of poets, his whole relationship to the problem of memory was complicated and not without a certain coquettishness.

In other words, long before the disease had broken out, or in any case long before it would have progressed very far, he was already *rehearsing* it, and it was impossible for him to find exactly the point at which fantasy shaded over into reality, or where the rehearsal turned into full-blown performance. Of course he surmised how strong this made him, but the full extent of this strength was not quite clear to him.

Obviously, a vulgar and superficially powerful enemy like, for example, Dr. Ernst Lutweiler would hardly be able to understand what a formidable adversary he'd taken on.

Their latest telephone conversation had been bizarre, to say the least. It had ended with Dr. Lutweiler, in a very faint voice, offering the old poet, as he said, "five percent of the street price" (whatever that might mean) if only he got his briefcase back. In that case, this briefcase should be left, almost right away, at betting window number five at the Täby racecourse, a place Bernard was not in the habit of frequenting. The briefcase was of the new, square kind, made from swanky, gaudy, yellow pigskin.

Bernard was not the least bit interested in this damn briefcase, which he'd never asked for and never been able to find again after it had come into his possession due to an idiotic mistake two weeks ago.

But what fascinated him most of all was the possibility of not knowing who you were, for one minute it seemed to him that this would be a terrible and incomprehensible state of affairs, and the next it seemed as if this were the state he'd been in all his life, and everyone else too, as far as that was concerned.

Some days, and after reading certain encyclopedias, he was firmly convinced that he was suffering from Alzheimer's disease; other days, after reading other encyclopedias, he was just as firmly convinced that he was the healthiest person in the whole library.

It wasn't easy to make up his mind. In fact, that was the way it had been his whole life. It had been impossible to decide whether misfortune had in fact overtaken him or whether he was simply trying out what it would be like.

Silently and energetically he quoted Socrates to himself—that magnificent passage where the philosopher says that he, he alone, is proceeding toward health while everyone else remains among the sick—but the consolation was not great.

Just the same, damn it, he'd become very forgetful. And now he was daily being importuned by the gentleman who, because of Bernard's annoying forgetfulness, had lost his briefcase.

There was no doubt that this gentleman was a gangster whose path Bernard had happened to cross, seemingly by pure chance. But what did he mean by saying he'd send "torpedoes"? Bernard would have to ask Simmerling, the bizarre old submarine mate who'd been his household helper for twenty years and who came by subway from Hässelby every Tuesday morning to vacuum his and Amelie's old armchairs and curtains, what might be the significance these days of wanting to take torpedoes along.

In the conciliatory spirit characteristic of very old men, he'd pointed out to Mr. Lutweiler on the phone that he himself was just as sorry, but that right now he was in the process of examining both the garbage can and the attic storeroom, and that he'd be back in touch with a report as soon as possible, if only Dr. Lutweiler would be as kind as to give him his telephone number. Oddly enough, this made Lutweiler hang up with what sounded very much like hysterical laughter.

He had the greatest trouble concealing both this conversation and earlier ones from Amelie. He didn't like to worry her. He imagined that he loved this white-haired woman—in spite of her white hair and indifferent hearing, almost ten years his junior—too much to want to worry her about anything whatsoever. In this manner, he'd long ago started developing his own secret life, half against his will.

How much did Amelie know about his bad memory? Perhaps as much as he knew about her bad hearing, her taste for ladies' magazines and for royalty, her sudden, lengthy depressions which she tried to hide from him behind a shy smile? In a sudden attack of tenderness and anxiety, he went out to her in the kitchen.

Small and white-haired, Amelie was sitting, as she often did at this time of year, at the kitchen table, very still, resting on her elbows, completely engrossed in some article on Houston, Texas, in *Månadsjournalen*.

Bernard found this as it should be.

She was one of the most illiterate women he'd known in his whole life, and he wasn't sure she'd ever done more than leaf through one of his books, including the autobiography. This was something he'd always seen as profoundly soothing.

When he came out into the kitchen, she looked as if he'd come upon her doing something forbidden, and he couldn't understand why.

To combat his embarrassment he asked for a cup of coffee.

She then pointed out, not without a certain injured dignity which he recognized only too well, that just twenty minutes ago, he'd had a large cup of coffee carried in to him and put on his old mahogany table, where numerous brown rings on the green felt testified to other coffee orgies.

It was the same desk at which once poetry collections such as *Ditties in Minor and Major Keys* and *Days of the Year* had been composed. Perhaps one should add that neither did it want for accomplishments these days. The only thing was that nowadays, those accomplishments belonged to Bernard's secret life. In fact, hadn't he just finished an exciting spy thriller? In greatest secrecy, that's true, and hidden from all the world, but still something that showed he still breathed, he still existed.

When he refused to accept the truth she might, as she was doing now, reluctantly leave her warm corner next to the radiator and, without a word—for they didn't speak much to each other on an everyday basis, since they understood each other just as well without words—lead him to his study.

That was what she was about to do now.

With an impatient and tremendously characteristic gesture, which he'd loved for a very long time, she pushed a white strand of hair behind her right ear and made as if to rise from the table.

"Don't bother, my dear Amelie, I believe you," Bernard said with surprising warmth and kindness.

She looked up from the magazine with her kind Danish eyes, framed by tiny wrinkles.

From the kitchen they could see in the light of the street lamp opposite that large, heavy snowflakes had once again started falling over the city, one by one.

The beginning of March already, and no sign of spring, Bernard reflected. He lost himself in thought. Amelie had already finished her tour of inspection. In addition to the coffee cup she'd gone out to find, she'd discovered two others behind the curtain, and furthermore a very old water glass whose contents looked as if they'd be good for growing cultures; also a plate of biscuits behind the curtain. He must have put them there rather recently, for at least they weren't moldy, the way some other things had been that he in his turn had found behind the curtain.

Putting bread and milk out overnight wasn't good. He'd learned that as a young art student on an excursion to Sicily. Bread and milk attract the dead. What dead might awaken here? More than one, it might seem. Not such a small number.

> The early dead are easy to remember.
> The early dead carry death in their faces.
> Like a shadow. Like a sadness.
> The early dead are the only friends
> who'll never fail you or deceive.

Veronica? No, he didn't want to think about her today.

Or Hans, vanished in the early summer of 1928 in the polar ice, after having capsized with an Italian zeppelin, snow-blind, on his way through the pack ice, dying, and with the disturbing thought that if one of his companions died some time later than he did, that one would eat him before the wild animals did.

He was a hero at the last, Hans, when the Russian icebreaker *Krassin* came through to the men and when the story then reached Uppsala, in bits and pieces,

"From swarms of flickering sparks, telegrams," as Silfverstolpe would write when the statue at the corner of Skolgatan and Börjegatan was finally put in place.

There weren't that many heroes then. He got his statue, Hans, in the strange little park in front of the Västmanland-Dala student association. In bronze fur coat with a husky at his feet.

How fast it had all gone! Putting bread and milk.

October days: 1920, 1921, 1922, when Hans hadn't yet started on his career as a glaciologist, a career that would end on the great ice, and before he'd started to dream about his dissertation, *On the Properties of Sea-Ice*; in those days, they'd mostly associated on canoe trips. They were both shy at bottom.

He suddenly wondered if he shouldn't take a walk after all. On ordinary nice days he'd walk all the way to Engelbrektsgatan and back, with a brief stop at Rönell's antiquarian bookstore on Birger Jarlsgatan on the way, sometimes even making a beeline for Augusta Jansson's candy shop. Mostly for the sake of the smells. For the warm light there would be in the shop.

His legs and knees were still excellent, and he wouldn't have minded a walk three times as long if it hadn't been that the city was so damn dull on late winter afternoons; or perhaps you should say early spring afternoons, when the diffident March light created a porcelain sky over the naked trees of the city.

Only some solitary magpies in a tree, or the red breast of a robin in Humlegården might, for a few moments, catch his attention. Other than that, everything had turned so oddly strange and dull. It was a strange city, and he had no clear concept of what he was doing in it; perhaps there was something there, but not for him.

The only alternative to a walk in the snow, apparently, was to stay home. But that was just as deadly dull.

The heavy old silver clock on his desk had a hard time *getting the hours out*, as he sometimes expressed it to Amelie. How deadly dull wouldn't this winter have been if he hadn't hit on the splendid idea of writing his spy thriller. And that had kept Amelie quiet. She knew nothing about the increasing extent of his secret life.

(The cool wind, the '20s October wind across Lake Mälar, always the same. Floating yellow leaves the wind absent-mindedly pilots across the water. The yellow leaves of September. The red leaves of October. Those fine, clear days in the middle of October when you go to the club and chat a bit and wash the boat. The smell of the Mälar water down by the Academic Canoe Club on Ekolnsfjärden.)

> Homeland, I knew all the birches.
> I could point out the stones

the gentle Silfverstolpe once wrote.

Bernard might had said something similar, for example about Lake Mälar. Perhaps he'd even said something similar and forgotten it.

He remembered all the smells. The shoals in the lake he could point out. The stillness before thunder and the stillness before winter. He remembered everything. The cool drip of cold water from the paddles into your sleeves if you hadn't made sure the drip ring was fastened properly.

The pain in your knee when you'd been kneeling too long paddling a canoe through the autumn waters.

The cries of black-throated divers and cranes.

No. There really wasn't anything much the matter with his memory.

2. October Exercise

They'd been shooting in the valley at Håga, the company of student recruits together with the whole regiment; they'd walked along the river in swiftly falling darkness and camped for the night on the west side of the bridge at Flottsund, to make their way at five a.m. to the other side, where a cluster of red screens designated hostile battalions.

Now, in the year after the World War, and with Hindenburg's impressive successes in the Masurian bogs fresh in their memories, daring night marches like this one, along lakes and rivers, were much in fashion.

After that they went on into Lunsen on narrow, difficult paths where it was easy to lose your footing on the slippery rocks. For Bernard it wasn't that difficult; from boyhood, he'd been used to the immense Västmanland forests around Svanå, but now the strain was starting to tell in his shoulders and lower back and in his legs, and the heavy Mauser '97 had a tendency to put a different kind of weight on each shoulder. After a few miles, your body felt lopsided.

As luck would have it, Bernard, going down a mossy rock, put his foot on a loose spot; he slipped quickly and incontrovertibly, did not fall but had a sharp, disagreeable pain in his left knee for the rest of the day.

They were only students, not real soldiers. Compared to what real soldiers of their generation had had to endure on the European battlefields, there wasn't much for them to complain about.

Should I give up, he thought. Should I talk to the lieutenant and at least get a ride on the baggage cart? (The baggage cart, pulled by a reliable dray, was already carrying several student soldiers with blood blisters, properly attested to by strict officers, in addition to milkpails and boxed tents. It was supposed to meet them at the Bergsbrunna station.)

Then he didn't bother.

At that age, he was very much against making a fuss or doing anything that would make him look squeamish. He punished his own sensitivity as if it were a secret vice. He'd drink the traditional arrack at student parties until he got dizzy, in spite of the fact that he hated it and it always gave him a headache. He'd smoke fat Brazilian cigars, especially if somebody older offered him one, and on principle, he took only ice cold showers. The smell of sweaty wool, Armol gun oil and autumn smoke from the others' clothes, mixed with the forest smells, oddly pharmaceutical, of bog myrtle, bilberry, and damp moss, intoxicated him. They were permitted to talk and smoke during the exercise; someone was smoking Kalmare Nyckel tobacco in his pipe.

A few years ago this had constituted an olfactory chord strong enough to make him feel sick. Now he could control such feelings.

When they got onto the plain everything was quite different. They walked under a big, red, menacing sky across yellowing fields, already bare, and in the October dusk the sun was very red and slanted over the Danmark church. Out in the world, a red and menacing sky had been burning for four years, and millions of young men like them had died, probably for no good reason, on still more naked and desolate fields.

"You're walking so badly. Do you want to change with me and take my bike?"

Hans von Lagerhielm was the company orderly today and had the benefit of a bicycle. The whole day, he'd been dashing up and down at the edge of muddy roads, going between the company commander's place at the head and the rear of the company. He must be quite tired, too. He was a nice young man, with carefully cut blond bangs under his sweaty peaked cap. He belonged to the Sörmland student association, and Bernard remembered having seen him at some party there the year before.

"That's decent of you," Bernard said. "But don't you have to have the bike if you're the orderly?"

"What the hell," Hans said. "They picked the captain up in a car at Bergsbrunna, and it'll soon be too dark to see who's who anyway."

Bernard hesitated. The simple truth was that his knee hurt quite a bit. Still he hesitated, without quite knowing why.

Meanwhile Hans walked beside him leading his bike. The heavy orderly's map folder banged against his right thigh at every step. His gaiters were covered with mud. Like the baggage cart, the company staff had taken a different route through the woods; a muddy timber track, it might be.

There was a space of time when neither one found anything to say.

"Isn't it strange, really, that we're walking along like this," Hans said.

"And that we're alive," Bernard said.

"Have you read Arthur Schopenhauer?" Hans said.

"I know of him," Bernard said. "But I haven't actually read him."

"You should," Hans said.

(The first drops of heavy, cold rain were starting to fall.

As they were finishing their march, the sergeant seemed to be the only officer left in the whole company; somehow, the others must have been picked up by car at the last crossroads. He gave the order to don coats. There seemed no danger of the orderly being needed again on this march. They could go on talking to each other without worrying.)

"He says some interesting things. For example, that life consists of either suffering or boredom."

"I'd say, either anxiety or boredom," Bernard said.

How had that conversation continued? The rain had intensified, and they'd been very tired when at last they reached the regiment. The October storm had raged furiously all night, and Bernard had lain awake for a long time, in spite of his weariness, and pondered, partly on the new friend he'd made.

114

In the storm outside, which made the old trees in the middle of the barracks yard drop their last leaves and the rope knock violently against the flagpole on the roof of the regimental offices, out there was his, Bernard Foy's life, his whole life, as a part of the storm, but also as something that had to endure the storm. And he didn't know what to do about it. The October night sighed anxiously about him, about his new friend Hans von Lagerhielm, about the millions of dead young men now buried in the enormous, dark battlefields of autumnal Europe. And nothing would be like itself any more in this world.

Had they spoken of Rilke as soon as that?

That was hardly possible. There could hardly have been anyone in Sweden that year who'd read Rilke. Or could there have been?

He remembered Hans's apartment very well; it was on Järnbrogatan; the year was 1920 or '21. They'd talked a lot about poetry in that apartment. It was very modern for those days, with central heating and what ten years later would be referred to as a "kitchenette." Bernard couldn't remember that Hans ever used the kitchenette for anything but making cognac highballs, as they called them in letters to each other, somewhat arrogantly. (At that time they wrote terribly Byzantine letters to each other, making very intricate, inanely complicated allusions to sexual encounters with shopgirls and nursing students and, in Bernard's case, one has to admit, with Dragarbrunnsgatan's rather dubious whores, not to speak of the awful little Finnish girls on Ofvandahl's attic floor. Bernard always had bizarre problems with those girls: they frightened him. However, his firm determination to turn into—no, to be—a new Baudelaire made him return there time after time. Eventually, they became less frightening.)

All this confidentiality was in fact quite dishonest. For each other, they played two personalities they'd learned in the world of literature. Hans, the somewhat melancholy English gentleman poet in pullover and plus fours, with slicked-back hair. Bernard, the darker, quicker, and more passionate character, must, as far as he was able, take on the role of symbolist, decadent, and *poète maudit*. Behind those masks there was, however, an honesty, an agreement, between two very shy young men, one nineteen and the other twenty when they first met.

And one would live to be eighty-three at least, the other only thirty-two. Bernard sometimes wondered if it wouldn't have been better the other way around; if he, Bernard, had died and Hans had lived. But of course Bernard would never have tried anything so crazy; he even detested biking in the wintertime in Uppsala, with a double layer of mufflers on; Hans found that a bit feeble.

Anyway, had they talked about Rilke or had Bernard just imagined it afterward?

Right now he could remember two worn but pleasant leather armchairs which Hans's father had let him bring to town from Flogsta Manor so that his student apartment would be a bit more personal and cozier than the other students'.

Also a handsome "Turkish" (as they called it then) brass coffee table.

But mustn't they have discussed Rilke as early as the first evening? Bernard remembered as clearly as if it were yesterday something Hans had translated from *Sonnets to Orpheus*. Or had he translated it himself and, perhaps only in his thought, dedicated it to the already dead, no, not dead: to his friend Hans, greatly missed, vanished among the polar ice, when he did the translation?

A god can do it. But can a human follow
him through the strings, the narrow lyre's door?
Cleft is our being. At the heart's mute core
there is no crossroads temple to Apollo.

Song, as you teach it, is not of desire,
nor striving for what hasn't come to pass.
Song is Being. Easy for gods. Alas,
when can *we* be? And when will *he* inspire

the earth and all the stars, so that they turn
to us? Young man, it's not your loving, even
were your voice forced out of you—learn

to forget what you have sung. It'll fade.
To truly sing demands a different breathing.
A breath of nothing. Wind from the god conveyed.

One summer vacation, it must have been 1924 or '25, Bernard had managed to talk his mother and his sisters, who were then living in a rather cheap apartment on Karlsgatan in Västerås, into his not having to come home. He wanted to sit in the Carolina Library instead and write an article about the Worpswede painters. Normally, he'd give up his lease every spring and take a chance on finding another rental in the fall. The landladies were so ridiculously like one another, anyway. The rooms, too. But this summer he stayed in Uppsala.

Evenings, he'd often sit in Hans's apartment, talking. Sometimes they'd go to Gillet or to Flustret and have a cognac highball. But not often.

"Nothing is as degrading for a creative person," Hans would say, "as forced social intercourse."

(With a twinge of conscience, Bernard would think of his mother and sisters in Västerås. Perhaps they missed him a whole lot. Or perhaps they didn't miss him at all?)

The trees on Skolgatan and Järnbrogatan had never been as deep, as devout as on warm summer nights that year. It was the summer that ended with Hans finding Elisabeth Frejer, the daughter of the great Orientalist François Frejer, who honored Uppsala University Library with his presence for a couple of semester.

Elisabeth had brought about an end to canoeing; not only that, but she had once and for all, in a profound and permanent way, disturbed the contact between Bernard and his friend, driven them from each other, yes, to the brink of enmity.

It had taught both of them much that they didn't know: about themselves and about each other. And after that it was almost time for Hans to start serious work on *On the Properties of Sea-Ice*. Elisabeth Frejer, this beautiful young Frenchwoman with the reddish blonde braids, was, one might safely say, the *limit* of what they'd be able to control and not control in their lives. She was the limit of their youth as well.

But before this shadow fell, they'd been able to realize their last big canoeing project: going up the narrow, reedy Örsundaån.

3. Putting Out Bread and Milk

Bernard's first visit to the von Lagerhielm family had been absent-minded and happy. The old house was situated on Lake Mälar; it was beautiful with its yellow front and big French windows under sheltering awnings and a view across a neglected garden that seemed to plunge into the lake. The terraces disappeared into the depths, one after the other, down to the shore, where alders replaced the oaks, giving the impression of a sea, now yellow, now wine-dark, with frozen billows down to the Mälar shore with its reeds and gentle waves. ("There blows a wind across the ravaged terrace")

Down there was an old-fashioned bathhouse, a sailboat no one ever seemed to sail; it lay there mostly as a decoration, and Hans von Lagerhielm's canoe, with red-lead paint on top of the taut sailcloth body, the way it was supposed to be in those days, lay neatly pulled up on sawhorses when it wasn't being used.

Here he met Veronica von Lagerhielm for the first time, as she came strolling slowly along the narrow path with a bouquet of carefully picked red, orange, and brown autumn leaves in her hand.

("Unaware, pure and happy you once walked/ An autumnal path./ The red leaves turned to spring/ In the narrow bird's nest of your hand.")

She hadn't been present at the luncheon, a somewhat old-fashioned, solemn occasion after the custom of that time, with the young men in ties and pullovers and the father in cravat and suit coat. There had just been a fat and rather charmless older sister with so many rows of pearls around her neck that they almost seemed to pull her heavy, melancholy head down to the table. A few hours later, when Bernard wanted to ask his friend why the younger sister hadn't been present (there were supposed to be two misses von Lagerhielm, weren't there?), phrasing his question rather facetiously, Hans had immediately put a warning finger to his lips. Bernard had understood at once. Here was one of those sorrows found in every family. But what? Was the younger sister some kind of monster?

Gradually, he found out.

Veronica von Lagerhielm, this frail, lovely, and strangely absent girl, was someone they preferred not to speak of. Not even years later, when the mental hospital finally and irredeemably closed its doors behind her, caught up as she was in apparently hopeless nervous melancholy, forever hiding her frail being from him, had he dared ask any member of her family what had brought this on, and what the last period before her commitment had been like for her. Still less had he dared to visit her.

Still ("Secretly my guilt begins/ And this guilt no one shall take away,/ It is mine and no one else's") this melancholy, rather tall girl with the cold blue eyes and a hint of red in her hair, this absent-minded being, at once hot and cold, was the entire reason why Bernard stayed in Uppsala for several years, in spite of the fact that he'd been offered a job in the capital as assistant curator at the National Museum. More than that: she was the entire reason he'd become a poet and not just an ordinary museum curator, entering some everyday bourgeois career in chilly comfort, the way other members of his generation strove after prebends, department chairs, and cold, meaningless medals to hang on their chests.

She'd given him the secret, tear-warm grief which made it possible for him to live without freezing to death. In fact, there wasn't much in his life that couldn't be traced back to this girl, in one way or another. She was his muse, and she was the only one who knew it. They'd only spoken a few times during an entire lifetime. When she died many years later, it was like a small grief, almost negligible in the beginning, and then suddenly insupportable. The notice on the obituary page of *Svenska Dagbladet* which at last brought the message of her death felt chilling, petrifying, and reproachful, and it rendered him sleepless for days and nights on end. How could she be dead, she, the immortal one! His own first important poems had been drawn from her slightly mocking blue eyes, at once ice-cold and *interested*, from her fate . . . Yes, much more than from his own father's tragic bankruptcy and suicide, his own fate had grown from this girl's. And this fate, which silently, hidden from the world, had been common to them both, the living and the dead, had shaped him, tempered him, had stratified and crystallized the metal in him into something hard enough to become poetry— real, resounding Swedish poetry, not just the confused poems of a young student, played on the usual keyboard of that time. The contrast between this girl and her fate was frightening: the contrast between her sensitivity and the iron-gray life awaiting her around the corner of the garden path of her youth, once and for all turning her into a terrible ice-maiden, an awful medieval instrument of torture, with all the spikes pointing inward, at herself. But there was more. In her fate there was something that in an obscure, profoundly disturbing fashion reminded him of himself. More than the warm, motherly Amelie in her weakness and strength would ever be, this young woman, whom he hardly knew in any reasonable sense of the word, was his wife. In some unclear fashion he had the feeling she was the frozen maiden present in himself; that her life had freed him from the dread, in some fashion or other, of suffering the same fate she had.

During the years after the war ended, almost everything had given him a feeling of brutal and inescapable betrayal. There were handsome young men like himself, as ready for and as uncertain about the true conditions of life as himself. Not far from the Swedish borders these millions of young men, who did not differ significantly from him as far as vitality, intelligence, or sensitivity to pain were concerned, turned into invalids dragging themselves along without legs, with the aid of wooden sticks, through ravaged parks, trying to reach the street corner where they hoped to beg their daily bread. Pianists returned from prison camps with only one hand that would always grope for the melody they'd lost. When such things happened, wasn't that enough to make you secretly suspect that the whole world lacked meaning? That it was all just a tale told by an idiot. He could-n't see Fritz Overbeck's wonderful *Summer Day in the Hamme-Niederung,* one of the best paintings of the Worpswede School (painted in 1900), without imag-ining that through the Great War the world had, once and for all, lost its primeval happiness, the innocence that it must once have possessed. The early summer clouds blew so gently across the sky of the marshland, mirroring themselves in the brown water of the turf canal, Weyerberg stood still and solemn on the hori-zon, bathed in the warm light of late afternoon. Just like his own world, this one was forever lost.

Of course his youth had also been full of personal disappointment. Abominable competitors for professorial chairs, veritable gangsters equipped with academic walking sticks, academic cutaways and cravats, but gangsters just the same, they would gradually, in the '20s, not just try to but succeed in wresting from him the meager living he attempted to make for himself and Amelie. And in the back-ground the completely unexpected and horrendous catastrophe from his gradua-tion year, 1917, continued to reverberate: the catastrophe of his father's loans, bad checks, bankruptcy, threatened imprisonment, and consequent suicide. This, too, was a betrayal. He felt he deserved something better, and he considered that his father, too, had deserved it. The two of them were equally betrayed, it seemed to him. (How grotesquely, how provocative and bitter he found it in the 1980s when the ignorant youth of the day, in culture pages of the newspapers and in the music programs on the radio, would speak assuredly of the "Roaring Twenties.")

But among all those betrayals there was a single one, his own, which would give all his mature poetry the melancholy tone which then, at the end of this unhappy decade, would make it so much admired. It was beautiful like Anders Österling's and Gunnar Mascoll Silfverstolpe's; rhythmically it danced more like Sven Lidman's collections from the first decade of the century than Karlfeldt's heavy farmer's feet, but that was as it should be. In Bernard there was something additional: there was a note of well-controlled despair, the practically weightless balancing across an abyss which almost immediately had aroused the sharp atten-tion and fascinated admiration of critics and readers alike. (Of course it had also occasioned some well-concealed hatred among the older poets of the period, except of course for the generous Silfverstolpe, who saw in Bernard a successor to his own Västmanland poetry.) Yes, betrayal had early become familiar to him. And where he was sitting now, chin in hands and elbows moodily supported on the heavy desk, looking out through the porcelain-colored net curtains at the snowy park, where the first big snowfall of the week was falling in heavy flakes through the blue, gentle, humid-smelling March evening, with its faint intima-tion of spring, he felt, for one infinitesimally brief moment, the whole weight of this memory in its close-knit union of pain and jubilant joy. In spite of every-thing, it's hard to deny that I have lived. I've existed, after all, he thought.

He wasn't quite sure what had triggered those memories this afternoon. Right then, he heard the solid old Stjernsund clock whirring with its brass weight in the drawing room, soon to sound its five strokes. She's managed to get them out of her, Bernard thought. In other words, Amelie will come in any time now to say that tea is ready. And then I won't have to sit in here pretending to work. Not today, at any rate. That'll be a relief, Bernard thought.

As often happens with old men, Bernard had few and rather bizarre pleasures, the kind of pleasures people who aren't old and who still feel that life offers them a lot of interesting, albeit urgent and pressing tasks, cannot possibly understand. One of Bernard's pleasures was to sit in a handsome old white rocking chair Amelie had brought with her when they married, watching the brass pendulum, not unlike some mystical sun, move back and forth inside the old clock. He liked to do it after his afternoon tea, when he no longer had to create a false impression of being occupied. At such times, there was a possibility of *identifying* with the pendulum, this small, totally empty space in his remaining life, the short life that might be left for him, and which now, rendered visible, passed at even intervals in front of the small window in the stomach of the clock. And this identification with the moment, which to an outside observer might seem odd and pointless, spelled considerable relief for Bernard. When he could become one with the pendulum and move with it, back and forth, he felt no time, no defeat, no victory. He was in the movement of the pendulum, and he was at one with it.

4. Dress Rehearsal

According to Amelie, it wasn't that easy to reconstruct what had actually happened, but one theory was that on a Thursday about two weeks before, he'd gone to the Royal Library as usual, and done exactly what he usually did, which included having a long conversation with his old friend, the bald, pince-nezed reading room supervisor Dr. Lennart Rodin. Of course he'd carried his usual old briefcase to the library, the one of worn black oxhide. This much-mended briefcase had been a present from his father, stern old Chief Forester Foy at Svanå, in the beautiful August of 1914, when he was about to begin his studies at Västerås *gymnasium.*

When it was time to go back home to Amelie and his waiting dinner, he'd noticed that the coat room attendant, some kind of foreigner he hadn't noticed particularly, didn't want to give him his briefcase. Bernard, who was getting tired of all those peculiar foreigners who nowadays seemed to inhabit every post office in Stockholm, and who seemed not to possess even ordinary politeness, told him firmly that he really wanted his briefcase, and to his surprise, the foreigner had indeed produced a briefcase.

Initially, Bernard hadn't paid much attention to it; he had enough trouble with his heavy winter overcoat, Amelie's two hand-knitted scarfs, his mittens—and, of course, the damn galoshes. Bundled up at long last, he exited the library grumbling discontentedly, and only when he got home did he discover to his surprise that the briefcase wasn't his usual one. This one wasn't black and made from oxhide; it was new, elegant, and made from light-colored pigskin. Where the hell could his own briefcase have got to, with all his notes about the airship *Italia* and the wreck due north of Foyn Island 1928? (One of the personages depicted in his autobiography, the von Lagerhielm brother, had participated in that expedition.) He opened the strange briefcase without enthusiasm and, to his complete disgust, he found that it seemed to contain nothing but a number of small bags; small plastic bags with some kind of white powder inside.

Some samples, probably, he told himself. It's too bad that I've taken his samples away from some traveling salesman. But what the hell is a traveling salesman doing at the Royal Library? No matter: it's my duty to return it to the Royal Library the next time I go there. I'll take it tomorrow.

The bizarre thing was that from that moment, he had no idea where that blasted new briefcase had got to. Amelie had just shouted that dinner was ready, and in his haste, he must have put it down in some inconceivable spot.

(For a while now, he'd been putting things down "in some strange place" and subsequently not been able to find them.)

It would transpire that he'd prevented one of the great benefactors of humanity, Dr. Ernst Lutweiler, from carrying out his humanitarian tasks.

Dr. Ernst Lutweiler had started calling. Extremely polite to begin with, Dr. Lutweiler had during a series of telephone calls run the gamut from politeness to slight irritation to open threat. At first he'd hoped that Bernard would realize his responsibility. Children in Africa, in particular, were dependent on his preparation in several different ways—it had to do with a new drug for tropical fevers. The contents of the briefcase represented fifteen years of hard work in some of the best pharmaceutical labs in the U.S. and in Europe.

Bernard regretted deeply and assured Mr. Lutweiler that if he'd only be good enough to call again tomorrow afternoon, everything would be all right.

But such was not the case. In the meantime, Bernard had been to the Library and found his old briefcase. Like any scholar, he hadn't left it in the coat room at all but had carried it with him into the reading room, where his admiring young friend, the former student at the Västerås *gymnasium*, Dr. Lennart Rodin, had preserved it respectfully and tenderly on behalf of the old poet and member of the Swedish Academy.

Bernard triumphantly carried his beloved old briefcase home, only to find that the strange yellow briefcase with all those valuable medical preparations seemed to have disappeared completely. Could it have passed through some strange door into another universe?

The great scientist and benefactor of humanity, Dr. Ernst Lutweiler, was less polite that evening. He intimated that someone who prevents the development of an important new drug which might have been used to save the lives of hundreds of thousands, perhaps millions, in Africa, might not have that large a claim to staying alive much longer. Bernard Foy asked his pardon a thousand times and said, a bit lamely, that if only Dr. Lutweiler would be so good as to phone again the next evening, he'd surely have found the briefcase and all the hundreds of thousands of suffering Africans could sleep soundly.

At seven o'clock the next evening, Dr. Lutweiler called again. This time, when he got the same answer as the night before, the discussion took on a noticeably vulgar tone. Bernard Foy was nothing but an *old clown*, for decades he'd been nothing but a completely insignificant poet whom he, Dr. Ernst Lutweiler, would delight in *taking care of personally*. He'd throw Bernard Foy down his own steps it he didn't immediately stop making a fool of himself and produce the *cocaine*!

But, Bernard Foy countered, if *cocaine* were that good for fever, wouldn't it have been used long ago in Africa for the poor suffering Negroes? Didn't the young Sigmund Freud write an important treatise on the advantages of cocaine, and hadn't he eventually contributed to the death of at least one colleague—also, of course, to the development of the mild and harmless zylocaine? In reply, Dr. Lutweiler informed Bernard that Bernard would soon see that it would be the best thing for his health to stop acting the fool. He was well acquainted with small dealers like Bernard. Tomorrow at three o'clock the whole thing had to be turned in at the ticket booth of the short-term parking lot at Arlanda airport, where Dr. Lutweiler enjoyed long-time contacts.

Oddly enough, Dr. Lutweiler sounded more respectful the next day.

For his part, Bernard had forgotten the whole thing. Or had he? I don't think we'll ever be able to differentiate among the parts of his being consisting of coquettishness, ambiguity, and the poet's fugitive, mild, but terribly superior strength, the triumphant power of the imagination to forsake the world.

This time, Dr. Lutweiler intimated the possibility of certain negotiations. It might be very unpleasant for an honored older member of the Swedish Academy if other members found out that one of them dealt in such merchandise. It might easily become one of those unpleasant *scandal sheet* items, and it was no secret what those papers were like.

If, on the other hand, Bernard were to be reasonable, one might think along the lines of five to eight percent. But in that case the briefcase had to be delivered at 2:30 a.m. to a white panel truck which would be parked on European Route 18, right where a handsome bridge arches almost a hundred feet above the picturesque depths of Ryssgraven.

It's certainly natural, Bernard replied, to get both nervous and angry when you lose the results of years of research and then can't get them back because some old man takes your briefcase at the Royal Library and afterward can't, no, not for the life of him, remember where on earth he put it. But that did not preclude trying to keep your patience. He, Bernard, would keep looking for the briefcase most energetically, and if only Dr. Lutweiler would be kind enough to leave his telephone number and a plain address where he could be reached, either at home or in his office, Bernard would send the briefcase along quite without any percentages or any strange ceremonies.

If this was not satisfactory perhaps Furtfeiler would be so kind as to call again the next day. He was sure to have found the briefcase by then.

Five minutes later the man called again. And this telephone call was, one might say, the point at which Bernard seized the initiative in this campaign, which had only alarmed him and distressed him up till now, but whose stimulating and entertaining qualities had grown more obvious with each passing day.

(The only important thing was to keep Amelie in the dark, by the grace of God.)

If Bernard Foy had been Napoleon, no doubt this would have been the battle of Marengo:

"Foy. Hello. Pardon? No, *actually* I don't remember your name. Oh, Professor Furtwängler? Yes, we've spoken earlier. At the Exchange, isn't that right? And what can I, poor old poet, do for you? Right away? Funny; I don't have the slightest recollection of anything like that. Nooo. Not at all. Isn't that strange. You think so? Pardon, I don't follow. *Briefcase?* I don't think I've heard a thing about a briefcase. Are you quite sure, Professor Dorfschwängler, that you've got the right number?

"Oh, really? *Come up? With torpedoes?* Just imagine, my cleaner who's here right now is an expert on torpedoes. Although these days, he mostly vacuums. He was torpedo master on board the little steam-driven submarine *Starke*, the first steam-driven submarine in the Baltic. I think it would make him happy and call up a lot of old unforgettable memories if he got to talk about *torpedoes* again. He once got an honorable mention from Prince Eugen, the Painter Prince, you know. After a most successful assault on the battleship *Victoria* in the course of naval exercises with the Baltic squadron. Of course I've forgotten what year it was. Yes, there aren't that many people who know it nowadays, but in fact, the Painter Prince was once the commander of the Second Torpedo Boat Division.

"Yes, that's how it was, I myself made the acquaintance of the Painter Prince much later. It was when I was on the board of the Artists' Association for a couple of years, but that was later on, in the '30s. Twice a year the Prince would have the board members over for dinner at his home on Waldemarsudde. I remember him well, his heavy, kindly head with the silver hair, his exquisite pronunciation which did not drop a single consonant. (Well, modern people slur a lot nowadays, as if they all belonged to the lower classes. Isn't it strange that it has to be that way? You can hardly understand what they say on the phone anymore.)

"Of course the thing I remember best is the wonderful spring nights on Waldemarsudde; the linden petals like a carpet over the garden paths, the thumping of the boats passing in the Sound, the blue hyacinths in the Prince's library. And the exquisitely set dining table.

"Perhaps it's never come to your attention, Dr. Grossweiler, but the Prince had quite a taste for the wines of southern France. Yes, he preferred Côtes de Rhône to Bordeaux wines. Oddly enough. It was probably a recollection of happy painter summers in his youth, in Provence.

"Another thing which might not be so well known about the Painter Prince is that he had a very fast repartee. His ability to improvise little profound and amusing verses was actually magnificent. No, I don't think that his biographers have even done justice to that trait of his.

"*Unforgettable moments.*

"For example, I remember one of those beautiful May evenings when the guests, Prince Vilhelm, Karlfeldt, and some other member of the Academy I don't quite remember, it may even have been Fredrik, Fredrik Böök that is, and nobody wanted to leave. The Prince ordered a late-night snack with meatballs and little sausages and Pripp's beer and nice chilled schnapps, but he was probable sleepy and wanted to get rid of us.

"But those damn guests didn't want to leave at all; they and the conversation went hither and yon in pleasant, labyrinthine paths, just the way good conversation among intelligent people should. And at long last we started talking about Fontaine de Vaucluse, this wonderful spot in Vaucluse with its crystal-clear, deep, and swift mountain brook where Francesco Petracra—Petrarch, you know—retired the last few years of his life, replete with honors, rich from the important diplomatic duties he'd been entrusted with and had just brought to a glorious conclusion.

"And the conversation had got around to the huge, dark *trout* that would stand in the water outside the terrace of the small tourist restaurant, waiting for the guests to throw bread to them. They'd come to the surface the way deep, not unfriendly, but awfully big thoughts might for a moment surface in human consciousness, only to disappear again swiftly into the deep, primeval, instinctual zones where they normally live and have their being.

"Someone—it can hardly have been Karlfeldt, who was quite unsophisticated, in spite of his Latin—more likely it was another of the poets of that time, the sometimes surprisingly subtle Gunnar Mascoll Silfverstolpe—*anyway,* this *someone,* whoever he was, mentioned those giant trout in the dark green fresh waters issuing from the mountain in the verdant spring far in the valley of Vaucluse, *Vallis Clausa,* 'the enclosed valley,' as its Latin name was.

"And the Prince, who'd been resting for some time with his white head on his arms at the kitchen table (the whole time the gigantic brown kitchen clock, the kitchen clock at Waldemarsudde, which otherwise kept track of the cooks and the butler and the kitchen maids from Karelia with narrow thin arms and blonde braids and maids from the Scanian castles the Prince liked to visit in the summer, this clock was ticking away more and more distinctly), then the Prince suddenly looked up and said: Apropos of those *trout* I'd like to say this:

> Good to be full and be uneaten,
> Better lusty and unbeaten,
> Best is free, unapprehended,
> Trout like that are truly splendid.

They'd laughed all the way into the coat room, and the waiting hansom cabs had had to stand for a long time before they piled in and departed, each in a different direction, in the dawning, immensely shy May morning.

"Did Professor Furtwängler realize how amusing this was, actually? Was he still there?"

But the only thing he could hear on the line was a strange ticking which reminded Bernard of the old kitchen clock at Waldemarsudde.

5. The Tribulations of a Prince of Poetry

Was he, as the saying goes, "happy?"

Sometimes he was happy, sometimes less happy. Actually he'd never really understood the concept. Often you'd be in both states at the same time.

It hadn't been different for him at any age. There was a state Amelie called "The Tribulation," and there was another one she called "The Royal Puff."

She regarded both with a mild skepticism which allowed her in the first instance to retain a supportive distance and, in the second, to avoid being drawn into the transcendent vanity which undoubtedly was an unavoidable consequence of this condition. Mystics tend either to turn into insufferable ascetic bores or else into blatantly self-righteous puffballs.

Bernard was familiar with both states of mind.

The Tribulation mostly hit in the morning, especially on black winter mornings when, at his age, one tends to wake up much too early, without anything sensible to do. (For a few happy weeks during the past winter, the terribly vulgar and one-dimensional spy thriller, *Bernard Foy's Third Castling,* which Bernard had been writing in secret and which he still kept in his bottom right-hand desk drawer, had been his salvation. Now he'd finished it a few days ago, and he had to find something else to amuse himself with.)

Svenska Dagbladet wasn't always the best thing. The newspaper, especially if he read it in the early dawn, would remind him of the Enemies, the Plagiarists, and most of all of Death, the cruel master who treated everyone so much the same that he might well subject Bernard to the same justice he meted out to everyone else.

The Plagiarists, to take the scourges one at a time, were those blasted young men whose books he was always reading about in the newspaper and who were obviously stealing from his poems, even from his old newspaper articles, without feeling any obligation to indicate their source.

For example, that young whippersnapper Fredrik Westholm, in his recent volume of poetry, *Incisions, Fractures, Joints* (evidently a painfully amateurish book which got tremendous accolades in the paper) had the audacity to allude to the Virgin Queen and the Bull, yes, actually to take the whole mythological idea from his own volume *Pasiphaë:*

> O Queen Pasiphaë!
> Rider! You forty-year-old needing the Beast
> to slake your mighty lust!
> Lust that does not stop at the human
> but must look into the mild dark eye of the bull
> (Westholm 1984)

> Echo of great depths, sound and reverberation:
> Thirst desiring the bottom of the well,
> Thirst desiring still greater depths.
> Oh, those are the dreams, the thirst of Pasiphaë.
> (Foy 1928)

Was there any need for further proof? And that was just one example. He could show, practically line for line, how this young man, with matchless impudence, had copied his own *Pasiphaë* from 1928. And it kept happening all the time. There wasn't a year when someone didn't steal another motif from his early poetry. If he'd at least had a real circle of devoted friends who could have done something about it! But he'd always been alone, a solitary in Swedish literature, a solitary in art history, a solitary in the Academy.

> Fresh water flowing over my hands.
> It's an ordinary Tuesday morning
> And I can't find my way.
> The apartment I wake up in
> belongs to a strange woman.

According to the regular poetry reviewer in the newspaper, that was the writing of the "promising and exquisite young ironist" Per-Ola Eriksson in his second collection of poetry, *Lived Through*, which has just been published. Dear God! Isn't there *anyone* who's well read enough, sensible enough, to see the *model*, the obvious, the almost great, he might even say *The Model*, in Swedish poetry, for this:

> How gently my spring would flow,
> The only moving thing in this white snow.
> How gently your waters would well forth,
> in a strange life, seeking the last of lakes!
> (*Ananke and Lyre*, 1932)

It wasn't just that if you told anyone about it, you always ran the risk of being considered querulous, or, still worse, you'd be accused of suffering from a persecution complex. There was hardly a theme he'd worked on in his life that some young idiot or other didn't seem to be taking over. He often had the feeling you have when you come upon a patch of wild strawberries only to find that stinkflies have invaded one berry after the other.

But the worst thing was not his suspicion that people were sitting there, brazenly copying some of his most beautiful sonnets from the '20s and '30s, insolently patching and sewing and fitting them into dull contemporary homespun suits. There were even worse things. And that thought, naturally, was so unpleasant that he preferred not to think it; it just might be that those stupid young poets with their pretensions, their strange airs, their mottoes from Jacques Lacan and Julia Kristeva, from Jacques Derrida and whatever they were called, quite simply and impudently, had never read his work.

Alas, he'd think: What *will become of me* when everyone seems to have conspired to steal from me. Someone save me, but quickly, before I'm stolen altogether, before I'm unraveled the way an old pullover is unraveled and turned back into yarn.

Worse than the whole thing with the *Plagiarists*, however, was the thing with the *Competition.*—What competition? the meek, innocent reader will ask. The only competition that's important in the long run, of course, The Competition for Survival. Oh, if he could only give up his unfortunate habit of reading the obituary page! Then it wouldn't have been a problem at all! But this uncertain, nervous anxiety, the failed hopes, the long drawn-out wait and the few, short triumphs when *the right* obituary at last appeared was almost too much for Amelie to keep up with.

One of the most bizarre of Bernard's many bizarre pleasures consisted of reading the obituary page in *Svenska Dagbladet*, hunting for familiar obituaries, those of friends or enemies, to see *whom he was surviving*.

This strange sport had the same importance for him now as love does for the young person and political passion for the mature man. He was at an age when he'd almost always encounter one or two names which awakened at least a transient memory, a face in a schoolroom, a voice on a committee, a half-forgotten irritation that would surface again for a moment, to turn swiftly into triumph as Bernard realized that this irritation would never return to his life. It was the weakest form of enjoyment.

Then there was enjoyment which was a degree stronger; those names that you read and reread, and where you felt positive relief. Bernard might yawn in his armchair with pleasure, not unlike a big, fat housecat with his white mane.

But not even those moments were the greatest. These would occur perhaps once a year, perhaps not even that often, and they were immediately recognizable from the brief, gusty, quickly suppressed laughter Bernard would send forth from the depths of his armchair on such occasions.

When Amelie came rushing in, he was very solemn and told her in a hushed voice that now, *sad to say*, Skunk, the editor of *Skandia*; Bladh, who used to be a taxation officer and who'd refused Bernard's deduction for a study trip to San Remo (to go to the beach, yes of course, but also to hunt for papers that may have been left behind by the *Italia* expedition); his former landlord, the coleric colonel Sigvard Silverben on Banérgatan (who'd had the audacity to claim that he, Bernard, a great Swedish poet, had called his wife "you furclad sow" on the stairs): now they had, all of them, *to our inexpressible sorrow,* left this life.

From the slight, almost unnoticeable clucking emanating from Bernard and his armchair on such occasions, Amelie would draw her conclusions about what had occurred. The vitality he'd radiate would remind her of a younger, much more vigorous man. Secretly, as of course any real woman would, she loved those traits of warrior, hunter, and gangster which at such times came to the fore in this descendant of innumerable generations of Västmanland foresters and farmers.

Suddenly, one gray winter morning, to find the obituary of an enemy in *Svenska Dagbladet* was one of the more pleasant sensations life could still offer Bernard Foy. The feeling of (once more) being in a world where divine justice— only partially, that's true, but never mind—had been restored because "an old publicist ganger boss" like X., a "self-enamored old queen and embroidery cushion" like Y., or "a horrible old pacifist pike" like former woman councilor Z. (he kept track of everyone, all the way from the '20s and provided them with his own labels, the way a housewife does her jam jars) had turned in their earthly equipment for good at the rough warrant officer's table of history, this was something that filled him with a quiet, pious admiration for the harmony and beauty of the created universe which would last for days. He almost felt like going to the Stockholm City Library on Sveavägen and take out some good books on galaxies so as to preserve the pious feeling a bit longer.

No idea seemed more distasteful, unhygienic, and generally repugnant to him than the idea of personal immortality.

"It's nothing but thoughtlessness, a lack of ability to envision the consequences of your own ideas," Bernard would say, "for someone to want the dead to be resurrected. A resurrected, fairly decent aunt, whom we'd have to be prepared to put up with forever, subsequent to the Day of Resurrection, already represents a considerable strain. Will we think she's as funny in three hundred years as we did the first seventy-five? If immortality is to have any kind of meaning, people can't be allowed to change a whole lot. If they go through a lot of change, perhaps they aren't really immortal any longer. So we have to suppose that they'll remain the same, by and large. She'll have the same irritating habit of dropping ash from her cigarettes, which she smokes in long amber holders, as she always has, the same lisp, the same awful ignorance of geography. We're always going to have to inform her that Roskilde is in Denmark, not in Norway, and that Franz Josef Land is not situated in Austria.

"All right then! Suppose we accept the aunt. But what are we going to do about our real enemies? Does a pious, decent person really want to see hundreds of happily dead and vanished SS soldiers resurrected so that they can start their pogroms and atrocities all over again? Who wants to see Attila and his Huns storm some timeless Europe, drowning peaceful French wine growers in the rivers? Or the Swedish plunderers of the Thirty Years' War for that matter. God, what vulgarity is concealed in this unfortunate belief in immortality.

"I assure you," Bernard would say, "that *nobody* who has seriously considered the problem would ever get such a silly notion as to wish for immortality. Still less anything so horribly destructive as to wish for the immortality of all kinds of unpleasant people. Grotesque!"

That his enemies no longer *were part of the connections of existence* would in some secret way give Bernard a taste of paradise. Because those who disappeared did not only, day by day, confirm the value of his own existence.

They restored the world to its original purity.

But there was one name he secretly looked for on this page and which he desired to see there with a hotter passion than all the rest of them together. It would never have occurred to him to divulge this name to anyone. And there were times when he wouldn't even have divulged it to himself. But every day, he continued to look for it, with an obstinacy whose strength surprised even him. For not that many strong feelings remained to him.

("You'll only be really happy when there aren't any people left at all," Amelie used to say.)

On the other hand, there were moments when Bernard would feel very great and above everything. That might happen in the dusk of late winter afternoons when he succeeded in being one with the movement of the pendulum in the old Stjernsund clock. This contemplative exercise even made him feel physically large. Like a very old lion, he'd sit there expanding in his armchair, he'd slowly "puff" over its edges. That's what Amelie called "The Royal Puff."

He liked to believe that such moments were the most noble ones in his life, and he wished he could regard the Swedish Academy banquet in that light, but he didn't quite succeed. On such occasions, there'd always be something that wasn't quite right. His underpants would pinch him under his evening trousers, his cuff links with the insignia of the Royal Uppland Regiment would be upside down, and it was much too late to try to do anything about it. Or someone had uttered an annoying sentence or one that might be interpreted as annoying, on the way in to the Börs Hall with its lighted candles.

At such times, when he actually managed to realize The Royal Puff, he often wished that Mrs. Elisabeth Verolyg would drop in. He knew he'd be sexually successful at such a time. If only Amelie would go shopping, or to the post office. Or to Beata von Post's. But Amelie was difficult. She hardly ever went out.

I'm old, Bernard thought, I'm weak, surrounded by young, determined people. I've never known how to surround myself with a small group of worshipers and young men who know they can get fellowships and other advantages if they write nicely about me in the papers. Good God! I've been a solitary man. I've never had the sense to organize my literary work into a working concern as so many of my colleagues have done. Good Lord, why should they write nicely about me, anyway? For many years, I haven't written anything that would be worth commenting on, nicely or not, to review, that is. *When Petals Still Fell in the Spring*, which was supposed to be the first part of my memoirs, was published when the young men of today had barely learned to read.

There's no doubt my books will have disappeared two years after my death. They still speak nicely of me in the newspapers, because they know I'm very old and will soon die and I'm no danger to anyone. But as soon as I'm gone they'll be able to keep silent about me in earnest. They'll unravel me like an old pullover. There won't be anything left.

Some absent-minded obituaries, and then it'll all be gone.

And by and by an article in the *Swedish Biographical Dictionary*, of course. And an issue of the *Minnesskrifter* of the Swedish Academy. But good Lord, nobody reads that. I don't even read it myself, Bernard realized. Or perhaps still worse: they'll *talk a lot of garbage* about me. Up there, in the daylight. And I won't be able to make myself heard all the way up there and answer them.

I'll be resting deep down in some gloomy grave where no protest can get out. Lutweiler will spread it about that I was a drug smuggler. Svenholm will spread it about that it was I who caused the death of Hans von Lagerhielm, that it was I who forced him to go on that awful zeppelin expedition because I took away the only girl he ever loved, or had a chance to love, in his life, Elisabeth Frejer. But that is wrong, wrong, wrong. Listen to me!

And they don't listen.

Deep down I know that I'm being punished. Punished because I betrayed Veronica von Lagerhielm once upon a time, betrayed and abandoned the one I loved because her absence, her bewitching somewhere-elseness frightened me. ("O forest witch, green-eyed and gentle,/ Witch, do not approach too close to me.")

6. Visit from a Literary Admirer

Bernard's depressing train of thought was interrupted by the ringing of the doorbell. Who could it be, so late in the afternoon? he asked himself. Perhaps it's just one of those funny market researchers who run around trying to find out how you do the dishes or what you watch on TV? I only hope it isn't that tiresome old accountant across the landing, because then I'll go crazy.

Amelie soon announced the visitor, who swept into the drawing room with an emphasis not unlike the way a racing yacht will approach the mooring in front of a club house. She even managed to give the impression of taking in her sails, one by one. Long before anyone had time to ask himself whether she was welcome or not, if it was the right time or if another time might have been better, Elisabeth Verolyg was already lying firmly at anchor in the drawing room. Amelie, who almost seemed to disappear under her fur coat, with its strong smell of not just one but of several fragrances, vanished in the direction of the kitchen. She was back in a moment to ask whether perhaps some tea . . .

The simple truth was that the Foys usually had tea at this time of the afternoon. After too many cups of coffee, Bernard would rather have gone for a walk, or even taken a nap, but just the same, he wasn't able to defend himself against the fascination emanating from their guest.

Elisabeth Verolyg was no insignificant force in the game which seemed to be in progress around him; like it or not, it was something he had to admit.

He didn't know why she'd started calling him and even writing little friendly, warmly appreciative letters in the last six months—this sudden interest from the great, fashionable woman critic had, so to speak, struck like lightning from a clear blue sky (or from a "bare" sky, as Bernard used to say; he loved to distort idioms). When he was feeling good, Bernard saw her interest as a sign that perhaps he wasn't as totally neglected and forgotten by the younger generation as sometimes seemed to be the case.

"Dear Amelie, what an honor," Bernard said in passing to his wife, nervously kissing Elisabeth's hand, which was still covered by an elegant black glove. He could feel the heavy rings under the black leather.

"It's so quiet at your house." (She spoke in a pleasantly low voice, which, however, had a veiled quality, probably due to heavy cigarette smoking.)

"I'm quite content, you know, just to *sit* here with you, enjoying the quiet."

She was dressed in a leather skirt, and her eyes glittered with dark make-up above a heavy, wide, sensuous mouth. The many wrinkles around her eyes revealed that perhaps she wasn't quite as young as the leather skirt, straining across her Junoesque hips, would seem to indicate.

"You create such quietness around yourselves, you two. I don't think you're conscious of it yourselves."

"But my dear Elisabeth, can't I offer you a small brandy at least," Bernard tried.

"Thank you so much, but I'd prefer a whiskey in that case," Elisabeth Verolyg answered with one of her strange smiles.

She had a very wide mouth, the mouth of a tragedy queen perhaps, and when she smiled, the corners of her mouth were pulled so far to the sides that the smile concealed some sad thought, a pain, a bitter memory, which she surmounted, proudly and silently. But perhaps it was only a peculiarity of her facial muscles?

"I only come here for the peacefulness. This, you see, this is one of the last really serene old-fashioned poet's homes in Stockholm, did you know that, Bernard? And I've had such a difficult day you can't imagine. You've got whiskey, haven't you, dear Amelie? Brandy is supposed to be so bad for your heart, haven't you heard?"

"Of course," Bernard said. "I'll look in the kitchen."

He belonged to a generation that kept brandy in a crystal decanter in the dining room next to the sherry and the vermouth. Whiskey, on the other hand, was something you didn't keep at home. It belonged more in bars.

Fortunately there was Amelie's bottle, that one she supposedly used for her rheumatism. Of course there was a risk that the Submarine Seaman, as he called him, Corporal Simmerling from the *Victoria,* had put the bottle in some unsuitable place. For years it had been one of his perks to have a small whiskey in the kitchen after he finished work. The man was energetic and effective, dashing about like a fury when he was in the apartment, and he demonstrated emphatically what all sensible people knew in the nineteenth century, which is that when all's said and done, there's no one to equal a sailor when it comes to cleaning. Bernard wondered silently whether it was tomorrow or Wednesday that he was supposed to be coming back.

Amelie was already in the kitchen. It was a bit strange. He'd never seen her leave the drawing room. He must have been more preoccupied with Elisabeth Verolyg's wide and tragic smile than he'd wanted to admit to himself.

It struck him that compared to their quest, Amelie suddenly looked small, thin, and transparent. Like a mosquito made of glass, he thought. And against his will, he noted that the comparison was not in Amelie's favor.

It may be that Elisabeth Verolyg is unbearable, power-mad, voluble, and perhaps a little stupid. But undoubtedly, she has a kind of Junoesque charm. She's very earthy, Bernard thought. I wonder, anyway, if she isn't shy behind all of her masks.

"You might as well take care of her," Amelie whispered, tense and nervous.

It often happened that Amelie said things which gave the impression that she'd heard his thoughts long before he'd thought them.

"What do you mean, take care of her?" Bernard said.

"You take care of her. Give her a glass of whiskey. Talk to her. Otherwise she'll start calling you again and talking on and on. I'm going out for a while anyway."

Amelie didn't like Elisabeth Verolyg.

"Where are you going?"

"But my dear Bernard, it's *Wednesday.*"

"So what, what does that mean? It means Simmerling's coming tomorrow, by the way. But why are you going out on the town in the evening just because it's Wednesday? Watch out, it might be slippery. And I thought you'd stopped going to those dull movies at the Alliance Française with Kerstin Löwenadler."

"But Bernard, dear, you aren't getting *senile,* are you? It's my ladies' bridge. I've played bridge every Wednesday for three winters now."

"I see. Then I'll be alone with her."

"I'm sorry, Bernard, but it's too late to say I can't play.

"Nooo."

Sometimes his wife could be extraordinarily difficult. Like now. Was it absolutely necessary to leave him in the lurch like this?

He was all set to return, with a bottle of Glenfiddich in his hand, and three glasses. He replaced one of the glasses on the kitchen counter.

Bernard's feelings were more ambivalent. Elisabeth Verolyg always radiated a scent of massive femininity, stale whiskey, and heavy Shalimar. She had to be about fifty.

"You go on," he said. "She won't stay long. God knows what she wants. In any case she'll be gone when you get back."

Still, she has magnificent posture, he thought, as he returned with a bottle and glasses on a tray, prepared to make the excuses for his absent wife. And magnificent thighs, you've got to admit it. It's a pity her neck's so *wrinkled,* he quickly added to himself. Or perhaps that's an illusion.

"It's so dark in here," Bernard said. "Just a moment, I'll turn on the ceiling light."

"Oh, I was enjoying it," Elisabeth said. "Can't you turn on that little table lamp instead? It looks as if it would have such a *warm* light."

If I only knew what this woman wants from me, Bernard thought.

Just as he'd put down the silver tray with Glenfiddich, the ice bucket and—for safety's sake—two glasses, he found her engrossed in one of the few truly interesting things available for study in the apartment.

In the dark passage between the kitchen and the dining room were two carefully framed, rather yellowed, enlarged photographs. One represented a zeppelin, hovering in unreally still air above what had to be an Arctic sea with masses of drift ice under it. Down on the horizon to one side was a gleaming white, majestic mountain range. The airship, magnificent in its loneliness, its oneness, seemed to reflect all the light.

In the other photograph the same airship was hovering above Stockholm. For some reason, this picture was more melancholy, more rainy; it didn't have the same immaterial character as the other one. The Essinge industrial area was plain to be seen, still virginal, undeveloped, but with the small vacuum-cleaner factory already in place.

"Is it really the airship *Italia?*"

She examined the photograph with unfeigned interest, nearsightedly leaning forward in the dark passage in a way that made her leather skirt strain across hips and buttocks. It was the Arctic picture she was examining.

"Yes," Bernard said. "It's the *Italia.* It's in 1928, it was in May that the airship passed over Stockholm. Hans von Lagerhielm threw a capsule, by the way, to an aunt who lived in Äppelviken. The other picture was taken by the expedition's expert on atmospheric electricity, Professor Běhounek. During the ascent, he made friends with Hans."

"Hans von Lagerhielm was the poet, wasn't he?"

The picture was very beautiful. It was the silvery shimmer, the whole character of something strange and wonderful visiting a sterile, desolate landscape, which made it beautiful, Bernard thought.

"The *Italia* expedition took place in 1928," Bernard noted dryly. "It was an Italian attempt to repeat Amundsen's exploit a few years before with the airship *Norge,* namely to sail across the polar sea. The *Italia* was captained by a man, General Umberto Nobile, who'd distinguished himself on the Amundsen expedition. He probably had the ear of the Fascist regime in Rome. Or perhaps he just had contacts in the Italian air force. Be that as it may, he was entrusted with the leadership of a new expedition that was to explore the great, still uncharted expanses of sea to the east of Amundsen's route."

"And it ended in catastrophe?"

He nodded.

Once more he asked himself what this woman really wanted from him. Aside from her Junoesque hips, she wasn't particularly appealing. Or, even if she were, she was still a total stranger. Her activities as literary critic on *Dagens Nyheter* must have been going on for the last twenty years. Her basic principle seemed to be to praise everything issuing from the small group of upper-class Östermalm families which, for her, was the real Sweden, and where everyone knew everyone else; even the novices could be placed within the circle of cousins. Nowadays, this circle conceived of itself as "radical," liberated, and emancipated; they liked showing up at Social-Democratic dos at the Modern Museum.

As a critic, she was cooler to what came from elsewhere: from those strange foreign countries or from the still more bizarre provincial districts she mostly knew from ski vacations at different mountain hotels, spent with various more or less successful lovers from the younger, upward-bound portion of the staff on the paper's cultural page.

In her criticism, she was profoundly ignorant and made a virtue of it.

In brief, she was the kind of critic whose activities are based more on social merit than on a reading of texts and books. And that's why she was so influential.

She can topple me or make me immortal with her left hand, Bernard said to himself. With her left hand . . . But would she really be willing to do something? She couldn't be very impressed with a bourgeois '20s poet like Bernard, who'd procrastinated for twenty years over such a simple, uncomplicated task as writing the second volume of his memoirs. What she, the daughter of an insurance company president on Karlavägen, really admired was managing directors of mining concerns, captains at the First Cavalry Regiment who greeted the ladies with a saber salute at the corner of Sturegatan and Karlavägen, white-haired, apple-cheeked corporation presidents sitting at their heavy manager's desks of antique oak. *That's* what she admires, he thought.

It struck him almost immediately that he'd forgotten one category: Finnish-Swedish *poètes maudits*. Where they were concerned, she had a patience that verged on the incredible. When she was younger, she'd married them one after the other, only to find some subtle organic flaw: here a failing liver, there a weak heart; all those wildly passionate marriages always ended in the premature death of her spouse. It was like a curse. And they were all brilliant poets.

"She has the knack of bringing on premature death in her husbands," the malicious Amelie would sometimes say.

"You're unfair, bordering on tastelessness," Bernard would answer. "Besides, you have to realize that there are a number of species where that's quite a common occurrence. Female spiders, for example, often kill the males after intercourse."

Or perhaps the males die from overexertion? He couldn't quite remember. Her somewhat mysterious but evidently great influence as a critic might, in the last instance, be due to the fact that she shared all the arrogant, narrow-minded prejudices of her readers to the last detail.

Her readers seemed to be those innumerable experts, committee secretaries, country councilors, state department councilors of the increasingly prevalent type who—under a Social-Democratic egalitarian reform system which, according to some observers, could afford nothing more than pocket money for the children of the system—had succeeded in acquiring ten-room houses, English nannies for their children, and annual family grants from the Julius Bär Bank in Zürich.

That was what her readers were like, and it was their prejudices she affirmed. At the same time, she always managed to disguise those prejudices and extremely right-wing positions as expressions of an almost *dangerous* radicalism. (Hadn't her grandmother, the Baroness Oehl-Friss, née Bebra, once in her youth, as a romantic young girl, carried a letter to no less a personage than Prince Kropotkin in Paris when she traveled there from Riga?)

Why should the working class have cars? It just made the pollution worse. Wouldn't it be better if *society* took charge of that money and gave it to disadvantaged groups? And what was the point of all those horrid and *ugly* little summer houses the working class insisted on hammering and sawing on in their spare time? They were spoiling natural beauty. Wouldn't it be much better if *society* could get them together in little villages so at least you wouldn't have to have them right on top of you?

Also, as far as Israel and the Middle East were concerned, she herself was of course a warm proponent of democracy and anti-Fascism and she had *so* many Jewish friends. Some of them were among her closest friends, and no one in her family had seen through Hitler as early as her father did, but was it really necessary for them to carry on like impertinent U.S. lackeys, imperialist and veritable *Nazis* in their unwitting, brutal demands? If only they'd *know their place* a bit better.

For decades, books had sold if they were praised by her and didn't sell if they didn't meet with her approval. In the midst of her warm contemporary feelings and her fervid engagement in the big questions of the time, the Third World, women's rights, the necessity of profoundly *pacifist education* of the young, this remarkable lady also found time to study and critically analyze the classics.

Her book on Petrarch was unconventional, but important. Not just important. It was considered *brilliant* by those, one would assume, who'd read it. It had even been translated into German. She'd also written an important book on Skogekär Bergbo's sonnets, this extraordinary Baroque work in which, despite much effort, it had proved impossible to get a glimpse of the creator behind the genteel pseudonym. (In her preface, Elisabeth hinted that he might perhaps be a forefather of hers, and not one of those dull brothers, Schering and Gustav Rosenhane, who were usually cast for the part. In her books, she often hinted at access to unique family documents which she was unfortunately prevented from making public.) It's true the book was not an *academic* success. Not unexpectedly, the envious, male-dominated circle of dull professors of the Baroque were up in arms about it, but as one of her admirers, young Tom Wedelin in *Aftonbladet,* had put it: "Before Elisabeth Verolyg took on this task no one knew who Skogekär Bergbo was, and everyone knew who Elisabeth Verolyg was. Now everyone knows who Skogekär Bergbo was and no one knows who Elisabeth Verolyg is."

To get praised by her was to be carried on the wave of contemporary fashion. Not to be noticed by her was not to belong, really. Stern and eager, she liked to celebrate novices who showed serious commitment and feeling, even though they might not always be as talented as she liked to imagine. The very few young writers who seemed to possess true originality she seemed—at any rate that's how it often appeared to Bernard—not to see, or to pass over in deliberate, almost offended silence.

If she was strict with the young, she was even stricter with the representatives of older literature. Debunking criticism of canonized poets was one of the many expressions of her lack of conformity and her refusal to accept "the petrified values of male society" and "the dead conventions of the literary establishment."

If this remarkable lady really wanted to lavish her benevolent attentions on Bernard, it would be a blessing.

She was also, in spite of her prejudices, her ignorance, and her limitations,

138

with her still firm bust, her carelessly flopping reddish-blonde hair, her unfortunately too made-up face, her Shalimar scent, and, above all, her Junoesque hips, what he used to call "a damn attractive woman."

Absent-mindedly, he put his right hand under her leather skirt while she was still watching the zeppelin's unreal hovering above the Arctic sea and got inside her elegant silk panties. To his surprise, she was already quite wet between the legs. She let it happen; only a slight trembling of her solid body actually betrayed that anything unusual was happening in this passage.

One can always hope, it struck Bernard with a sudden feeling of conviction, that she'll write a really extensive and lively obituary about me.

7. A Sight of Undeniable Beauty

Once upon a time Bernard Foy had been, if not a great, at least a thorough lover. However, that was some considerable time ago. When the important female critic and literary personality, fifty-year-old Elisabeth Verolyg, quite unexpectedly turned into a willing, trembling reed in his arms, just because he'd touched her between the legs as she examined one of the few surviving pictures of the airship *Italia,* this caused him a moment of embarrassment.

A clump of softened clay was an adequate expression for the state of this remarkable lady. More by her own, now very soft bodily weight than by force, she pushed Bernard into one of his old, deep leather armchairs, pulling down her pretty white silk panties with decisive movements, not unlike an experienced old whore. Her leather skirt had meanwhile ridden up to her navel, and her carelessly flopping red hair seemed to have loosened as of its own accord and appeared to encircle her. All this was a sight of undeniable beauty, and Bernard said, somewhat embarrassed, "I think you'll have to blow me a little. Unfortunately, we old men need it."

This speech only seemed to increase her trembling excitement.

With a kind of soft, catlike purr she undid his fly buttons, one by one. The moment when she closed her full, bitter lips on his manly organ, unused for such a long time, with its eighty-three years of hernias, old pimples, and healed lesions, not unlike an old pickled cucumber that's been left in it jar over the winter, he saw her one eye look up at him, blue, skeptical, and friendly, through the tendril of red hair. She seemed to be laughing softly.

"Why are you laughing?" Bernard asked.

For obvious reasons, there was no answer.

"My dear Bernard, I write this to you at an altitude of twelve hundred meters, somewhere between Katowice and Köningshütte. We have just been in radio-telegraphic connection with Stolp, where we are supposed to initiate our landing maneuvers, maneuvers which, I hope, will be the calm conclusion to what I believe to be the thirty-one most dramatic hours of my life, thirty-one hours when I, more than once, feared we would not survive.

"You get cold and frozen, let me tell you, from standing in the little boat-shaped gondola; if you want to sleep you have to lean against a window, for there is no place to lie down. In addition, there are the regular instrument readings which must also be handled in a satisfactory manner.

"But let me tell you briefly about our principal adventures after our start from Milan. We proceeded all afternoon through gentle, still spring air, until we were over the Czech border. Only the regular drone of our three 250-horsepower Maybach engines, hanging in their engine gondolas, and the sound of the bells on the telegraph machines would interrupt my thoughts from time to time. My thoughts were going back home, of course. But to my friends in Uppsala as well.

"One sometimes wonders, for instance, whether Elisabeth Frejer and her French Papa are still in town. Do you still go for walks with her on Sunday afternoons to Islandsfallet? Does she still wear white gloves and that large picture hat? And do you still have to take that awful chaperone along? What was her name again? Miss Engström, was that it? The one with the teeth, I mean.

"At any rate I think it is time for me to return to our awe-inspiring adventures. (I have not tried to write a poem about it yet, so far there are only electrostatic protocols. But the poem may come. There are still quite a few thousand kilometers to Kungsfjorden and much may yet happen.)

"The first night the wind was weak and calm. It was a fantastic sight, all the Italian cities spread out underneath us with their thousand gaslights like big, reddish-yellow jewels. Someone who has not seen it simply cannot imagine how beautiful it all is!

"Then we passed over the cities of Brescia, Verona, and Padua, and it felt as if we were looking into a mirror of those sounds of barking dogs and voices from the distant darkness.

"In one way it reminded me of a strange passage in Meister Eckhart I found last winter during my time of sadness (which you are certain to remember, such as it was): 'God looks on us with exactly those eyes with which we look on God.' It reminds me forcibly of something I am about to relate. You know that the old cabalists considered it a sign that a man was very close to God if he met himself, literally himself.

"For the only way in which God can show himself to a human being is through the labyrinthine structure of the world. A wonderful, deep thought, isn't it? You will remember Goethe relating to Eckermann how he met himself, coming toward him on a path. This, I like to tell myself, reveals something of how the world is in fact constructed.

"(When I think of these things, I sometimes imagine an endless number of reflections of the image into itself, *involutions,* as the topologists call it. The world does not exist anywhere, it is only a point in the Divine Consciousness, and the point-shaped existence of this point consists of its ability to reproduce itself innumerable times. But let me close quickly, because I know, my dear Bernard, that you find such thoughts abstruse.)

"About this and other, similar thoughts I have had lately I do not want to say anything more at present.

"Back to our adventures. We proceeded through the thinnest spring air until night fell. When we passed over the lagoon at Venice, the first, slanted sunbeams fell straight across our cabin, throwing an eerie light over the faces of the crew. Zappi and Trojani, concentrating on the altitude and lateral controls, General Nobile himself, with his expression of manly concentration, as if hewn in Roman marble, leaning over the magnificent, large compass that is bolted down in the middle of the gondola. Admirable and singular, a late descendant of Florentine condottieri, that is how he often seems to me when he sits there in the middle of the gondola (the only one who is allowed to sit on a small pedestal), in control of immense powers. That's exactly how modern man, envisioned by such poets as Marinetti, Mayakovsky, and Gabriele d'Annunzio, should look. Someone who has seen the beauty of modern technology and can control it, the way he controls the world of new speed with its sensation of simultaneity, controls the air-ocean and the deadly weapons of a new era.

"After that we could look down on the blue-green surface of the water and on Trieste, and then we steered northeast to initiate the large circling movement around the Alps, which of course was necessary, and which would bring us up through the young Czech republic, Franz Běhounek's homeland. (Franz Běhounek is my new scientific comrade. He participated a bit at the end of the *Norge* expedition. More of him later.)"

(He'd been wrong. It wasn't that difficult to get an erection. The one he had now was impressive, surprising even himself. That was no longer the problem, which was how to push her down on top of him somehow, so that the arms of the creaking old leather armchair wouldn't get in the way. With the guile and calculation of someone who now knows that he's in complete control of the situation and will be for some time to come, Bernard wondered, How would it be if she'd just sit facing forward. Then I'll take her from the back.)

"East of Laibach we passed over the Sava River, encountering a certain amount of turbulence: the pleasant, calm flight, the regular humming of the engines, were replaced by violent movement that made us hold on white-knuckled to any fixed object that came to hand—I to my instruments—and soon the telegraph was ringing almost without pause as the General alternately tried to increase and decrease our altitude in order to accommodate ourselves to the hazardous air currents.

"It was admirable to see how he maintained the, I do not hesitate to say it, stature and countenance of an old Roman centurion. When it was at its worst, the General himself silently took charge of the altitude controls. Without a doubt, this is a man with whom you could weather storms.

"Then everything quieted down. We flew over Steinamanger, where we went down for a moment, reading the sign at the railroad station to convince ourselves that our navigation was correct. (We must have frightened a solitary inhabitant considerably; he happened to look out his window at that very moment, our immense, silver-gleaming cigar over the little house roofs in the moonlight.)

"The closer we got to the Schleswig border, the denser the clouds became. We had weather reports every half hour via the radio telegraph, on this occasion principally from the Czech weather stations of Prague and Lindenberg. Soon Prague announced that a big thunderstorm was approaching to the southwest at a velocity of thirty kilometers an hour, and the noise from our three powerful engines increased to a mighty crescendo as we tried to escape the rapidly advancing storm. Radio contact was already impossible due to the violent electrical dis-

142

charge, and the activity on my atmospheric gauges was, for the same reason, comparatively meaningless.

"After barely half an hour, we simply had to acknowledge that there was a thunderstorm in front of us as well as another one rapidly approaching from behind.

"There was nothing for it but to manfully enter the eye of the storm. It turned completely dark inside the gondola, although there should have been moonlight up to midnight, and the violet light from giant lightning flashes illuminated the white-painted canvas walls almost continuously. To start with, we were practically at the center of the electrical discharge, and I do not think there was a single one of us who did not think of the unfortunate French airship, the *Dixmude,* which was demolished by lightning over the Mediterranean.

"The lurching, the panic fear of a fall without end, the sudden ascents, yes, this whole wondrous air circus is something I have a hard time doing justice to in the shape of a letter, yes, in any shape whatever."

(Bernard, too, had difficulty doing justice to the situation at this moment, truth to tell, for in the moonlight in his dark drawing room Elisabeth Verolyg, not unlike some strange, large witch of passion, was straddling him with her long, wild hair loose around him in an ecstatic ride that made her profuse saliva drip onto his hairline. Neither that nor the fact that a wicked little square object of some kind, fallen off Amelie's sewing table as it overturned, kept Bernard from enjoying the situation with audible grunts and cries.

Not unlike a Roman centurion, he steered his ship through the storm.)

"When the immense airship at last emerged from the clouds and all of it was illuminated by the profuse moonlight: this was a sight of undeniable beauty.

"I and the Czech physicist Frans Běhounek leaned against the thin, linen-cloth wall of the engine gondola at the same time, looking out through the isinglass that served as the forward window of the airship."

"(Běhounek is a man I have become more and more friendly with on board. As the only 'foreigners' we tend to turn to each other. I suppose we both have a feeling that the Italians would like everyone on board to be Italian, and we are very conscious of being here solely in consequence of General Umberto Nobile's wishes; we are old experts from the airship *Norge.*)

"In front of us the monotonous cumulus clouds of the morning were rolling like a sea of immense, silver-colored waves, a very slow sea. Now and then the landscape underneath us would become visible through some surprising opening or other in the fabric of wet, heavy, early spring clouds over this Central Europe we all loved and which we were all leaving behind for other, more Arctic regions. Who did not feel a sense of loss at such a moment? Perhaps even sorrow?"

"Bernard, my poor darling," Elisabeth Verolyg said, wiping his forehead with a pungently perfumed handkerchief that seemed much too small for such a large woman.

"Bernard, my dear, I hope you're feeling well. I had no idea there was such stormy passion in you."

Bernard hoped so too. His heart felt fine, there was lots of time before Amelie would be back from her bridge—to his amazement, he saw from the Stjernsund clock that only twenty minutes had passed since they entered the room.

I only hope, he thought quietly, and not without a certain desolate self-esteem, that this will get into her memoirs. It would undoubtedly improve my standing with posterity.

"Now, my darling, I have a special little request for you," Elisabeth Verolyg said. "A small thing I'm sure you won't deny me."

8. More about Forgetfulness: Art and Life

Poor Bernard! Once the words started abandoning him—the speed at which they did so seemed to increase with each passing day—it was the same as when a chess player, confronted with a superior opponent, starts to lose his pieces. It begins with the light noun pawns. Gradually, the swift adjective bishops and adverb knights go too. Until the time has come for the heavy verb rooks to be discreetly put on the sidelines. Then the experienced chess player knows there isn't much he can do.

Soon there are rows of captured words standing at the side of the chessboard, and only a spectator can see how poorly the game is going for one of the players, how much he's already lost to his evidently *much* superior opponent.

Three weeks after the incidents we touched on lightly in the preceding chapter and which ought not to come to Amelie's knowledge (but perhaps we ought not to exclude the possibility that in the previous chapter, we were duped by Bernard's lively old man's *imagination*, not to mention our own prurient novel reader's imagination, for the manly capability he excelled in throughout important portions of the chapter seems to us, after due consideration not quite consonant with what's been said about his age), Bernard discovered the lost pigskin briefcase.

For many years, he'd kept his rhyming dictionaries discreetly behind the heavy curtains of Chinese silk in his study. He had no reason to hide the fact that he, like most other poets of his generation, had used a rhyming dictionary for his poems. Who the hell hasn't? Silfverstolpe? Nonsense. Österling? Österling probably used an entire shelf of rhyming dictionaries. Bernard hardly ever consulted his rhyming dictionaries, but there they were, had been for at least a decade, covered by a thick layer of dust, on the wide windowsill, together with a very dusty palm tree that Submarine Seaman Simmerling watered. If you, a great Nordic poet, happen to have in your library, left over from your youth, six or seven volumes of rhyming dictionaries, it isn't absolutely necessary to place them in such a way that they're bound to be noticed by every magazine writer who happens to enter your study.

A few weeks before, he'd been visited by the youthful, brilliant critic Elisabeth Verolyg, with her long, flapping red hair and large, soulful blue eyes, a lady with whom he had felt a surprising, deep inner connection, not least in her capacity as a representative of the younger generation of critics. This incident had made Bernard feel the need to write a poem. It must have been the first time in a very long while. He had some vague ideas of something about fall, about how burning the fall sun can be. On certain surprising October days. But also the incomprehensible but sweet attraction which mature age, under fortunate circumstances, may exert on youth.

(We are still allowing ourselves a neutral attitude as regards the weight Bernard wanted to give the events of the previous chapter.)

At any rate, he'd started off pretty well with something like:

> My autumn days are once again aflame,
> and rowan berries of enormous size
> on which the sparrows soon will gormandize
> bode a severe winter. But my lame
>
> and anxious spirit was consoled . . .

Here it started to get difficult. The Petrarchan pattern he'd selected, abba, abba, now required two more rhymes for "size." What he wanted to say was that such large, burning days had a greatness ordinary summer days don't have. Of course he might try a slant rhyme, an assonance like "vitrified":

> . . . and anxious spirit was consoled: a light
> day of spacious sky that's vitrified

One doesn't have to be a professional poet to realize that in this situation, Bernard found himself in a somewhat precarious position. Frankly, it looked as if the damn rhymes, with the willfulness characteristic of such unruly little monsters, were getting him further away from what he wanted to say, rather than closer. (If only there were a spray against rhymes as there is against mosquitoes!) What should the next rhyme word be?

It ought to be discreet, inserted as swiftly and effectively as the thrust of a foil, and it should place a large rose of heat in the autumnal landscape he'd sketched in the first quatrain. "Hide" didn't seem particularly promising. ("From death does hide") "Tide" was already an improvement, but with the same malicious precision, it would bring him still further away from the enclosed heat that was the secret heart of the sonnet. Tide has to do with the sea, and that doesn't imply heat. And vitrified by what? Frost? That would hardly be present until December at our latitude.

God how strange, Bernard thought, I want to write about warmth and my poem keeps getting colder and colder.

But wait, did he have to stick to the Petrarchan pattern? Couldn't he do a Shakespearean sonnet and rhyme the second quatrain cddc? And he might try putting in a *sizable wave,* a *billow* (of course Erik Lindegren had done something like it in his "Arioso," without any great success, but anyway).

> . . . by frost. Billow, rising on the tide
> and capped with froth, at your passion's height . . .

That isn't bad for my first poem in twenty-two or twenty-four years, Bernard thought. I have every reason to feel satisfied with myself.

And it *wasn't* that bad when you considered that someone who'd seemed

146

almost lost at the previous turn was now in this excellent position for the end game:

My autumn days are once again aflame,
and rowan berries of enormous size
on which the sparrows soon will gormandize
bode a severe winter. But my lame

and anxious spirit was consoled: a light
day of spacious sky that's vitrified
by frost. Billow, rising on the tide
with froth, at your passion's height . . .

It was at this point, at the last moment before the sestet took hold of him, that Bernard, seized by a weakness understandable even in a great lyric poet, felt a strong need to consult one of the numerous rhyming dictionaries which, for years, had hidden behind the curtain in the shadow of the palm tree.

There stood the mysterious pigskin briefcase that had given rise to so many strange telephone calls from that unpleasant, aggressive pharmaceutical expert in the last few weeks—was it Lutweiler his name was? It stood in the shadow of the lyrical palm tree together with a well-watered and -tended hibiscus behind the curtain in the north window of the study. A small spring breeze of a kind more typical of April than of March had started to blow, and the birches had assumed their first violet tint. It seems we're going to have spring this year, too, Bernard thought.

"Oh, that one," Amelie Foy said. "Yes, of course I've seen it. I was thinking of taking it up to the attic."

"Don't do that," Bernard said. "There's something important about it, I can't remember what. Yes, there is a man who calls here and shouts about that brief-case all the time. He says I took it by mistake from the coat room at the Royal Library."

"Shame on you, Bernard," Amelie said. "Of course you've got to return it."

"I suppose," Bernard said. "Strange, though. He didn't want to leave his telephone number. If I remember correctly, he just said I'd hear from him again. Perhaps we should look in it. There might be some clue."

At this moment, faint as a shadow, discreet as a stag moving through the forest to its watering hole, but very distinctly, Bernard became conscious of a feeling that he'd opened the briefcase once before. But where and how he couldn't remember. And not what it had contained, either.

Alzheimer's disease, if that's what I'm suffering from, is a game of chess, and the opponent is truly terrible. If you let your attention slip for a moment, there's another piece gone. At one fell swoop, it's gone. One moment it's there. And the next one it isn't. The long, complicated words are the first ones to go.

"Pneumatological" and "homology" vanished into darkness, side by side like two melancholy, exotic elephants. I wonder where they might be now. And which riders they carry in their howdahs now. Anyway, nobody uses words like that anymore, I guess everybody nowadays would think the "pneumatological" has to do with tires. They don't have the slightest idea that it is the doctrine of the Holy Spirit. Or the Holy Ghost, as older texts have it.

It does make a difference in which order you forget things, Bernard told himself. Somewhat systematic forgetfulness is as important as somewhat systematic learning. If you forget in the wrong order, you're doomed to lose your dignity.

I don't want that to happen.

He could go on like that. Amelie called it his *rummaging*.

"But don't you ever forget something, Amelie?"

She looked up at him with a bewildered expression, small, white-haired, and completely trusting.

"No. I don't feel that I do. You're the one who forgets things. I hardly ever forget anything. But," she added, "I'm no poet either."

The noise from a heavy bus in the street made the windowpanes in the old house vibrate slightly. A flock of restless gulls circled above the trees in the park.

"Sometimes," Bernard said abruptly, "I have a feeling that everything has changed very quickly. Like in a country where new rulers have seized power overnight, taken over the radio stations, the newspapers: everything. And they try to give the public the impression that nothing whatever has happened. Everything is to be perceived as unaltered. That's the idea. But I can remember when it happened. I'm sure there's something obvious here that other people know, and I'm the only one who doesn't."

"Poor Bernard."

She took his hand pityingly.

"A good example," he said suddenly on this peaceful Wednesday afternoon when the trees in the park were already beginning to assume the light brown-violet tint which is the first harbinger of spring, and the shadows of the trees lay long and blue in the natural complementary color of the snow, across the hard white crusted snow in the park . . . "A good example of . . . that is . . ."

Then there was silence again for a while.

How long will it be before the king, his own name, has to be given up, squeezed into a corner? And abandoned by the queen, who is . . . what? If only I could remember who the queen is.

"A good example of my forgetfulness is that briefcase. It contains something criminal, something that has to do with drugs. Cocaine, perhaps. It belongs to a gangster. An awful gangster of the modern kind they have nowadays. He's called me several times and threatened me with horrible consequences if I don't return the briefcase to him. The strange thing is I haven't heard from him for weeks. And of course I've forgotten his name now. Otherwise I could at least turn it over to the police. But if I turn it in now, I'll be suspected of having something to do with it."

"But *poor* Bernard," Amelie continued, still pityingly. "Do you mean to say that you've been carrying such a secret all by yourself? It's no wonder, my little Bernard, that you've seemed unhappy lately."

"I'm not unhappy at all," Bernard said, quite definitely. "I'm writing a poem."

"*A poem?*"

She wasn't able to suppress a shrill cry of surprise.

At this moment, the bell in the vestibule rang. (Over the years, he'd learned to distinguish it from the bell in the kitchen, which had an old-fashioned entrance for delivery boys and handymen.) It wasn't strange that it should ring, because it was the time when people paid visits, three o'clock in the afternoon. The light fell in behind the curtain where the mysterious briefcase was still standing, stubbornly silent about its riddle.

The cheerful, fluting voice now making itself heard in the vestibule, quickly approaching, could not be mistaken. It had to be Elisabeth Verolyg. Now she was already in the drawing room, just as the sad old Stjernsund clock struck three times with much whirring and booming. (Like a very old poet trying to extract the fourteen lines of a sonnet from his rusty works, Bernard thought.) Did he, or did he not, want to receive this visitor, who both disturbed the work on his last sonnet and who was the cause of that sonnet?

He already, not without a faint and happy shudder that would remain his secret, heard her soprano voice which might cut glass if required to, assuring Amelie with hypocritical benevolence of something or other. What a horrible woman, he thought. Why should this particularly affected, licentious, slightly alcoholic, and furthermore red-haired tigress of a literacy critic be the one to occasion what would surely be the last sonnet of a great poet? But wasn't there *always* something disturbing, almost embarrassing, about trying to find out the circumstances in which an important work of art had originated? Anyway, that was what Thomas Mann had once said, when he wanted to explain one of his novels to American students in his Princeton speech.

With an old steel comb he'd had since his Uppsala days, Bernard neatened his hair, which had become disheveled during his lyrical efforts, and quickly put a few drops of Watzin's Keratin on his white temples.

There's nothing I dislike more, he thought to himself, than this rooster part, the role of poet prince that poor Swedish poets feel they have to assume when they're around sixty—if, by that time, they still have a decent suit of clothes and haven't ended up in the detoxification unit yet. God, how much rather I'd have been a rich old lawyer.

Like the count, Hans Hansdorff, J.D., who has his office here in the house right underneath us. He'd do everything I do, but better and with much greater ease. Besides, he's rich. *He* has young, incredibly doe-eyed *models* come visit him sometimes. Or perhaps they're his grown daughters? Strictly speaking, daughters might turn into models, isn't that so?

With a discreet, dark blue corduroy coat across his shoulders, his hair carefully combed around his white temples, the long, narrow, sensitive hands held out; not so far that it looked feminine, just enough so that it looked sensitive, not at all affected, Bernard Foy entered his drawing room with perfect timing.

> You were not easy,
> fate that turned into mine,
> but sometimes I would find
> the honey of an unknown sweetness.

9. What the Briefcase Did Not Contain. And What It Did Contain.

My autumn days are once again aflame,
and rowan berries of enormous size
on which the sparrows soon will gormandize
bode a severe winter. But my lame

and anxious spirit was consoled: a light
day of spacious sky that's vitrified
by frost. Billow rising on the tide
capped with froth, at your passion's height . . .

"That's it. *A poem,*" Bernard said.

"And," he added consideringly, "I'd like to finish it before we open the damn briefcase. I was right in the middle when I caught sight of it. And I'm hunting for the last six lines of my last sonnet."

"*Last,* Bernard? Why do you say an awful thing like that?"

"It feels like the last one," Bernard replied. When I write a poem it *always* feels like the last one. I think I'll have to ask you to leave me alone. It would be such a pity if I should forget my *last* poem. But maybe we *have to* open the briefcase first? Perhaps you're curious."

"Not at all, Bernard dear. Go on working on your poem. It's such a long time since you wrote one."

He felt a twinge of conscience. It *would* have been better if the poem, after so many years of her patience, had been directed to her. But it wasn't.

Hardly had he completed this thought before he started to feel the poem slipping from his hands. He'd already started to forget it. Very often when you start to forget something, there's a fantastic moment reminiscent of those terrible incidents that occur when little children flush things down the toilet (he'd never done it himself, for he belonged to an earlier generation, but he'd seen it.)

Not uncommonly, it's their parents or other relatives they're flushing down. And there always comes a moment when they'd really like to stick their hands down and get it back. But the thought of all the stinking, messy, and disgusting things there *are* in the toilet keep them from doing it. And they see the beloved object, the little teddy bear or the little car or the small stuffed bird or whatever it was, disappearing beyond hope. And of course they know it's themselves they see disappearing down there.

To be an artist, Bernard thought, is in some ways the same thing as sticking your hand resolutely into *that thing,* trying to grab hold of the past before it's gone. The exact moment when it *slips down* is, of course, the pleasurable moment. As a small boy, he'd often stood on the bridge across Svartån at

Västerfärnebo, watching the pike lure disappear into the darkness, glinting mysteriously. What a pleasure when it disappeared! What a pleasure when it reappeared, becoming visible again.

Of course forgetfulness was a form of pleasure, the way all relinquishment is pleasurable in some way. And of course all retention—whatever it was that you retained, bodily fluids, memories, bitter thoughts—had to be connected to pain and suffering.

Didn't the great Jorge Luis Borges write a shadowless, terrible, and immortal story about a man who had some kind of head injury and who afterward could never forget? A man who remembered the slightest nuance of the shifting wind, of the falling rain, of the sunset's way toward darkness. A poor unfortunate whose sleepless world always crawled with a horrible ants' nest of meaningless telephone numbers, the idiotic replies of equally idiotic people, the price of light bulbs in provincial Skåne shops in 1923, the recipe for Punic wax a friend at the Västmanland-Dala student association had once told him about at an art history seminar—how terrible it must be!

A man who could recreate a whole day in his memory if he wanted to. And of course it would take a whole day to remember.

And *that* was the point. It was the hinge, the catch, the dead angle at which the arm can't be bent without the fragile elbow breaking, the way in which the paper can't be folded without breaking:

What happened to the day you spent remembering? To what white and inaccessible backside of the world did it escape?

It wasn't possible to spend even a single day of your life remembering without creating the same amount of emptiness in the world of future memories, that is, the thing that's referred to as the present, or reality. Every moment contained every past moment the way rings on the water contain all new rings within their periphery. All life was actually one single time, all life penetrated itself in every direction. Because of that, it was more important to learn to forget than to remember. Where there was forgetfulness, there was hope as well. Remembering always meant preventing something from happening that might otherwise have happened.

This new discovery overwhelmed him, and Bernard, not unlike a schoolboy who, for the first time, feels with secret joy that he has understood the way second degree equations should be handled, walked back and forth excitedly in the room Amelie had just left.

The awful thing that threatened him, he strongly felt these days, was not Alzheimer's disease, not forgetfulness at all. The awful thing consisted of that fact that he seemed involved in some terrible choice, where it appeared that some dark power, one inside himself perhaps, forced him to choose between forgetting all and remembering all.

It was as if the normal proportions of forgetting to remembering had been forbidden him, and only the extremes were left.

At this moment he again grabbed resolutely for the long tail of the sonnet, which was just about to slip into the moist, warm cavity of forgetfulness with unfeigned, sensual pleasure.

First of all, he had to get rid of that annoying billow, no, not get rid of, because that was already too late (for according to Bernard's way of thinking, it had already happened, if only with an alcoholic, red-haired, and quite terrible poetry critic who, however, might become useful in connection with the necrological fame beckoning him some time in the future) but to bring the poem to its poetically optimal conclusion. If a billow has risen it's got to fall, Bernard thought. That's clear as day.

The risk will be that people will say I've copied Stagnelius' "The Mystery of Sighs," but that can't be helped. (He felt he didn't have much time left. If the slippery, elusive, strange object, the component not only of one world but of many, as a true poem always is, got away this time, it would be for good.) Frantically, he groped for the fountain pen on his desk and for an envelope which had contained an invitation to the Italian Cultural Institute, C.M. Lerici, and hastened to put the sestet down on paper. Did it or did it not exist in the world at this moment? An ancient Chinese tradition says that all real poems are written not just once but several times, for they are written in all possible worlds simultaneously, and right now, he was firmly convinced of the correctness of this theory. Still, he couldn't help taking a quick last look—the way Lot's wife couldn't help turning around—over his shoulder; what in God's name did *"vitrified by frost"* mean, he asked himself.

Probably something significant. Or at least something that was *recently* significant to me. Perhaps everything in a poem has to be significant at the same time?

If this slimy object, the sestet of his poem, could be brought up from the steep, dark bend it had already started to slip down a few tenths of a second ago, he couldn't let his consciousness stand in his way. *"Vitrified by frost"*—that was as crystal clear as it sounded. Take it or leave it—it's still my last poem, Bernard thought. And you, stupid readers, will never be able to tell the difference anyway between what's really meaningless and what only seems to be meaningless in my poems. Neither can I, for that matter.

Enough of this adolescent talk about *meaning. From sounds to things,* as the English say.

From his youth, Bernard had detested a too detailed rhyme scheme in the sestet. Letting the last six lines rhyme with each other in every line was something only practiced by very insecure sonnet makers. Just as a vibrato mustn't be made too insistent, since it would then sound something like a Hammond organ, two lines in the sestet that are close together should never rhyme.

The rhymes are just the way I want them. Not insistent. But at the same time, not so subdued that they can't be noticed. I like the "forgetfulness-nothingness" in-rhyme, and the division of "forgetfulness" into two lines is a nice casual touch. No, rhymes are no longer a problem for me, he thought. My problem . . .

My problem is that somewhere, I've got to say something true about my life. Something that isn't just poetry.

What on earth can I say? Suddenly I don't remember anything that's true about me. Yes. *It's been painful.* All of it has been painful. That's something I can say, anyway: *Every stone was sharp.* Calm, dignified. Not exaggerated the way it is in that tiresome Gunnar Ekelöf. Calm, like in Gunnar Mascoll Silfverstolpe. Noble, like in Arvid Mörne. And a nice little bit of exoticism (description of desert) as in Hjalmar Gullberg of blessed memory.

And the best thing is that it's true, he thought. Every stone *was* actually sharp.

Now at last, there's just one thing left.

And that's to provide a contrast for all the wetness in the poem. That contrast is a lot more important than the one I thought of at first: between cool autumn and hot passion. I wanted to write a poem on the difference between warm and cold, and, strange to say, I've written one on the difference between wet and dry, Bernard Foy told himself, nearsightedly turning the old creased envelope from the Italian Cultural Institute, C.M. Lerici, with its innumerable hieroglyphs and crossings-out, under his gold-rimmed pince-nez.

He heard Amelie's entry perfectly well. From her step, he could already tell what she was thinking.

"Now I know what the briefcase contained," Bernard said. "A sonnet. A sonnet, nothing else. *Only* a sonnet, you might say."

"Oh," answered Amelie without the least surprise but with the very slightest tinge of irony in her voice. "Only a sonnet, really? I looked in that mysterious briefcase, by the way. It's empty. Quite empty."

"Well," Bernard said. "Time tidies everything up. Only time will obliterate all traces."

In a low but distinct voice, he read the precious contents of the envelope:

> My autumn days are once again aflame,
> and rowan berries of enormous size
> on which the sparrows soon will gormandize
> bode a severe winter. But my lame
>
> and anxious spirit was consoled: a light
> day of spacious sky that's vitrified
> by frost. Billow rising on the tide
> capped with froth, at your passion's height
>
> cresting and surging, freedom absolute.
> What if the wave will sink and turn to foam?
> Our memory is unshadowed desert land
>
> where every stone was sharp. Oh sweet forget-
> fulness, deep source of night and nothingness,
> my one desire. Come and make me mute.

10. The Sweet Draught of Forgetfulness

"Mr. Lutweiler, I know that the gesture you're making once had some significance for me. I distinctly remember that it signified something in particular. To that extent, my memory works quite well. But I can't possibly remember *what* the significance was. Why don't you explain yourself more fully? And I remember that small, gleaming object of bluish metal as well. I've seen it in the movies. *That's* where I've seen it, of course it is. If you could just help me out a bit. Oh, Mr. Lutweiler, if only you'd explain in words what it is you want, instead of using such strange gestures, I think we'd understand each other *much* better."

(Of course he knows quite well that it means death. But there are things we want to remember and things we don't want to remember. Besides, for someone who no longer feels that his consciousness has any coherence, there's no reason to fear death.)

When he entered the apartment, after a strange, gloomy evening walk, which in some odd way seemed to want to prolong itself indefinitely, the lights were on all over the apartment, but Amelie was nowhere to be seen. It was late, surprisingly late; it must have taken him much longer to get home than he'd counted on. The Stjernsund clock showed a quarter past six.

Perhaps he should have taken a cab instead? Perhaps Amelie was out looking for him?

But I can't understand, he said to himself, why she's left so many lights on. An any rate, here's *Svenska Dagbladet* on the library table.

He thought that was peculiar but still sat down to read it. Perhaps it had taken him several days to get home? Or perhaps it was just the usual thing: he would read the paper in bed in the morning; in the evening, he'd find it new and interesting again. The terrible thing about this forgetfulness was that you'd sometimes feel that you were close to an immense empty space, as empty as the space between galaxies. And the awful thing was that this emptiness was inside you. Consequently it would be quite possible to fall into yourself and to keep on falling there forever, without even knowing that it was inside yourself you were falling.

It's odd, he thought, when I was writing poetry in my youth I had the most banal, uninteresting ideas to write about. And now, when I have quite original ideas, I've no real desire to write them down.

Those awful empty spaces one is walking around in at my age is nothing but death, actually. Shouldn't one write a "deeply moving" or "simple and human" and perhaps even a "bloodcurdling" volume of poetry about them?

Imagine, there's nothing I feel less like doing now than writing about my experiences. I really wish there were something I hadn't experienced I could write something about.

Here I sit with my miserable old memory, with its banal, vague contents, and right beside me there's Forgetfulness, which isn't banal in the least. It's just that if I step into it, I'm lost forever. Here, where I can still exist, everything's dreary and uninteresting. And the fascinating crevice opening up inside me, inside the large, growing hole in my own memory, I can't be in there, either. Isn't it strange and bizarre and horrible all at the same time?

Suppose I go out into the kitchen, he thought, and make some tea. I wonder how that would be? If I start making tea, perhaps Amelie will come home while I'm doing it, and she'll finish the job.

However, Bernard was not alone in his kitchen.

The man who was sitting on the kitchen table, in a flawless chalk-striped suit, one leg crossed over the other, swinging slightly, was totally unfamiliar to Bernard. He looked like some older, not altogether philanthropic lawyer or businessman, his hair cut short in a way that made his ears (very hairy on the inside) look absurdly large.

"Dr. Lutweiler, I assume?"

"You aren't mistaken, Mr. Foy."

In reply, the elegant older men in the chalk-striped suit unsentimentally produced a heavy revolver with a bluish sheen. Bernard was honestly surprised that he should have chosen such a banal weapon. But fundamentally, perhaps it's their banality that makes our enemies our enemies?

But could Dr. Lutweiler seriously believe that this threat would mean anything to a man who was balancing on the *crater rim* of nothingness every day?

(Damned metaphors, Bernard thought, adjusting his tie, a habit he'd started in youth whenever he was thinking of metaphors; what I mean, of course, isn't a crater rim but the edge of an old-fashioned sandpit, one where you can hear the sand hissing and whispering and running under your feet as you stand at the top. And you know that only a few tenacious blueberry roots and a bit of grass separate you from a plunge into a *slide of quicksand*.

But who ever heard of a stupid metaphor like *the sandpit edge of Nothingness?*

In this kind of landscape, the way back becomes tremendously difficult. God, where do all those phrases come from?)

For some days, Bernard had had a strong, upsetting feeling that he wasn't able to be the same person all the time. Could that be connected with Alzheimer's disease? Or perhaps he'd always been this way? There are times when he feels like an entire busload of people. Except for the peculiar circumstance that not all the passengers occupy the same landscape at the same time. They seemed to be dispersed as much across time as across space.

Now there's a quiet October evening somewhere, and not, like here, a dark, blustery April evening with a spring storm raging among the trees in the park, a door banging, the door to the delivery entry, the errand-boy's entry to the kitchen, and inside the door, a silent, menacing Lutweiler dourly brandishing a heavy gun in the gloom of the kitchen. What in the world has happened to Amelie? For some time, her bridge clubs and exercise groups have constituted an impenetrable labyrinth for Bernard. He has the feeling that she's subjecting him to some kind of subtle injustice any time she isn't there when he gets home. It never happens that she gets home and he isn't there.

(But somewhere it's a quiet October evening, an Uppsala evening in the mid-'20s. They're standing, Bernard and a girl only vaguely glimpsed, both in student caps and both with bikes, neat and trim as a picture in a guide book, looking at the steeples illuminated by the strange red glow of the vanishing light.

And in a solemn double whirl the jackdaws, indefatigable, visitors from another world, or else the restless spirits of the dead, keep doing a helpless dance around the steeples, emitting raucous cries for air or for meaning—it's hard to tell which—continuously in flight from their own instincts.)

Here is a small crystal ball, quite heavy actually. It's got a number of small holes. You're supposed to put the first birch twigs or perhaps the first pussy willows into it, to get a nice-looking table decoration for the dinner table.

Suppose this crystal ball could exist in two, or perhaps three, worlds simultaneously. Suppose Lutweiler, in some other world entirely, is in fact standing there looking into a crystal ball which some other Bernard Foy is holding up in the gloom, and that he can see both of us right now, reflected as in a small window, Bernard Foy visible in his red dressing-gown, not unlike a sorcerer with crystal ball lifted in his hand, but Dr. Ernst Lutweiler, too, a very small man, visible in the projection of the ball, in his chalk-striped suit, holding a revolver.

And why would this gesture of holding a crystal ball be less frightening, less incomprehensible than the obscene, childish gesture of pointing this bizarre little bluish male organ at another person's face? How beautifully the ball reflects the red of Bernard's dressing-gown, red as blood, or perhaps like some mysterious fire. Doesn't he look like the high priest of some secret society that's been in existence since the beginning of time, a kind of policeman present everywhere in time and space, always in the right place at the right moment?

Thoughtfully, Bernard looks into his red ball.

"Dr. Lutweiler, do you think a ball like this might exist in several worlds simultaneously?

"I don't mean the same kind of ball, but literally the same ball. Do you think it might exist, hanging perhaps in the top of an immense mast in a world, circled by big, awful birds that fly about in the dusk, and lying quite still on a kitchen table with a red-checked tablecloth in a different world? In my youth, there was such a ball in a story by H.G. Wells.

"Do you think a crystal ball can lie still in one world and be carried about in another one? Or won't the world in which it's lying still have to make some kind of movement to compensate for the fact that the ball is lying still on its tablecloth in one world and moving in the other?

"Do you know what I think? I think everyone lives many lives at once, and that the red shadow falling into a piece of crystal like this one is actually the shadow or the reflex of something that's already happened somewhere else.

"Perhaps a bloody deed?

"It's funny, but when I say 'bloody deed,' I have a definite sense that I'm touching a memory. But I can't have any memory like that. I've absolutely decided that I'm nothing but an old poet who's become somewhat confused lately.

"You see, Dr. Lutweiler, one of the most difficult things about a condition such as mine is that it's not as easy for me as it is for other people to distinguish between memories of what's happened and memories of what's *going* to happen.

"For example, I have a very distinct, very sad memory of you that I just can't place in the circumstances of my own life, so that means it has to belong to the future. I see you lying battered and ugly at the bottom of the kitchen steps where, for some obscure reason, you've entered from the street and evidently fallen down after you discovered that the steps led to a private kitchen.

"I see my excellent cleaner leaning over you. He was probably the one who discovered you when he came to clean. He's leaning over you to see whether you're still breathing. But you aren't. Oh, what a sad story!

"Pardon, I didn't quite catch what you were saying. My hearing isn't that good either, you see. My father? Did you say *my father?* Strictly speaking, he can't have anything to do with this. Or does he?''

(When his father died Bernard hadn't been told right away. Only on the second day did they call the *gymnasium*.

He remembered that he was taking a Latin test—it was his third year—and looking out through the windows in the hall at the big, heavy, autumnally yellow boughs of elm and oak outside the main building of the Västerås *gymnasium* and how the wind would intermittently pass through the foliage, which was already half blown apart. He knew what it would sound like in the woods on a day like that, organ works of wind from hill to hill, and how the dark gusts of wind would ripple the surfaces of the large Västmanland lakes, and he thought how boring it was to have to sit here, translating a long, dreary text by Suetonius, when he might have been walking in the Haraker woods, hunting for big yellow chanterelles in the soft, deep moss.

One moment the day had been very yellow, and he already knew his father had shot himself, long before someone came and told him.

And then the feared principal, Fåhreus himself, had come in, in his severe dark suit with waistcoat and pocket watch. Gently, almost absent-mindedly, he asked young Bernard to come out and to come with him to his office.

The very fact of being fetched from a Latin test, and by the principal himself, was something unprecedented, and forty young heads lifted from dictionaries and blue books to see what was going on. What strange offense might this boy have committed?

Of course it couldn't be anything minor, or the principal himself wouldn't have come. The sunlight had shone through the chalk dust in the second-floor corridor, with its unvarying smell of marble and scouring powder; on the way to the principal's office, the stern, eccentric old man had put his right arm protectively across the boy's shoulders.

You cut chanterelles with a knife. You never pull them up. That might damage the sensitive mycelium. That's what Bernard had thought. Why had he thought that?)

The way back was tremendously difficult. The ice changed every moment. Where there had only been a crack just before, there was now a channel ruffled by the wind. The channel you'd just crossed, with immense difficulty and with the aid of a board you'd dragged along, was now completely gone. It was as if this entire labyrinth of cracks, ice blocks, crevices, and wind wells had their own will and wanted to play a joke on the helpless men dragging themselves along on wet feet through this shadowless world under a porcelain-colored sky.

(It was in this kind of landscape—although the few survivors would only learn that long after their rescue—that Hans von Lagerhielm and his two Italian comrades had discovered that they'd only moved three kilometers in a very hard day's march. Sometimes, because of the movements of the drift ice itself, those three kilometers had brought them farther from their goal, the island of Foyn, than they had been on the previous evening.

When you look at the map and see the spot where Mariano and Zappi left Hans von Lagerhielm to die in a depression in the ice, with a couple of coats over him, blind and apathetic, you're surprised it's so close to the island.

For someone not familiar with the circumstances, it seems almost incomprehensible that Hans didn't just get up and continue walking.)

Of course the way back was tremendously difficult. It was still going on, actually. The principal had said that he didn't have to go back to the hall if he didn't want to, that he could have the rest of the day off. Bernard had interpreted this to mean that he might go back to the hall *if* he wanted to. Head high, he returned there. Every pair of eyes turned toward the door: you felt that even the teacher who served as proctor would have given a lot to know what it was all about.

Through a mist of tears which he only managed to suppress with tremendous effort, Bernard Foy had quietly finished copying his Latin translation into his blue book and with measured steps, revealing nothing whatsoever, carried it to the teacher's desk and with a polite bow handed it to the pale, grayish, nearsighted, and generally unattractive physics teacher, Nilsson, who could hardly contain his curiosity, intensified into hatred.

Perhaps it was at this moment of outwardly perfectly normal, exemplary behavior, but for someone who knew the background the wildest, most improbable of improvisations, not unlike the mad aria in *Lucia di Lammermoor* or the last great leap of the trapeze artists under the circus top, when all of them change places at once in a dizzying performance, that made a poet of Bernard Foy.

> (Calmy, autumn wind, you passed,
> calm and implacable,
> through the greenwood of my youth
> ravaging its crown.)

"No, Mr. Lutweiler, you can't frighten me, not even with my father."

(What had his father looked like, actually? The only thing he remembered was the pale, grayish face of the physics teacher, his awful glasses with nickel-plated rims. His father gone, and in this kind of landscape only Time, Weight, and Death in his place.)

11. Winter Resort

If he could only stop acting so terribly affected, Bernard thought.

"Then perhaps it's time to go into a very interesting period of your life, your mature age. It occurred toward the end of the peacetime period, just before World War II. Just as you were getting recognized as a poet. There was even a play produced by the Royal Dramatic Theater, isn't that correct?"

"Oh, you know my play *Ice Light*? I didn't think many people knew it, these days. It wasn't any great success."

"Oh, Mr. Foy, you're being modest. Prince Eugen was there on opening night. The receipts went to the Red Cross action. The reviews the next day were glowing. Absolutely glowing. W.W., for example, wrote in *Morgontidningen* . . ."

"Yes, I know," Bernard said. "I know that kind of success: I've had a few in my life. They're more bitter than failures. There's nothing more bitter. A week later, they had to close *Ice Light*. There's no reason to sit here in my kitchen now, many decades later, hashing over an old failure nobody remembers, is there? I can tell you I haven't even included that piece in the list of my works in *Who's Who*."

"There may be," Dr. Lutweiler said in slow tones, as if taking sadistic pleasure in every word, "there just *may be* a reason."

(The crystal ball in Bernard's right hand still radiated a mild red glow. Dr. Lutweiler was still sitting, just as carelessly, on the edge of the table. His well-shod right foot was moving up and down with a trace of impatience. Who the hell does he think he is? Bernard asked himself fretfully. Some kind of interrogator? The question of how long I'm going to let him sit there talking garbage is only a question of how far my own curiosity extends. He should be grateful that I'm listening to his ridiculous twaddle.

Dr. Lutweiler didn't appear particularly grateful. His face had assumed the virtuous expression of an auditor intent on examining a major customer's accounts.)

"Where was this hotel? The ski hotel? The winter resort? Was it in Engelsberg or in Svärdsjö? You must remember? Where you went to rest up after the play closed. With Helena Roge, the young blond actress who played the sister of the brave Arctic explorer in the same play?"

"A small, blond, pleasant girl everyone expected to become one of the great tragic actresses at the Dramatic Theater, in ten years perhaps, when she had acquired more presence and more heft about the middle, when one of the gentlemen she granted her favors to had become more influential with the court, the newspapers, and the Minister of Educational and Ecclesiatical Affairs.

"Amelie is still a woman in her prime, while you're a bit too old to be called up for military service a few years later. With handsome brown hair framing a face that's a bit on the pale side, perhaps. Why pale? You don't remember. Do you remember, Mr. Foy, what Amelie was doing that week? You don't remember that either? Bernard, you're a terrible hypocrite."

They came down early from their room that afternoon. It was nice. With the exception of that awful Mrs. Mannfeld, the wife of the cathedral dean, always knitting away in a corner of the sitting room, there was nobody to stare at them. The guests, fortunately neither very numerous nor very interesting, didn't bother them much.

There was a hearty, probably slightly Nazi *gymnasium* teacher from Västerås with his wife and three strictly brought up boys in their late teens. You'd only see them in the morning and in the evening. And there was the obligatory Stockholm businessman, probably with a liver scarred from lots of drinking, who was supposed to go out on "regular walks," as it was called, to get some exercise and fresh air but who mostly seemed to sit there half asleep over the financial pages of *Svenska Dagbladet* and *Göteborgs Handels- och Sjöfarts-Tidning*. The exchange was fluctuating. The world was moving again.

But that did not bother Bernard Foy, the poet, and his young mistress with her dancing steps and wide, womanly hips. They came and went as they pleased. When they weren't out skiing, they were in bed together. Bernard was deeply in love.

The blond, short-haired, light and lively Helena Roge was a different kind of girl from any Bernard had known previously. She was a little bit dangerous, a little bit hysterical, and precisely this dangerousness meant that she suited him somehow, like the key in a lock.

"Look, here's *Svenska Dagbladet*," said the young lady who'd followed him into the library of the hotel. He loosened the blue band around the paper carefully. Always a day late in Svärdsjö. Bernard couldn't find anything to read. There were just some very trivial periodicals, *Tidsfördrif* and *En rolig halv-timme*. Reading matter suitable for the maids, Bernard thought. "But it isn't that bad, Bernard," Helena consoled him. "Why do you have to complain about everything?"

"Do you think so, darling?" He put his arm around her slim waist, feeling her girdle plainly under the silk. She slipped from his grasp.

"Bernard, you boring old thing, are you just going to sit here reading the paper?"

"What do you want to do?"

"Go out. Some way or other. Skiing, walking. Or perhaps going for a spin in the sleigh. What do you say? *Darling?*" She loved little Anglicisms like that. They were fashionable in Stockholm at the time.

The hotel arranged sleigh rides where, bundled up in furs, you'd go along the lake and then under the rime-covered trees in the timber forest on the other side. But it probably wouldn't be easy to get hold of a sleigh as quickly as Helena Roge thought. Bernard was happy. It was true there was something trying about Helena. She'd get sudden migraines, get into a bad mood, "bitchiness," as Bernard's father called that condition in ladies.

For him his adultery had the charm of novelty and of the forbidden. Among its many exquisite ontological, or perhaps one might even say metaphysical, pleasures was the fact of being so close, so familiar with someone whose whole point was that she was a stranger. In this blend of the familiar and the nonfamiliar, he almost fancied he got a faint, momentary glimpse which reflected the mystic's relationship to God.

On the whole, this was a year when Foy often felt completely happy. Due to his friendship with Prince Eugen, he was a frequent guest in the best families. And his play *Ice Light* had of course been accepted by the Royal Dramatic Theater. He was on his way into a social career, that was obvious. He was getting over certain wounds from his youth.

The exquisiteness of carrying on a love affair with a young actress who in his play had the part of the person he'd loved deeply in his youth, the sister of his late best friend, did not escape him. In fact, it conferred a special dimension of excitement on the relationship.

"Make up your mind," Helena said. "Otherwise I'll go skiing by myself. I can do that perfectly well."

A smile was playing around the corners of her mouth, the sunlight from the window made the golden hair shine around her narrow (and rather determined) face. I really like her a lot, Bernard told himself.

"Telephone for Dr. Foy," the hotel hostess said in the door.

He felt a frisson of uneasiness. What could have happened? Was it something with Amelie? Had his mother fallen sick? His guilt feelings surged up like a black fountain.

On his way to the telephone in the hotel, a venerable old-fashioned instrument placed on the wall of the vestibule just inside the front door, so that you felt a cold draft around your temples the whole time you were on the phone, he suddenly became absolutely convinced that Amelie had committed suicide. It wasn't the least like Amelie to do something like that, but just the same. Could she have found something out? Perhaps someone had talked out of turn? Perhaps she'd become totally dejected?

But if she'd committed suicide, how would she have done it? The gas stove?

There was a buzzing on the line. At last the voice of the telephone operator said "Stockholm on the line" in singing Dalecarlia dialect, or was it a Västmanland dialect; it wasn't easy to remember forty years later, and then—thank God, Amelie's voice.

"What is it, has there been an accident?"

"No, silly. It's nice and sunny here. Is it nice and sunny in Svärdsjö too?"

She had to repeat her question several times before he realized how trivial and inoffensive it was.

"What's it like up there? You're going for long walks, I hope?"

163

"Yes, yes."

"You aren't depressed?"

"Not at all."

"Are you homesick?"

"Yes, a bit," Bernard answered politely.

"I wouldn't have called except that the Royal Marshal, Count Bonde, wanted to talk to you."

"Really? Did he say what about?"

"No. He just wanted to get hold of you."

Bernard had met him once, at Prince Eugen's, a charming, not very remarkable nobleman, who evidently had certain literary interests apart from the bridge table but who otherwise was rather a quiet individual. One of those big, everlastingly boyish gentlemen often encountered among the highest nobility and the Stockholm world of civil servants. What could he want with Bernard?

A list of pleasant alternatives ran through Bernard's head. It might be that the Master of Ceremonies at court, an influential man, wanted to know whether some more or less respected colleague of Bernard's was married or had a doctorate or something else along that line which might be significant for the seating at some palace dinner.

But since there were a lot of calendars and handbooks to tell you that sort of thing (this was in '30s' Sweden, which considered itself extremely *modern, forward-looking,* and a *people's home,* with *ceiling organizations* for everyone in a spirit of *national solidarity,* but where the pretense that everyone was *equal* hadn't yet gained a footing), it seemed odd to Bernard. Perhaps he and Amelie were to be invited to a *palace dinner,* with all the social prestige that would of course accrue to it? The more important not to have it become public knowledge that he was here on a ski vacation with young Helena Roge, who'd received enough notice, because of her stage appearances, that the newspapers might be interested in her.

Hadn't *Idun* published a rather long interview with her in one of the last issues before Christmas? It was obvious that scandal, and social misfortune along with it, was lurking around the corner if you thought about it. Bernard was sensitive to those issues. He'd never forgotten his father's last days and his death. He'd have to watch his step. Every bend of the road he was traveling was booby-trapped.

"Bernard, are you still there?"

"Should I try to call him?"

"You might try. He has an office at the Palace. There's no number, you have to ask the operator to connect you with the Palace. But how are you feeling?"

She sounded disappointed that he wasn't more interested in her but so entirely preoccupied with this prestige-laden telephone call.

Their goodbyes were rather brief. Now he knew what it would be like. That *small* feeling of guilt, the faint but always present feeling of betrayal, which would accompany him (and consequently Amelie as well) from now on, would grow between them the way invisible cracks grow in a damaged glass.

It would make him *stupid,* for stupidity (he knew it well from his childhood, when he was often stupid, almost bordering on idiocy) is of course nothing but a refusal, minted in our own coinage, when we realize that we receive more of the world than we can give back to it.

Always in the future, there'd be something hard and wooden between them because of this.

And he didn't regret it?

No, he didn't regret it for a moment. If he had, things would have been different, it had become trivial but not . . .

"You're through to the Palace."

There was no doubt the telephone operator in Svärdsjö or Engelsberg was full of respect after this call had been placed. There was a buzz on the line. Outside the window, heavy snowflakes started falling. While he'd been on the phone to Stockholm, the blue sky had disappeared, "like magic," as the saying was.

He wondered a bit what might have become of Helena Roge. Perhaps she was sitting in the library? Or had she been wise enough to order some tea and sherry? They'd already acquired some minor habits. One of them was to have tea with a small glass of sherry after the short ski run they made each day after lunch. Tea with a small glass of sherry would taste very good right now, when the weather was turning nasty. Unquestionably, there was a snowstorm on the way.

He pushed the curtain aside. The fat hotel cat who'd been sleeping on the windowsill leapt onto the rag rug. The snow out there was moving in rapid little whirls across the carefully shoveled and swept yard. The Swedish flag flapped hard, straining on its pole.

It was February 5, 1938. Only in a vague and so to speak spiritual fashion did he distinguish a voice that had to belong to the marshal's female secretary over the buzzing, snow-laden line. Oh yes, His Excellency would be free in a moment and would like to speak with Dr. Foy.

After a wait that felt unconscionably long, the great man's voice came on the line, just the kind of boyishly cheerful, high, almost feminine voice typical of the highest nobility and the most prominent officeholders in Sweden. As usual, Count Bonde was extremely polite and courteous.

"Oh, Dr. Foy, I'm so sorry that you've had to wait such a long time. I had *no idea,* you see, that you were calling all the way from Dalecarlia. How's the skiing up there, anyway? Oh. Yes, I imagine you're having a good time up there. Anyway: I'm really embarrassed to disturb a poet during one of his periods of creative tranquillity.

"This is just something trivial. The thing is, yesterday when Prince Eugen had me and some other friends over for bridge, *he was playing with his brother,* we started talking about a sonnet by a French poet. But no one could remember past the beginning. And it was embarrassing. Nobody could remember whether it was by Baudelaire or Mallarmé. His Royal Highness had often heard it quoted when he was studying in Paris.

"However, His Royal Highness was firm in his belief that it was Dr. Bernard Foy who had once translated it into Swedish. And I promised, a bit arrogantly it may be, that I'd find out all about it by this morning. 'And if such an important poet and someone so familiar with French poetry as Bernard Foy has translated it, then he'll remember it straight off,' I said to His Royal Highness. 'First thing tomorrow morning when I get to my office, I'll call him and ask him.'"

" 'In that case, give him my warmest regards,' His Royal Highness said. 'I'll ask the poet, first thing tomorrow morning,' I said to His Royal Highness, but of course I didn't intend to disturb you *right in the middle of your ski vacation* like this."

"Oh," Bernard answered, flattered as had been intended, "that doesn't matter in the least. Please convey my respectful greetings to His Royal Highness. But tell me, how does that poem begin? I've translated a few, actually."

"I've got *that* written down, very carefully," His Excellency said. "It starts like this: 'La rue assourdissante autour de moi hurlait . . . ' "

"Oh, then I know just what it is. I translated it in Uppsala, actually. For me it's connected with a sentimental memory from my earliest youth," Bernard said, with sincere emotion in his voice which, however, did not prevent him from also *playing* the easily moved, warmly sensitive poet, one of the friends around the Painter Prince Eugen.

"It's by Baudelaire: 'A une passante,' from *Tableaux Parisiens*. A very well-known poem," Bernard added, perhaps rather incautiously.

"Really?"

"Oh yes. The translation is still present in my mind."

(And Bernard did still have it, not only *then,* on the snowy February morning in 1938, but now, at this late, strange midnight hour, in the kitchen of his last apartment, in 1983. A night in late winter, or early spring, whichever way you wanted to look at it.

And it struck him that at that time, when he translated the poem, it was less than a hundred years old, and now—at least a hundred and twenty. He was no longer in the middle of the twentieth century. This strange night, this "night at the horizon," as Mallarmé would have called it, was only seventeen years from the end of the new century. I'm a complete stranger in the time I'm living in now, Bernard thought. Only a kind of whimsical *biological* comtemporaneity, a tie more fragile than a silken thread, connects me to what's happening now: computers, astronauts, software programs.

As a matter of fact, poor Baudelaire would have liked it much better than I did. He was the first to write "the *clamor* of the street." And somehow, he was always prepared to *say yes* to that clamor. A hundred years later, I and my provincial friends could only write about "old houses and old trees." Isn't it annoying to be so completely *trumped.* We're nothing but shy boys with childish voices up here in the north. *We'll never amount to anything. Not one of us amounted to anything. They won't even remember Silfverstolpe.*)

This chilling realization brought him back to his own '30s, happy in spite of everything. The time when he'd still been able to hide his own mediocrity, his lack of depth and real poetic originality by indulging in boyish expectations of royal favors and the respect of princes. What a benevolent illusion. And oh! how short-lived.

"I'm all ears," said His Excellency, who couldn't be expected to know that Bernard had simultaneously been making a brief but intense visit to the remote 1980s and that he was soon to return there.

"But perhaps it'll be too long?"

"Not at all," his Excellency answered, with unvarying boyish courtesy. "Poems travel in time more easily than other things do."

"Pas de problème," Bernard continued. This is how I translated it in 1927:

(I published in in *Ord och Bild* somewhat later, the '80s Bernard added to himself.)

> "The clamor of the street surrounded me.
> Slender and tall, a woman passed me by,
> dressed in stately mourning, lifting high
> her ruffled dress's hem disdainfully."

"Magnificent, that's it precisely," His Excellency shouted remotely in the crackling, buzzing receiver.

> "A glimpse of sculptured leg, her noble poise,
> I, trembling like a fool, drank from her eye
> the tempest brewing in a livid sky,
> enthralling sweetness, pleasure that destroys.
>
> "A lightning flash—And then the night. Your glance
> O fleeting beauty, brought a second birth.
> Say, won't we meet until eternity?
>
> "You're gone. Too late. My fatal ignorance
> of where you've gone, and yours of where I am.
> O you I might have loved, O you who knew it."

"A charming translation of an equally charming poem," His Excellency screamed benevolently. "Just the poem His Royal Highness had in mind. He will be delighted."

When the conversation was concluded, there was no Helena Roge to be found. It bothered him.

"Helena. Excuse me, it was such a stupid little thing . . . Helena. Are you there?"

No. She couldn't be in the library.

How strange, he thought. She can't have gone skiing in this weather?

But that was just what she had done.

12. Death and the Maiden

Lutweiler, who was still sitting on the edge of Bernard's kitchen table with perfectly demonic stubbornness, was relishing all the most humiliating, the most insupportable, the most unendurable moments of the old poet's life with unseemly, obscene satisfaction.

Yes, he did relish it. The way a coyote, the evil desert dog, relishes the marrow of his victim's broken bones in the moonlight of the mesa, where only the crickets sing among the mesquite brush. Relished, and did not want to leave at all. On the contrary, the highly polished shoe in the gray spats was swinging up and down at the kitchen table with unbroken, almost frenetic energy and alertness. Perhaps he was some kind of *cricket?*

"What a sad story, Dr. Foy. She died, didn't she? She went out in the gathering snowstorm, disappointed that you kept speaking to your wife over the hotel telephone and, when you weren't speaking to your wife, to various functionaries at court with whom you wanted to curry favor. Isn't it just like a novel by the elegant Henning Berger or perhaps a short story by the melancholy, clever Adolf Johansson? You don't have to say anything, my dear Foy, I know the story as well as you do."

When he hung up the phone after his call to Stockholm, in every way a more expensive phone call than he could afford, carefully terminating the call by cranking the handle an exaggerated number of times, Bernard looked out the window and found that the snowstorm had turned into a white inferno.

To his dismay, he hears that Helena Roge, impatient and unwilling to wait any longer for the continuously telephoning Bernard, has gone out on her own on the "easy run" that the hotel provides for its guests in addition to the "hard run."

He looks for her in vain, and other people also look for her. A group of hotel guests, experienced skiers among the local population, the country commissioner, and the local police—everyone is looking for her, but without result.

Only when the storm has died down on the third day and a pale winter sun appears, with rime and powdery snow over heavily laden fir boughs, do they find her dead under her covering of white snow, an ice maiden, a snow saint, just a few kilometers from the building. Those things happen.

Bernard, inconsolable, disregards the gossip and the rumors of scandal, he doesn't close his eyes for the three terrible days that pass before a local ski patrol at last finds the young dead woman under a fir big tree where, at the end, she'd tried to find shelter from the roaring snowstorm. *Death and the Maiden* is the title of a well-known string quartet by Franz Schubert.

Bernard has such a clear memory of how it was played at her funeral where he sat, silent and pale at the very back, his black hat pulled far down over his forehead, somewhat protected, he thought, from the overly curious glances of photographers and reporters.

Consideration for the young, prematurely dead actress and for the condition of inconsolable grief her death had evidently brought on in the sensitive poet (who was soon afterward elected to the Swedish Academy, succeeding—if we remember correctly, which we seldom do in the company of Bernard Foy—Henning Berger, who had lived in Denmark for a long time and who unfortunately suffered from a weakness of the lungs) resulted in the newspapers exercising a form of highly considerate discretion. The thing gets talked about, however.

A bittersweet memory of his youth is completed.

But the annoying Lutweiler shoe is still swinging.

"But Dr. Foy. Can that be true? Helena Roge, I remember that name. Helena Roge, isn't she the fat actress who eventually married the millionaire millowner, Consul Fimmersten-Hansson?

"And went with him to Mexico on board his yacht *Ixthapa* when the Second World War at last started threatening Sweden?

"A lady featured on a lot of society pages of that time, literally garlanded with pearls. That was just after the war; 1955 or something like that, and the lady seems to have returned from Mexico with her elegant husband with the gray temples who was on the boards of various corporations.

"The question is whether your memory is correct, Dr. Foy. Or are you suggesting that Helena Roge had a *twin sister?*"

No. That's not the way it was. He hears sounds. That's the way it was. *He hears sounds.*

By the time Bernard had pulled the wool gloves on his cold hands, the snowfall had already stopped. A pale red winter sun came out of the clouds, light powdery snow blew across the trail Helena must have swept along, at most twenty minutes ahead of him.

It was a good trail. First it went through relatively open country, then it followed the complicated curves of the lake shore, and then, at a reasonable gradient, it went into real fir woods, heavy, old-fashioned fir woods, a true primeval forest of a type hardly found any longer in the southern or middle parts of Sweden.

Now the shadows are falling, long and slanted across the trail. The waxwings in a large birch tree right at the edge of the woods fly up when he appears, pushing himself along with his poles; silent like fluttering omens, they soon return.

Had Helena skied along here a few minutes ago? Not just she, but many skiers seemed to have used the trail; you could tell from all the pole marks. Now it's getting dark. And here the track disappears into the woods. Up and down, and you have to watch out as you pass the big boulders so you don't get your poles tangled up in them.

He heard a sound and at first perceived it as mournful. For a brief moment, he must have thought that she'd had an accident; the sound came from under one of the really big, heavy fir trees. Then when he saw the two pairs of skis, carefully planted, with the poles amicably linked, he realized that the sounds weren't mournful at all.

What he heard was Helena Roge crying with lust, crying out in the moment of passion in the arms of some other man, under the sheltering shadow of the big, dark fir tree.

She hadn't just gone ahead. She'd given herself to someone else, the little whore.

When Bernard returned to the hotel, pale and cold with sweat, he couldn't even get a cab to the station. He started making a fuss about getting one. They were all taken and, furthermore, nobody could understand why he was in such a rush all of a sudden.

If he hadn't been so firm, he'd never have got the sleigh that took him finally. And something that belonged to the absolute point, to the most dreadful edge, of his humiliation was the fact that Bernard actually saw them returning just as the last of his two suitcases was being lifted into the sleigh by the coachman. Helena must have seen him. Of course he remembered the man she had with her from the dining room, some insignificant Stockholm engineer, very silent, with some gray in his beard and gold-rimmed glasses.

That man, it struck him with quiet triumph, who was probably ten years older than I at the time and who acted with the false authority of an old man, must have died long ago.

The road back was tremendously difficult.

He remembered sitting very still at the train window. He was alone in his first-class compartment, and he breathed cautiously, as if afraid he'd choke if he weren't careful.

Endless fir woods and fields out there in the darkness beyond the smoke from the locomotive. But the only thing he saw when he strained his eyes was his timorous face reflected in the dirty windowpane.

Death and the maiden. It was something that would hold him captive for a long time, but Bernard Foy never wrote a poem on this theme.

The very attempt caused a metallic taste in his mouth. Perhaps that was the way death tasted?

And on this day, deep in another time, he could still feel his helpless rage at this girl, this death. If only she could have died like other people, an ordinary, real death, he thought, *the little whore.*

The question was whether he'd ever loved anyone else.

"The question is, Dr. Lutweiler, whether when we love somebody, we actually love a person or a concept. Can you answer that?"

Rather surprisingly, the man who answered to the name of Ernst Lutweiler replied immediately,

"People die and they change. Concepts never die."

Oh well, Bernard thought. Then we know how it is. *That's how it is.*

13. Master and Servant

One morning some time back, Bernard got a phone call at eight from his publisher, Baron and Dr. (Ph.D., *honoris causa*) Sven Kolzack. This surprised Bernard since he couldn't remember when he'd last had a call from Kolzack. It seemed to him that the last time he'd seen his publisher in person was at some Swedish Academy banquet in 1952 or 1953. On that occasion, Kolzack in rented tails and with the correct doctor's collar, had been sitting in one of the front rows in the Börs Hall, smiling encouragingly at Bernard when he delivered the director's speech for that year, but of course there was the possibility that the man he'd seen had actually been Prince Bertil.

For Prince Bertil was also someone who was capable of showing everyone he met warm and generous appreciation. Kolzack and His Royal Highness Prince Bertil of Sweden enjoyed the advantage of similar looks; they were men of mature charm, with white temples and round, ruddy, kindly faces where a life of pleasant memories had left a smile behind.

Kolzack, like many other prominent and capable Swedes a descendant of Baltic nobility from the time of the Teutonic Knights, was a much occupied man. For the past ten years, he had not only been managing director of Victor Hagerberg, Publisher, but also a most appreciated opera critic in *Svenska Dagbladet,* where he primarily focused on a simultaneously broad, acute, and detailed surveillance of the big international music festivals: Bayreuth, Glyndebourne, Salzburg and, of course, the Metropolitan season.

Sometimes he even managed a first night or two at the Chicago opera; perhaps there weren't that many among his *Svenska Dagbladet* readers able to heed his admonition to rush off to the travel agent's and book tickets for the flight to Chicago and to Placido Domingo's next performance at the Chicago Opera. The readers of the opera page loved Dr. Kolzack anyway, since he gave them the feeling that they belonged to the people who *could have gone* to the new Chicago production, if only they'd had the time.

Certain kill-joys, jealous people, and others of that ilk, would insist that it wasn't good for Victor Hagerberg that Dr. Kolzack, the chief editor for literary publications, was always in Salzburg or New York. It was said that this somehow had a detrimental effect on his ability to manage the affairs of the publishing house.

For his part, Bernard was unable to share this opinion.

As a matter of fact, he was scared to death of meeting Kolzack; it's true that the advances he got during the '60s for the new volume of memoirs he'd promised must be written off by now. However, contact with Kolzack would still have meant a dreary reminder of what a promise this autobiography had once been, with *When Petals Still Fell in the Spring* as a joyous beginning and its presumably fascinating continuation, *The Age of Maturity* and *October's Roof Hangs Low,* to follow in the near future.

A future which, one is forced to admit, seemed to retreat the moment Bernard approached it.

In brief, Bernard was of the opinion that the more time Kolzack spent in the lobbies of international hotels and the brightly lit foyers of opera houses, sweetened by perfumes and by wonderful ivory breasts glimpsed in ebony decolletages, the better it was not just for Hagerberg, Publisher, and its employees and authors in general, but for Bernard Foy in particular. The rumor was that Dr. Kolzack was about to assume the presidency of the International PEN association, with all of its burdensome round tables, executive meetings, and world conferences, spread from Riga to Tokyo. To Bernard, this appeared as a particularly forward-looking and wise measure, not only on the part of the renowned doctor but also of PEN International.

The voice that now, full of youthful freshness and pulsing optimistic will to life and so-called room for living, boomed at him through the telephone receiver Amelie passed him with the utmost reluctance, belonged to a man who, strictly speaking, was only twelve years younger than Bernard. If he'd counted right, that is. Incredible but true.

Bernard could not conceal, either from himself or from Amelie, that his hand trembled a bit at this moment.

"*Hello,* Bernard," the voice said, as familiar, as real, as present as if the two gentlemen had been speaking to each other just a few days ago. "I hope you're well, Bernard. I'm so sorry I haven't been in touch for a while—it's because I've had such a lot to do, you see."

"Me too," Bernard said. "An *awful* lot to do."

"I see that, in *Aftonbladet.*"

"Really? Are they writing about me in *Aftonbladet?*"

"Haven't you seen it? It's like a whole novel. It's intimated that you have very close connections to—some segment of—industry."

"I don't understand a word," Bernard said.

Kolzack had the ability of the seasoned publisher, honed by long and bitter experience, to know when to pursue a topic of conversation with a venerable old national poet and when not to. If Bernard hadn't read those articles, with their somewhat immodest hints about Bernard's intimate connections to the blackest part of the business world, especially the cocaine trade, the best thing would be for him, Kolzack, not to have read them either. It had even been hinted that an entire briefcase with a consignment of cocaine had been received by Bernard in the presence of witnesses in the vestibule of the Royal Library. To print such strange things about a revered old poet seemed a bit odd even to Sven Kolzack.

But nothing was the way it used to be anymore.

"I didn't have the slightest idea," Bernard said.

"Oh, you're *current* everywhere just now," Kolzach said swiftly. "Did you see in *Svenska Dagbladet* the other day that no less a personage than Elisabeth Verolyg mentioned you? In her review of Vera Flyger's latest poetry book—which, sad to say, she didn't think a lot of."

"Just imagine," Bernard said with sudden sincerity. "What did she write?"

"That you're one of the *great hidden resources* of our national literature, if I remember her wording correctly."

"That's not bad."

"And that actually, there's *no* young author who can be *compared* with you. When it comes to *the naked truth.*"

In the somewhat confused silence that ensued when the two gentlemen—not unlike two wrestlers watching each other from their respective corners, each trying to find the most advantageous point of attack—at their respective ends of the telephone line, were sunk in speculation about what might be behind what the other one had just said, nothing was heard except the low buzzing sound you always hear over the worn, inadequate Stockholm telephone lines. Behind this sudden laudatory mention in a newspaper that had hardly concerned itself with Bernard's work or with his person since the '60s there was, Kolzack thought, one or two possibilities. Either there was some bizarre misunderstanding or else, a thought that produced a chilly fear in him, the taste of the times was shifting and everything Kolzack had backed the last ten years, in the shape of beginning authors and geniuses and doctoral dissertations and national editions, was all wrong.

If that were the case, he realized with death in his heart, not only would Bernard Foy have to be published in gold-tooled bindings, but probably Gunnar Mascoll Silfverstolpe, Sven Lidman, and Hans von Lagerhielm would have to come out in paperback. And of course somewhere there was a rival publisher with better contacts among the younger critics who, at this very moment, was finishing up the page proofs of those editions. Damn it all. Of course it was because his duties had kept him so long in Paris this spring.

To his own surprise, Bernard was the one who recovered first.

"Can I do something . . . for you . . . in some way?"

"Absolutely, Bernard, *absolutely.* You can have lunch with me. At one o'clock tomorrow, at Operakällaren."

"Has it opened again?"

"What do you mean, *opened?*"

"Wasn't it closed for repairs a while back?"

"But my dear Bernard, that was late in the '50s."

Regarded with a mixture of respect and slight suspicion by the gold-festooned doorman, Bernard arrived the next day in a cab at the famous restaurant, where he could not remember having set foot since it closed in the late '20s.

It was obvious that it had opened again.

There were throngs of people, young and old, everyone very elegant, some of the men strikingly feminine in their manner of dress and in their gestures.

Somewhat upset by Sven's telephone hints that he seemed to be turning into a celebrity these days, that his poetry, not unlike a butterfly emerging from its chrysalis, was now emerging from a forty-year period of latency, Bernard was quite content to see that people didn't point him out, whispering to each other.

They're educated people, Bernard told himself. Discreet.

Of course they must also be very used to literary celebrities in the lobby of Operakällaren.

In my youth, this was the *obvious* place. With arrack and strong cigarillos. Everybody in Stockholm sat here in those days. Some brought young opera singers and some brought seamstresses. It was that kind of place. Now there seem to be more queers than there were then. But it's fashionable.

At any rate it's a relief that nobody's pointing and whispering. The fact is that everybody here pretends they don't know me.

Not even Sven is here. Or am I early?

This thought momentarily made Bernard feel anxious.

I hope I've got the right day. With effort, he produced his pocket diary where his elegant handwriting, rather large nowadays, had noted the name Kolzack and the word "lunch" for this particular Thursday.

Of course he needn't have worried. Elegant as always in a gray-blue suit from Karl Lagerfeld in New York, with a discreet tie and a well-polished bald head, the publisher literally *floated* into the vestibule where Bernard had sunk into one of the sofas, glumly pondering a work of art on the opposite wall he thought he'd seen before, but without being able to remember where.

Suddenly, all those previously absent waiters seemed to be assembling from every direction.

There's no doubt, Bernard thought, that he's here rather more often than I am.

They sat down.

Kolzack ordered Campari and soda for himself and for Bernard, after some discussion, something Bernard insisted on calling a "cognac highball."

"That hit the spot," Bernard said, leaning back in his chair with the magnificent menu whose prices appeared to him altogether unreal.

Buoyed up by his cognac highball, he continued (would it be presumptuous of him to order another one?):

"So you want to publish my collected poems?"

"Did I say that," asked Kolzack, whose playful charm in dealing with authors was generally admired.

"That's the impression I got when we spoke on the phone," Bernard said. "That you thought the time was ripe."

"Yes, we've got to do something," Kolzack said. For the last thirty seconds, his absent-minded gray eyes had been following a person who was at least a hundred meters further down the dining room.

"Frankly, I think two volumes would be the most reasonable," Bernard said. "Perhaps even three. I think they should look something like the national Karlfelt edition. But that wasn't brought out by your publishing house."

174

"Of course," Kolzack said.

There was some indication that right now, he wasn't very interested in his guest. If the one he was looking at had been a beautiful woman, it would have been more understandable. But the one he followed so stubbornly with his eyes seemed to be a man of his own age, evidently about to sit down to have lunch with a somewhat skinnier and more battered individual, but by and large the same type of older gentleman.

"Please, Bernard," Kolzack said, "I hope you won't be offended, but over there I see someone I've been trying to get on the phone all week. I'd just like to tell him something briefly. Would you mind if I went over there for a moment? It would save me an annoying letter later on."

"Not at all," said Bernard, who had the feeling that he was controlling his fear well. "No problem. I'll have a drink and look at the murals on the ceiling. They're so nice and indecent."

His gaze lost itself among the fauns and nymphs who once, in the infancy of the current century, had occasioned a serious moral debate. One of the nymphs reminded him of Elisabeth Verolyg. She had the same kind of calves.

If it weren't for that odd man, Lutweiler, with his unpleasant threatening telephone calls, one might say that this spring had turned out well.

Two or three volumes, he thought, available in both hard- and soft-cover, perhaps with a nice preface by some suitable professor, perhaps some young colleague in the Swedish Academy, or perhaps by the charming *Dagens Nyheter* critic, Elisabeth Verolyg. Wouldn't that be something? Perhaps as early as next Christmas? Wouldn't that give him the feeling of being the classic he in fact was?

"Would you like anything else from the bar?" a solemn headwaiter asked.

"Yes, yes," Bernard said. "Let me have another of your excellent cognac highballs. With a lot of water."

"Mineral water? Ramlösa? Club soda?"

After thorough consideration, Bernard, to the unfeigned surprise of the waiter, asked for ordinary tap water.

He wasn't the least bit put out because his publisher had disappeared in this rather inconsiderate manner, practically as soon as he'd arrived.

There seemed to be a lot of gentlemen having lunch here, and the buzz of voices in the room started having the same pleasantly soporific effect running water does. Like running water, Bernard thought. But wasn't the current a bit strong?

Why, he asked himself, is there a waterfall in here? How have I ended up among those strange cataracts?

My boat is drifting toward a waterfall, more and more swiftly. I hope the waterfall won't be too big.

14. Bernard Foy Meets a Stranger

(A drop of blood
moistened the brain's fine roots to uncertain end . . .)

The light from Strömmen was porcelain colored, Arctic, and weak. For a moment he could clearly feel the collected melancholy weight of all his years flying up within him, like a flock of raucous gulls flying up out there in the porcelain light, only to sink back again. Once more, without knowing how he had ended up there, he found himself in the well-known landscape of his own melancholy. Neither the thought of the national edition nor of Elisabeth Verolyg's fat, friendly thighs on top of his own skinny, hairy old man's thighs could bring him back from the strange landscape where he now found himself.

For Bernard Foy, melancholy was often a polar landscape, drift ice at the beginning of June under an Arctic sky. And the awareness that this white, evenly distributed light would never stop to let through sunshine, contrasts, sharp shadows. It suddenly seemed to him that he'd been moving in this landscape all his life: at the same time as he'd given the outward impression of walking around in the street, in libraries, and in academic processions, he was actually shipwrecked on the drift ice.

The ice changed every moment. Where there had only been a crack just before, there was now a channel ruffled by the wind. The channel you'd just crossed, with immense difficulty and with the aid of a board you'd dragged along, was now completely gone. It was as if this entire labyrinth of cracks, ice blocks, crevices, and wind wells had their own will and wanted to play a joke on the helpless men dragging themselves along on wet feet through this shadowless world under a porcelain-colored sky.

From that moment to this much more time must have passed than Bernard had thought. For suddenly there was Sven Kolzack leaning almost across his chair, asking:

"How are you, Bernard?"

"Quite well, thank you," Bernard said.

"Pardon my asking," Sven said. "You seemed so absent. And so pale. All at once."

"Oh," Bernard said. "I was just thinking about a passage in my memoirs. When I concentrate deeply that's what happens."

"Well, pardon me for asking," the publisher said, in the slightly offended tone often used when people have been frightened for some reason or other and don't quite want to admit it.

"It's just that I asked you four times if you'd made up your mind about an entrée. And you just kept looking out the window. I thought you had a pain some place."

"Please order for me," Bernard said. "I've got to disappear for a moment."

At last he found the very elegant men's room. It was upstairs and not that easy to find.

Just as he was about to open the door to the palatial men's room and enter with a sigh of relief, he met a man, dressed like himself in a dark gray suit, white-haired like him, with bluish sides carefully brushed over his temples, and quite a few wrinkles around blue eyes that looked more sad than happy. The stranger walked with slow steps, as if stepping through slush rather than across elegant wall-to-wall carpeting. The man gave Bernard a mildly ironic smile, as if he knew something the other man didn't. *Where* had Bernard seen him before? The man seemed familiar in some strange way. There was a mixture of melancholy and deep friendship in this meeting which, even in his present situation, momentarily distracted Bernard's thoughts.

Leaning across the probably very costly wash basin of black marble, he examined his face with a pained expression in his eyes. It looked the way it usually did. Just a bit pale. He repeatedly threw ice-cold water on his face.

Every time there was a new visitor to the elegant men's room, he pretended to be washing his hands.

He didn't want to attract any attention.

He wanted to know whether it was a temporary or a permanent phenomenon, the fact that he didn't feel anything of the cold water on the right side of his face.

A cerebral hemorrhage. A stroke, he thought. I've had a stroke at last. I've been waiting for a long time. But now it's come. Damn it!

Cerebral hemorrhage. Strange that I can actually move. And when the cold water didn't help he tried hot, as hot as he dared. Horror-struck, he realized the next stroke might occur at any moment. In a second of panic, he felt he had a terrorist bomb, a dynamite charge, inside his own head.

But no matter how much he sluiced cold water from the faucet over the criss-cross of wrinkles on his face, he couldn't restore the feeling in the right side of his face. On the left side, the cold water was cold and the hot, hot. On the right side nothing happened.

It didn't hurt at all. It felt numb, the way it usually does when you've had some novocaine at the dentist's, only spread over a larger area.

There can no longer be any doubt. I've had a small stroke. My first stroke. It's lucky it didn't go deeper. I can still control my hands. My feet obey me.

There was no denying that it felt as if the world had changed. As if the color had changed. I'll go back to Sven now so he won't worry.

Just as he came out of the men's room he met an older man, very pale, dressed in a rather nice dark gray suit with waistcoat, evidently going in.

Something about this gentleman was vaguely familiar to Bernard. That way of combing his white hair which, aided by Watzin's Keratin, acquired an almost bluish tinge around the temples. Where had he see it before?

I might go on forever, Bernard thought, meeting men I recognize and yet don't recognize. Strange.

Bernard politely held the door for the gentleman, who not only nodded gratefully but who also gave him a brief but strangely expressive glance. In his grayish blue eyes there was, for one hundredth of a second, an expression of mild irony, as if he wanted to say, "But don't you recognize me?"

Only when he was entering the dining room to join the impatiently waiting publisher (by this time probably furious at not having his lunch served in reasonable time or at least, polite as he was, not able to start devouring it) was he struck, with the force of a hammer blow, but the sudden realization that the man he had met *could be none other than himself,* the poet and memoir writer Bernard Foy.

I think, therefore I am,

Bernard told himself in a moment of panic. That's all good and well. But there's still something that has to be cleared up, isn't there? Of course there is. For if the kindly ironic and well-dressed gentleman I just met, this apparition of melancholy and happiness, of deepest lust, of tragedy and of farce, whose pupils for one moment looked into mine with a darkness that was the entire, deep darkness between galaxies, if this stranger was the poet, the popular autobiographer, the favorite of the ladies, one of the eighteen members of the Swedish Academy, Bernard Foy,

who am I when I'm thinking?

From the table down at the far end of the large room his publisher watched him intently, with a mild expression of friendly skepticism. Everything suddenly looked very small and remote. Like in the kind of old-fashioned contraption, a stereoscope, that's what it's called, where you put in a postcard and you suddenly get a three-dimensional picture, Bernard thought.

15. There's Something Profoundly Demonic about Mirrors

There are, as Baudelaire correctly remarks, moments when the most trivial scene before our eyes somehow seems to encompass and contain your whole life.

The way back . . .

At this moment, Bernard had the feeling that he'd started sliding down an endless slope. Still worse, that every movement he made might well bring him still further down.

Because in a single moment, the scene has assumed the right to become a symbol of everything we are. And that's because every moment of our lives of course encompasses all other moments, in the figure of a circle, the way rings on the water contain each other.

The rather boring publisher with his high, naked forehead and his large, tired blue eyes, not unlike his own oil portrait in some board room or other, the impeccably set table with its crystal vases, its flowers and its artfully folded napkins, the Stockholm Palace in the background with its restlessly circling gulls, everything suddenly seemed to Bernard to contain everything he was.

In the publisher's blue and somewhat alcoholically rigid eyes (like an old officer's) he seemed to see all of Swedish literature, not just the poets, from Stiernhielm to Silfverstolpe, but also the critics, the magazines, the long, drowsy director's speeches in the Swedish Academy, the smell of very old dust in the country library in Västerås, his slow boyhood leafing through a well-worn copy of Horace where his pencil had written and then carefully erased childish attempts at translation, the unwritten lines, the prematurely dead, the forgotten poets, the great unhappy ones who had become the objects of veneration too early and had been deified. Yes this gaze was the gaze of the teacher who only wanted one thing from him: that he should perform well.

The whole time the gulls were circling behind them, and they seemed to want something else. They weren't a part of it.

(Lieutenant Einar Lundborg landed on the ice floe twice. The first time was June 23. It was a hazardous but successful landing, with the somewhat surprising outcome that the leader of the expedition, General Umberto Nobile, had himself flown out first of all.

There were no Swedes left to save. About twenty days earlier, Hans von Lagerhielm had gone out on the ice excursion from which he alone would never return.

Soon after midnight, that is June 24, Midsummer's Day, the pilot returned in the white porcelain light of the polar night, carefully waited until the fog had lifted, and made a landing during which the plane turned over in the last few sec-

onds; the propeller broke, and the skis were smashed. Lundborg was now as
much a prisoner as the distressed party he'd recently tried to rescue.

Almost silently, the men went to the smaller ice floe where the orange tent was
still standing. The wounded Cecioni, who was to have been flown out, was left
in the shelter of the wrecked plane's double wing. Fear of polar bears prevented
him from sleeping.

The way back was tremendously difficult. The ice changed every moment.
Where there had only been a crack just before, there was now a channel ruffled
by the wind. The channel you'd just crossed, with immense difficulty and with the
aid of a board you'd dragged along, was now completely gone. It was as if this
entire labyrinth of cracks, ice blocks, crevices, and wind wells had their own will
and wanted to play a joke on the helpless men dragging themselves along on wet
feet through this shadowless world under a porcelain-colored sky. They moved
under the ice-cold, humid early summer sky of the Underworld. And they feared
that they would continue on this endless walk forever.

It was in this kind of landscape—although the few survivors would only learn
that long after their rescue—that Hans von Lagerhielm and his two Italian com-
rades had discovered that they'd only moved three kilometers in a very hard day's
march. Sometimes, because of the movements of the drift ice itself, those three
kilometers had brought them further from their goal, the island of Foyn, than they
had been on the previous evening.

It isn't that easy to decide what is the use of a human being.

The way back was tremendously difficult.

Bernard was honestly surprised and relieved to find that he was still able to
speak. The right side of his face felt stiff, but no worse than after a visit to the
dentist's; his voice was a bit croaky, but Bernard had always had rather a croaky
voice, he fancied; it had to do with the fact that his mother became hard of hearing early in life.

"I'm sorry I've been so long," Bernard said.

"Oh, I've spent quite a pleasant hour," the published replied with absent-
minded affability. "But I allowed myself a little shrimp cocktail. I'm always so
hungry at this time of day. And then I talked for quite a while to some business
acquaintances. Have you heard that there may be a new bond issue at Uddeholm?
Isn't it fantastic? After all these years. But perhaps you'd like some herring now?
And caraway cheese? And a schnapps? And a couple of cold beers.?"

"Thank you," Bernard said. "I don't think I'll have lunch today. Perhaps tea
and toast. Will that be all right, do you think? Tea and toast?"

(He definitely remembered that that was what it was called.)

"Now where were we? You're going to publish my collected works? In three
volumes?"

"Did I say that? I thought I'd said that considering the depressed situation in
the publishing market I'd like to, but unfortunately I'll have to limit myself to a
pretty little selection which would be appropriate for the Christmas market."

I no longer know who I am, Bernard thought. One half of my face is paralyzed, and I no longer know who I am, and for the first time in my life, I've met myself. Many people would despair at less.

And if that Other One I met in the door was Bernard Foy, then who am I? *There's something profoundly demonic about mirrors.*

Or if he was Bernard, then am I not The Other?

"Don't you think that'll work?" the publisher asked anxiously. "A nice little volume, let's say fifty poems. Perhaps with some period vignettes."

"Excuse me, what do you mean by *period?*"

(Bernard was pleasantly surprised to hear himself utter this sentence, even if his articulation was somewhat slurred. There evidently was a corner of his brain which, in spite of the fact that he no longer knew whose brain it was, functioned excellently. No better than usual, and no worse, Bernard considered.)

"When you say *period,* do you mean typical of this period we're in? Or do you mean something else? I think you have to give it some more thought, my dear Sven."

What actually occupied Bernard's mind at this moment was quite a different problem, of greater weight and importance than how his ridiculous early poems might fit into next year's Christmas book list, to lie like corpses on the book section counters of dreary department stores, the kind where the salespeople never read books, and where all the customers look like county councilors, with wide, ugly, lying mouths and dull camel's hair coats. The kind of store where he himself never, on principle, set foot. And whether his poems sold or not, were available in communal libraries or not, together with handbooks on embroidery and dog training, he actually couldn't care less.

And those readers, a group of dunces and blockheads, in principle of as little concern to him as the Moroccan cleaners in the Paris Metro, let Sven Kolzack worry about them.

There's something profoundly demonic about mirrors.

For if Someone once folded the big sheet of paper that's the world in the middle to make it reflect itself and become visible, then people ought not to destroy this work by folding it over once more.

Bizarre, strange, frightening thought, where did you come from?

The question presently occupying Bernard Foy was this:

If I am part of someone else's dream, how can I know that this is the case? Only if I wake up. But the waking, too, might be a dream that someone else has, or that I myself am having.

Hah, all the philosophers have already written and talked about that.

But suppose The Other is part of my dream at the same time, so that we are mutually dreaming each other? Then it must be like some kind of *Möbius strip,* where you walk in and out of the dream without knowing where the boundary goes, and where you return to the same place forever.

Then there's no way out. The dream will change, but we'll be dreaming forever. Where are you, stable world? Reality, the thing all the dictators refer to when they want new laws, you looked so firm and stable—were you nothing, then, but a surface slowly turning, so slowly that we can't see it, a slope we inexorably slide down?

Where are you hiding, you soft furry animal?

And suppose the one who's dreaming me is myself, but in reality quite different from the way I am in my dream. How can I know who I am?

If I can dream that I'm a butterfly, can't I just as well dream that I'm a tired old poet who's just had his first, slight stroke. And who I really was, and who dreamed me, I'll never know.

Strange, Bernard thought, here are thoughts of a different kind, of a type I've never had before. If there were anything to me, I'd try to write a poem about it.

> (A drop of blood
> moistened the brain's fine roots to uncertain end
> and straight the mirror's surface misted over,
> losing its power to reflect.)

"Excuse me, Bernard," the publisher said surprisingly, "I didn't mean to hurt you, not at all. We're old friends, aren't we, Bernard?"

He paused briefly. For effect, Bernard thought.

"If you really want it, we'll do the collected poems in three volumes for next Christmas. I think that'll be better. Let's do that, Bernard: when all's said and done, we should take better care of our classics."

The way back was tremendously difficult. The ice changed every moment. Where there had only been a crack just before, there was now a channel ruffled by the wind.

"Bernard, aren't you feeling well?" Sven Kolzack asked anxiously.

He had half risen from his chair. Bernard imagined he was hearing a waterfall of voices: complaining, laughing, loudly arguing voices, the voices of men, women, children. The mocking laughter of demons, the helpless, drawn-out crying of women, the heavy, powerful sound of big windmills driven by a strong wind, the hollow crash of ocean waves beating against poles down in the darkness under some pier, everything filled his ears at once.

> (Over empty April fields
> the harsh light of hope
> was falling, one last time.
>
> The lark hangs in the sky and falls in flight
> across still-brown and waiting fields,
> as in my restless youth.
>
> I see a youth that once was
> and I know I will never be his friend.)

"It's nothing, Sven. Just some kind of buzzing in my ears I get now and then. It doesn't make me feel very well. I think I'll go home and rest for a while. If you'd be kind enough to get me a cab I'd be grateful. We've already agreed on three volumes, isn't that right?"

"But of course, Bernard. We'll be in touch soon again, my dear Bernard. I'll have my secretary write up some notes on this productive and pleasant discussion."

> (What do you want from me, images?
> Faces, still and immobile like African masks?
> Demon faces from the dark stairs of childhood,
> cataracts of faces?
> Perhaps you only wanted this:
> to say that you were all my own mask?)

He got his coat, his hat and his stick and hurried out into the blue spring-winter dusk.

It had melted and frozen over again, and it was so slippery that he slid back a little with every step. He walked with uncertain gait, slurring and mumbling to himself in a loud, almost merry fashion. Nobody he met bothered about him. There are so many drunks and peculiar people walking the streets of downtown Stockholm. It can't be the job of passing pedestrians to take care of people who are the responsibility of the social services.

The way back was tremendously difficult. The ice changed every moment. Where there had only been a crack just before, there was now a channel ruffled by the wind. The channel you'd just crossed, with immense difficulty and with the aid of a board you'd dragged along, was now completely gone.

It was as if, in this kind of landscape, this entire labyrinth of cracks, ice blocks, crevices, and wind wells had their own will and wanted to play a joke on the helpless men dragging themselves along on wet feet through this shadowless world under a porcelain-colored sky.

16. A Zeppelin Rises, at Long Last, through Clouds of Restless Birds

In this kind of landscape.

If only I could remember what it's supposed to mean, this idiotic phrase: *In this kind of landscape.* What's it supposed to mean?

Now the wind picks up, tearing poor Bernard's memories into thinner shreds, like the clouds above the blue ridges and ruffled lakes of northern Västmanland on a gusty October day. Big and small, everything's torn apart, and when it's put together again it doesn't quite fit into the old torn places.

Bernard Foy, poet and member of the Academy? No, we haven't forgotten him.

It amazes me that he hasn't gone mad in the course of the last few weeks, as he sees the wind pushing him in every direction. Poor Bernard, now his memory is being blown apart like a spider web in the strong Alzheimer wind.

"Dr. Lutweiler, I'm afraid it's time for you to go home now," Bernard said, turning to his demanding guest.

"What makes you think," Lutweiler said, "that I've got a home? That it's easy for me to call a cab or go to the nearest subway stop and get home right away? Where do you live, by the way, Mr. Foy? How do you know, Mr. Foy, that I'm not the one who lives here, and you're the stranger?"

There was a certain logic to his question. For Bernard dreamed, night after night, about a strange plague that had descended on the city. It caused no boils, not even a fever. It struck all the people *in the center,* in their center, that is. There were no dramatic manifestations. It was just that one morning, people would wake up to the feeling that, strictly speaking, they might have been anybody, and that the person they were didn't in fact mean anything.

They wandered around like sleepwalkers, precise and silent in the performance of their ordinary tasks, with a small movement around the mouth of each one which betrayed their knowledge that, from now on, they were totally meaningless.

Quite different words and phrases of what they said became important. It was as if a mask had been removed, so that it suddenly became visible to everyone that people had been speaking in a secret code all the time. Now this code became visible:

Lundborg was sleeping in the tent, to the left of Viglieri, who kept complaining all night of rheumatic aches and pains. Lundborg sometimes took morphine tablets and seemed a constant prey to melancholy thoughts.

"It amazes me," he said, "that you haven't yet gone mad in the course of those last few weeks on the ice floe, *when you see the wind pushing you in every direction.*"

It was in this kind of landscape—although the few survivors would only learn it long after their rescue—that Hans von Lagerhielm and his two Italian comrades had discovered that they'd only moved three kilometers in a very hard day's march. Sometimes, because of the movements of the drift ice itself, those three kilometers had brought them further from their goal, the island of Foyn, than they had been on the previous evening.

When you look at the map and see the spot where Mariano and Zappi left Hans von Lagerhielm to die in a depression in the ice, with a couple of coats over him, blind and apathetic, you're surprised it's so close to the island. For someone not familiar with the circumstances, it seems almost incomprehensible that Hans didn't just get up and continue walking.

(In this kind of landscape.)

"Furthermore, it'll be to the advantage of the expedition as a whole if you come along," von Lagerhielm continued, making one of his usual jokes, which always referred to my rather considerable corpulence.

"If we meet with misfortune," he continued, *"at least we'll have something to live off."*

They came out of Örsundaån one Sunday evening at the end of August 1925. It was the last summer they were friends. They came out in the dusk, among the last mallards that hadn't yet flown, through close stands of rushes still, yellow only in spots. Before the rain of the August evening increased, falling cold and heavy, the stalks sang against each other in the wind. The stalks are singing their half-finished song, Bernard thought. The last swan flies up from the rushes.

There was already something unsaid and strange between them which prevented them from finding natural topics of conversation.

They'd been paddling since Friday afternoon, when they'd carried the canoe the comparatively short stretch from the Örsundsbro railway station down to the river. Then they'd been filled with optimism, drive, and hopes of good weather. It hadn't turned out that way. It had been drizzling most of the time, and the temperature had dropped to seventeen or sixteen degrees Celsius.

It must have been the most silent of all their excursions. They even pumped up the old-fashioned Primus stove, cleaned it with the cleaning needle, and lit it without any of the merry comments they normally made.

Higher up in the river, at the mouth of the first small lake, the old men catching crayfish in their black-tarred rowboats had sworn at being disturbed by those students in their student caps and canoes. They were the kind of fishermen who, as late as the end of the month, would offer the black, rustling crayfish for sale at the stalls of the Uppsala market. Bernard and Hans had waved back at them, affable and somewhat superior.

Only farmworkers would catch crayfish in the daytime, probably with pieces of fish dipped in kerosene. Summer people always caught them in pots that were put out in torchlight in the August darkness. It was more romantic that way.

In spite of the drip cuffs, the water found its way into your sleeves sooner or later. Bernard's coat was wet all the way up to his shoulders when they got onto Lake Mälar in the steady rain. Hans von Lagerhielm had providently put on a wool sweater.

"It's just as well for me to experience some hardship."

He'd already received an offer to participate in the Amundsen expedition, and this made him an important man in the department of geography. That was the expedition that would later become the triumphant voyage of the airship *Norge* from Kungsfjorden on Spitsbergen via the North Pole and for a short distance across the uncharted Beaufort Sea.

"In principle, an airship like that should be able to shut off its engines when the winds are blowing in the right direction and let them waft it across Greenland, all the way to the mouth of the St. Lawrence. Yes, if you had enough provisions and favorable June winds, it should be possible to drift across the Pole from Svalbard all the way down to New York. To fly across the Pole to America!"

In spite of his matter-of-fact realism, Hans would sometimes have those outbursts of—what would you call it—fantastic imaginings. Bernard would often think it came from his sister. He didn't like to think of her these days. When the rain plastered Hans's hair over his blond head, he might briefly remind you of his sister.

That was a sight which always sent a shiver of unease through Bernard. He didn't quite know why.

"Half past three," Hans said, putting his pocket watch back into his wet pants with some difficulty. "In two hours, we'll be on the bus."

(*In this kind of landscape.*)

Letting the wind waft you from fragment to fragment. How easy it was. How pleasant when, once and for all, you've accepted the idea that you're nobody in particular.

"If you don't leave soon, Mr. Lutweiler, I'm afraid I'll have to kill you."

"But my dear Dr. Foy. You've done it so many times before. Don't you remember? And your crystal ball is nothing but a silly little flower holder, nothing else."

He paused for effect.

"But perhaps . . . that is to say . . . Undoubtedly, you do have something of interest to me. Just one thing. If I got that, perhaps I'd leave . . . voluntarily."

"By the kitchen stairs?"

"That's it. By the kitchen stairs."

"You're referring to the yellow pigskin briefcase?"

"That's it."

"You'll never get it," Bernard said in a tone whose determination surprised even himself. "I know your past history only too well, Dr. Lutweiler. You'll never get that briefcase. It contains my own self. I'd sooner you killed me."

"That's just what I'm going to do," Ernst Lutweiler answered.

Bernard asked himself where the strange tone of moral indignation in Lutweiler's voice could have come from. Perhaps all murderers feel moral, he speculated.

Soon this thought, too, was forgotten.

If only I could figure out what it's supposed to mean, this idiotic phrase: *In this kind of landscape.* What's it supposed to mean?

I can't have written anything so stupid? Remarkable. I forget everything. I even forget death. (*In this kind of landscape.*) But when all's said and done, is death really that extraordinary? Hasn't it been exaggerated somewhat? I have the feeling that all those living have felt dead at some point. And that all the dead have felt alive at some point.

And there are evenings, you see, crazy evenings, with many birds in naked trees against a red sky, when everyone knows that it isn't easy to tell one thing from another.

Eventually, Amelie returned from her bridge club. She always paid the cab driver a little something extra so that he'd wait until she'd unlocked the door to the building. Stockholm is an unsafe city nowadays. Amelie went looking from room to room, turning on lights, crying the name of the man she'd been married to for more than fifty years and whose absence now filled her with mounting anxiety.

There was still a light on in the kitchen.

To her horror, the door of the kitchen entry was unlocked. She found him dead at the foot of the steps. His face was that of someone who's sleeping peacefully. In his hand he held the red ball of Bohemian glass you were supposed to put flowers in. He squeezed it so tightly in his death that she had a hard time getting it out of his hand.

Of course there are those strange evenings. Of course there are those evenings when all the birds go crazy? But look, there's the airship *Italia,* rising through clouds of restless jackdaws. How *big* it looks up close.

The cathedral steeples are blazing red in the twilight, and the city looks quite different from the way it did just before.

The old Gubbhyllan restaurant on Öfre Slottsgatan has a black metal roof which, on such evenings, looks as if it's heated from inside. It glows for a single minute at sunset, and then it dies down. Come, porters with big-wheeled carts, come bourgeoisie, come pale students on ladies' bikes, come revelers, night walkers, and boulevardiers! Don't you see? But you have to see it. Over *there,* right above the roof of Gubbhyllan, which is glowing red right this minute, a glow that'll soon die down again.

It's the airship Italia *passing over the city on its way to the North Pole.* And everybody's on board.

Now you see it, don't you, how majestically it's moving among the fading evening clouds? You can't be that nearsighted—you must see it.

The three engines roar mightily, but of course it's impossible to see individual passengers at this distance.

"Caratti's engine was still laboring, and Nobile leaned out the window of the gondola, shouting, *'Ferma la macchina!'*

"I looked out beside him and saw the rear of the airship starting to list and sort of slide downwards. I also saw Mariano wearing an oddly *embarrassed* expression, but otherwise he was calm. Everything I've related here happened very quickly; in two minutes, we were on the polar ice. At the last moment, I took a firm grip on the guide rope of the gondola and looked down again.

"The aspect was terrible. The ice seemed to be flying toward us, and, as we approached it, it was transformed from its original unified surface into hundreds of blocks of ice, thrown about chaotically, separated here and there by water channels. I pulled my head back and closed my eyes, with the thought: 'This is the end of everything.' "

The third gate is opened:

THE AGE OF
MATURITY

1. The Last Swan Flies Up from the Rushes

Such was the astonishing novel which the young Bernard Foy was writing. What's more, the end of it will take place underground. We will now relate how such strange happenings came about.

When Hans von Lagerhielm eventually realized that Bernard had in fact disappeared—not just gone off on one of his ordinary boyish adventures, but disappeared in a more serious sense—at first he wasn't as downhearted as he'd expected. Bernard Foy had played hooky since the spring, when his father hanged himself, so for him it wasn't a problem. But for Hans von Lagerhielm, who had a few more ambitions at the Billsta Central School, it wasn't easy to find enough time when he was going around with Bernard.

A ring, forged through someone else.

Spider web in spider web. Mirror mirroring another mirror. Bernard found the poem in the communal library. In the end, Hans von Lagerhielm would be the one to reconstruct it.

This was how it all began:

Those days during a gray, rainy, and windy August when he first unpacked the wonderful stolen machine and dragged it up to his room in the attic, where you could hear the twigs of the large, desolate pear tree scratch against the roof and where the rain squalls from Bockstensfjärden streaked the windowpane, had liberated a poet in him, whose existence no one had suspected, least of all himself. He bought out Hans, who was a bit skeptical, with his moped and a car stereo he'd salvaged from a different context in his life.

Thus Bernard Foy ended up sitting at his little table in the attic all through the dark, rainy August night while the branches of the tree knocked heavily, uneasily against the windowpane, as if they didn't like it out there any longer and wanted to get in.

Not unlike willing soldiers, the small letters aligned themselves in rows each time he pressed the right key. It made him strangely happy. For the first time in his life he was able to *see* his own language. The heavy express train that passed just a few kilometers north of the residential district in Billsta, after crawling across the immense bridge that spans the canal, just getting its steam up again, made the old '30s ceiling fixture vibrate. The bulb flickered over the table, the radiator clattered. He didn't notice. He saw his language and that was enough. It lived its independent life around him. Like the amniotic fluid around an embryo, he thought.

Day after day, low, restless clouds wandered across the bitter conclusion of a windy summer.

"Only now do I know who I am. And no one will be able to take it from me again."

His face was pale and pimply, his hair much too long. He had no life so he had to write it; for the passing wind, clear and cool, for the water creased and darkened in the shadow of the wind squalls; for the wind, for the water, and for no one. Perhaps he really was the last swan flying up from the rushes.

In spite of his sixteen years, Bernard Foy could sometimes be a considerable tyrant. He wanted others to keep him company and always got moody and contrary when they showed a tendency to go home and take care of homework and other, in his opinion totally irrelevant, duties. Bernard's disposition was such that when something had caught his interest, be it a game or a whim, there was nothing in the world that mattered to him other than that single thing. With dogged perseverance, he followed things to the bitter end, and his friends knew that when he was in that kind of mood, there was no way they could persuade him to let go of it.

When, on the other hand, he felt *done* with something, then nothing in the world could make him take an interest in it again. That was how it was with school, that was how it was with the catastrophic scenes that had taken place in the yellow house on a gray winter morning in 1983 and which had ended with his father, that same afternoon, swinging back and forth in one of the rooms, like the pendulum of an old clock. Hanged, dead, and finished.

In some strange way, Bernard seemed to be done with all of this. Those things, too, were clean, dead, and finished.

"My problem," he said to his best friend, Hans, the first time they met after Bernard's father had committed suicide, "my problem isn't that at all. It's something quite different: the whole time, I've indulged in childishness. But I think I'm getting more mature now. I'll never again hope that something will get better than it is."

Of course it felt emptier. There was nobody Hans could drop in on after school. No one to sneak home to in that yellow house behind the pine hedge in the fall dusk. No reason anymore to creep uneasily through the back door of the house (the front door was still bolted and locked since the spring) with its eerie creaking noise, listening for some life in the darkness of the house. No reason anymore to find your way in the darkness through the kitchen which now, the fall of 1983, was frighteningly messy and unused, with old cartons and empty bottles strewn here and there. (The water had been shut off a long time ago, but Bernard had managed to provide himself with electricity by plugging into the transformer at the end of the old pine hedge.) Up the steep stairs, where the emaciated housecats would streak past, noiseless as ghosts in the darkness.

No Bernard looking up with large, friendly eyes, bloodshot from the small, cosily green-shimmering computer screen, smiling a shy welcome.

While Hans von Lagerhielm was rather tall, thin, and lanky, Bernard had a low-slung, broad, sturdy body, his rather heavy head placed close to his shoulders on a short, muscular neck. There was something of the gnome about him, one of those small, powerful men equipped with a double axe one might imagine encountering in a deserted mine far underground.

When Bernard had looked up, smiling his shy, bloodshot smile, it had always made Hans feel happy. Now there was no one to visit and the whole house was empty and dead. No one to play the more and more intricate and labyrinthine computer games Bernard learned to make, more and more quickly, on his small Atari, and which often constituted bizarre continuations of games he'd originally pocketed at the Galleria in Billsta.

Making extraordinary new computer games was an art Bernard had quickly mastered. Hans was convinced Bernard would have been able to make his living from them if he'd wanted to. One was called "Triple Spies," and another—to Hans's mind rather boring—was called "Sonnets and Sestinas." There was another game that was a lot of fun, called simply "Zeppelins." (*A zeppelin has crashed somewhere between the west side of Spitzbergen and Jan Mayen. You can choose to stay on the drift ice, and try to walk somewhere, but you have to calculate the amount of the provisions you will be able to carry very carefully. The drift ice the players are walking on is continuously carried in different directions by capricious winds, and consequently it is sometimes more advantageous to sit still than to walk. Airplanes and icebreakers from different nations are trying to rescue the players, and they complicate the situation.*) The latter was Hans's favorite game. He never tired of playing it with Bernard, even though he'd almost always lose.

But one thing has to be admitted: Hans's life was undoubtedly simplified by Bernard's absence. He could associate with his sister Veronica again, a large, rather aggressive and robust girl whom Bernard detested. Most of all he detested the pimples on her back, which were particularly noticeable in a bathing suit. Even the bathing suit was old-fashioned and stupid-looking. He detested the braces on her teeth, and he detested her silly way of pronouncing the letters "ö" and "ä" in a ridiculous kind of Stockholm accent so that they became "u" and "e." She was also, in Bernard's opinion, fat.

(Hans's and Veronica's parents had been divorced for some years. The mother and daughter lived in Billsta; Hans and his father, a bit older than most fathers of schoolboys, lived in what used to be a summer cottage, down by Lake Mälar, more precisely by the Flogsta shore toward Bockstensfjärden.)

On the other hand, Veronica detested Bernard with the same youthful abhorrence he felt for her. She seldom passed up an opportunity to ridicule the small mannerisms characteristic of him, his rather dragging gait, his forward-leaning head, his heavy, sleepy-looking eyelids.

There were other things as well.

If Bernard had been content to sit in the small room high up in the otherwise frighteningly desolate yellow house, inventing more and more complicated computer games, he wouldn't have been a particularly difficult friend. But he didn't hesitate to introduce his games into the larger world. Those games Bernard loved to play in the heating culverts of the County Council under Billsta Center had something exaggerated and desperate about them.

Bernard loved playing them in teams of two and two, and preferably, the members of each team would be a boy and a girl. You had a head start of a specified number of minutes, often ten, and then you tracked, hunted, and surprised each other according to complicated game rules in the long, meandering heating culverts that stretched underneath a rather extensive area of communal and commercial institutions in Billsta. (Bernard had found an entrance in the heating plant of the school while he was still attending the *gymnasium;* he had a certain acumen where things underground were concerned.)

Those underground culverts were rather pleasant in their own way, since they had a temperature well above normal room temperature even in the coldest weather—in certain spots (close to the heat pumps and at the larger intersections) the temperature was so high that it felt unpleasant to walk through. They were color-coded, presumably so that repairmen and maintenance people wouldn't lose their way so easily: the passages were painted green, red, and blue.

There were also intersections where the colors faded into one another. Bernard's rules, which he enforced with brutal and rigid stubbornness, meant that you were allowed to do some things in certain color zones which were absolutely prohibited in others. (For example, all the other players had to obey him blindly in the red passages, but they acquired a similarly blind command over him if the meeting took place in another color zone.) Since the different players did not have the same ideas about what was pleasurable and what wasn't, certain zones, for example the red ones, turned into a kind of war zone which the girls in particular had to get through as fast as possible.

There's no reason to go into those childish games. In the rather restricted group of schoolmates who were parties to the secret, there were quite a few who, more and more frequently, would find excuses not to participate once they'd tried the game. Others, Hans for instance, were indefatigable. Hans's sister Veronica believed that after his father's death, Bernard had started taking the games too seriously. Bernard himself wasn't content with even the culvert system. In his eyes, it was too restricted: he'd calculated that in its entirety, the system hardly extended for more than about fifteen thousand meters.

He didn't think much of that. He dreamed of finding secret connections between this underground system and others: the tunnel of the southern railway branch just before the Södertälje Canal, with all its access points and maintenance tunnels, the underground mains of the Botkyrka community electrical system, the Billsta-Flogsta electrical plant, drainage tunnels, even the kind of ancient shafts that had been used by dour Russian prisoners who had built canals and port structures here and there in the Mälar district during the eighteenth century. After his father's death, the dream of exploring and controlling all of this extensive underworld dominated Bernard with an almost manic eagerness.

In brief, Hans had reason both to miss and not to miss Bernard.

Of course he asked around. Down by the Galleria shops in Billsta Center. On dark October nights he biked along the shorewalks where, at this time of year, the heavy waves of Bockstensfjärden pounded in the darkness. He asked his father to inquire among the circle of ancient but often surprisingly well-informed old gentlemen he played cards with every Tuesday—Preference, his father insisted on calling the game—down at the Billsta Home, the last private nursing home for older people in the district. He didn't even hesitate to ask the insufferable gang of unemployed alcoholics who'd gather outside the state liquor store in Flogsta in order to inveigle young people biking past into acquiring the tranquilizers they got at the alcohol clinic across the town square, trading them for bottles of red wine the young people would go in and buy for them.

Neither did Hans even hesitate to make a polite approach to the tough Finnish whores who warmed their feet on the subway grates on cold winter evenings.

But where could Bernard have gone? If he wasn't still in the Billsta-Flogsta district, there was undoubtedly a lot of area to choose from. A persistent rumor had it that he'd been seen on an old sand barge with black sails, out in Lake Mälar. One rumor related that he'd been seen under the pillars of Västerbron. Another reported a sighting in the foyer of the Royal Library in Humlegården. At this time, there was actually no end to the rumors.

Naturally, Hans returned more than once to the yellow house. But nothing had changed there. Cardboard boxes and empties stood in the kitchen as before. Outside the triple-locked door of Jacob Foy's office, there was an empty black plastic bag apparently left behind when the police took away the older Foy's records and books. It flapped in the draft when Hans entered and almost scared him out of his wits, for he imagined he saw an agitated black hand signaling for help.

Only the starved cats stroked against his shins with embarrassing persistence. This house was dead, and every living thing had abandoned it. Apparently.

It's obvious, he said to himself, that my investigations have to be carried further afield.

Three days later, he unexpectedly found a new clue. A little guy he knew from the sixth grade, Leffe—for some unscrutable reason, he was called Leffe Twelvefoot—turned up to beg him for money for a cup of coffee. Leffe was a burn-out, one of those kids who'd become totally empty due to the incredible amounts of bad weed he'd smoked in Billsta Central School as a child. He'd fallen or, rather, sneakily slid out of school at a very early age. The social worker and the school psychologist and the teachers must have given up looking for him by this time.

But sometimes this boy would have oddly precise information as to what was happening around Billsta. No one knew why; no one knew where he got his information. He just knew.

A priori, the philosophical former submarine mate and, later, radio store proprietor, Torsten Simmerling at the Billsta Home, would have said. He was one of Hans's father's card-playing cronies.

2. Sentimental Landscape Description

After the continuous rains of August there are frequent days of silver-colored light over the great Bockstensfjärden baywaters, and a sharp, nearsighted wind passes through the September rushes, which are already getting brittle. It makes everything in its way clear as glass and superficial; it knows what it wants, and it does some damage to everyone it encounters.

That was the time when our pockets bulged with fallen fruit, muddy from the rain—and the pockets of some of us bulged with other objects as well. Some of those were so strange that, with the best will in the world, we were unable to find words for them. Some, of course, for such is the way of the world, have to leave with empty pockets. Provided we have succeeded in persuading you to be patient, the time has come for us to provide some further details.

The landscape is extensive, and it doesn't hang together very well.

Let's suppose that the main railroad between Stockholm and Södertälje, where the fast trains pass continuously over the tall bridge at the Södertälje Canal, is in the middle: that'll make it easier to point things out. The place where the canal passes under the railroad between tall rock embankments will then form the center of a cross with four sectors.

In the upper right-hand sector there's the Flogsta Marin Company, situated on a deteriorating inlet of Lake Mälar, where ancient concrete barges still rot among yellowing reeds. Now, in early October, there isn't much left of the forest of masts which fill the pier of the marina in the summertime. The small gas station on the pier has already discontinued service; only a few young men on motorbikes test their engines down by the row of restrooms next to the sandwich shop. In the bushes behind the crane used for replacing masts are the last of the summer's used condoms along with the strange, brown-black mushrooms which, at this season, seem to spring from the earth with each night's rain.

Flogsta Marin Company was initially conceived as something a lot more impressive, more southern and elegant than it turned out to be. At this time of year, a few old wooden boats lie submerged at their moorings, like prisoners who, even in death, have not been liberated from their bonds. An old man sits fishing at the end of the pier. He pulls white-gleaming, flat-bellied bream from the rather polluted water, one after the other, putting them into a cheap imitation-leather shopping bag patterned with chess squares. God knows what he intends to do with these dreary fish who live in polluted, shallow waters and who almost always carry flatworms in their unknowing white stomachs.

The only other person in sight is a man in a sports jacket and plus fours walking along the pier, very systematically noting the dock numbers of the few boats that are left. It's probably a tax investigator on some routine mission, looking for undeclared boats.

There are those who say that the reason Flogsta Marin doesn't get many boats—above all, not such large boats as were originally expected—at its expensive, communally subsidized pier, is that the whole place is too easily accessible from the County Government Board. It's too close to the Government Board, that's the whole thing. There may be something in it. Although it's debatable whether you'd fare any better at a greater distance, nowadays. For several years, the former district tax director used two large helicopters in his hunt for hidden property. Hugin and Mugin, they were called. Low and ominous, they flapped across the landscape the previous summer. When the sun suddenly streamed down through some silver-glinting well of light, their large, fantastic shadows passed over forgotten bulldozers behind rotting outhouses and thrown-together summer cottages at the edge of abandoned sandpits. You might say that their shadows passed over the district the way centuries pass over the country. But they're gone now.

Sometimes they'd be far out across the Mälar bays, spying out some forgotten summer cottage; sometimes they hovered above the immense forest around Sjunkarmossarna down in the remote lower left-hand corner. God, but hardly anyone else, might know what they'd be looking for out there in the marshlands. Sometimes you'd see them hovering motionless for a long time above the water holes, the way dragonflies will sometimes hover pensively above summer lakes. As if they wanted to see their reflections in the polished shield of the water hole.

Sjunkarmossarna constitutes the beginning of the real Sörmland wilderness. Not only does the strangely used-up, worn, and nowadays almost forgotten landscape of the Mälar district end there, but also the Flogsta shopping center, county council buildings, protected workshops, and endless, gray-concrete apartment complexes. Out there goshawks still fly above the marshes that stretch for many miles, now overgrown with cloudberries, meadowsweet, and bog myrtle, now dotted with treacherous water holes. In the parts closest to the Billsta-Flogsta community, confusing objects may sometimes be seen floating on these water holes; a lady's shoe, an abandoned suitcase like a pike gasping for air, a yellow pigskin briefcase that might once have contained something valuable but which now only bobs up and down on the cushion of stuffy, enclosed air ingested at the moment when it was thrown into the water hole, emptied of its original contents.

Further out there are no more traces left of what modern, concrete housing developments, planned for cozy living, can transfer, furtively and imperceptibly, to the world of fragments, remnants, and never quite articulated secrets. Beyond this indistinct zone another one begins, one which does not quite belong to the human race: the undeveloped—and forever undevelopable—large marshland called Sjunkarmossarna; the name "Sinking Mosses" may derive from the fact that people have always claimed just about anything can sink in there and be lost forever.

The only people who come here are those familiar with the faint, winding paths

197

from childhood, or else those who want to risk their lives trying them out. Out here, only the goshawks seem to reign over an extensive wilderness, but the impression that they reign alone is perhaps also somewhat illusory.

Out here in Sjunkarmossarna, on warm, solitary July days, life may seem as primeval and untouched by history as during the early Scandinavian Bronze Age. Out here in the still weather on such afternoons some very large butterflies appear, butterflies that otherwise only seem to exist in gaudy entomological handbooks in the community library. Out here in the glades, flying ants still swarm over some dried-up log from what must once have been one of the few trees in the marshland. One has to assume that this was once alive: forested lake, perhaps a deep Mälar inlet which the rapid land elevation has turned into marshland.

Out here there are traditions, legends of bog people, Stone Age hunters in cloaks of coarse-spun cloth who've been killed by their enemies and, through the millennia, have sunk deeper and deeper into the brown humus of the bogs, preserving them forever. The legends—we don't quite know *whose*—claim that these strangely well-preserved bog corpses rise from the depths of the marshes on dark November nights in order to mingle their ghostly lives with those of the living for a few hours. Then the lives of the living can no longer be distinguished from the lives of the dead.

We prefer not to speculate on what those living dead, those eternally wandering bog men, may have been up to on their extensive wanderings in the November darkness.

Baron Carl Rutger von Lagerhielm, the last private owner of Flogsta Manor, always used to soothe people by stating that he was sure there were more dangerous things about in the district than the bog people. If anyone has *really* seen them out there in the marshland, they were more likely to be Soviet parachute troops, *Spetsnaz* troops from Riga or Leningrad preparing for an eventual Russian occupation and listening to radio messages from the Swedish civil defense, rather than primeval figures from some remote prehistoric period. People are welcome to believe whatever they like.

"At any rate, hopefully the devil'll get them. Whoever they may be," Carl Rutger would say, blowing his nose rustically straight out. In spite of his undisputed learning, this gentleman has never had any manners.

With this personage, we have moved from the most desolate corner of the landscape, the lower left-hand one, back to the most civilized one, where we started, the upper right-hand corner. (For we love diagonal movement. Our attitude toward pendulum movements is, for reasons that may eventually become clear, more ambivalent.) Flogsta Marin Company, Flogsta beach, all of Flogsta, has of course taken its name from Flogsta Manor, built by the baron and Caroline colonel Karl Larsson Lagerhielm in 1706, burned to the ground a few times, but always rebuilt.

The old house was situated on Lake Mälar; with its yellow front and large French windows overlooking a terrace, it was just as beautiful as one expects such a house to be. The terraces disappeared into the depths, one after the other, down to the shore, where alders replaced the oaks, giving the impression of a sea, now yellow, now wine-dark, with frozen billows down to the equally wondrous Mälar shore with its reeds and gusts of clear blue air. Of course Baron von Lagerhielm no longer lived in the house. In connection with his latest bankruptcy, he'd retired to a more modest abode which we will try to find an excuse to describe later on.

It was rumored that Flogsta Manor was used as a home for a voluntary drug detoxification program run by the Södermanland county council. But no substance abusers were ever seen there. Perhaps they'd gone quietly back home.

Some years ago, a few unusually silent old men with stiff, immobile faces were noticed being walked around the park and the terrace with its broken marble statues and smashed garden urns. Perhaps those gray individuals taken out on apathetic morning walks in a long, winding line by some caretaker youths were actually dope fiends. Perhaps they were criminals. Perhaps sex fiends. There aren't any completely normal people anywhere. For that matter, they might also have been bog corpses; it would hardly have made any difference. Now the Gray Ones hadn't been seen all summer. Instead one of the area bike gangs had celebrated orgies in the empty rooms and caused a fire which, strangely enough, had petered out. Perhaps it happened on a night during a sudden thunderstorm.

"No," Baron von Lagerhielm said. "Somehow it's the destiny of this house, that it isn't supposed to burn down."

Not before its hour has come.

Carl Rutger von Lagerhielm never visited Flogsta Manor after the sale. He kept much more to the south, in a very small, only partially winterized summer cottage which one of his ancestors, probably his grandfather, had portioned off from a small peninsula sold in the '30s to a Stockholm buyer. It was a quaint little cottage that almost looked like a lighthouse and was sometimes mistaken for one by swift motorboats out in the bay. For only one of the four walls had windows: two narrow portholes facing the bay and Bockstenssundet.

All the other walls were windowless.

This suited the baron, a learned and eccentric man in his seventies. It was said that he'd lined the inner walls of this minute habitation with the remains of the old manor library which had ended up on the dump in the summer of 1961, when the county council took over. He'd gone there picking all summer, the baron had, as if he'd no shame at all. But perhaps the books came in handy for keeping the cold out when the winter storms blew across the bay.

Quite a number of rumors circulated about this Baron von Lagerhielm, actually. Only a few people had been in his cottage on the point. One of those who had gained his confidence and been admitted to this strangely salvaged library was the sixteen-year-old, already orphaned Bernard Foy.

The son, a tall, healthy, red-haired youth called Hans von Lagerhielm, lived with his father only intermittently, and he'd usually avoid it when the winter storms raged. Then the winds would go right through the former summer cottage; you had to carry in firewood, even in the middle of the night. Hans would then prefer to live in the central heating at Billsta-Flogsta, where his mother, a very fat and—as distinct from her son—wheat-blond woman, kept a tobacco store. It was said to be the hub of illegal liquor sales to the helpless and burned-out alcoholics who did not have the strength and the money to cover the fifteen kilometers to the state liquor store in Södertälje.

"The boy has discovered," his father would say, "that it's only a prejudice to consider human warmth superior to mechanical warmth. In the winter it can be the other way around."

This woman will only have a peripherial part in our long narrative. She is considered slightly mad, and her dirty blonde hair flies in tousled, uncombed strands across a broad, imposing forehead when she answers the phone in her tobacco store. She detests Carl Rutger as much as she loves her son Hans. Somewhat schematically, she refers to the baron as "the male parent."

On principle, the degraded nobleman never again went up to Flogsta Manor after the bankruptcy and the auction. Nor was there much to see up there: only the last traces of an ice-damaged and, finally, burned-down bathhouse of the old-fashioned kind. There were also the muddy remains of what must once have been a sailboat, which evidently one fall had simply been left to be broken up by the ice, to sink and turn into a monster: a baleen whale and skeleton out there in the mud. Nowadays it was mostly a wonderful haunt of perch and stickleback. On fine days, the small Turkish boys from the Billsta-Flogsta development would come out, fishing for them with bread dough on their hooks. However, the sailboat seemed to be done with sailing.

"My old boat I had such good times in as a boy has turned into Charon's ferry," Carl Rutger von Lagerhielm would say to Hans. "A ship that only sets sail when someone hands the ferryman an obol. I have nothing to leave to you, my boy—after a whole life, after three hundred years of Lagerhielms. It's terrible."

"It doesn't matter, Father. We can be friends just the same."

Carl Rutger von Lagerhielm's canoe, which had once had red-lead paint on top of the taut sailcloth body (the way it was supposed to be in those days), lay neatly pulled up on sawhorses when it wasn't being used. The painful thing was that it must last have been used more than thirty years ago. Grass and epilobium coexisted cheerfully, sticking up through the holes in the rotted cloth. The canoe itself was no longer a vessel but rather a log, a natural object, a cadaver. Why not bog corpse and *bog man* as well?

When the young Bernard gradually became more familiar with the Baron and dared joke with him, he might answer this way when asked how things were at Flogsta these days:

> "The wind blows across the ravaged terrace.
> The light plays wildly on the lyre of the poet prince.
> The last swan flies up from the rushes."

Such things would create a closeness—unusual considering the time, the place, and the situation—between the tired, already seventy-year-old aristocrat in the windy summer cottage on the point by Bockstenssundet and the almost seventeen-year-old poet.

This was, as has already been mentioned, the year when Bernard Foy, sixteen years old, would turn seventeen. He entered that year without a mother, and from May on, his father wouldn't be alive either. It took the entire fall, the long, rainy, stormy fall of 1983, to rid himself of it by writing it all down.

The writing would finally take—something which we will also recount in this narrative—an unexpected turn and go underground. There it would grow like a spider web, layer upon layer. He became a poet, but of course it cost something: eventually, we will tell what.

3. It Was the Time When Our Pockets Bulged with Fruit . . .

Of course there's a lot more to be said about the landscape. Of the four sectors in our diagram, we've only really touched on the lower left-hand one: the desolate marshland southwest of the railroad, called Sjunkarmossarna, and the upper right-hand one, where Flogsta Manor is the center of a shore landscape moving down toward Lake Mälar in a series of terraces.

To the west of this area, looking toward the mighty Bockstensfjärden, where right now a lone blue freighter with a cargo of concrete, flying a Dutch flag, is about to disappear in the silvery shimmer of the horizon, lies the old residential district of Billsta. At a distance, it still looks idyllic. But it's nothing but a dream that's failed, the dream of a happier, more egalitarian Sweden, where the working class would also be able to own houses, and where the common people would have access to light and air and pear trees.

The little houses with their carefully tended garden plots came into existence in the 1930s, when diligent and enterprising foremen and supervisors from the Scania-Vabis factory in Södertälje arrived here to get air and light and to be close to Lake Mälar. They dug in the soft clay slope toward the lake, they planted their apple trees and pear trees. These are now to a large extent decimated by winter storms, but some giant trees still remain.

Some of the houses have started falling into disrepair, now that their owners are no longer young and don't have much money left over for repairs and maintenance. Some of the houses have asphalt shingles on top of their original wooden boards, and some have chimneys that look about to fall down. Some have yards cluttered with the most singular objects: plumber's benches, old English Fords from the late '40s, locomotives, automated potato pickers of the Olsén and Hagwald patented design.

To the east everything slowly changes into an industrial area which is the horror of the county council and of the health services. On small lots, not much bigger than the garden plots close by, strange one- and two-people businesses practice a number of specialized trades. There's an angry Finn whose office, decorated with pornographic tool company calendars, is guarded by two attack-trained German shepherds who are said to have cost visiting tax and health inspectors their trousers.

He buys up old cars, either incredibly rust-eaten or else those that have been in wrecks. His customers, mostly young people, are allowed to detach the parts they think they might have a use for under the eyes of his stern associates. In the next shop there are some older men from Dalarna in an indescribably smelly shop yard. They are the only ones in the community able to repair the tipping device on the new garbage trucks the county council ordered from West Germany.

Every time a truck like that comes in for repairs, a fair amount of garbage will end up in the untidy yard. There's quite a smell in the spring when the thaw starts, and it's better not to try to determine what it's doing to the subsoil. (For, as Carl Rutger von Lagerhielm says, in this world there are things one should inquire into and things one should not.) This results in Andersson's Tip Repair getting a notice to stop operations every New Year's from the Sjunkarmossen Health Department, then getting a dispensation from the same department the next day. How else to avoid the much greater discomfort of not having enough functioning garbage trucks in the community?

On the whole, this is not the kind of area where the authorities like to interfere a whole lot. By and large, it's an area where people have a strange tendency to disappear, only to resurface in the most surprising and puzzling guises. Berry pickers, retirees on bus excursions, owners of frankfurter stands: there's no limit to how many people disappear. Sometimes children who've gone swimming will find the swollen corpses in the reeds, sometimes they're found crouched behind some rock in the woods on the edge of Sjunkarmossarna in April. Sometimes they'll look brooding, as if they're still searching for the road they lost one day in May.

A sheriff, too, easily gets lost out here. One was seen by some boys late in the spring, sitting in a toilet for the handicapped down by the Flogsta beach. Strictly speaking, there aren't many handicapped who go that far from town to have a swim. His wrists and ankles were carefully tied with prime quality anchor chains that looked as if they had come from some shop in the area. Then he disappeared from there, too. Evidently someone had carried off the old guy entire.

The rumor that young Bernard Foy was instrumental in disseminating claimed that when he, Bernard, discovered the dead man ahead of anyone else, angry black little forest bees were already coming out of his nostrils. Later the old guy had disappeared, so it wasn't easy to check on the truth about the bees. A persistent rumor pointed to Bernard as the one who'd dragged the dead man off before the police came. This was a rumor that Bernard did his best to promote, standing on this street corner or that, by means of rhetorical brilliance with effective pauses and digressions. He'd supposedly inherited his rhetorical ability from his mother who, when she was alive, had been a renowned seller of embroidered cushions and other curiosities in the Södertälje market square. According to what Bernard imparted to a breathless crowd of his contemporaries—little leather-clad bikers and moped-riders—down by the notice board at the beach, the dead man's cranium was already polished to a shine by the wild bees who'd made it into a hive. Bernard, at this point still unaware that he was a poet, but already a devotee of detail, would stress that he'd seen a bee emerge from the dead man's nostril, seen it with his own eyes, and then seen it return inside the cranium.

Again according to young Bernard, the subdued buzzing inside the sheriff's cranium was supposed to make the most singular music. Some thoughts were going on in there that seemed to be the absent-minded and absent voice of God rather than of anyone else. A low, droning, primeval music, not to be disturbed by any temporary whim or fancy crawling in or out of a swiftly disintegrating human skull. You might say that for the first time in its existence, this skull had a really sensible task. Only now was real thinking going on inside. For everything serves.

"Nature," the boy had added as he reached the conclusion of his narrative, turning confidentially to his two most fascinated listeners, Hans von Lagerhielm and Kenta Holm—who leaned so far forward over the seats of their mopeds that their fair and reddish heads almost made a unity, a strange flower pattern, in conjunction with Bernard's dark hair—"nature, you see, isn't just lettuce and tomatoes and larks and crested grebes, nature also encompasses things like this. Someone who believes that nature is beautiful hasn't seen much of nature. Or else he's started to realize that beauty doesn't have to be beautiful.

"The question is if fucking nature isn't most itself when it's like this. Once I saw a cow that had gotten mired down in Sjunkarmossen. That is, I saw her the next summer. It was almost the same thing. There was buzzing and singing in the swollen stomach of that cadaver, too. And that wasn't all. She spread her legs like a damn whore."

At such times, it wasn't easy to tell what was truth and what was only little Bernard's fantasy, primeval, unpruned by formal education and generally high-spirited.

You might ask yourself, for instance—if it were true that Bernard had in fact, and not just in his hectic puerile fantasy life, found a piece of a sheriff eaten clean and polished by bees, whose brain had been replaced by a clump of energetically buzzing and honey-gathering insects inside his skull, chained on the stinking, terrible old handicapped toilet down by the Flogsta beach, with innumerable traces of the activity of young pyromaniacs and the resolute sexual attempts of very immature teenagers—why on earth hadn't the police come and picked up the old guy? Before Bernard and his little friends found him and took him over.

Of course our quick-witted Bernard had an answer to this question as he did to every other question: because of the interesting sound, he'd wanted to keep the old man as a kind of oracle, and so he and his friends had dragged the skeleton off one fall night, in his chalk-striped suit and silver tie and his briefcase, *the whole ball of wax,* in fact, and sat him down on a tree stump in one of the southernmost and most desolate part of Sjunkarmossarna, far from all paths and footbridges. There he sat, solemnly buzzing in the summer and more difficult to wake up in the winter. And gave answers. In the winter, however, you had to knock lightly on his forehead with a piece of dry wood Bernard had broken off from the stump he was sitting on.

"Some kind of *deity* you mean?" the fanciful Hans asked.

"Absolutely not," Bernard answered very seriously. "Just an oracle. Like a tarot deck my mother used. A *mediator* of voices from outside. Neither more nor less. A carrier of thoughts, tea leaves to read in. Neither more nor less."

What made his little friends still more unsure than the sovereign assurance with which Bernard used to dish up such stories was the fact that they knew what a frighteningly perfect memory this boy had. For Bernard never forgot anything. In the days when he still visited the Billsta Central School he'd almost scared his math teacher, who was not easily intimidated, with his incredible mnemotechnical skills. There were teachers who'd use him instead of the logarithm table. He was an embarrassing witness to conversations, for there was no promise, no formulation, which he didn't retain forever once he'd heard it. Like all people with shadowless memories, Bernard Foy naturally suffered terribly from the merciless clarity, the frighteningly clear daylight of the pictures from his life that he possessed. He was trapped in the clear light of his own unfailing memory, which tended to make the world overexposed. He'd often dream of forgetfulness.

"The truth about Bernard," the school psychologist, fifty-one-year-old Elisabeth Verolyg, Ph. D., said on a certain occasion in the fall when the conversation got around to Bernard—he hadn't been in school for six months—"the truth is that he can probably get along equally well on his own. With that remarkable head he's got. He doesn't forget anything. But we'll have to assume that Social Services have arranged for a foster home for him by now. But," she added in her breezy girlish Djursholm accent, "*if he knows* anything about this strange disappearance, *then* I'm sure he'll make an excellent witness. The truth about Bernard is that he's never actually understood how it's possible to forget something. He lives in a *shadowless* world, that boy does."

At the end of August 1983, Bernard was still happily not conscious of this conversation.

"A shadowless world?"

(Sture Lannerstedt, the headmaster, had never enjoyed particularly quick comprehension, and his ability had not increased with the passing years. Furthermore, he frankly disliked anything he didn't understand. He was the permanent substitute for the real headmaster, the much more original, bizarre Måns Wedelin, who was on sick leave for an undetermined period because he'd had a nervous breakdown in which, oddly enough, Bernard Foy and Hans von Lagerhielm were peripherally involved.)

"Yes. In the shadowless world of memory." Poor Lannerstedt shook his head. He didn't think it sounded particularly *therapeutic* to use such expressions as Elisabeth Verolyg did. On the whole, he found her unpleasantly upper-class. She belonged to the generation before teachers' colleges.

"The fact is," the still striking-looking fifty-one-year-old school psychologist continued (her long, magnificent reddish-blonde hair was combed into a long braid worn over her shoulder, which made her look a bit like the most famous portraits of the great actress Sarah Bernhardt), "the fact is, several times during my explorative sessions with him, I'd realize *that he will sometimes lie and say that he's forgotten something*. In order to appear more normal. He pretends that he's forgotten things just so his teachers and classmates won't know that he's never had the experience of forgetting. In general, he's afraid of being suspected of not having had an experience other children consider natural and commonplace. On one occasion, when he was about twelve, he discovered that some of his classmates liked to talk about ice hockey results, and he wanted to make some kind of contact with them. Then it turned out that he'd spent an entire Sunday afternoon memorizing all the results and goal scores in the whole Swedish ice hockey series and, in addition, the names of all the players. That didn't get him far, and soon he was back to his usual autistic behavior. Not talking to anyone. Also his father—who's *out of the picture* now—is supposed to have used the boy as a telephone book. He'd often sit on the floor of the office when he was small, playing for hours on end."

"Are such things *common*," the frightened Sture Lannerstedt asked, reluctantly seeing his question expanded into an *unplanned conversation*, "or is this a special case?"

"I think it's a *very* special case?" Elisabeth Verolyg answered. To Lannerstedts's surprise, she smiled an astonishing little smile.

Still, in Lannerstedt's opinion, a lady should not wear blue eye shadow to work.

"It's important to remember that until he reached prepuberty, Bernard was a very *autistic* child," Dr. Verolyg continued unconcernedly. She assumed that everyone was interested in the psychology of a child. "Actually, according to what I've been told, no one except his father seems to have had any real oral contact with Bernard before he was twelve. Unfortunately, we know very little of what takes place in the strange world of the autistic child," Elisabeth Verolyg concluded with a sigh, skillfully catching a hair pin that had just slipped from her magnificent braid. She held it between her full lips while she quickly fished for an elegant little ivory comb in her large, motherly handbag.

("Full," without a doubt, but perhaps *sensuous* as well? Lannerstedt asked himself. There was something about this unmarried school psychologist with her powerful, handsome body and the reddish-blonde braid down her strong back that disturbed him profoundly, as if she were connected with some catastrophe that hadn't yet occurred but which would do so sooner or later.)

As far as the story of Bernard Foy and the Polished Sheriff is concerned, the former used to claim he had evidence of actually having found the latter. He had the dead man's briefcase. It was the kind of elegant, square affair you see here and there nowadays, and it had been leaning against the sooty inner wall of that horrible handicapped toilet.

It was supposed to have been full of some strange auditing papers which Bernard, in the interest of the whole district, had submerged in one of the deep-black water holes in Sjunkarmossarna.

Hans von Lagerhielm would point out that this whole story might be nothing but pure invention. There were just the same kind of briefcases in Billsta Center, and last spring it had still been quite easy to steal things from the Leather Loft, as the shop was called.

4. Medusa and the Mirror

The black waters flowing between bog myrtle, meadowsweet, and cloudberries are called water holes. When the wind doesn't ruffle them, they can look like the dark, polished surface of a shield that doesn't mirror anything. A person who's ended up in them doesn't have much of a chance of getting out. The edges recede, soft as veils, if someone tries to grab hold of them. Like clear, black eyes, these water holes mirror clouds, the sky, even the stars, until a sudden breeze ruffles them. Then they themselves turn into *surface* and are no longer mirrors.

(Breathe on the surface of the mirror and the image disappears.)

Making your way, one afternoon of pale sun at the end of October 1983, across endless, swaying, and unsafe cloudberry bogs, between quagmire and open water holes, across rotting log causeways and small wooded islands smelling strangely of bilberry, all the way to the place where the Polished Sheriff sat on his stump, was a rather precarious, not to say positively hazardous, thing to do. Bernard did it a couple of times that fall; each time seemed more difficult than the last. But he had to get there. It was his inspiration. The place drew him with irresistible force. He got a bit of color in his pale, still boyish face that fall.

It was difficult to know what lured him there. Perhaps this polished cranium of an erstwhile tax investigator was truly an oracle? Was there a sentimental connection between Bernard and this strangely wind- and bee-eaten skeleton? The old man didn't look like much by now. Had he died out here in thrall of the bees, struggling vainly, with his wrists held by heavy chains? Or was he already dead when Bernard, Hans, and the other boys found him at the handicapped toilet by the Flogsta beach?

Perhaps it no longer mattered how he had died. Or who he'd been. In any case, he was something different now. For one of the rumors was true: a community of wild bees had made themselves a hive in his clean-eaten cranium. And where his poor brain has been, once upon a time, there were now sweet honey and the mysteriously rising and falling song of the aggressive forest bees. Their songs were about quite different, more fascinating things than his dried-up and evil zombie brain had ever conceived of. His once elegant chalk-striped suit had weathered the summer sun and the autumn rain surprisingly well.

His silver tie, on the other hand, was moldy, and the whole figure with the still chained wrists leaned forward at a more acute angle than the last time Bernard had been here. If nothing were done in the near future, the Oracle Sheriff would fall forward and be devoured by the soft, brown humus water of the bog. Yes, he'd become a bog man, a ghost, one of the silent ghosts of history. Perhaps archaeologists of the future would carefully poke in the creases of his wool suit, preserved by the bog water, searching for his fatal wound? What could have killed this man from the later part of the fifth millennium? Was he a hunter, a gatherer, or a farmer? Neither: he was a nothing, a parasitic growth on a society that had lost every trace of inner connection and meaning. And now? Now he was great, horizonless Nothingness itself, and consequently he was something new and promising.

What few pieces of wood and branches there were, this far into the bog—pieces of root from long-since vanished birches and the strangely shaped bilberry roots—had all acquired a strange, appealing, silvery surface. The humus acids seemed to do the same thing to craniums and to tree roots out here.

Bernard looked around. It wasn't altogether easy, for all the root pieces were so crooked, but he finally managed to find a couple of approximately equal length. With the top ends in his armpits—like crutches—and the opposite ends firmly pressed into the soft turf, he managed to stabilize the Oracle Sheriff. It looked a bit pathetic, but it ought to work pretty well. For a while, at any rate.

Bernard sat down on the stump in front of the Oracle Sheriff, who was now leaning over the bog the way an invalid leans on his crutches in the standing-room balcony at a football match. Right now, he seemed to want to have the whole world under surveillance.

Bernard looked around in the bilberry shrubs and found the short, club-shaped bit of silvery white wood he used during his visits to attract the attention of the Sheriff. Sometimes you had to knock three whole times. Sometimes once would be enough. This was especially the case before a thunderstorm. However, there wasn't much danger of thunder on a cool, clear October day like this one.

He knocked cautiously, first once and then once more, on the Oracle Sheriff's forehead. The angry buzzing of the dark wild bees who lived out here in the bog and gathered their honey from bilberries and heather was not slow in coming.

"Sheriff," Bernard said in a low but audible voice. "What do you know about the death of Medusa?"

(The small tendril of lighter-, of light-red substance in a marble top, something that's a vein in the marble, but perhaps also a tendril of hair, where had he seen it before? In a café? In one of the waiting rooms and corridors of the County Council, not uncommonly decorated in marble?

Was it a piece of living hair which, in a woman's sleep, clung for a moment to her pillowcase?

Or was it something he'd in fact seen *underground?* But now the swarm of bees had started to speak. When the dull buzzing turned into words, it would lecture like a real old fashioned German professor:)

"Different authors have different opinions on how Perseus actually killed Medusa. Hesiod says that it was with an ordinary sword, and all subsequent authorities that what was used was the kind of short Greek curved sword, the *harpê* that looks more like a scythe than an ordinary sword, and which later on in the labyrinthine history of weapons turns up as the scimitar or the short Turkish curved saber.

"According to Herodotus, the terrible severed head of Medusa is buried at Chemmis in Egypt, an ancient and awe-inspiring cult place, where the Gorgons are still said to inhabit underground caves. According to some authorities, Perseus brought the severed head to the goddess Pallas Athena, who affixed it to her shield. According to Pausanius, the head is buried forever under a small knoll in the market square of Argos, an insignificant place in ancient Greece.

"The connections between this mythology and the Mithraic can only be touched on here. Let us remember, however, that the oldest Greek name for the moon, *gorgonéon*, with its allusion to the dark, menacing face the Old Ones fancied they could see in the moon's disk, naturally has a connection to the above. In truth—the well of the past is deep! And what strange connections cannot be glimpsed between the Mithraic hero Perseus and a rising moon goddess. How deep the well is, and how strange the original spring must be, constantly filling a world empty of significance with the innumerable, sometimes menacing, sometimes benignly watching faces of myth. Significances, gestures, liberal arts, fill the once empty and meaningless world.

"Fundamentally more interesting than the severing of that horrible head is of course the version found in Lucian, which states that while Athena guided the hero's arm as he cut off the horrible head, Perseus *held a mirror* up to Medusa's face. That is how he conquered her. Ovid and Lucian are both agreed that in the vicinity of Medusa, 'all living things she regards: humans, plants, and animals' are turned to stone. Since the gaze of the Gorgon petrifies anyone she looks at, Medusa, according to this simple and seemingly logical reasoning, *must also be able to petrify herself.*

"For those among our future readers having some familiarity with self-referential systems of the type which, for instance, Dr. Kurt Gödel treats in his powerful 1931 essay 'Über formal unentscheidbare Sätze der Principia Mathematica und verwandter Systeme I' this, however, might not be obvious. (Submitted for publication November 17, 1930; furthermore, we ask our honored audience—companions on the road through these extensive connections—to note the supreme irony the late great mathematician has embedded in this 'I': an indication of a second part, a 'II' of this essay which can never be realized in this world.) Against the background of Gödel's results, it does not seem altogether certain that a procedure such as the one outlined above would be successful. Perhaps the gaze of the Medusa, too, might be gödelized? Of course there's a risk that Medusa, when she looks in the mirror, will perceive neither her own gaze nor that of anyone else, will neither be petrified nor not-petrified. It's possible that in that moment, Medusa sees nothing whatever. And that what she sees is the *truth* about herself.

"When something is mirrored, it is easy to lose sight of the essentials (to take just one example, the right side will become the left, and vice versa), and the essentials that are lost might have been just the thing that would cause petrification.

"The ancient horror we connect with the third of the Gorgons (as we all know, the other two were Stheno and Euryale), a horror of *the petrifying gaze* the reader is himself able to experience right now, is somewhat ameliorated by the concept of a Medusa who petrifies herself in the mirror. Considering Gödel's result, it is not at all certain that Perseus' dark mirror shield provides much of a consolation.

"In some accounts," the bee swarm pursued its lecture with undiminished energy, "that of Strabo, for example, Medusa is no longer horrifying. Her hair does not consist of snakes but of wonderfully flexible reddish tendrils which momentarily seem to have a life of their own. The Medusa of this atypical mythology is actually beautiful. Her beauty then becomes horrifying in itself. For beauty is—as all sensible people know—the beginning of horror. And we don't notice it. Just as the surfer wants to stand on top of the wave forever, this experience of beauty wants to stand, hovering, breathlessly still, in the tremendous moment before the tragedy has become fact, before horror breaks in. This Medusa might be described as *the Medusa of literary modernism,"* the black forest bees continued undaunted, at the same time flying in and out of what had once been the nostrils of a quite uneducated, malicious, and narrow-minded tax director, with progammatic unconcern.

They were momentarily silent. The sun was lower over the marshes now, and the shadows of the low shrubs started creeping further out over the water holes. Homeland, I knew all the birches, Bernard thought, once more knocking politely but firmly on the shimmering white forehead of the Oracle Sheriff.

"An ancient myth which we latter-day humans, conversely, do not find it as easy to deal with as the idealized, beautiful Medusa with her tendrils of noble hair," they continued with the experienced lecturer's feeling for effective pauses, "is the one that tells us that the dead body of Medusa is immediately transformed into two new beings, Chrysaur and Pegasus. Pegasus, yes, that is easy to understand. But Chrysaur—what use do we have for this seemingly whimsical emanation?

"(For us, living in much later times, and also so much farther away, it is often difficult to understand such things as the apparently easy and obvious logic with which the figures of ancient Greek mythology always stand ready to emanate from one another, as if they were only waiting, so to speak, for the liberating cut of the sword which will transform one deity into two new ones.)

"Let us then return to what we are better able to understand: *petrification.*

"Of course we have all observed *petrification.* Perhaps we do not primarily refer to such innocuous experiences as the familiar 'freeze' sometimes experienced by a tennis player before the net when he is about to deliver a smash, or by a hockey player who cuts loose with an excellent goal opportunity right in front of the opposition goal. In either case, the outward appearance is of a completely incomprehensible failure.

"At the critical moment, the ambitions of the respective athletes become so great, their exertion so immense, that it turns into its own object, and from the plane of the object, where the living, soaring ball in its trajectory ought to be the all-dominant content of his consciousness, its natural goal, his action is elevated to a sterile metalevel. Here *Success* suddenly takes over the role of the *Object*, not unlike the usurpers in stern Merovingian tales who imprison young princes in fortified and well-guarded towers in order to take over their legal powers under false pretenses. In a similar manner, Success, the dour usurper, seems to imprison the original impulse to movement of those athletes in a dark tower so that to the outside world, the once primeval impulse to movement seems in some mysterious way to be devouring itself.

"However, this kind of petrification

> ('And thus the native hue of resolution
> Is sicklied o'er with the pale cast of thought')

of course is not the same as the one threatened by Medusa. Medusa transfers to us the awful fear of being seen, which we all recognize from the horror-struck early moments in our lives when, one day, our mothers watch us with a new, cold gaze that tells us we *aren't* our mothers but rather this mysterious and deter-minedly enforced *Other* whom we get to know in the tired bathroom mirror of our mornings, and whose connection to ourselves we are never quite able to grasp.

"However, the question which for us must be the most profound, the most fundamental, is more precisely this one: What would be the appearance of the mirror that Perseus aims at Medusa? It doesn't help us much to know that it is his dark and polished shield. Does it resemble ordinary mirrors? What does it mirror when it isn't mirroring the horrifying aspect of Medusa?

"What's Perseus' dark mirror shield doing when there's no Medusa to look into it?

"Consequently, it is not entirely satisfactory to claim, with Ovid and Lucian, that 'all living she gazes on turns to stone.' What the Gorgon does with every-thing else is insignificant. The only significant thing is the moment *when her milky-white, oddly frozen gaze meets our own.* From the night table, for instance, a ranunculus, radiating an immense, milky-white emptiness, an emptiness like that of the world before Creation. From the slowly disintegrating eyes a gaze emanates which no longer seems to see anything. Or rather: it looks into the absolute nothingness which is the other, obverse side of the world. Consequently it is not true that Medusa turns us to stone.

"We ourselves carry out this transformation."

5. The Pit and the Pendulum

He didn't have a chance in the long run, and he should have realized it. But it's always difficult to see when the moment has actually arrived

All during September and October, Bernard lived in the yellow house, only avoiding the room, the office in the north gable, where he'd last seen his father. In order not be tempted to *look in there* again, he'd locked up very carefully after he'd pulled down the blinds and taken everything of value that was left. Of course there wasn't much left after Tax Director Lutweiler and his crew had emptied the contents of every drawer into their big, black plastic bags. They'd put the key in the mailbox. He didn't know why they'd left it there, exactly. Perhaps the idea was that it would be easily accessible if the authorities should find further action necessary.

When the harvest of apples and pears came like a scented wave across the garden at the end of August, things got easier.

The harvest was quite large this year, so he was able to stay for weeks in the yellow house without going out. Of course he had stomach pains from eating such a lot of windfalls. But there was nothing else he could do unless he wanted to go down to the Galleria in Billsta or to the Fast Food store in Flogsta and hook a few franks and some canned goods. That in itself wasn't easy since by now, they'd started to recognize him in quite a few places.

Bernard discovered that, with a certain amount of effort, it was possible to live at one end of a house, to sit there writing and listening to the branches of the old pear tree scratch against the roof and still be able to avoid the other end of the house completely. The border between the two parts of the house was everything to the north of the kitchen. At night, especially, he was careful not to step across the border. Not because he was superstitious but because nighttime had the ability to call up memories. And if there was anything he didn't want to remember it was the *pendulum movement,* not unlike that of the pendulum movement in an old clock, his father's dead body, hanging there for hours, had made from the chandelier in the office.

This movement was somehow incorporated in his own being, and sometimes in his imagination he'd see all kinds of objects around him repeating it. (He didn't even like to see children swinging in the park.) He'd felt like that from the moment he'd discovered his father's death and seen his dark-blue face with the oddly empty, white eyes, not unlike the eyes of a dead perch that's been left too long in the bottom of a rowboat.

He didn't like to leave the house. Partly he considered it unnecessary to show himself much in populated areas. He had a distinct feeling that there were some people who believed they had some claim on him and who'd make trouble for him as soon as he showed himself. The other thing that kept him in the house was the increasingly ambitious and interesting literary efforts which preoccupied him. In a pleasurable way, they seemed to open the doors to another world. This other world gave him a feeling of certainty, of security, of protection from everything else.

He started by writing six quite voluminous collections of poetry. He himself thought they were *solid,* but what he didn't know was that some critics might have found them somewhat obsolete. He only had a fly-blown and dog-eared copy of Bertil Malmberg's *Poems at the Border* and a much better preserved one of Gunnar Mascoll Silfverstolpe's poems to go by. After his third collection of big, visionary poems predicting the downfall of Western civilization, he tired of it. For two forceful diskettes, he became a regional poet.

Mostly because he didn't give a damn if Western civilization went under. He'd never noticed whether it had in fact penetrated all the way to the Billsta-Flogsta area. The question was whether it had ever crossed Öresund before starting to shrink back in the other direction. Anyway, the result had been some magnificent poems. But then it became clear the time had come for something a bit more nostalgic, autumnal, and regional, that much was clear.

Right at the moment, though, his poetry was in abeyance. For a few weeks he'd been engaged in a rather extensive and complicated spy thriller to be entitled *Operation Medusa.* He thought it was quite exciting, but he really missed some of the opportunities the poems had given him. He had the feeling that poetry provides more of an opportunity to sort of say different things *at the same time.*

(But he was already getting tired of the thriller, too, and he wondered whether there might not be some way of combining the poetry collection with the spy thriller.)

Everything looked the same, and yet it was quite a different house from the one he'd lived in as a boy. He could walk along the dilapidated fence at the bottom of the garden in the deep shadow of the large pine trees his father had once planted and see the huts he himself had built on the heavy bottom branches. He saw, once more, the surprising formations of chanterelles his mother once used to pick and spread out to dry on old newspapers in the kitchen, saving them for winter soup.

The chanterelles were older now, bigger and wearier. They stood there rotting away, getting larger, blacker, and more and more shapeless, and there would never again be anyone to care about the chanterelles in this garden. He remembered the small bonfires Jacob Foy would make in the fall, where leaves and twigs he'd raked together would send a melancholy smoke into the air. He could still see the half-overgrown traces of the small cold frame where his father used to force plants in the spring, before it was warm enough to put them into the cold soil of the flower beds. Now they were all overgrown with unhealthy-looking giant wild chervil that disseminated a strange odor of poison, rottenness, and autopsy room over the whole area down by the end of the garden fence.

It's odd, Bernard thought, *the way everything's getting overgrown.* In just

213

those few short years between *then,* when I was a boy, and *now,* when I'm getting to be a man. Soon all the zeppelins of my childhood will be sailing through clouds of stone.

When he turned to the house and saw the light in the kitchen, he was able to forget momentarily that the light up there was just a naked bulb and to remember for an instant the voices of his parents the way they had been just a few years ago, quarreling in a friendly manner, worried, sometimes planning for the future and sometimes analyzing what had already happened.

At any rate: he didn't have a chance in the long run, and he should have realized it.

One beautiful, clear Monday morning—it was one of those crystal-clear October days when the sparrows, like swarms of crazy punctuation marks, will suddenly fling themselves out of the rowanberry trees as soon as they hear a noise—a car drove up to the house. A youngish man in a camel's hair coat and thick-framed glasses whom Bernard had never seen stepped out of the car, also someone he'd started to recognize by now, that is the Jug.

You could see from far off that the man came from some kind of *service authority,* probably something to do with *youth care,* possibly the police. He moved with a very determined, slow step. With a small, rather thin, smile of recognition Elisabeth Verolyg, the school psychologist he'd had some dealings with that spring, stepped out of the other door of the car. Evidently it wasn't her car. The guy from the service authority had driven her.

Today she was dressed in a black winter coat and kept her long, red braid, whose firmness Bernard had admired from the first time he'd seen her, tucked up in an elegant silk scarf. She wore black gloves against the October chill.

Say what you want, but this school psychologist was undoubtedly *someone,* not just one in the row of faceless zombies, bog corpses, and ghosts whom, at earlier times in his life, Bernard had become used to seeing in such circumstances.

Bernard realized that what primarily mattered was preventing them from entering the house. That would only give them a lot of silly notions and the idea that perhaps he was still *living* in his father's house, dangerously and antisocially, and also of *how* he lived there. Above all it might—as things stood at present—lead to the discovery of the computer, this valuable stolen Atari on the upper floor. At this moment, Bernard perceived a threat to his entire literary activity. He swore that if he succeeded in getting out of this fix, he'd make sure the texts he'd already keyed in would never again be in danger of being plucked away before his very eyes in the shape of small $5^1/4''$ floppies.

Quick as a flash, Bernard jumped out on the other side of the house, rattled around the corner with the intention of getting out into the road, but was caught by the raspberry canes.

"Hello, Bernard," Elisabeth Verolyg said, not without some warmth in her voice.

The gentleman in the camel's hair coat was evidently less talkative. One glance was enough to show that he was *nobody*. The raspberry canes had more characteristics than that man's soul did, asleep or lost along the way.

"You aren't *living* here, are you?" Dr. Verolyg asked, with a trace of horror in her voice when she got to the word "living."

Bernard shook his head with practiced, pretend childishness. (How could anyone believe something so absurd?)

"No, I've got a foster family. I'm living just outside of Södertälje. I'm living in a big house. It's a family that's got a barn. And a tractor, you know. And a binder. And they've got dogs, too. Big, big dogs. Brown dogs . . . I've got a lot of nice brothers and sisters."

"What do you mean, *a lot?*"

"Four, I think. I don't know if I've met all of them yet."

"You're not used to having brothers and sisters, are you?"

"No. I'm unique."

Bernard knew quite well that this answer wasn't what was wanted. It showed he was a problem child, lacking the ability to live in a collective. For this reason precisely, his answer might lead the attention of his dangerous opponents away from the risky notion that perhaps he was still living here.

"Have you been inside the house?" the man asked in inquisitory tones. Bernard could feel, almost physically, in his wrists, what a pleasure it'd be to approach this man—some late night, say—from the back with quick, determined steps, down in some small road close to Lake Mälar where heavy waves drowned the sound of your steps, while the guy was standing there, absorbed by something in the trunk of his car, and then swiftly put a piece of heavy, rusty chain around his neck, tightening it. His movements would be jerky and violent at first, then get stiffer and stiffer. This *same* sly Bernard answered with great politeness that it wasn't that easy. Everything was locked and nailed shut. He'd only, Bernard continued, looked into the garden for a moment, while his foster father was doing an errand in his truck at the former Flogsta Manor.

"Why?"

"To look for a ball in the garden, an old football."

He wanted to give it to his new baby brother. He was a great little guy, really—liked playing ball, he did. This socially exemplary answer caused a certain amount of confusion. Bernard felt quite satisfied. There was no doubt he'd made a point. An *autistic* child taking his first stumbling steps on the road to the higher spheres of *collectivism*.

"Don't you want to sit in the car while you wait for your foster father, Bernard? It's chilly out today, don't you think?"

Bernard decided to take the risk. When all was said and done, there wasn't much he could do in this situation. Running away would be a big mistake. He sat down in the back seat next to Elisabeth Verolyg. Close up, her scent was heavy and convincing. There was also, however, a faint smell of alcohol and of mouth wash which told him she probably had a few drinks during working hours, too. She had a very wide mouth, like the mouth of a tragedy queen, you might say, and when she smiled, the corners of her mouth were pulled so far to the sides that her whole smile concealed some sad thought, a pain, a bitter memory which she surmounted, proudly and silently. But perhaps it was only a peculiarity of her facial muscles?

This, Bernard thought, is a fundamentally unsatisfied woman. This makes her doubly dangerous from my perspective.

"This, Bernard, is Inspector Karlström."

"I see. From my old school?"

"No. You've misunderstood a bit, Bernard. Inspector Karlström is from the Homicide Division of the State Police."

This close up, Bernard noticed in the rearview mirror that the man had a very narrow head. The distance between his eyes, in fact, was so small that it gave him a surprising resemblance to a flounder. For some reason, it calmed Bernard. A man who looks that ridiculous will never be able to hurt me or my plans, he thought. To be dangerous to me he'd have to look quite different.

"Awesome," Bernard said, raising his eyebrows charmingly.

"Inspector Karlström would like to ask you some questions. It's about something very tragic that happened here last spring."

"Yes," Karlström interjected. "The thing is, someone disappeared around here."

"What was his name?"

"That doesn't matter."

"Well," Bernard said, *competently,* "it might make a certain difference. There was a rumor around Billsta Center that a tax director by the name of Ernst Lutweiler had been found by the shore. Dead. Well, that's what I heard."

"When?"

"A couple of weeks after he—he'd visited my father."

The detective's ears seemed to prick up.

"Who did you hear it from?"

"Some guys down at the Galleria."

"What kind of guys? Names?"

"Allow me to say something," Dr. Verolyg interposed in a mild, firm voice.

"Do you have to right now?" Inspector Karlström said, almost angrily. "I've just gotten to a very important question . . ."

"At the time we're talking about I knew about this strange story, too. By that time, it had been in the evening papers. *Expressen* ran pictures of the burned-down toilet at least three days in a row."

When Bernard stepped out of the car, it at first became very silent in there. Elisabeth Verolyg was the first to break the silence.

"I wonder," she said in an affectedly interested tone, "why he returned?"

"Who? The Foy boy?"

"No. The other one."

"Lutweiler?"

6. Hans von Lagerhielm Goes in Search of Bernard Foy

Leffe Twelvefoot—could the name have anything to do with his small size? Or had he been involved in some episode connected with twelve feet of water? Be that as it may, this Leffe Twelvefoot spoke very quietly and indistinctly, with a rather garbled syntax. In Hans von Lagerhielm's experience, this was the kind of small, bashful guy who had a particular affinity for water. Perhaps for fire as well—but that was not as clear. Not at all for air and earth. Air and earth, Hans thought—that's Bernard. But to return to Leffe Twelvefoot, the fact was that you'd often see him down by Lake Mälar. He always seemed to be walking around on his own by the shore.

Flotsam and jetsam, cigar stumps that had floated ashore from the summer sailboats: broken little dolls who'd lost their heads or arms after weeks in the water; books fallen from the laps of the elegant sailing ladies of late summer when some sudden gust had caused the boat to pitch and the book had slid from the usually sunny foredeck. Those books could be dried out, and the leaves with some effort could be separated, so it was possible to see what the book had once been about . . . Gone for such a long time: the scent of suntan oil on their tanned backs. That is, if you didn't have the incredible luck to find just such a bottle of suntan oil in the rushes, a blue glass bottle, dark blue like the most ancient sea, with a few drops of musk-smelling elixir still preserved in the bottom.

Carefully sealed dark-brown hemp bags, insulated with asphalt and containing the finest raw Afghan marijuana, had been thrown overboard: deliveries from the old, loaded-down, heaving East German freighters going along at half speed across Bockstensfjärden's lead-gray, silent October mirror. A spinnaker pole that had broken off, thrown overboard by some hurried, exasperated regatta crew member, once he'd cut the new one.

Here high and low mingled, great and trivial were mixed the way only a large body of water can mingle objects and bring them together in new combinations. In brief: Leffe Twelvefoot walked around all day picking among the flotsam and jetsam with his poor, empty, hollowed-out marijuana-brain where only the indistinct feeling that something had been lost, something important, remained and kept him alive. It wasn't easy to know what he was actually looking for. Perhaps everything at once? Perhaps he'd recognize what he was looking for and only realize what it was in the moment of discovery?

No matter: Leffe Twelvefoot had got fifteen kronor for coffee and Danish, or whatever he wanted to use them for, and Hans had tried to formulate the question of where his friend Bernard Foy might be in four different ways when, to his surprise, he received—not quite an answer, but something pretty close to it.

"Gåsholmarna. You know, the other side of Björkölandet? The pits. Fucking weather. Cement barge? Black sails. Fucking rags. Beached three days ago. But he isn't there. Never has been. That fucking boat's sunk by now. Just the tips of the masts sticking up. Bernard isn't there. No, no. He *isn't*. Now you know that. Well. There were some motorheads in a plastic boat who took him from here all the way to the Strängnäs bridge. He stayed there. Had a fight with the motorheads. Just a nosebleed. Slept under the bridge last night. Damp and cold."

"And then?"

For Hans, as for anyone else who'd ever had anything to do with this bizarre and seedy teenager, with his poor burned-out brain, lacking in synaptic trigger substances, it was a complete mystery where he got his often detailed and up-to-the-minute information from the great landscape around him. If the boy had been able to fly—best of all perhaps, in some slow and low-flying vessel, an air balloon or a helicopter—across the Mälar bays and hopelessly dull suburbs, there might have been some natural explanation for all the things he knew. He would in fact have been an unbeatable tax director: thank God, no one would ever get the idea of offering him either that job or any other.

He'd have needed ravens for friends to know all the things he did know. Perhaps he really did have friends like that?

(For some time, Hans had had the feeling that everything was possible. There was a sea, an ocean on every side.)

Hans von Lagerhielm knew where the motorboat was; deep in one of the large reed banks below Flogsta Manor. A typical stolen camping boat from the summer. Quite a number of boats were stolen each summer, and they were usually left in the reeds. And if it *had* been left in the reeds it was a sure bet it wouldn't have any gas.

He'd counted on that, and when he biked down to the old beach jetty, rotting among the reeds, surrounded by the black poles of the vanished bathhouse, poles that stuck up from the water like teeth in the mouth of an old bag lady in a subway station, he didn't just carry a backpack full of useful items: marine chart, compass, parallel rule, and his father's sturdy old mooring line. He'd even put an almost full twenty-liter container of gasoline on his bike carrier. A little had splashed out—the bike trip had been quite perilous, going one-handed down the last few hills—but most of the stuff was there.

With his backpack and his shorts, his anachronistic long socks, his tool box and his gas container, Hans looked like an old-fashioned boy scout. A young man who performed everything he undertook with the utmost precision and determination. Somehow it showed that his father was older than other people's. If there was anyone suitable for conducting a real search for a vanished friend, he was the one.

If anyone had a chance of success, he'd be the one. Perhaps his task was not the easiest: the traces of his vanished friend and schoolmate, sixteen-year-old Bernard Foy, were not exactly fresh. Strange feet had trampled back and forth, turning the tracks of the solitary boy into a veritable labyrinth. Perhaps someone would get there ahead of him and ruin everything?

Actually, Hans had taken most things into account: that the boat would be half full of water, that the battery of the start motor and the pump would be stone dead, that the steering gear would be tangled. But he hadn't counted on all this mud which two months of waves washing over the boat had deposited in the poor, beached mahogany vessel. Some loving but not particularly maritime idiot of an owner had, to top it all, put *carpeting* on the cabin floor of the blighted vessel.

Hans tries to dig, bail, and scrape away the tough, blubbery blue mud. It wasn't easy to understand how such a thick, horrid layer could have made its way into the boat. But there it was. And it took time. Shoveling mud from carpeting is no easy task. This mud, and the hard, gusting wind with drops of rain which penetrated all the way into the reeds, put Hans in rather a melancholy mood.

There was no use trying to get the start-up motor going with a battery like that; Hans was steaming in the midst of the increasingly heavy and cold afternoon rain, when at last, with just the string, he managed to get one of the two Archimedes engines to fire. The other one seemed quite impossible, but it didn't matter that much, strictly speaking. It was a sort of triumph, anyway.

Hans was ready to go. His vessel was set. At that moment, he started thinking about Leffe Twelvefoot and his strange talents once more.

Perhaps Leffe Twelvefoot was actually *flying?* With some other, turned-away side of his poor, empty, chemically washed-out teenage brain? It's unwise to underestimate the talents of our fellow human beings, for we know so little about them.

Hans was more or less ready to leave shore. The engine was running; there was just a question of poling his way out of the reeds with his oars so that the propeller wouldn't get caught and entangled; there was only a bit of poling left before he'd be out in the inlet and round the headland. If the boat didn't leak too much he'd soon be out on Bockstensfjärden, at present sporting rather off-putting whitecaps. Then a short little guy in a worn wool sweater comes running down the slope, running so fast that he actually falls down a couple of times in the mud on the slope. It doesn't seem to affect him particularly. And of course it's Leffe Twelvefoot. Who else would it be?

He had to get all the way up to Hans and lean close to his ear: the noise from the newly awakened engine in the stolen and painfully emptied boat was that loud.

"What are you saying? Speak louder! I can't hear because of the engine!"

"There was a car finally that came and picked him up. A big old blue Plymouth. A lot of people in there. They let him off after. Now it's down by the hamburger joint the bikers use. You know. By the big Shell station at Björklunda Backar."

"What's *it?*"

"The thing that moves. The thing you wanted to get hold of. The thing in the middle of the narrative. The white spot."

"Hell, then time could be short," Hans von Lagerhielm thought, jumping on his bike. The hill up to Flogsta Manor seemed impossibly steep and muddy as well. He decided to hell with the gas container and threw his backpack on. He didn't dare leave that behind. It was a very old, heavy, black man's bike, so tall that Hans had trouble reaching the pedals.

"Why is it so important to you to get hold of him?"

Surprisingly, it was Leffe Twelvefoot who had contrived a grammatically correct sentence from down the jetty. It was so unusual that Hans did a double take.

"I have to find him before someone else does."

But Leffe Twelvefoot didn't seem particularly interested in waiting for Hans's answer. He was already practically *underneath* the old dilapidated jetty. He seemed to be hunting for something the storm had driven into the shallow water down there. Evidently this, and nothing else in the world, was absorbing his whole attention. Hans didn't take the time to ascertain what he might have found, still less to thank him.

7. The Hierophant

He didn't have a chance in the long run, and he should have realized it. But it's always difficult to see when the moment has actually arrived. This happened the day after Bernard's bizarre meeting with the detective inspector. It was the last Tuesday in October, shortly before Bernard, for various reasons, decided literally to go underground.

Down at the ICA food store, which is not situated in the Flogsta passage like the other stores but instead lies aristocratically removed down by the Billsta highway, right at the intersection of the roads to the Flogsta beach, there's a delicatessen counter. It doesn't have anything out of the ordinary, like goose liver or Swedish crayfish or eggplant, but it still has things to tempt the local inhabitants. Barbequed chicken, Swiss cheese of quite acceptable quality, expensive but fairly tasty little patés, pickled herring with onions, of course, and a few other things that pleasure-loving people tend to buy on Friday afternoons.

This particular Tuesday in October, Bernard Foy would again catch sight of his former school psychologist, Dr. Elisabeth Verolyg. This happened just as he was quickly turning back to the delicatessen counter after having put two cans, one of Portuguese sardines in oil and another, bigger and more difficult to handle, of fermented Baltic herring of the excellent Röda Ulven brand, inside his leather jacket.

He was not surprised, not frightened either, but instead regarded the Jug (as they called her at the Central School) with a winning smile while he remained standing in the open door. It's always a big advantage to stop and start a friendly conversation with someone you know as you're leaving a store where you've hooked something.

Today she was dressed in a severe gray wool skirt which showed off her round, generous hips. A freshly ironed white blouse. An elegant dark-blue jacket rested on her powerful shoulders. A multiple-strand pearl necklace, evidently not of real pearls, adorned her strong, only slightly wrinkled neck. She had an unusually long and beautiful neck, a real Djursholm neck, you might say.

Elisabeth Verolyg was now regarding Bernard with her cool gray-blue eyes, not in an unfriendly manner, not intimately either, but with the kind, scrutinizing expression she used for her clients. Bernard, on the other hand, had eyes for nothing but her neck. Of course this was a moment when they tested each other's strength. Both of them already knew that.

Elisabeth took the initiative, perhaps a bit brutally, with the practiced professional ease in sorting out situations and making swift cuts through the external layers of human contact to essentials that is habitual with the experienced therapist, psychiatrist, and psychologist:

"You were really fibbing yesterday, weren't you. You lied like a used car dealer, falsified like a counterfeiter, charmed like an actor, went on just like the completely false, lying, autistic little creep you've always been. How would you have managed if I hadn't helped you out, you little liar?"

Bernard didn't answer. His silence was not discourteous but forced on him. He was completely absorbed in his admiration of this still firm fifty-year-old body, with its evidently still virginal breasts, long, powerful thighs, and erect, almost queenly posture. Actually, he was completely or almost completely absorbed in increasingly bizarre fantasies about what he'd do to her if he could have her to himself. Women often provoked Bernard to lively fantasies, but hardly anyone he knew did it as intensely and consistently as this school psychologist.

Earlier, he'd had so-called "talks" with her. The first time it had been in connection with a certain incident that happened in the seventh grade. He'd gone for a walk on a snowy day with some friends on top of the school building and had gone through a glass roof, not readily noticeable in the new-fallen snow. He'd ended up in the school attic after a rather unsuccessful climbing expedition. It had annoyed the then headmaster, Måns Wedelin, enormously that Bernard and the two friends who'd been with him hadn't been killed in the fall, especially since they'd happened to surprise the headmaster in an astonishingly private situation in one of the small, dusty cubbyholes up in the attic.

The three schoolboys had found the fact that the headmaster indulged in such practices as natural as they'd found his horror, indignation, and rage unnatural. What had really confounded them had been the extremely peculiar and bizarre *picture* the headmaster had used as a foundation for his evidently failing fantasy life as he practiced his autoerotic contemplation. The picture was so surprising, so bizarre, so completely revealing, that for weeks after, the three youngsters were able to collect a sizeable audience in corners of the schoolyard, describing this picture. Of course they were not readily believed, but on the whole, this only increased the entertainment value of what they had to offer.

(A recurring high point of this story was when Hans von Lagerhielm, one of the three, was said by Bernard to have shouted, *"Stop the machine!"* right after the three boys' perilous landing, which, however, had been softened by some rolls of carpeting that had been delegated to the attics.)

Of course Headmaster Måns Wedelin knew this, and he hated it. Just a few days later, he'd sent Bernard to the school psychologist. His rather obvious hope was that Bernard's fall through the attic roof might be interpreted as a symptom of such profound cognitive, emotional, and social disturbance that it might lead to his removal from the school. It was a brash attempt, based on the supposition that the school psychologist would do what the headmaster wanted. What he forgot, however, was that this particular psychologist belonged to an older, and consequently not politically adapted, generation. She had her Djursholm accent and her Djursholm neck.

The headmaster's clumsy tactics, explicable only if you assume an intelligence which couldn't for a moment be compared to Bernard's, and which was also too limited to realize this fact, were founded on the circumstance that the headmaster expected Bernard to tell the school psychologist *exactly what he'd seen*. Of course Bernard would then be unmasked as *a pathological little liar* if he tried to explain the picture to the school psychologist.

Wedelin's plan was simple, ingenious, and certain to fail when applied against a youngster such a Bernard Foy.

Naturally, Bernard didn't say a single word either about the horrible *picture* or about the headmaster's bizarre autoerotic activities.

Bernard and his friends had never been up on the roof. He had no explanation to offer as to why it had broken. Perhaps the weight of all the wet March snow up there.

On the other hand, the headmaster had offered the boys certain economic incentives if they would come with him up to the attic—to do what, Bernard didn't have the slightest idea. They had, however, become somewhat bewildered and frightened by his agitated demeanor and had left the attic through the ordinary staircase to the passage outside the headmaster's office. They had only found out about the big crash of the glass roof when other boys told them once they were back in the schoolyard.

According to Bernard, nothing further had occurred, actually, except for one peculiar detail. What was it? Well, after this incident, Bernard had several times heard the headmaster's voice crying from the attic, "Stop the machine!" That was all. No. Bernard had no idea what he could have meant.

The story, of course, was perfect. It was sufficiently murky, sufficiently disconnected, to place exactly the right associations right where they should be, as far as a normally trained school psychologist was concerned. Not many weeks passed before Bernard and his schoolmates had the satisfaction of seeing Headmaster Måns Wedelin apply for leave of absence due to serious symptoms of stress. The illness seemed to be a protracted one, for since that winter nobody had seen him, and nobody missed him either.

The second time Bernard had been called into the Jug's pleasant consulting room with the many binders on the shelves and the plants in the windows, he'd cast a glance of recognition at two details which had fascinated him on his first visit: the analyst's couch, which confused him a lot since he couldn't guess at its purpose, and the Jug's paperweight of red Bohemian glass on a corner of her desk.

It wasn't that long since this conversation had taken place; it was some time in the spring, and what was involved was the catastrophic tax review visit at Bernard's father's house and all it might have brought in its wake. There was also a rumor already circulating in the school about the briefcase which had been found in such a strange way. For example, what was the meaning of "The Polished Sheriff"? A strange expression which had even been found as graffiti on a lavatory wall.

This time Bernard didn't feel he had the same rapport with Elisabeth Verolyg. She had received him sitting behind her desk, not sitting next to him on the couch the way she had the first time, something Bernard had noticed immediately. The consulting room, with its smell of floor wax and coffee brewed in a coffeemaker, also had a faint smell of medicine, of iodine, or carbolic acid, of disinfectant.

She hadn't been as elegantly dressed, and when she had leaned down across a document drawer in the large fire-proof cabinet where student files were kept, her shirt had slid up, revealing a piece of rather tanned skin between the waistband of her pants and the back of her bra.

They hadn't gotten far with their problem that time, either.

He'd had an easy time convincing her that the whole story of The Polished Sheriff and his mysteriously recovered briefcase was nothing but a typical schoolyard tale. What else could it be? Made up by some admiring eleven-year-olds, most probably. That he himself had been assigned a part in the legend was something he couldn't take responsibility for.

(Absent-mindedly, he took the small red Bohemian crystal ball from her desk, a paperweight. It was beautiful, surprisingly heavy.)

"Put that back, if you don't mind. It's very valuable."

"Why?"

"It's a memory of my father."

She had told him this in a voice that said it should be obvious that no outsider could be allowed to touch memories of her father. At this moment she, of course, appeared to be the neurotic one, and Bernard appeared calm, manly, and convincing as he carefully replaced the small ball on her desk. This was a kind of breakthrough, a moment of contact. But what kind of contact was hard to say. The ball had a row of small holes. Perhaps the idea was that you could put twigs in there, the first birch twigs of the season or perhaps the first pussy willow twigs, to get a tasteful and appealing table decoration.

Suppose this crystal ball could exist in two, or perhaps three, worlds simultaneously. Suppose Mr. Lutweiler, in some other world entirely, was also staring into the very same crystal ball. Suppose some Third Person was, right now, able to watch them both through the dusky red twilight of the ball, and that far away in another world a Fourth Person could watch the three of them . . . Reflected as if in a small window. Where Bernard Foy is visible in his leather jacket and his worn jeans, not unlike a sorcerer with a crystal ball lifted in his hand, but where Dr. Ernst Lutweiler too, a very small man, is visible in the projection of the ball, in his chalk-striped suit, holding a yellow pigskin briefcase in his hand.

The autistic boy had unexpectedly spoken, and Elisabeth Verolyg had listened, watching him with the same blue-gray, clinical gaze which for a brief moment had assumed a different, warmer, more cat-yellow shade.

8. The Voices of the Whist Players in the Arbor

It's doubtful whether Hans Hansdorff had ever really been a poet.

"Poet—baloney, he was no more a poet than my coachman or my cook at Flogsta,'' Carl Rutger von Lagerhielm would say to the card players in the arbor at the Billsta Home when one of the trembling old men with worn playing cards in his hands started to bring it up.

Of course the issue was old Hans Hansdorff's pretensions to the title, as usual. In his far advanced senility, Hansdorff was still a man with quite a strong grip and an extremely choleric temperament; consequently, no one would hint at it except on the regularly occurring occasions when he had to leave the arbor to go inside the Home and take a leak. But then, they took the opportunity of calumniating him all the more.

"Poet like hell,'' shouted the former submarine mate, later radio shop owner, Torsten Simmerling from Göteborg, who was rather hard of hearing. "He was Gunnar Mascoll Silfverstolpe's chauffeur. That was what he was, his chauffeur, nothing else. I have that on good authority, *very* good. And it was there, at Stora Åsby, that he picked up everything he knows about his so-called poet friends and Prince Eugen and that whole gang. A bluff, a mythomaniac, that's what he is. He never tells the truth.''

"I doubt that very much,'' said Carl Rutger, examining the poor hand he'd just been dealt by the conceited little radio store owner. In the first place, if he's lying when he says that he's a poet, it's a kind of argument for him being one. So whether he's a poet or not, he's still a poet. This is what's called a 'constructive dilemma' in medieval logic.

"Apart from scholastic logic, however, there's quite a reasonable empirical argument for him. What you say about him being the chauffeur is totally unreasonable. The Silfverstolpe family at Stora Åsby was never able to afford a private chauffeur. Åsby was no castle. It was a rather modest captain's house. You can see that from Sten Selander's foreword to Silfverstolpe's poems. Unfortunately, young Bernard Foy has borrowed my copy, or else it would have been easy to end the argument. Confound the boy!''

"How do you know that?'' asked the man from Göteborg, the former submarine mate and, until recently, radio store owner Simmerling, in his most old-mannish, cranky, and insistent manner. "And besides, what *confounded kind of logic* is it, anyway? Do you really mean to say that everybody who hasn't been the chauffeur of a poet has to be a poet? Either you're a poet or the chauffeur of a poet? What happens, for example, if a poet is the chauffeur of a nonpoet? To take just one example of the fallacies in such a negative, circular argument.''

"But I happen to know for a fact,'' Carl Rutger continued unabashed, "that the great poet Gunnar Mascoll Silfverstolpe, one of the eighteen members of the Swedish Academy, never lived at Åsby once he got out of the *gymnasium,* except once in a great while, for some holiday or other. He had an apartment on Kungsholmen, in fact."

"I'd really like to know how you know that," the querulous old man continued uninhibitedly.

Carl Rutger used to say that he *loved polemics,* and once he got started, there was really no way to get rid of him except to say that everything he maintained or believed he remembered, or wanted to prove, or had experienced, *was exactly the way he said it was.*

"Oh, I've forgotten how I know. Who's got the king?"

"And the *Italia* expedition?" former police constable Sverre Ståhl asked from his corner. "Didn't he go on that, either?"

"Don't forget," said the terrible Simmerling, banging the ace on the table so that the old men's spilled afternoon coffee splashed over cards and table ribs and over a copy of *Södertälje Post Tidning* the fresh autumn breeze had riffled apart, "that I was the one who was at the southern tip of Greenland that time with *Starkodder* from Sundsvall, Sweden's only ocean-going icebreaker at that time. We were the ones who fetched the Swede back, Lieutenant Einar Lundborg.

"That damn Hansdorff has been sitting here, hearing it all from me thousands of times when we've been playing cards, every detail about the drift ice and the airship and the Italians who ate up the Swede when he couldn't get any further, everything, no, not everything, for there's a small detail he's got from Mrs. Bouveng, the rest he got from me." (Mrs. Claire Bouveng was the benign manager of the Billsta Home; once, when she was a schoolgirl, she'd been ordered up on the terrace roof of the Detthow school to watch, together with the other girls in her class, the white, fantastic, silver-gleaming airship pass over the city on its northward journey.)

"And then, damn it all if he doesn't sit there and tell it all back, right to my face. Because he's—I *can't* put it any better than that—so damn senile he simply doesn't remember who he heard it from."

"Calm down," said Carl Rutger von Lagerhielm, always courteous. "We all have our little weaknesses. Anyway, we're here to play cards, not to argue. But look who's here, it's Hans coming back. Then we'll see who takes the trick."

Mrs. Claire Bouveng was not all that fond of the card parties. On the one hand, she was afraid that the old men might get pneumonia in the drafty arbor. It might be all right on warm days in July. But now, at the end of August, it was rather hazardous, even if they did have blankets over their legs. On the other hand, she feared that their horrible quarrels might lead to strokes or possibly aneurisms in their fragile, alcohol-soaked arteries.

It struck her the old men were lucky to be in one of the last private old people's homes in the district. If it had been one of the awful communal old people's barracks with eight oldsters in every room, they'd have been tucked into bed by this time. And never, by the farthest flight of the imagination, would they have been allowed anything as daring as dragging blankets into an arbor. Then they'd have been properly tucked up in their beds at four in the afternoon, willy-nilly, since that the employees left at this time of year. One could only hope the State wouldn't get the idea of forbidding frivolous private nursing homes like this one, with the dangerous lack of *societal control* it must entail.

Such dark thoughts did not disturb the warm and friendly Mrs. Bouveng for long. However, there was something about this socializing in the arbor that created disorder in her arrangements, without her being quite clear about how it happened.

It was the same thing every year. The arbor created disorder; it was a power center of a different kind than the ordinary ones, and if it hadn't been for the nice Mr. von Lagerhielm, who had such a wonderful knack of dispensing calm and of keeping quarrels and contention among her old men to a minimum, she'd hardly have countenanced an *outsider* coming here to play cards.

But he was a baron, after all, and such a wonderful person besides. In addition, he had such nice little jokes. Once, last year, around midsummer, he'd made her laugh, old as she was, by comparing her to the major's wife at Ekeby, in Selma Lagerlöf's *Gösta Berling's Saga,* and the senile old men in the arbor to the cavaliers at Ekeby.

Now Hans Hansdorff was coming back. Whether he'd been a poet, or only the chauffeur of one of the great '30s poets, was not so easy to determine. But he really looked like a great poet, strolling down the garden path. His fly was undone, and there were visible spots of an old man's slow-running urine on his trousers. His shirt bore traces of the pea soup at lunch, but his mane, the handsome mane of white hair, large blue eyes, and imposing nose, might have belonged to a great and important poet. Or were there no poets left in the country anymore?

Hans Hansdorff cleared his throat loudly, spat three times into the flower bed, did not let on for a moment that he'd seen the newly arrived Mrs. Bouveng, and picked up his cards with the dignity of a man who knows that his presence makes every social occasion a little bit more important, perhaps even historical: more memorable, anyway.

"It's a pity about Foy," he said, surprisingly. "So stupid and unnecessary. I wonder what happened to his boy, by the way?"

"I did see him a few times this summer," Carl Rutger answered affably. "He sees my son Hans some, and sometimes both boys will come to my house and get help with this and that. I teach them how to snare pikes instead of catching them on a hook, things like that. But I honestly don't know where he's living now. One has to assume he's been taken care of somehow. He should be in some kind of foster home by now, the way things are. But I don't know where his foster home is. I can ask Hans if you're interested."

"I ask," Hans Hansdorff continued gravely, "because I came upon him in a very bizarre situation yesterday afternoon, not far from here."

"Really?"

"*Extremely* bizarre."

"In what way?"

"He was sitting on a park bench, down by the shore walk in Flogsta. With a very well turned-out, reddish-haired lady in her fifties."

"But isn't it a good thing for the boy to have some human contact after all the sad things he's been through? I don't understand what you mean by *bizarre.*"

"No, but if you'd seen *the way* they were sitting, you'd have understood."

"Really?"

"More *on top* of each other than next to each other. Yes. *Straddling* each other. That's how. Young people have no shame nowadays."

"Oh?"

(As often happened to Hans these days, the old man with his gorgeous white poet's mane of hair forgot what he had to tell just as he was going to tell his story. Or else he might forget that he was the one telling the story. He'd suddenly assume the pose of interested listener just as his listeners were waiting for the point.

This made his conversation into a rather tragic series of great, always unfulfilled promises. On the other hand, one could not claim that he was trying to dominate the group he was in. Although there was a certain dominant quality to him anyway.)

"Well, since my old woman died I think almost everything's meaningless," Simmerling said. He had the kind of loud voice often encountered in older marine officers and people like that. "I should have shot myself with my old service pistol from the navy long ago. Since everything's gotten so damn boring. But I can't for the life of me remember what drawer I've put the confounded pistol in. I've looked for it like crazy. But once I find it, then you'll see something."

"*The drift ice,*" Hans Hansdorff suddenly said. "I remember it now. No, not the *drift ice,* but the *icebergs,* southeast of Greenland, that's what fascinated me. Enormously. They had that thing. They had meaninglessness."

"They fascinated *you,* did they? I wonder how *that* came about? *I* was the one who was south of Greenland with Vice-Admiral Wrangel in the *Starkodder.* That's *my* experience you're trying to steal from me. Well—what the hell does it matter, anyway. What is it that's occurred to you?"

"It's one of the most important memories in my life. You know, you think everything in your life is going to mean something special. That everything has some significance. But those enormous, beautiful, white, dangerous icebergs, gliding solemnly toward us through the seas, one by one—as if there were an infinite number—meant nothing at all, really. I've never in my life seen any objects that made it as obvious as those did. Nothing at all. They just were there. Or they only signified themselves. Those of the mates who didn't have anything to do just then were standing on the foredeck, spellbound, trying to read some kind of meaning into them. They wanted to see human shapes, faces, profiles, animal shapes, the way people like to see human and animal shapes in cloud formations. But the main thing is that there was nothing there, then, except those icebergs. They were meaningless, quite meaningless, and that was their meaning. I was twenty-one or twenty-two when I stood there at the rudder on the bridge of the old State icebreaker. The bridge of the *Starkodder*—just imagine—under a plume of graphite-black engine smoke, and I saw them come gliding, quietly, one by one, in the solemn, frosty, strangely hazy June air, just south of Greenland . . . I'm sure you realize that summer isn't much of a summer up there. And I thought: they're coming like the years of my life. Since that time, I haven't been easily frightened. I've sort of become friendly with His Majesty Meaninglessness."

"I think you've spoken well," Carl Rutger von Lagerhielm said with sudden emotion, which manifested itself in his gray-blue eyes looking more glazed than usual. "It reminds of those bog men, dead for such a very long time, that archaeologists find from time to time, wrapped in ancient mantles of coarse fabric, with a hole from their enemy's flint arrow, which was their bane, still visible at the temple, like a dark shadow. They're so well preserved by humus acid in the bogs that it seems as if they'd stand up at any time and start waddling about the bog again. And that inspires a feeling of the most profound horror."

He made an exquisite rhetorical pause.

"But isn't that just the horror of an old, lost *significance* starting to move again?"

"I don't think you've altogether understood me," said the former poet, possibly only manor chauffeur, Hansdorff, in a slightly injured tone. "You haven't understood me. Not at all, because you see something negative, something threatening and frightening, in the fact that more and more of the world, of people's actions and words, seem to be losing their original significance. I, on the other hand, don't you see, I see the mystical, the grandiose, in life's lack of significance. God wants nothing. Because if God had wanted anything, then it would have come into being long ago. God only means himself. That's what I realized that Arctic day in the early summer of 1928, when I saw the big icebergs gliding through Dansköbukten, one by one, large, dramatic, and completely meaningless."

"But my dear Hans, you weren't the one who was there. I was the one who saw those icebergs in 1928." Torsten Simmerling couldn't keep quiet any longer. "You've never been north of Grisslehamn! You're taking *my* icebergs!"

"Don't carry on like that, you damn *long-term-care patient*. Let's say they're your icebergs. Yours, and everyone's, and no one's. But just the same, it's in *my* memory they keep coming. Gliding in the crystal air, through deep green water that looks almost as sluggish as oil because it's so close to freezing, a June day in 1928, in Dansköbukten. Searching for Lieutenant Einar Lundborg, the Swede, and for wreckage from the tragically lost air ship *Italia*—well, you already know the rest, don't you, gentlemen?"

Among those sitting in the arbor only the old poet was standing up, with shaking hands and a tremble that seemed to travel through even his enormous, white mane of hair. At this moment, his face wore a pleading expression. As if he were someone asking for mercy at the last minute.

9. The Hanged Man

The Jug had put her Volvo where the "No Parking" zone began; there wasn't anyone around on a night like this. It was already quite dark and unpleasant. Gradually, after having given him a protracted blow job with the pedantic thoroughness of a middle-aged woman, she pulled her skirt up and placed herself so that she was straddling him. He came very quickly, but to his surprise, not so quickly that she wasn't with him. He felt he was ready to start over again right away.

Meanwhile, he absent-mindedly bit the heavy braid of red hair on the right side of her strong neck, where an artery could plainly be felt against the left corner of his mouth.

He'd never had a woman who seemed to get so much out of him. She seemed capable of subjecting herself to him in everything.

The wind pulled at her reddish hair, and her face was wet, whether from saliva or from tears wasn't easy to know, and there was an intense smell of sex about her. He had a feeling that these fifty-year-old genitals, apparently involved in their own labyrinth of violent orgasms, wanted to swallow his own painfully erect organ, a part of his body which right now didn't know where it was: in heaven or in hell. He was sitting very uncomfortably and had a feeling that his back might break at any moment, but that's the way it had to be.

The whole time short, nervous waves were pounding the shore. Gravel rolled back and forth at the shoreline, an empty bottle beat against a rotting pier support, a dead fish floated belly up, and its corpse smell was noticeable through all the other smells, perfumes, scents which filled this moment.

At such moments the Pendulum Movement might unexpectedly return to Bernard, at first very slowly and then livelier, until he could actually see his dead father hanging from the ceiling in his modest office.

Sometimes he had the feeling that it was the whole blind, implacable energy of the universe which slowly rocked his dead father with his swollen blue face. In some strange way, this unendurable pendulum movement reminded him that at the same time as it was going on, elementary particles were disintegrating at immense speed. Distant galaxies rotated in implacable, lazy movements, hundreds of thousands years old. The quantum mechanical wave functions oscillated in their Hilbert spaces. The Fourier components marched with tin-soldier movements in their much denser momentum space; the multiparticle configurations swept ahead in their phase space:

"Like cloud shadows across the countryside"

and it was all implacable and unwanted by everyone. Actually, it only existed to distract his attention from something else that was more important. There was no

230

order to geometry, or to space, any more than there was to anything else in the world, loudly resounding with pendulum movements. In brief, his was a rather uncommon spiritual state. Approximately the state some people call ecstasy, and which, in the opinion of other people, absolves one from legal responsibility. In the world it was only one state among all the others.

He felt a panic that was not unknown to him: *Breathe on the surface of the mirror, he told himself, and the terrible picture will disappear again.*

What force was it that made the dead man swing back and forth? Did he really swing in the wind? Was there a window still standing open after the sheriffs had gone? Their cigar stubs could still be seen here and there on the worn carpet. They'd been ground into the pattern while the sheriffs stood there filling their black plastic bags with accounting books, salary lists, and receipts. They'd even packed an advertising calendar from a bulldozer company, the kind that promotes lightly clad ladies in jeans on every page, and taken it along. Perhaps in the belief that there would be some notations which might throw some light on the extensive crimes against the State his father had apparently engaged in for a long time; he'd paid people's salaries under the table and kept his little concern going, giving work to twenty people by avoiding the crushing employment tax.

A few loose pages had floated back and forth along the floor in the strong cross draft. A fig tree that seemed not to have had enough water withered in a corner.

The food bowl of the dead German shepherd was still there in another corner. As far back as Bernard could remember, it had belonged to the dog and to no one else.

To the last, Jacob Foy had been a methodical and practical man. Before he stepped on the chair, pulling the noose around his neck, he'd taken off his rather worn shoes (with traces of wet mud) so they wouldn't leave spots on the worn but solid leather seat of the office chair.

For weeks, the then tax director, Ernst Lutweiler, had searched for the three remaining bulldozers and the two tractors, down by Lake Mälar and also from a low-flying helicopter far out over Sjunkarmossarna, but without finding them. It was all in vain. It was clear to Bernard's father that what couldn't be saved had better be destroyed, rather than end up in the hands of the enemy. The operations he'd carried out the last few weeks had been extremely effective. As far as his father's bulldozers were concerned, they probably reposed far in the depths of Sjunkarmossarna by this time, Bernard thought, not without admiration for his father's resoluteness in his last days. The same thing was repeated in so many places in Sweden in those terrible times. Actually, there was nothing special about either him or his father, Bernard thought.

I'm quite ordinary. Actually I'm a very trivial, completely commonplace human being, Bernard told himself. Nothing remarkable has happened. Absolutely nothing at all. Once again, he felt panic, which was not unknown to him. *Breathe on the surface of the mirror, he told himself, and the terrible image will disappear.*

10. Images at the Beginning of Night

In order to, as the saying goes, get the show on the road, and at long last ensure that we get somewhere on the journey toward dusk and slowly approaching night, which you have evidently decided to undertake in our company, we still have quite a few things to relate about the landscape.

To do a brief recap and to say whether, contrary to expectation, you've managed to learn something, we first of all want to remind you that at an early stage, and due solely to pedagogical concern for those who will one day find this manuscript and, against their will or not, have to become our readers, we've divided the landscape into four segments:

The bottom left-hand segment, or, more scientifically expressed, the southwest segment, of this rectangle encompasses nothing but the endless marshland of Sjunkarmossarna, which eventually and gradually evolves into the forests and high plateaus of Östergötland, difficult and dangerous terrain, where the inexperienced wanderer does not go with impunity.

The upper left-hand corner is the, at least in former days, idyllic Billsta area of small industry. Down by the shore of Lake Mälar, it gradually turns into shallow, reedy inlets, fingers from the extensive Bockstenssundet. Here there are not only small industries, quaint little workingmen's cafés, piles of trash, graveyards for junked cars, cement bags, and all kinds of peculiarities. Here, too, are cosy little supervisors' houses, smallboat docks, verandas, and arbors which even today spread a mild scent of white lilac through the long May afternoons. But now the lilac bushes are ravaged and empty. Great autumn, with its pale light able to reconcile almost everything, is already on its way, and the wind blows savagely through the apple trees, making the fruit hit the ground by the dozen.

Far out on Bockstensfjärden where a lone West German steamer is beating its way into larger and larger inlets which, far to the west, lead first to the port of Västerås and then to that of Köping, the waves have already assumed the white beards they normally only assume by the end of November.

There'll be an early fall this year. A lot of fruit as well. Plums are ripening in the old, neglected castle garden which once belonged to the proud Flogsta Manor, which is still the only building of any size in the upper right-hand rectangle of our four-segmented landscape scheme.

Here the landscape reaches down to the calm, shallow inlets of Lake Mälar; here dramatic cliff terraces fall down to the water. Here are all the traces of an older, kinder time: dilapidated bourgeois summer houses with bathhouses and yellow wooden fences down by the water, chimney stocks and wild apple trees from vanished houses, garden plots and outlooks.

In addition to Flogsta Manor, which, as we have said, belongs to the County

232

Council, and which was used for drug rehabilitation for a time, but whose use might at the moment seem somewhat indeterminate, there is the Billsta Home, a small, private nursing home and, strangely isolated in the countryside, almost as if it were a prison, Billsta Central School, a huge concrete building on one of the hills, to which Bernard had an opportunity to make sporadic visits during some absent-minded years in the early '80s.

As we've already remarked, the name of the acting headmaster is Sture Lannerstedt, and the school psychologist is Dr. Elisabeth Verolyg. We already know the name of some former pupils. Other than that, this institution is rather foreign to us.

The lower right-hand landscape segment, which we have not touched on so far, must now be described. It contains the residential district of Sjunkarmossarna, a few hundred concrete blocks of up to twenty stories, primarily inhabited by melancholy immigrants who don't seem to have a whole lot to say to one another, and not to anyone else, either, and whose only social ambition seems to be to occupy all the available parking places in the area as soon as possible with large and small campers, all of which disappear out on the roads during the July vacation.

Of course there are many more things in this district. There are pockets here, secrets, invisible ties and unclear connections between people, terror and lust. It only lacks its poet.

In the intersection of the four segments there's the railroad crossing the Södertälje Canal on a tall, dizzying cast-iron bridge from the turn of the century. The canal runs into Lake Mälar here, and to the left of the bridge is the Sjunkarmossen Center, with subway station, bus terminal, and a shopping arcade which, among other things, sports a shop which at present supplies young Bernard Foy with some equipment for his increasingly resolute literacy practice.

There are also a few street market stands where the foreigners buy tropical fruits and vegetables by the case and the Swedes buy one or two tomatoes, where deals in old cars are struck, and where, in the evening, low-keyed commerce in drugs and teenage prostitution is routinely carried out.

The fact is that Bernard Foy knows at least one of the girls. That's not so strange. She sat in front of him in class, diagonally to the left. At the time, he liked her skinny, pale neck a lot. He can still remember how she used to play with her small gold confirmation cross, how she kind of let it disappear to rest in there in the warmth of her lips. Things like that would give the then twelve-year-old Bernard furious erections. He'd often lean forward as far as he could to get a glimpse of her still virginal breasts through her sleeveless summer dress.

Like everything else he's ever seen in his life, he remembers every detail of this neck, remembers a small, round liver spot high up under her left ear, and her special way of inclining her head. She hasn't been seen here for a while, Bernard notes, as he comes sauntering in the windy furor of the autumn evening. He walks with a rocking step—he always has. Self-absorbed perhaps. The elbows of his black leather jacket are very worn, and his jeans are more white than blue. He's exactly the kind of person who will be denied entrance by guards, no matter how sober he is. He's a young man compact rather than big, that is, what he lacks in height is compensated for by a kind of inner density. Not seldom, he can be seen in the Sjunkarmossen shopping arcade. He has some things to take care of there, but now no one has seen him for a while.

This time, he's actually on his way to the community library. He still has the feeling that he has too little *to go by*. To create literature demands other literature. He's been sitting at his keyboard for quite some time now, longer than he'd originally intended. Something, perhaps the feeling of having access to another world, or anyway to another galaxy that's easy to enter, and so getting away from the ordinary world, fascinates him to such an extent that he forgets the passage of days and of weeks.

Now it's suddenly night in the abandoned yellow house with all the echoes of voices and shadows of people who are no longer there. Bernard felt a big emptiness in his head. Wind and rain in the trees out there. No, he really needs something *to go by,* or else his book will be destined to come to a standstill.

He knew just what he needed: another poet, a bit more dangerous, a bit less well brought-up than Silfverstolpe, something at the same time more poisonous and more beautiful, something that came closer to the world *the way it actually looked.* Nature that wasn't just vegetables, people that weren't just noble, passions that weren't just edifying. His poet had—in spite of all the pleasant poems Bernard had given to him—started to get awfully boring, and he had a good mind to shove him off for good into the fictitious and stylized '20s from which Bernard had conjured him up.

It was with great reluctance that the fifty-three-year old community librarian, Mrs. Evelyne Björkquist, gave him the book. It's true the library had bought it because the translator's Dante translation had been so highly praised a few years before. Bernard, on the other hand, was ecstatic. A glimpse of two or three poems had convinced him that he'd found the right one.

There were things in that book which she, for her part, did *not* consider suitable in a book of poetry. No social responsibility. No education for peace. No concern with the problems of the handicapped. In brief: no real literature. And what a strange title! Evil couldn't have flowers! On the other hand, no visitor other than this determined little gnome had ever borrowed the book, and no one was likely to, either. People here mostly concentrated on novel sequences set in poor, unhappy nineteenth-century or turn-of-the-century Sweden, things of that kind. Anyway, she made out a new borrower's card for Bernard and lent him The Book. She was probably the last socially responsible person to see Bernard for a very long time. With a shudder of God knows what, she let Bernard and his book out into the autumn rain—he didn't even seem to want a plastic bag— turned out the lights in the library one by one, and prepared to go home.

11. Invitation to the Voyage

There's nothing particularly appealing about Björnlunda Backar. A big, ugly Shell station where truck drivers, motorheads, and bikers would hang out at an indescribably greasy and smoke-filled hamburger joint that stayed open practically around the clock. It was reminiscent of the way animal species supposedly have free access to water holes. Four or five different species of travelers jostled each other in there while steaming coffee cups and electronically defrosted hamburgers passed over the long, dirty counter in a never-ending stream.

It got quite noisy for a couple of hours between ten and twelve at night when the motorcycle gangs erupted from the movie houses in the surrounding communities: the night's first wave of long distance truckers thundered in; a gang of motorheads cruised to a stop in some lovingly repainted, softly sprung old Plymouth, the radio playing at top volume. People sat at different tables, some timid souls closest to the door, the regulars furthest in. The line to the cash register where you paid for gas and where the charge card customers took the opportunity of charging cans of coffee, evening papers, and groceries to the accounts of their employers went straight down the middle. A collection of timid, stingy souls who thought they still had something to gain from their one-track, petty-thieving lives. They narrowed their eyes, already surrounded by wrinkles from much narrowing, and pretended not to see the bikers touching the unconfined and still youthful breasts of their chicks under the leather jackets, fumbling at the zippers.

The sly, contented petty players of the welfare state would soon disappear into the fall darkness once more, into the square, gray Volvo loaves they were paying for in hefty installments; they'd cast a quick glance at the evening paper where huge black headlines told of yet another tragic, headless female corpse found in the southern suburbs and gingerly put paper and tax-free coffee cans on the passenger seat. Then, safety belt securely in place, they'd glide discreetly into the line of cars slowly moving north in the raw, gathering evening fog. Meanwhile the rebels inside, the owners of flame-painted cars and perversely swollen and fatally fast three-liter motorbikes out there (how the hell could they afford those things?) turned up the volume of already thundering hard rock on the jukebox so that the windowpanes of the hamburger joint rattled. The bikers jangled their iron chains lightly on the table when they wanted more coffee. The rest of the time, they wore the chains wound a couple of turns around their waists. It wasn't always easy to understand them.

The food in the place wasn't anything to write home about: it was something called "hamburgers," mostly plasma and variety meats, everything ground three times and mixed with cheap wheat flour, frozen and defrosted by microwave, served with fried potatoes that, for some reason, always tasted of leftover fish. Nobody here particularly cared what he ate. You just shoveled it in. The truck drivers, with their funny T-shirts and caps with advertising logos they never took off, ate the most. The motorheads and the bikers mostly consumed coffee, Danish, and cigarettes.

The microwaves were a constant joy. Their combined radiation was so great that it produced extreme readings on all the radar detectors several thousand meters down the road. Small boys would stand there on warm Sunday afternoons, rejoicing in the sight of Stockholm drivers who could afford such devices standing on the brakes on their way toward Björnlunda. Evidently, a field of ominous microwaves surrounded this place. The police, who had also become aware of this circumstance, had lately started placing their radar speed traps close to the gas station, something that made it even more fun to live along Björnlunda Backar, particularly on Friday afternoons, when many arrogant Stockholm drivers were on the move.

The junk food that came out of those frighteningly active microwaves was not what primarily attracted people to this place. For most of them, it was more the warm, smoky light from the windows which contrasted sharply with the autumn fog outside; the homey cigarette smoke among the tables, the thundering of the jukebox, loud laughter from some table or other. In brief: it was somewhere to go. If the food was terrible, at least the girls at the counter were impressive. They handled the food with swift hands and with a precision which, in earlier times, would have been referred to as "clockwork." Most of them were round little Finnish girls, but not all. There was one who, against all odds, constantly managed to exchange a couple of words with each customer. Long-distance truckers, motorheads, punks, leaders of biker gangs who would have inspired fear in anybody, with their skull-decorated leather jackets: it made no difference, she had something to say to them all.

She was a bit fat, plain rather than pretty, with shaggy dark blonde hair and a face with a fine pallor. She pushed forward plates and cups in a seemingly inexorable rhythm, exactly like a table tennis player in a final higher division game. In contrast to the other girls, who were both absent and grave, she smiled a small smile from time to time as she pushed back a tendril of hair from her forehead.

When Hans von Lagerhielm entered the Björnlunda Grill, dressed in ski pants, model 1952, a gray, worn windbreaker from about the same era, a blue ski cap with a cracked visor and the silver emblem of the Swedish Ski and Outdoor Life Association pinned above the visor, the whole place fell momentarily silent. What probably saved him from a lynching was the hard rock—it came back on the jukebox, blowing across the room like a gust of wind—and everything returned to normal. They'd never seen anything like him in here, that was certain. When the music came back on, however, there was no acoustical space for comments. Whether they wanted to or not, they all had to return to their own concerns.

It took Hans several minutes before he figured out how to park his big, old-fashioned bike; finally, he'd simply leaned it against one of the gas pumps. Now he walked straight up to the counter. His shoes left a lot of mud on the floor, but nobody seemed to notice that. With instinctive certainty, he hit on the right girl. She was prepared. Perhaps her life had been a preparation for this moment?

"Hi. I haven't got any money. But I don't want to order anything, either. I'm looking for—someone."

"You're some *new* guys starting to come here, right? With funny-looking jackets and pants and like that."

"What do you mean?"

"There was a guy looked about like you came by yesterday."

"Did he say what his name was?"

"No. But he was coming back. He was kind of a neat guy. We got talking . . . about a trip it might be fun to make. Like that."

(In the middle of this sentence, she managed to push two gluey fried eggs onto a mound of fried potatoes for a trucker at the far end of the counter and take an order from a traveling salesman in a camel's hair coat at the other end.)

"He was neat. He wanted to take me on a trip, he said. To some warm country in the south. With large, quiet rooms. Where there's furniture gleaming with nice old polish. Under beautiful molded ceilings, with big, deep, mysterious mirrors."

She smiled her big, beautiful, inward woman's smile again. "*That's enough,*" Hans said. "It's perfect."

It was Bernard. It couldn't possibly be anyone else. Bernard had been here; Leffe Twelvefoot had been right. Incredible. It was difficult for him to keep his enthusiasm under control.

"And something about big ships, big, beautiful ships sleeping on the canals."

"No question about it. You've seen my pal, the poet Bernard Foy. Did he say when he'd be back?"

"No. Just that he'd drop by some day. He knew a guy in a travel agency he'd talk to. Then he'd be back. Is he really a poet?"

"Yes. But he's too shy to write the poems directly. Instead, he's writing a novel about a poet. The poet is shy, too, but his poems have to be in the novel just the same. It's a way he's hit on. Clever, isn't it? He didn't say where he was headed, by any chance?"

"Yes. But he particularly asked me not to say."

After a pause the girl continued:

"He's coming back, anyways. If you just wait long enough."

Intentionally or unintentionally, however, the attention of the dark blonde waitress was now completely taken up with a heavily made-up blonde in a leather jacket who wanted more potatoes. She got lots of fried potatoes. The longer Hans looked at this remarkable waitress, the more beautiful she became. There are girls who are like that.

He felt a wild jealousy burning inside his eyelids. It was a while before he found his big bicycle outside. An offended driver had thrown it behind the serv-

12. Guide to the Underworld

It was very easy to walk the first ten or fifteen meters onto the railroad tracks on the bridge—it was no more difficult than walking along any kind of railroad embankment; at regular intervals, everything was illuminated by strong, yellow sodium-vapor lamps of the kind used in ports and oil refineries, so there was no difficulty about seeing where he was.

He couldn't see the abyss under him, but the terrible thing was that he could *feel* it more and more distinctly. Between the tracks and the outside edge of the bridge there was only a tall fence, and there was barely room between fence and tracks to walk clear of the trains. The bridge was open between the crossties. The rain and wind of the early October night didn't just come toward him: with each step, it grew more and more frightening because it came from underneath with equal force, in some surprising manner revealing that apart from the railroad ties, there was nothing at all under him.

Thirty meters below, the slow top lanterns of freighters were moving. There were at least three hundred meters of railroad before them, and if a train should come through the night at this precise moment (there were a lot of trains, and they went very fast at this point) he didn't quite know where they'd go. Perhaps it would be possible to hang by your arms from the iron structure *under* the bridge for the time it would take the train to pass? Or wouldn't you have sufficient strength? And how would you get from the top to the underside of the bridge?

It was best not to think about it right now.

Presumably you risked falling all the way to the night-dark water thirty meters below the bridge if you didn't manage the crossing. That would still be preferable to being run over by an express train going south.

Everything had looked so much easier when he'd stood at the northern end of the bridge, doing this walk in his imagination. He suddenly felt completely naked, exposed, and visible to all the powers that hunted him and wanted to annihilate him. He felt a wild longing to turn back, but he could no longer do it; he felt shaken by the immense difference between the airy constructions of his imagination and the much more vulgar, palpable and, each in its own way, unique confrontations which the cruel outside world incessantly forces on us.

The green signal lamp at the distant other end of the bridge flared up and then faded, like the menacing pupil of a lurking beast of prey.

Bernard would have turned back if it hadn't been for the light steps of the girl behind him. He still couldn't understand why she'd wanted to come along.

What business did she have with him? How could his adventures, his destiny, be any concern of hers? But her determined little steps sounded stubbornly behind him.

There was a slight vibration running through the metal structure: he wondered whether she was walking here in high heels. Perhaps she assumed that he'd done this thing many times before? In actual fact, Bernard had never previously been on the bridge. That he knew he'd find what he was looking for was due to the fact that he'd once seen it from the other end. It was in the fall of 1980, when he'd once, under the admiring glances of his school friends, climbed down the opposite slope to fetch a football that had gone over the tall wire fence and was lying against one of the bridge pillars at the point where the steep concrete wall started, dropping dizzily down to the waters of Lake Mälar thirty meters below.

That time it had been easier than Bernard had imagined, for there was a coarse web of wire sort of woven into the ground, evidently put there to prevent gravel and rocks from hurtling into the abyss. The tall, red stalks of epilobium, and a few thistles, grew unconcernedly through the wire web.

When he'd gotten so far down this dangerous and presumably seldom visited slope that he only had to stretch his hand out to reach the ball which still, with an annoyingly calm aspect, was resting against the solitary pillar which prevented it from disappearing into the abyss for good, then Bernard had, for a brief moment, been unmanned by momentary, needle-sharp dizziness. For of course he couldn't help seeing the similarity between the position of the ball and the equally exposed position of his own fragile life.

Instead of looking down toward the abrupt end of the slope (the same for all but right now visible to the thirteen-year-old boy) he took a few calm breaths and then looked up the slope instead of down. He was so far down that his friends had disappeared on the other side of the crest. He couldn't even hear their voices. A warm, gentle October wind came in from Bockstenssundet. It had been one of those warm, clear October days that sometimes occur in the Stockholm area in the fall, like a belated autumn gift. The impression it gives is of trying to surpass the bygone summer in rhetorical fervor. This day in 1980, when Bernard was just thirteen, such a gentle, unreal, summerlike October wind passed in waves through the reddish-blonde carpet of *Agrostis tenuis* (as we learned men call this grass). Right then, there was one of those rare moments of complete stillness and peace.

When Bernard's calmed eye, again turned away from death, looked at the slope right next to him, he made a fascinating discovery. Three years later, he of course retained every detail in his memory: an iron grate, cemented right into the slope and hidden in the shadow under the bridge. Evidently the end of some kind of culvert, the mouth of a tunnel in other words, so large that a grown man could easily stand upright in there.

The grate was a door. But that wasn't all: he'd seen how it could be opened. There was a ladder, evidently intended for maintenance, leading from the bridge itself straight to this point. A narrow, dangerous-looking ladder, girded only by some kind of protective metal spikes, but still a ladder. Bernard committed it all to memory—but of course, there wasn't much "committing" involved. Everything remained with him the way objects remain in photographic emulsion, and when one October night three years later he wanted to use it, it was all in place there, just as it should be.

"You'd better hurry up now," he called to the girl behind him. "So the train doesn't catch you."

Her light steps in the darkness behind him became swifter. She was rather a courageous girl, really. He imagined that he could hear the distant ticking in the rails that might mean the next train going south was on its way. But when the train passed above their heads with deafening thunder, casting a flickering, slanted light from its windows, they were already on the slope. The lock clicked as Bernard put his jackknife into it. The grate opened just as it was supposed to, and to the girl's astonishment, there was an ordinary light switch to the right of the entrance.

A faint but discernible wind came from the depth of the tunnel. It was pleasantly warm, warmer than normal inside temperature, and it carried a faint smell of cellar, dried concrete, and electric insulation. There was no longer any sound from the express train that had just thundered along above them.

"What *is* this?" she whispered.

"An entrance to the underworld," Bernard said.

The girl examined him with large, serious, cold blue eyes. At this moment, he looked like a compact dwarf, triumphant, legs wide apart, with his hands in the pockets of his leather jacket and a slanted smile on his face, strangely experienced for such a young person.

Actually, she thought, he's rather a fun guy.

13. In This Kind of Landscape: A Walk Underground

In a discreet and fleeting manner, the bulbs grew dimmer and dimmer until they could only be seen as faint half-moons against the pressing mountain darkness behind them. Bernard had noticed this for the last half-hour but he didn't want to speak of it. In general, the underworld tended to make him at once taciturn and happy. After about an hour of weary trudging—weary because it was so late in the silent night, but also because of the tunnel's continuous upward slope—it ended so abruptly that in the very faint light, Bernard almost walked into the solid steel grille that blocked the tunnel. He jumped up on the bottom parallel bar of the grille and looked down. The sound of the rushing water was heard from the other side.

"Oh," Bernard said, "now I know exactly where we are. It's the old Billsta Brook. When they built Billsta Center, they had to make it go underground. It goes from west to east, and it runs into Lake Mälar just south of the Flogsta subway station. Down by the Flogsta Beach, actually. But we're going south, so we'll only follow the brook for a short distance."

"Is it deep?"

"I don't really think so. Now let's see if we can get over this grille."

There seemed to be a tiny opening between grille and ceiling. Bernard pressed through first. When the girl tried to take the same route, she had trouble with her heavy handbag. In the sound of flowing water both felt, for a moment, the immense weight of rock above and around them. In different ways, however: to Bernard, this situation was much more familiar. He felt he'd experienced it many times before.

In this kind of landscape

he thought. *If only* I could know what it means, this idiotic phrase: *In this kind of landscape.* What does it mean?

The water was ice cold, but it was only up to their shins. Like all rapidly flowing water, it was quite shallow. To flow rapidly and to be shallow is actually the same quality in water, Bernard thought.

They walked in the direction of the brook, that is to say, eastward; it's hard to know how far they might have walked when no fewer than three tunnel mouths—this time dark and of such small circumference that it became necessary for them to lean forward in order to get into them at all—were opening on their left.

"Nice to get out of that awful ice water," Bernard said. "Aren't your feet freezing?"

"Mine have gone to sleep."

"It's over now," Bernard said. "We'll just crawl for a short distance through

242

this middle tunnel. I've been here before, although then I came from the opposite direction."

"You're crazy."

"My memory's quite good," Bernard said shyly. "I mean, I don't forget many things. No even when it's pitch dark all around. That means I find it quite easy to move around in, what shall I say— *in this kind of landscape.* But if you don't trust me you should be able to feel that there's a draft coming through the third opening here. There's a slight air current. *Do you feel it?"*

She felt it, but very faintly, like the breath of someone in a deep sleep. The sound of running water made it impossible to hear, anyway. Amelie felt it against the back of her hand, against the palm of her hand, and she shivered—from cold because of her drenched stockings, but also from terror. In this faint, faint breath she could feel how far it was to the surface, to daylight, to the ordinary landscape.

"Where do the other two lead?"

"The one on the far left leads to somewhere very dangerous, a kind of very deep pocket. Perhaps it's always been there, or perhaps it opened up after they blasted down here. I've no idea how deep it is. The one far to the right gets so damp and unpleasant when you get into it that you don't feel like going on. I think it goes under Lake Mälar. That would explain the dampness. The only time I tried it there was something . . . something I didn't like."

"What do you mean?"

"I don't know. *Something.*"

"And the one in the middle?"

"It isn't long at all, and it leads back into the Flogsta culvert system. It's warm and dry. But there's one difficulty. Somewhere in the middle you're going to feel sand, very fine sand, underfoot. Then you have to lie down on your elbows and your knees, and crawl along. It's quicksand. I don't think it was there from the beginning, but the insulation in the tunnel must have burst and let it in. It doesn't go on for very long, but it's dangerous to sink into it. You don't get up again, you see what I mean? Something's happened here after the system was built. It may be only the start of bigger changes—what do I know? The thing is to get across the quicksand slowly, calmly, but not to linger."

In spite of the darkness he felt that the girl was frightened.

"Do you think it would be easier to go back?" Bernard asked her.

"What do you mean?"

"I mean: do you think it's easier to go back than to go forward?"

"What do you mean?"

"I mean: *do you know what changes may have happened behind us?"*

She preferred not to say anything. It was no longer possible to see her face in the darkness, but it *felt* bitter right through the darkness. What I can't tell her, Bernard thought, is that actually, we've been incredibly lucky. Everything down here has changed a lot since I was here last. Perhaps everything will gradually cave in? It's lucky, too, that we don't have to climb very far. The system's much bigger, actually, than she's able to grasp. But the left-hand branch is almost incredibly difficult. There's something—stern and frightening about it, and I've never tried the right-hand one. The only one I've actually tried is this one, and I've never seen it as changed as it is now. Also, I've never walked it from this direction.

If only there aren't any tremendous difficulties somewhere in this tunnel, I know that we'll get to the branch down under the new Flogsta subway station. Just north of it, there's the substructure of the freeway intersection. From that point, it should be possible to climb diagonally to the right or diagonally to the left through various district heat culverts into the new County Council system.

The problem is, of course, that one doesn't quite know what's in there. Some of those tunnels are old sewer lines, as old as the South Railway line, originally built to drain it, and some are just made to dispose of rocks from other tunnel construction, never used after they were built. Some are like the old Billsta Brook, streams flowing underground, and then there are all the small drainage tunnels that carry additional water to the underground streams.

Higher up there's the modern system of heat culverts, electrical cable tunnels, and the tunnels that belong to the telephone company. It wouldn't be hard to keep it all in your head, every branch, every bend, if you could just be sure *it would stay the same behind you.* But you can't know that. Where once there was a fragile bridge that you could negotiate if you were careful, there might be a bottomless abyss the next time around, a crevasse wide enough to drop an entire truck into. The next time you pass this place everything might be different. *In this kind of landscape.* What was open and negotiable just a short time ago, clear as sunlight and as easy to travel as a highway, can suddenly close up. Some of the ancient pockets of quicksand in the rock, the pockets of never-resting, continually seeping postdiluvial sand, might make their way through narrow cracks, and all of a sudden, there's a gigantic shaft full of quicksand, impossible to get through.

And just as suddenly, some day a huge hospital construction, a new, deep subway station of the southern subway network, or something else equally huge and monstrous, will have altered the water table in the area so that you'll walk dryshod through a place where the water used to reach the ceiling in a thundering, wild flood of sickly, yellowish sewage water. The silence in a tunnel that's suddenly become dry can be deafening and menacing.

There's no order at all. But of course there's an order. Both things at once, and intimately connected, Bernard thought. It's a system that's somehow made a system out of systemlessness. It's incorporated meaningless into itself and made it part of its meaning. It's unintentional and minutely planned at the same time.

There is—to make a long story short—no real chance to defend yourself against changes. *In this kind of landscape.*

He was interrupted by the girl crying out behind him. It was a sharp, anxious little cry. He didn't like it. Bernard wasn't sure it was a good idea to cry out in here.

"Quiet."

"But something flew past me in the dark. It almost hit my cheek."

"A bat. There are lots down here. And they get quite big."

"Are they dangerous?"

"Frankly, I don't know. I don't suppose they're any more dangerous than other things down here."

The quicksand under the palms of his hands felt like something much *cooler* than the ordinary tunnel bottom, with its rough concrete that pulled at your palms so that they burned and cut them with sudden, deep cracks and sharp small rocks sticking up, splinters from the original blasting in the tunnel, presumably. Compared to this hard and burning sensation, the quicksand would have been distinctly pleasurable if he hadn't been aware of how completely unpredictable it was. How it might give under them at any moment and let them fall, enclosed in an icy-cool impenetrable cloud of shapeless dust, fall—it was impossible to say for how long—until they reached a bottom that would clasp them forever.

Time went by excruciatingly slowly. Each movement they made was as cautious as the movement of the minute hand in an old clock which might start to strike at any moment. Bernard was actually enjoying the situation. He thought his life had really always been just like this, but that only now had that fact become apparent. He felt the kind of relief you always feel when a half-truth has come to an end and a cruel truth restores everything to your original understanding.

14. A World of Interiors

The girl was more observant than he was.

Bernard had already passed the spot when she stopped, indicating the ceiling with a shy gesture. Perhaps after all this night was not as much of a *useless, futile wipe-out* as he'd thought at first? Here was a large opening in the ceiling, pitch dark, from which a current of colder air plunged in a continuous down draft.

A ladder, of the same type as the one that had led down from the railroad bridge to the slope with the first tunnel opening, started in there. Since it had protective hoops to prevent someone climbing up from falling outward if he lost control, it might be a tall ladder.

"Step into my hands, so you can jump up. Then you'll have to pull me up as best you can."

He folded his hands into a step, and when she jumped up he felt how surprisingly light she was; very light; there wasn't the slightest problem getting her onto the first rung of the ladder. As far as he himself was concerned, he'd meant to ask her to pull him up, but it turned out not to be as easy as he'd thought, getting her to understand what he wanted. At last Bernard got impatient and said:

"Just keep on climbing."

"But where are we going?"

She sounded a little anxious. For his part, Bernard was in good form, merry now that he had the gusty, dangerous railroad bridge behind him and could move underground. He was convinced that this upward shaft would bring them, sooner or later, to his old familiar underground landscapes, and like all true speleologists, he was obsessed with the thought of establishing links between cave systems that had apparent communication.

He had exactly the kind of brain that's made for negotiating labyrinths of this kind. Not even the darkness bothered him in the least. With the girl's body, tense and yet full of secret energy, invisible somewhere above him in the darkness, he climbed cheerfully on.

Step by step, slowly, the shaft became horizontal, returned to being a place.

Fifty meters further on it seemed their journey would end. The girl seemed sure of it, at any rate. She was kneeling, exhausted, in front of something which in the beam of the flashlight gradually revealed itself as a huge block of blast rock. The size of a small frankfurter stand, Bernard thought. Evidently it had fallen since the tunnel was built and now blocked the path. At least that's what the girl seemed to believe.

"Now we've come to a stop," she said resignedly.

"Move over a bit," Bernard said. "This isn't the way I remember, you know. Since my memory isn't often at fault, it's worse than that. Somewhere around here something has changed since I was here last. But my experience is that where you can get your head through, the rest will go through, too.

"If you'll hold the lamp up a bit higher, yes, like that, we'll first dig into the mud the cloudbursts have left on the bottom here, and then we'll see if we can't *wriggle* through. I've done it before. You've done something like it before, too. Everybody's done it at least once before. Wriggling through is what you do when you're born, you see."

"Except the ones who died doing it."

"But you never meet those people," Bernard answered absent-mindedly. He was already on a different track.

He dug with both hands like a mole and was already a bit below the rock. In actual fact, neither one felt very cheerful when, after two hours' digging, they started wriggling their way underneath the rock. The minutes felt like hours, and the girl was close to panic when she heard Bernard's voice, strangely distorted and magnified, shout something encouraging to her.

She gasped for breath like a fish on dry land and realized that the air she drew into her lungs was rock air, the kind of raw, underground, rather oxygen-poor air you only find in underground spaces that have been closed up for a while. She'd never dare go back.

And of course Bernard would never be able to bring his Atari, or anything else for that matter, this way. It didn't make any difference.

All his talents and instincts for the underworld—his labyrinthine feeling for landscape—told him that somewhere ahead of him there was some communication between this unknown underworld and the one he already knew, where he used to play when he was fourteen. The old route, however, was much too heavily trafficked by repairmen and linemen for him to be able to plug his Atari into some disregarded power line and finish the narrative he'd started. And that was something he wanted to do. He'd just come up with a way of writing poetry—something he was normally much too shy to do. He'd simply made up an old poet who wrote poems as a part of his story about the old poet. This seemed to Bernard to be a brilliant invention, and he couldn't understand why some grown-up hadn't hit on it before.

Fundamentally, from his earliest childhood Bernard had been made for living in labyrinths, although nobody had ever told him so. Actually, this was the kind of landscape he understood best of all. "Homeland," he said to himself. For a moment, the girl stopped brooding.

"What did you say?" she asked, very cautiously.

> "Homeland,
> I knew all the tunnels,
> I could point out the stones."

He couldn't help laughing one of his short, funny laughs. The girl had a hard time enduring the strange echoes they caused down here.

Now the path became steeper until it was almost a vertical shaft. It was narrow enough, however, to provide good holds on the rough rock surface on both sides. The climb continued for a very long time with the most terrifying monotony. Nothing changed. The cooler air flowed downward, the silence was great and compact around them. No water could be heard either to their left or to their right. How high above the original level might they be? As high as a three-story building? A six-story building? The thought of the abyss under them, of the distance they still had to climb, only made Bernard more exuberant. On some planet or other, he thought with a new laugh, as abrupt, as brief, and as brutal as his previous one, on some planet or other in the galaxy, or at least on some planet in some galaxy, there must exist some heavy birds flying about underground, some heavy falcons of immense *density* who could fly as easily through rock as the birds of this planet fly through air.

Bernard would have liked to be such a bird.

"Wait," the girl said. "There *is* something here. Something strange."

"What? An opening? A new corridor?"

"I don't really know. Not actually. Come up yourself and feel here."

"Is there room for me, then?"

In the silence, he felt she didn't like that kind of joke. Our relationship, if you can call it that, Bernard thought, has already developed in a rather unusual fashion. It's at once intimate and platonic. Similar to the relationship between a person and one of his ideas. She might be a nice girl, or perhaps she's nothing but a little freeway whore. The fact is, it feels good that she's here. She might as well be here as somewhere else, that's what I think.

He climbed up beside her. The space was so narrow that he could feel her sharp little hipbones grate against his thighs without his having made any effort to bring it about.

"That thing, it's a door, and it's probably stuck. But wait, what the hell is this? It's fastened with wing nuts. I'll be able to fix that."

He took hold of the first wing nut and then instantly pulled his hand back very quickly.

"What is it?" the girl said, flinching with fear. From her stiffness, he could tell she wasn't far from panicking. He himself felt only a mixture of calm happiness and curiosity. Now he was convinced they wouldn't have to return by the terrifying route they'd taken before.

Cautiously, Bernard felt all four wing nuts in turn. All of them were too hot for him to keep his hand on for more than an instant.

"This," Bernard said, "means something bad and something good. The good thing is that we've made contact with the district heat system. The network of culverts is all around us here. We're in the right vertical shaft. And if my calculations are correct, we'll get out somewhere in the neighborhood of the Billsta intersection of the freeways. But we can't get in through here. There's hot water behind this door."

"What do we do now?"

"We'll continue upward."

"Whatever you like."

It struck him that they must have been in total darkness for twenty minutes or more, and still, they'd continued to climb and explore their surroundings without panicking. The faint light from the lamps in the tunnel under them was only the slightest indication of a reflex in the metallic walls. A thought that disturbed him a little.

Could it be that the shaft they were climbing up was some kind of overflow protection against flooding? Perhaps the entire horizontal tunnel they'd come in through was for that same purpose, to lead the hot water away if there should be a major leak in the system.

The thought of the horrendous surge of water at above-boiling temperature which could sweep them away was something he preferred not to communicate to the girl. A disturbing fact was that for less than a minute, he'd been feeling the extremely slight dripping of water against his forehead. What was happening?

But this water wasn't hot. It was more cold than warm, and it didn't have an industrial smell. He caught a drop from his forehead with the tip of his finger and tasted it cautiously. It didn't taste like rock water but more like ordinary tap water. And wasn't the air that was now coming through the shaft much fresher? Not real outdoor air, but anyhow much more oxygen-rich, much less rock-enclosed and raw than what they'd been breathing up to now.

"Be prepared for a surprise. The fresh air's coming back. The shaft's going in an outward direction now. And climb silently."

"What is it?" she whispered.

Was it an illusion, or did her face start to become visible down in the darkness? A very faintly drawn oval, at once expectant and frightened?

Five minutes later, with great effort, Bernard lifted the iron door that covered the upper part of the shaft. It was easier the higher he moved it. He looked around cautiously. What he saw was a room in early morning light. Now more and more details emerged. On elegant little bedside tables were neat ceramic teapots, appealingly shaped and glazed, and, something which particularly attracted Bernard's attention, here and there were real books standing on the white-lacquered shelves above the beds.

What did this puzzle picture signify? Bernard felt quite sure that he'd seen it all before. A beautiful wicker bed was in the middle of the room, nicely made with elegant, violet-colored sheets and a comfy crocheted bedspread invitingly folded across the foot of the bed. Around the walls, cupboards and chests of old, beautifully polished mahogany reflected the morning light. The ceiling was decorated with handsome stucco imitations, probably made from plastic, which made it look like the ceiling in a nice old city apartment. Deep mirrors occupied two walls. The whole room breathed of luxury, calm—even voluptuousness.

"Where are we?" the girl asked breathlessly.

"*In a bedroom interior*. We've come up right smack in IKEA in Billsta. In the bedroom department. Do you see? It's fantastic. We've *come out* into an *interior*."

15. Mysteries of a Bedroom Town

Sometimes he'd been seen in the most desolate parts of Sjunkarmossarna, jumping nimbly between perilous water holes with a heavy backpack and with the much talked-about pigskin briefcase in his hand, going across causeways so old and rotten they'd probably been constructed by elk hunters in the previous century. Sometimes a jogger had seen him peeping out of an iron door in a bridge support on Västerbron, and on still another occasion, a couple of Sunday fisherman in a wooden boat had seen him climb up through the aft cabin door of an ominously black, leaking old cement tugboat anchored by Gåsholmen, a depressing little islet far out in northern Björkfjärden.

For several years afterward, there were hordes of Bernard Foy's friends and acquaintances who imagined they'd seen him practicing the most surprising trades in different places, generally in situations which reflected the deepest fears and desires of the tellers rather than anything else.

Among the zaniest and most remarkable of those legends, schoolyard stories, and bedroom town rumors we've already mentioned are the stories of the Polished Oracle Sheriff. It might be called suburban mythology, bedroom town mythology of a type which a literatureless working class has always created in order to formulate a deep structure for their impoverished lives. Be that as it may: the way it developed in the Flogsta-Billsta area in the years after 1983, the legend of the Oracle Sheriff related that all of Bernard Foy's poems, later lost, and of which only a small part was recovered, were dictated by this sheriff's head, long since turned into a wind-polished cranium. Someone might object that of course this dead, slowly desiccating tax director couldn't speak after death.

Of course not. But the swarm of small black wild bees who had taken up their habitation in his skull could buzz. Mildly at times, wildly and agitatedly at others, it is to be assumed, if anyone happened to disturb them. If you knocked on the Sheriff's white forehead with a cautious stick, the swarm would start buzzing in a rising and falling rhythm that could go on for hours. Sitting at the feet of the Oracle and (as it was claimed) put into a kind of trance by the smells of heated bog myrtle, turf, and brown humus water, young Bernard is supposed to have composed his tale. (Later, he'd write down everything that had been dictated and, in this manner, verbally inspired, on his small, stolen word processor of the Atari brand, hidden in some warm hollow of the heating system under the Billsta IKEA.)

The strange thing about this story is of course that, if it's true, the whole protracted narrative you're reading now, the story of Bernard Foy's third castling, would have been dictated by one of its darkest and least sympathetic characters, the gentleman who, both in life and in fiction, appears under the strangely foreign name of Ernst Lutweiler. No, not by him, by the nameless bees of course, who would eventually make their abode in his skull.

At exactly this point we must, in spite of the danger of perhaps wearying some of our future readers, make another of the many digressions in our narrative. It is a proven fact that at exactly this time, books started to disappear from the elegantly displayed bookshelves in the recently opened IKEA complex in Billsta.

Poor, lonely, abandoned books like that, leaning against each other, provisionally held up by a blue ceramic vase in the elegant sitting room of a furniture showroom, in a way constitute the most pathetically abandoned of all books in the entire universe. Their task is more to *appear* to be books than to *be* books: they are symbols of themselves, so to speak, and no one attaches any importance to them. They're kept in cartons by the decorators who pick them up as needed; they usually originate among the publishers' unsellable remaindered stock which normally is shredded.

The fact is that this fall, 1983, so many books disappeared from the shelves of the elegant interiors at IKEA-Billsta that the person responsible, interior decorator Vivianne Söderberg, actually had to order a whole panel truck's worth of neat-looking but, as usual, unsold books from P.A. Norstedt & Söner, Tryckerigatan 2, Stockholm. In one of her ringbind folders, she still keeps the invoice that was sent later. However, Miss Söderberg is quite uncertain about the source of the first lot of decorative books. Apparently they came from the same source, the one she usually employed.

Was it Bernard Foy who transported all these books at night, one by one—or perhaps in bundles, laboriously tied together—and dragged through endless underground passages to the place, situated God knows where underground, which became his literary workplace? Or is the connection an arbitrary one? Did the books disappear due to some misunderstanding? Were they carried out in a couple of cartons along with trash by some careless truck driver? Or were they perhaps found on some dump? As we know, one tradition tells of their actually originating in the fine old library at Flogsta Manor, ending up as decorative volumes, their own substitutes, on those shelves. Perhaps because some energetic, recently hired young IKEA decorator wanted to save them from the communal dump after Flogsta Manor was taken over, or perhaps because Baron von Lagerhielm had sold them to IKEA during one of his recurrent economic crises?

The funny thing is that if—let's say hypothetically, *if*—that were the case, if the books Bernard Foy fetched in the night to his underground refuge had indeed originated at Flogsta, then we know approximately which ones they were. For among the papers of his late father, Baron and Colonel Henning Rutger von Lagerhielm, which Carl Rutger still keeps in his humble, drafty summer cottage, there is a list of the exquisitely selected library which belonged to this officer with broad humanistic and mathematical interests. He departed this life, by the way, in 1941, a long time before Flogsta Manor entered the tailspin of economic difficulties which would soon lead to bankruptcy and auction. First as an institution for serious repeat alcoholics in the early '50s, then for drug addicts, and at last only the ruin of a building with leaking roof, broken windows, and ravaged and demolished tile stoves, with painted Marieberg tiles, where birds started to live among the flaking gilded-leather wall coverings that hung in the damp and forever abandoned rooms.

The first four pages of this list which Hans von Lagerhielm's grandfather supposedly put together (a highly mysterious claim, as the reader will certainly note, since some of those books are obviously published too late to hold an authentic place in this list) looks like this:

Alexandroff, Alexander D.N. *Anaxagoras and Heraclites.* Cambridge University Press, 1931.

Silfverstolpe, Gunnar Mascoll. *Poems.* Selected and with an introduction by Sten Selander. Included in the series *Swedish Poetry.* Stockholm: Bonniers, 1953.

Malmberg, Bertil. *Poems.* Included in the series *Swedish Poetry.* Stockholm: Bonniers, 1952.

Ytterberg, Bernard O. *Poems.* Selected and with an introduction by Tom Hedlund, Ph.D. Included in the series *Swedish Poetry.* Stockholm: Bonniers, 1983.

Ytterberg, Bernard O. *When Petals Still Fell in the Spring.* Stockholm: Bonniers, 1961.

Běhounek, Franz. *The Men on the Ice Floe.* Stockholm: Wahlström & Widstrand, 1932.

Ben Abraham de Leone David Ben Yehudah Hehasid, Rabbi Jaakov. *Buch der Spiegel* [*The Book of Mirror*]. With the gracious permission of His Majesty the King of Bavaria. Die Güntzburg, 1536.

Rilke, Rainer Maria. *Worpswede.* Berlin-Bremen: 1903.

Richter Frich, Övre. *The Black Buzzards.* Stockholm: Fritzes Förlag, 1932.

Middleton, Christopher. *Operation Medusa.* Translated from English by Madeleine Lindbladh. Stockholm: Wahlströms, 1929.

Nouvelle Revue Française nr. 284. 1 Mai, 1937.

Gustafsson, Einar H. *Lüge und Sprache.* [*Lies and Speech*]. Munich: Carl Hanser Verlag, 1934.

Woodruff, Paul. *Instruction in Chess.* Translated from English by O. Björlin, lecturer. Lindbladhs: Uppsala, 1931.

Gödel, Kurt. *Über formal unentscheidbare Sätze der Principia Mathematica und verwandter Systeme I.* [*On Formally Undecidable Propositions of* Principia Mathematica *and Related Systems*]. *Monatshefte für Mathematik und Physik,* 38. [*Monthly Review for Mathematics and Physics,* 38.] Berlin/Göttingen: 1931.

Baeckström, Lena. *How To Take Your Flight Certificate.* Vol. II: Airships, Autogiros, and Helicopters. Kooperativa Förbundets Förlag: Stockholm, 1942.

"Arizona und Texas." Vol. VI: *Houston mit Umgebungen."* [*Arizona and Texas. Vol. VI: Houston and Environs.*] *Fremdenführer und Strassenkarte* von Dr. Chr. Schlotterer, Ordinarius für Erdkunde an der Universität Rostock. [*Guide book and street map*] Dr. Chr. Schlotterer, Professor of Geography at Rostock University. Verlag F. Feilhauer: Leipzig, 1933.

Diels, H. and W. Kranz, *Fragmente der Vorsokratiker.* [*Fragments of the Pre-Socratic Writers.*] Vols. I-III. 10th edition. Berlin: 1961.

There are other theories as well. Some of those are so confusing and strangely speculative that there seems no reason to immerse ourselves in them. Some of the others presuppose unicities, strange loops, pockets, and folds in the space-time continuum of normal physics: discontinuities of the type we only want to discuss with a more mature type of audience than the one available to us at the moment—readers who, above all, have access to more precise mathematical symbolism and are more used to handling a rather formalized and thoroughly defined topological conceptial structure. (The above-mentioned, unfortunately deceased Dr. Kurt Gödel would have been just the right person.) While we wait for another such reader to turn up and call himself to our attention, we prefer to maintain *epokē,* a skeptical holding back of all utterance. We simply wish not to take a position on the question of what space we occupy on the space-time continuum of normal physics. We're buzzing—let that suffice.

16. The Whist Players Move Up on the Porch

Now it's already early December or, as Carl Rutger von Lagerhielm likes to put it, in the words of a beloved but unfortunately dead member of his own generation, the poet Erik Axel Karlfeldt:

> Fall has come with blushing leaves.
> The sea's sad breast forlornly heaves.

The whist players at the Billsta Home have long ago moved in from the arbor, and now they conduct their afternoon game among all the potted plants on the big glassed-in porch. Just the same, Mrs. Bouveng has prescribed that they must all have blankets over their knees. An old glassed-in porch can be quite draughty, and the manageress comes in not just once, but many times, to make sure they don't lose their blankets. Those aggravating old men, who nagged for themselves the privilege of sitting and looking out over Bockstensfjärden, whose heavy and swiftly darking evening sky bodes snow for tonight.

Out there on Lake Mälar there are hardly any waves left. The time of autumn storms is already past, and the water seems to move with effort beneath a leaden horizon. These are the December days when the expanse of Bockstensfjärden prepares for the ice. The question is which will come first: the first snow or the ice. The old men at the Billsta Home rejoice like children those years when the ice comes first. It's so much fun to see the long distance skaters turning up in their red jackets down by the horizon, the wind skaters with their gaudy sails that move so swiftly.

On a winter night like this there are hardly any cars down on the shore walk. Just a slowly creeping police car.

"Not again," Carl Rutger says, and adds: "I wonder if I shouldn't turn up my cards this time."

"The police are down there again," Torsten Simmerling says. "I wonder what they're after now?"

"That doesn't surprise me," says the former police officer, Sverre Ståhl. "We've had a rather singular rash of unsolved crime lately. I must say I have the impression that in my time, on the Södertälje police, we solved a few more criminal riddles. The level just isn't the same."

"But weren't there rather simpler criminals you had to contend with? You like to tell the story about the safe-cracker who'd left his matches behind and who tried to throw a typewriter at your head, whatever he was called."

"I assume you're referring to *Jansson with the pants?*"

"Why did they call him that?" Carl Rutger interposes diplomatically. For he realizes that one of the not uncommon quarrels between Simmerling and Ståhl might well be brewing. It has been two weeks since the last one.

"I've told you that on a number of occasions: he was going to crack the safe in Jansson's Bakery in Traninge, using dough as precharge, but he couldn't get the dough to stick to the safe door the way it was supposed to. So then he pulls his pants off and fills them with dough."

"Professionals," Carl Rutger says. "People of a different time, with the interest in their task characteristic of a different time. So he pulls his pants off and fills them with dough."

"By the way, I remember when I was Gunnar Mascoll Silfverstolpe's chauffeur for a short time in my youth," says Hans Hansdorff. "Well, actually I was at Stora Åsby as his secretary. It was at the Agricultural College, by the way, that my father brought us together, since the regular chauffeur had problems with his rheumatism—at any rate I filled in, and what do you think happened?"

"Excuse me," Simmerling interrupts, "but isn't it about time for you to cough up a card, Baron von Lagerhielm? We're waiting."

"There are awful things happening, anyway," Mrs. Bouveng said, walking quickly through the room, checking the kerosene stove in passing so it wouldn't accidentally set fire to some old man's pants' leg.

"How you dare to live all alone out there in your little house, Baron von Lagerhielm, in the dark of winter, I simply can't understand. Would it be much better to live here at the Billsta Home?"

This was not a new issue. Carl Rutger always felt flattered and always answered in the same terms.

"But my dear Madame Claire, so far only women have been attacked, and," he added cautiously, "among the women only strange types like meter maids. And a school psychologist, is that right?"

"Of course I can understand," Simmerling said, "that people find meter maids disagreeable, especially if they have cars to park, which certainly isn't true of everyone in these times. But to go so far in your rage against them that you start decapitating them systematically, that's something I cannot understand." For the fourth time, he opened the evening paper with an irate crackling.

"As an old police officer and as someone conversant with human nature," Sverre Ståhl said, shuffling the deck with experienced movements, "I've got to say that there's no certainty the perpetrator has any special *distaste* for meter maids. It might be a positive emotion, a fascination. To decapitate someone might be the expression of a wish to have that person to yourself, so to speak. An infantile reaction, in short. Then there's the *irreversible* aspect of such an action. The head literally can't be put back. That's an important point, gentlemen."

"I wonder," former submarine mate Torsten Simmerling said, "if he, for I assume the perpetrator is male, has to have anything against meter maids or school psychologists. He may like them all too well. It may be that he views them with the greatest benevolence. Meter maids are usually young women. You can find them practically anywhere at any conceivable and inconceivable time of day."

"You meant they are *à prendre,* so to speak, sitting birds?"

"How you do go on, an old man like you." Mrs. Bouveng said irritatedly, and commenced an energetic dusting of the indescribably ugly pressed glass vases she'd already given a careful polish earlier that morning.

"That could be it. And the last time it wasn't a meter maid."

"But what can you say about the at once pedantic and esthetic way of arranging this last one? As a decoration in a bedroom interior? À la Baudelaire, with a night table, a red sock on her foot, and all the accessories . . . And a school psychologist, on top of it all."

"Nobody knows what people really want. And least of all what women want."

"But isn't this going rather far? Don't you think so?"

"*Prenez garde à Madame.*"

"Oh, don't be embarrassed, gentlemen," Mrs. Bouveng swiftly intervened. "As the saying goes, you have to hear a lot before your ears fall off, isn't that true? But I'll tell you this much, it never occurs to me to visit IKEA in Billsta after such an awful incident."

"For those of us who've read the poem there's no question but that someone tried to recreate it. At the terrible price of a crime. What an esthetic soul it must be, committing these horrendous crimes. What a strange passion for beauty there must be, hiding behind this brilliant way of deciding—on the poor soil of reality, under our Nordic homeland's concrete sky of prohibitions, police raids, controls, general poverty—to recreate one of the most beautiful poems of French pre-Symbolism in all its willful splendor. And right in a bedroom interior in one of IKEA's estimable furniture showrooms. Brilliant. Absolutely on target. Believe you me, only a true poet could have done it."

"Poor taste, my dear Baron, poor taste and nothing else. Esthetics as frowzy as the air in a Victor Hugo museum."

"I think you're the one who's in poor taste, former submarine mate Simmerling. Well. It's *remarkable.* I . . ."

"Look here. I think it's time for you gentlemen to retire to your rooms. My tolerance is great, but as you well know, it has its limits. Now you've been sitting up past nine o'clock two nights in a row, and perhaps I'll be forced to disallow not just the sponge cake but also the arrak with your Sunday coffee after the soccer game, if this is getting to be a habit."

"Dear me."

"And I just want to tell you, Baron, that I'm going to call you a cab right now. I don't want you biking home alone in the dark when there are so many horrid, terrible things happening roundabout."

"That's much too good of you, my dear Mrs. Bouveng, but I don't think I'm in any danger."

"And how do I know that?"

"Yes, how do I know that? I guess there are certain things you just know. *I* am not *à prendre,* for example. It's not so easy to decapitate me, not even to put me in a bag. Good evening."

256

She saw him disappear down the garden path with his bicycle clips and his flashlight, blinking and swinging back and forth in the December darkness, his checked cap on his snow-white hair. The thought she sent him was full of warmth and concern.

When he's gone, she thought, there won't be any real man left in these parts.

17. The Oracle Is Silent, Snow Falls

I'll go out to Sjunkarmossarna, he told himself. That's the only place I haven't looked. If there's a place where the old excavators are hidden, perhaps on one of the islands in the marshes, then it isn't impossible for Bernard to have left some traces out there.

It was a courageous decision. And of course it couldn't be put into effect until it had gotten cold enough so that you could get about among the water holes and the quagmire; the water in the channels had to freeze first.

In ski pants and the kind of windcheater jacket people used when they went skiing in the early '50s, with a twirling, unreliable scout compass hanging in a string around his neck and his father's old hunting backpack, one winter's day Hans walked into the marshes.

Of course he found Bernard at last in the early winter dusk, standing in front of the Polished Oracle Sheriff's tree stump. Exactly where Hans would have expected. Bernard hadn't changed much, but he had changed. His clothes were badly worn, he was red-eyed and rather pale. He seemed much calmer and at the same time more worn now.

"I'm glad I've found you at last. I'd almost given up hope."

"You should never do that," Bernard said.

His crooked, friendly smile was the same, and he moved with a new heaviness. His clothes were much the worse for wear. They looked as if he'd slept in them for weeks.

"Where have you been all this time?"

"Here and there," Bernard said. "The truth is, you see, that for too long I've allowed my attention to become focused on childish things. But now I feel a bit more grown up. There won't be any more now. Childish things, I mean."

He smiled his quick, shy, somewhat apologetic smile. He'd never looked as much like a gnome as he did now.

"And then, you know, I've written my stories down. In the end, there were quite a few poems. But I'm not quite sure they were all mine. It's not so easy to keep track of things like that. I've had so few things to *go by*."

"*For my part, I made a poem*," Hans said. "Just one."

"Oh well," Bernard said. "That's the way it *is*, then."

"You've got *him*. I had to invent everything myself. You've got to understand that it makes a difference."

He gestured toward the sunken, lightly snow-covered figure on the tree stump that had once been Chief Tax Director Ernst Lutweiler. It seemed unbelievable when you saw him now. He wasn't much to look at on a winter day like today. Hans felt disappointed and unhappy; he'd wanted something more from Bernard;

something terrible, or something enormously fascinating, admirable, but not this.

"Yes," Bernard said. "But he's stopped speaking to me now. There won't be any more stories."

Bernard found it difficult to think of anything better to say. Absently, he clapped his mittens together in front of him and saw his own breath in the dry, frosty air. Somehow his eyelids had grown heavier, his blue-gray gaze sharper. The young boy was turning into a man. It was one of the first days of Christmas vacation, when at last the water in the water holes had frozen into black, polished ice, when a light fall of snow hovers like a cloud of lead-gray India ink across the horizon, when the air feels sharp and brittle at the same time, and when the grass straws, crystalline in the first severe frost, crackle with every step of your boots like so many brittle glass needles.

There the two friends stand in the first frost, with visible breaths, and no longer know what to say to each other. All the cranes in Sjunkarmossarna have long since departed . . . The layer of new snow is like a thin veil over cloudberries already pinched with frost. Faint smell of bilberries. It'll be a while before spring comes back.

The Polished Oracle Sheriff, he sits out in the marshes on his stump. But he doesn't speak any longer. In his skull, now rather weather-worn and yellowed, where the first, shy lichens have started to take root in the zigzag lines of the fontanels, the bee swarm has gone into its winter sleep. Nowadays they only send a scout from the depths of the nostril if you knock on the forehead. In this manner, the woodpecker supposedly teases a whole swarm of wintering bees outside, one after the other. For of course each new bee wonders what became of the last one.

To get the old, familiar murmur going, the once so learned and voluble buzzing from this head, isn't easy any more. Principally because the whole polished glory has fallen down on the moss. The body itself is in somewhat better condition. It leans forward a bit in its chalk-striped suit, but it's still standing on the two crutches Bernard gave it to lean on in October. Like an invalid, but he does stand. The skull is in a worse case. It's fallen, bees and all, and now gleams whitely between two tussocks of cloudberries. A few cloudberries still gleam like amber. The fall doesn't prevent the bees from sleeping their winter sleep inside the skull. They don't care where they've fallen as long as it's nice and warm inside.

That old skull is theirs, and they feel as much at home there as my thoughts do in my head, Hans thinks. But of course it's impossible to know what my thoughts in my head are all about.

"What day is today, anyway?" Hans von Lagerhielm asked at the same time as he lifted—very gingerly, for he didn't want to wake the bees—this head. But the bees were sleeping and didn't allow themselves to be disturbed.

"Friday, I think."

For quite a while, Hans scrutinized the skull, holding it between his boyishly warty hands. Then he tried solemnly to restore it to its place. He tried not just once but several times. It didn't work. This head was tired and preferred to rest. It was obvious the Polished Oracle Sheriff would speak no more this winter.

And *if* he had in fact spoken—well, then that tale wouldn't have had the least idea who was actually telling it.